The Wedding Dress

For Hazel, my beautiful friend,
who wore a blush pink wedding dress

DANI ATKINS is an award-winning novelist.
Her 2013 debut *Fractured* (published as *Then and
Always* in North America) has been translated into
18 languages and has sold more than half a million
copies since first publication in the UK. Dani is the
author of several other bestselling novels, one of which,
This Love, won the Romantic Novel of the Year Award
in 2018. Dani lives in a small village in Hertfordshire
with her husband, one Siamese cat and a
very soppy Border Collie.

Follow Dani on Twitter @AtkinsDani.

ALSO BY DANI ATKINS

Fractured
The Story of Us
Our Song
Perfect Strangers
This Love
While I Was Sleeping
A Million Dreams
A Sky Full of Stars

The Wedding Dress

DANI ATKINS

HEAD
ZEUS

First published in the UK in 2021 by Head of Zeus Ltd

9 7 5 3 1 2 4 6 8

A catalogue record for this book is available from
the British Library.

ISBN (HB): 9781800246492
ISBN (XTPB): 9781800246508
ISBN (E): 9781800246522

Typeset by Divaddict Publishing Solutions Ltd

Printed and bound in Great Britain by
CPI Group (UK) Ltd, Croydon CR0 4YY

Head of Zeus Ltd
First Floor East
5–8 Hardwick Street
London EC1R 4RG

WWW.HEADOFZEUS.COM

PART ONE

Suzanne

1

The carpet was thick. And expensive. It was the type that left footprints in the pile when you walked across it. It was the palest of greys, the colour of a dove's wings or an iridescent pearl plucked from an oyster. Surely it was a ridiculously impractical colour for a shop? I looked up at the rows of dresses lining the walls: white, ivory, champagne and cream. It was a bit like being in Heaven; everything around me was coloured in shades of white and the palest of pastels. Everything was immaculate. Dirt, soil and everyday grime simply wouldn't be tolerated here. But just to be on the safe side, I spent much longer than usual grinding my feet backwards and forwards on the coconut doormat.

A woman emerged from a shadowy area at the rear of the shop. Tall and as thin as a crochet hook, she was dressed from head to toe in black. Even her hair was ebony, the kind of shade that nature doesn't do on Caucasian women. It was pulled back into the sort of topknot that surely had to hurt, and was neat enough to look as though it had been superglued into place. Absolutely no hairpins required.

'Suzanne,' she said, holding out a long-fingered hand to me as she crossed the distance between us. 'Welcome back.'

I smiled a lot more easily than I'd probably done on my first visit to Fleurs, some six months earlier. Of course, then I'd been facing the pressure of making one of the most important shopping decisions of my entire life, *and* doing it all alone. Except of course, I hadn't really been alone, and I probably hadn't even been the one making the decision, because Gwendoline Flowers, the indomitable owner of Fleurs Wedding Gowns, had pretty much decided on which dress I should buy as soon as I entered her shop.

'Have you brought anyone with you today?' Gwendoline asked, looking past my shoulder at the clearly empty space behind me.

'My mother and my best friend – Karen – will be joining me for the fitting,' I said, glancing down at my watch. 'I think I may be a little early,' I apologised, knowing that I was, in fact, a good fifteen minutes ahead of my scheduled appointment. Nothing new there. My fear of being late – for absolutely anything – was a phobia that at almost thirty-two I was probably never going to outgrow.

'Far better to be early than late,' Gwendoline announced archly, and I gave a small shudder for the foolhardy bride who failed to keep to her given appointment time. 'Except for your wedding ceremony,' she added. 'You definitely don't want to arrive early for that. And *never* get there before the groom,' she added, with a scarily witch-like cackle. And I would know, seeing as witches had featured so prominently in my formative years. And dragons.

'Take a seat, my dear, while we wait for your entourage to arrive,' Gwendoline invited, her arm sweeping like a conductor instructing an invisible orchestra towards the same velvet-covered chair I had occupied six months earlier, on my first visit.

As before, Gwendoline slipped behind the antique desk, and the memory of how our first meeting had felt exactly like a job interview came flooding back. I knew better than to expect any type of refreshments to be offered. There were establishments where the customers were offered a glass of champagne as they shopped for gowns, but Fleurs had a strict ban on food, drinks, small children and anything that walked on four feet.

'So, just three weeks until the big day,' Gwendoline said, smiling in a way that managed to reveal practically every one of her teeth.

I felt the nervous knot of tension in my stomach, the one that kept giving me sleepless nights the closer it got to my wedding day, twist and tighten. 'Yes. It's all gone terrifyingly fast. I just hope I haven't forgotten anything. You were absolutely right when you said six months wasn't long enough to plan a wedding.'

'All you really need are two things,' the shop owner declared. 'A magnificent dress...' – she inclined her head towards a curtained cubicle, where I guessed mine was waiting to be tried on – 'and a truly wonderful groom.'

I gave a small happy sigh and smiled. One of those, I definitely had. Although I knew the jury was still out on that verdict as far as some members of our wedding party were concerned. One of whom was my mother. It probably hadn't helped that she'd had so few opportunities to meet and get to know her future son-in-law before he officially became a member of our family. Or was I becoming a member of his? I really wasn't sure of the protocol.

Part of the problem was that my mother lived in Cornwall, and the other part was that she hated men… No, that wasn't entirely true; it was only my father she truly disliked. Which is probably part of the reason she also hated marriage, both as an idea and as an experience that having tried once she'd chosen never to repeat.

Darrell liked to describe his future mother-in-law as delightfully eccentric, a phrase I hoped for his sake he never decided to share in front of her. He also took considerable delight in her celebrity status, certainly far more than I had ever done. My mother is an author, a very successful one. If I told you the name on my birth certificate, you'd know instantly who she is. There's probably not a child in the country who hasn't read one of the books in her series about magic, witches and fearsome, molten-lava-spewing dragons.

I was uncommonly popular at school, which had nothing whatsoever to do with me. I was a quiet and introverted little girl, the kind who lurked at the edges of the playground; who never dared to hang upside-down on the climbing frame; who was the last child over every finishing line on sports day. But there was an almost obscene clamour to be my friend, to be invited back to tea after school, or even – the holy grail of achievements – to be invited for a sleepover. I've no idea whether my classmates were disappointed to discover we lived in a very comfortable, but otherwise boringly normal house, rather than the castle they were clearly expecting.

My father had bounced happily from one money-making scheme to another, doing his best to spend my mother's income at a rate that almost outpaced her ability to earn it. It was certainly a surprise when, after many years of living together, they chose to get married just before my fifth birthday. Far less surprising was their divorce, just after I turned eight. My father had disappeared to Spain shortly after that, taking with him a sizeable chunk of my mother's latest advance, which he'd used to open a bar in Malaga that unexpectedly became hugely successful. He'd left nothing behind except bad memories for my mother, and his surname, which I legally adopted; this at least prevented me from having to answer the inevitable '*I don't suppose you're related to…?*' every time I was introduced to someone.

It was difficult to know if some of my mother's anti-Darrell feelings were because – despite her objections – I'd asked my father to give me away at the wedding, thereby forcing my warring parents, who hadn't exchanged more than a dozen words in over twenty years, to spend a day in each other's company without killing their former spouse.

'Does the dress look good?' I asked, suddenly aware it had been several minutes since either Gwendoline or I had spoken. Normally I was comfortable with silence, but today I wanted noise and distraction around me.

'Are you worried you won't still like it?' asked Gwendoline, raising one perfectly threaded brow. 'Because you don't need to be. You will. It's going to look beautiful and will fit you perfectly.'

How she knew that was a mystery, but it was one I was prepared to accept without question. She knew it in the way

I understood a ledger book, or how to file a VAT or tax return. When, six months earlier, I'd sat opposite her across this same desk and admitted I really had no idea what kind of wedding dress I wanted, or what would suit me, she'd drawn herself up in her chair, and for just a moment her nostrils had flared, and I was reminded of the fire-breathing dragons who lived in my mother's imagination. And then Gwendoline had smiled and risen gracefully to her feet, declaring with a confident smile, 'I *do* love a challenge.'

She'd stood me on one side of the room and had walked slowly around me, as though I was a horse at a county fair. Occasionally she'd murmured instructions. 'Turn to your left.' 'Now your right.' 'Lift your hair off your neck.' 'Now let it fall.' It had all seemed a little arbitrary and when she'd disappeared, returning a minute or two later with three cellophane-covered dresses draped over her arm, I had had my doubts. Just three dresses? In a shop that surely held hundreds, if not thousands?

The first dress was 'the one'. I tried on numbers two and three, just to be polite, but I think we both knew my mind was already made up; it had been even before Gwendoline had finished lacing up the bodice. I'd taken far longer deciding whether or not to accept Darrell's – very unexpected – proposal, which was something that bothered me a little whenever I thought about it too much. So I tried not to.

Darrell and I had only been dating seriously for four months, and the very last thing I'd been expecting was to see him drop down on one knee in the restaurant where he'd taken me for Valentine's Day. Every table around us had fallen embarrassingly silent, forks poised halfway to mouths as they waited to hear my reply. There were waiters standing prepped and ready at the edge of the room with a bottle of chilled champagne in a silver bucket, so clearly even *they'd* known this had been on Darrell's mind for longer than I had.

I remember looking down into his large soulful brown eyes, and even while some part of me knew I should be saying something sensible like *We really haven't been together all that long yet* or *Why don't we just move in with each other?* or even *Hey, slow down, what's the rush?*, somehow none of those would have been what the waiters, the other diners, or Darrell had been expecting me to say. So I said the only thing I could, given the circumstances. I said 'yes'.

'Whoa, I'm seriously gonna need sunglasses before I look at that thing again,' my friend and colleague Karen had cried when I'd walked past her desk the morning after accepting Darrell's proposal. It was Monday and the first thought that had flashed through my head when my six a.m. alarm had sounded was *Oh my God, I can't believe I'm actually engaged.* I'd rolled over, reaching out for the man who'd placed the square-cut diamond on my finger the night before, only to remember that he hadn't been able to stay the night. 'I'm so sorry, sweetheart, but my flight to Berlin is crazy early, and I still haven't packed yet,' Darrell had apologised, kissing me very slowly and thoroughly just to prove how much he didn't want to leave.

'I understand,' I'd said with a regretful sigh, trying to ignore the voice that had whispered annoyingly in my head, the one that wasn't too shy to ask why he'd chosen a night when he'd known he'd have to pop the question and run.

Darrell travelled. A lot. I should know that better than anyone, because the first time I'd met him had been on one of his many business trips. I'd been on a company conference, and after an evening of less-than-scintillating conversation – there's a reason accountants have earned a reputation for being boring – I'd done something quite out of character and walked into the hotel bar alone. Just a nightcap, I told myself. I won't even put it down to expenses, and then I'll go straight up to my room.

I'd felt more than a little self-conscious as I crossed the room to the long beaten-copper-surfaced bar. A single woman in a hotel bar wasn't unusual, not these days – but it *was* unusual for me. I was seriously regretting my decision, when an attractive man in his mid-thirties, seated on a stool to my right, looked up from his drink and smiled. There was something about him, something engaging and warm, that made me think that, for just one night, it might be all right to be the kind of girl who could accept the offer of a drink from a good-looking stranger.

One drink led to three, then four, and then I lost count. The bar emptied, until we were the last two people in it. The hotel employee who'd been serving us had coughed discreetly, having wiped down and cleared away everything that needed tidying, tipped out the bowls of nuts, and switched off most of the lights.

Darrell had chivalrously taken my elbow as I'd climbed down from the bar stool, which certainly seemed a lot further from the ground than it had done when I'd climbed up on to it a few hours earlier. I'd intercepted a brief look of concern on the bartender's face as his eyes flashed from me and then to the man who was carefully supporting my weight. I was swaying slightly, and while logically I knew the floor was perfectly stationary, it still felt as though I was on the deck of a boat on turbulent waters.

'I'll see she gets safely to her room,' assured the man who'd been my companion for the evening. The barman frowned, making a single bushy monobrow form over his eyes. If there'd been a thought bubble above his head, it would clearly have said, *That's what I'm worried about.*

I don't remember crossing from the dimly lit bar into the overly bright hotel foyer, or summoning the lift. I'd closed my eyes against the disturbing image of the flushed-face young woman in the mirrored walls of the lift carriage, and only opened them again when we'd pinged to a stop at my floor. Darrell took the plastic key card from my hand, and after glancing down to check my room number, had taken my arm, as though escorting me into dinner in a period drama, and guided me to my door.

I do remember becoming almost-all-the-way-sober as he slid the card into the slot, withdrawing it smartly as the light turned green. What the hell was I doing? This wasn't me. I wasn't the kind of girl who picked up random strangers in hotel bars and took them up to my room. I didn't *do* this.

Neither, it turned out, did Darrell. He'd placed one smartly polished shoe in the opening, to prevent the door from closing, and bent to graze my cheek lightly with a kiss so fleeting I scarcely even felt the touch of his lips. Then he'd gently propelled me into the room.

'Drink all the water from the mini bar,' he'd advised, his

eyes twinkling warmly as I groped on the wall for the light switch. 'Sleep well, Suzanne,' he said softly, as he withdrew his foot and the door began to swing to a close. 'It's been really lovely meeting you.'

'God, you were *so* lucky,' Karen had declared, when I'd recounted the story to her several days later, on my return to the office. 'He could have been an axe murderer, or a rapist, or... or...'

'I think you've probably covered most of the worst-case scenarios,' I'd said, my voice a little brittle because I was embarrassed, and also because I knew she was right. I don't take risks, I think everything through, weigh it up carefully, and then always, always, play it safe. I am the epitome of careful. I'm made of the stuff that most likely earned accountants their reputation for being dull.

'It was a one-off moment of madness, a temporary lapse, which luckily I walked away from unscathed,' I said, gathering up the armful of files that I'd temporarily dropped on to her desk as we chatted. I picked them up and made to return to my own work station, at the opposite end of the huge open-plan office floor.

'Whoa, not so fast, Miss Reckless. What happened in the morning? What did you say when you saw him the next day? What did *he* say, come to that?'

I gave a small wintry smile, and brushed a long strand of chestnut hair off my face. 'Nothing. He said absolutely nothing.' I hoped I sounded as unconcerned as I was trying to look. 'I wanted to thank him, but couldn't find him anywhere, and when I asked at Reception later that day, they told me he'd checked out first thing that morning. I didn't see him again after that.'

A bell tinkled behind me, and I swivelled on my seat to watch my mother sail through the shop's doorway. She's a slight woman, half a head shorter and a whole dress size smaller than me, yet wherever she goes she creates an illusion of presence. People often say television personalities appear much smaller when you see them in real life. My mum is the exact opposite of that; her charismatic personality somehow appears to inflate her. If she ever committed a crime, every single witness would probably give an inaccurate description of her height and build.

A subtle waft of her familiar perfume engulfed me as she swept me into a hug. It was the smell of my childhood, and was more uniquely hers than even her signature. I've always hated smelling it on anyone else. When I first left home for university, I was so homesick that I bought a small bottle and inhaled sneaky draughts of it, like a junkie needing a fix, until the loneliness faded. I never told her that, and to this day I don't know why. She'd probably be delighted to find a sentimental heart beating beneath my pragmatic accountant's one.

'Am I dreadfully late?' she asked the room in general. 'I swear the taxi driver took me on the most *implausible* route from the train station to the hotel. I could have walked it quicker.' I glanced down at her small, dainty feet in their elegant suede court shoes, and turned my face to hide my smile. I suspected that, somewhere out there, a poor cab driver was now nursing a very large headache.

'We've not started yet. We're still waiting for Karen.' Rubbing Aladdin's magic lamp couldn't have been more effective, for virtually as soon as I spoke the words, the missing member of our party grinned at me through the shop's plate-glass window and hurried in to join us.

We were an unlikely quartet of women, as different both physically and psychologically as it's possible to get. And yet when Gwendoline and I disappeared into the changing room, there was an air of impending excitement that bristled like static electricity in the air. My designer-clad mother, with her immaculately blow-dried hair, should have looked mismatched seated on the antique chaise longue beside my very fashion-indifferent best friend. And yet, as they disappeared from view when Gwendoline swished the curtain into place on its rail, I saw the two women exchange an identical look of anticipation and then – unbelievably – clasp hands. There aren't many things in the world that have the ability to unite total polar-opposite strangers in such a uniquely emotional way. Newborn babies can do it, puppies too I suppose, but other than that, a wedding dress – or rather the first sight of a bride in her wedding dress – might possibly be one of only a few other situations when even the stoniest, coldest of hearts melts.

My fingers were trembling as I undid the buttons on my shirt and pulled it free from the waistband of my skirt. I kicked aside my everyday clothes with a bare foot, as though they were suddenly unworthy of sharing a changing room with the dress I was about to try on. Gwendoline reached for the garment bag that still effectively hid from view the most expensive and important piece of clothing I'd ever purchased. She paused with one hand on the zip fastener and glanced back at me over her shoulder. This was pure theatrics, and I suspected she'd done this not just once, but many times before. She was smiling in a Mona Lisa sort of way, but I was too busy trying to remember how to breathe to join in.

'Ready?' she asked.

I nodded, my eyes fixed on the zip as it crept slowly down on small white teeth. I thought I'd remembered the dress; I thought the reason *why* this had been 'the one' was securely locked away in my data banks. But I'd forgotten so many details over the past six months. I could have told you it was strapless with a sweetheart neckline, but the silver embroidery decorating the bodice was more delicate than I remembered, with a Milky Way of tiny crystals scattered across the fabric that glittered like the remains of a passing comet. I reached out my hand to finger the soft chiffon folds of the skirt that flared from the dropped waist, already knowing and loving the way it would swirl around my legs like a moving white cloud as I walked.

For the first time I was grateful that Fleurs insisted upon a strict no-photography-of-the-gowns rule. It would have ruined this perfect moment of falling in love with my dress all over again if I'd have been able to see it any time I'd wanted.

'Couldn't you have taken a sneaky photo on your phone?' Karen had asked, when I'd tried and failed to properly describe my dress to her.

'They don't let you,' I'd answered, 'and to be honest I was still in a state of shock when I chose it.'

'That was probably because of the price tag,' she'd quipped. It was hard to tell from her voice whether or not she was teasing. 'Did you stop to work out how cost in-effective it is spending that many months' salary on a dress you're only going to wear once?'

'Actually, I'm planning on wearing it to work every day, until I break even,' I'd said, laughing at how well that plan would go down at the weekly team meeting. 'I know you think I'm crazy – and not just because of how much the dress cost. But I only intend to do this once in my life. This is the only wedding dress I'm ever going to buy, so for once I forgot to be an accountant and decided to just be a girl.'

Karen had smiled then and given me a really hard squeeze, and when we'd broken apart I was shocked to see her eyes were glittering brightly. She'd been with her boyfriend, Tom, since university, and although she always claimed she wasn't bothered about getting married, I wondered for the first time if my whirlwind courtship, engagement, and now marriage was actually painful for her. And just like that, she wasn't the only one with teary eyes.

'Have you got it on yet?' called my friend's voice now from the main salon. 'We're practically dying out here, you know.'

'Patience, ladies. It's going to be worth the wait,' assured Gwendoline, slipping the dress from its hanger and holding it open, like a silken pool, for me to step into.

The fabric rippled smoothly against my bare legs, as I was expertly eased into the gown. Being dressed by hands other than your own is a strange sensation. Unless you're royal or exceptionally rich, most of us will probably only ever experience it as an adult on our wedding day. I shut my eyes as Gwendoline expertly hitched the strapless dress exactly where it was meant to go, and then kept them closed as she deftly laced up the back fastenings. If speed-lacing ever became a competitive sport, Gwendoline was a shoo-in for gold. Finally, she stepped back, ensuring her reflection was clear of the changing-room mirror.

'You can look now,' she instructed quietly. It wasn't just the dress, although that alone made me want to cry. I'm not vain, but most of the time the reflection staring back at me in the mirror is passably attractive. Today I looked beautiful. And it wasn't just the dress. Somehow, with just a skilful twist and two hairclips, Gwendoline had managed to secure my shoulder-length hair into a style that looked as though I'd spent an afternoon in a hairdresser's chair.

'Go and show them,' she urged, whispering as though we were in a place of worship, and even though Darrell and I had been in total agreement about having a civil ceremony, I suddenly regretted our choice, and wanted not the slimmed-down svelte service, but the pews, and the organ, and the peeling of bells and a hymn-singing choir. The whole big fat wedding.

'Oh, Suzanne, oh my God… you look… you look…'

'Please don't say "like a cupcake",' I pleaded. My voice, my lower lip, everything about me felt like it was trembling. Karen leapt from the chaise and came towards me with her arms outstretched, stopping just centimetres away, as though she'd hit a force field.

'You look so perfect and so beautiful, I'm afraid to touch you.' I solved the problem by closing the distance between us and hugging her fiercely. From the corner of my eye I believe I saw Gwendoline wince. 'You look totally amazing,' Karen whispered into my ear, before slipping out of my hold.

There was only one person left who still hadn't passed judgement, and three pairs of eyes went to her, as she sat straight-backed and unmoving on the velvet chaise. My mum didn't play poker, but should she ever decide to take up the game, she'd make an absolute killing. It was impossible to tell from her expression if she was moved, disapproving or just a little bit bored by the proceedings. No one could have seen the difference... unless they'd spent almost thirty-two years looking into a pair of cornflower-blue eyes that were practically identical to their own. Because when nothing else gave away her emotions, her eyes revealed her secrets. Karen and Gwendoline looked between mother and daughter and back again, like spectators at a tennis match, waiting for someone to knock the ball out of play. The longer the silence stretched on, the more anxious they looked. But not me.

I cracked first. I always did. I was good, but I couldn't beat the master at the game she had practically invented. I started, ever so slowly, to smile. 'You like it, Mum, don't you?' She blinked, just a little more rapidly than usual. 'You do, don't you?' She licked her lips but her mouth looked somehow softer now, and if I wasn't mistaken, perhaps not quite as steady as she'd have liked.

'I know you're disappointed that I picked the dress out by myself, and that you weren't involved. And I know you've got doubts, and they're only because you're worried about me. But putting all that aside, it would be really good right now to hear you say that I look nice.' Blue eyes on blue eyes, and still she stayed silent. 'Unless – of course – you *really* don't like it.'

'You look...' She sighed as though struggling to find

the right words, which as an author is not something she usually had a problem with. The one she eventually settled on was fine with me. 'Perfect,' she completed, wiping away a solitary timorous tear from the edge of one eye, before it dared run down her cheek and ruin her foundation. 'You look absolutely perfect, Suzanne.' Her hand reached for mine, and I gripped it tightly, noticing as I did two new small brown smudgy age spots. She was getting older, and I was getting married, and just for a moment I wasn't sure which of those statements terrified me more.

By the time I was back in my own clothes, Karen had already gone back to work. 'I told them I'd be back in the office by lunchtime,' she apologised, popping her head through a gap in the changing-room curtain. 'You're back in tomorrow, right?' I nodded, hunting on the floor for a missing shoe. 'Okay, well, I'll see you in the morning. Enjoy the rest of your day off.'

I gave her a watery smile from my kneeling position, where I probably looked like I was praying. And in a way I was. The first hurdle of the day was over; the dress had been a success. But there were further challenges that still lay ahead.

Darrell had booked a table for three at an expensive restaurant, where he had insisted we take my mother for dinner. He was on a full-out charm offensive, and had looked so crushed when I'd suggested somewhere less fancy that I'd swallowed down my objections. There was an almost uncomfortable urgency in Darrell's desire to change my mother's mind about our forthcoming wedding. In a way it reminded me of the speed with which he'd swept me off my feet, making it practically impossible *not* to fall in love with him. This was his greatest fault, if I had to admit that he had any: his impatience. When he wanted something to happen, or to change, he wanted it right now, instantly. But that strategy wasn't ever going to win over my mother.

'So, it's more softly, softly, catchee monkey, is it?' he'd asked, nuzzling against the side of my throat in the way he did that was guaranteed to render me virtually incoherent in seconds.

'Kind of,' I said, my response already sounding throaty. 'Although if you refer to my mother as *any* type of primate, she'll probably never speak to either of us again.'

Darrell had picked me up then, gripping my thighs as they fastened around his hips. 'Talking of animal instincts...' he'd said, striding towards my open bedroom door.

'That's not the most subtle or sexy segue I've ever heard,' I said, gasping as his hand slid smoothly beneath the fabric of my T-shirt and around to cup my breast.

'I'll work on it, wife-to-be,' he promised, his lips covering mine, making any further conversation impossible.

I was smiling when I emerged from the fitting room, and didn't really expect to stop doing that any time soon. Even the considerable outstanding balance on my bill didn't have the power to deflate my happy mood. Knowing that the two most important women in my life both agreed I'd chosen the right dress made paying for it a great deal less painful. I drew my credit card from my purse and laid it down on Gwendoline's desk, waiting for her to finish up with the paperwork she was currently filing away.

'Could you put the balance for the dress on this, please,' I asked, confused when she slid my card back across the desk towards me.

'I'm afraid I can't do that,' she said, 'because it's already been taken care of.' For just a moment I thought Darrell had somehow contacted Gwendoline and paid for my dress. Except he hadn't known which shop I'd gone to, nor how expensive it had been.

I'm not sure why the obvious answer took so long to occur to me. No, scratch that. I knew *exactly* why Mum hadn't been my first guess, because she'd spent the last twenty years or so of my life quietly brainwashing me *against* marriage. Darrell had seemed shocked when I'd said I would never ask nor expect my mother to contribute financially to our big day. 'If we do this, we do it by ourselves,' I'd told him unwaveringly. Darrell's own parents had emigrated to Australia, and all I really knew about them was that after some huge falling-out – which he was very reluctant to talk about – they hadn't spoken in years. It was one more thing that had drawn us together – a huge gaping chasm of a fault line that separated us from absent family members.

'I really don't give a monkey's who pays for what, or whether we're going against tradition,' he had said, pulling me into his arms. 'I don't care where we get married, or how many bridesmaids you have, or how many guests you want to invite. Just as long as you're there and I'm there, that's all I'm ever going to want or need.' We were writing our own vows, and I really hoped he was planning on including that line.

'Mum? Did you do this?'

My mother looked a little shamefaced, and I'm sure if

there had been another customer in the shop, she might have tried to let them claim the credit for the purchase of her only daughter's wedding dress. 'It's a very beautiful gown,' she said with a small artless shrug, as though that had been her justification in parting with not just many thousands of pounds, but also with her long-held principles.

I went to her and hugged her tightly, struggling to speak past the huge lump in my throat. I knew this didn't mean she'd changed her mind about marriage, or the wedding, or even about Darrell, but it *did* mean that even if she thought I was in the wrong, she was still on my side. She always had been.

'You do know, I didn't ask you to come here today to pay for my dress,' I said. From my peripheral vision, I was aware that Gwendoline had discreetly slipped into the shadows.

'I know that, Suzy.'

Suzy? When was the last time she had called me that? Not since I was in hospital with appendicitis, I thought, and that was when I was sixteen. It made me realise for the first time that today had been every bit as important to my mother as it had been to me. She just hid it better, that's all.

'Besides, *one* of your parents needed to contribute financially to your big day, and I'm pretty sure your father will have squandered every last peseta he owns on that damn drinking hole of his.'

My father's bar was actually quite upmarket and elite, but this definitely wasn't the moment to point that out, and anyway, I strongly suspected she already knew that.

'You do know Spain has been using the euro since 2002, don't you?'

Her eyes glinted with the wickedly dark sense of humour that always took people by surprise the first time they met her. 'Pesetas sounded pithier,' she retorted, with a brief flash of a familiar smile.

And there, as ever, was the chief difference between us: she was all about the words, and I was all about the numbers. I'd inherited none of her creativity, nor her unique and gifted way with words. Every B minus on my English school reports had probably left her wondering if there hadn't been some dreadful mix-up on the maternity ward. If I didn't look so much like her, I'm sure she'd have pursued it. Of course, in a world full of keyboards and spellcheckers, I keep my secret well hidden. But the notebook beside my bed, where I've scribbled down the vows I'll be declaring in three weeks' time, tells its own story. Each time I see the crossed-out words *With Darrell I've **definately** found the right man to **comit** to*, it looks as though I've changed not only my spelling, but also my mind.

2

It was three weeks after the sales conference where I'd first met Darrell when I stopped by Karen's desk on my way to the photocopying room. She looked up from her screen with a smile and pushed her chair back. There was a half-eaten doughnut on a serviette beside her computer mouse, and sugar everywhere. Her desk was nothing like mine.

'I think I'm being wooed,' I said without preamble.

Karen's eyes widened with delight, as though she'd just sampled something even more delicious than the confectionery beside her. 'Really?' she breathed, beckoning me to bend down a little closer. 'What are you *doing*, and more importantly, who are you doing it with?'

'Pardon?'

'Just how dirty are we talking here?' she asked, before waving her arms excitedly as a new thought occurred to her. 'Oh, is it with Paul?'

'Who's Paul?'

'The really fit guy from the post room, you know, the one with the body like a Diet Coke ad model.'

I shook my head, feeling like I'd accidentally stepped over into an alternate universe. It was difficult to know which of the many wrong tangents Karen was going down that I needed to correct first.

'Firstly, I have no idea who this Paul person is. And secondly, I didn't say "rude", I said "wooed".'

Karen flopped back against the worn grey fabric of her office chair and looked seriously disappointed for a moment, before considering what I'd said and deciding it was still way more interesting than whatever she'd been working on before I interrupted her.

She nodded to her colleague's vacant chair. 'Eric's in a meeting,' she explained, 'sit down and tell me everything.'

I folded on to the chair and rolled it a little closer to hers, although I don't think anyone – apart from her – was in the slightest bit interested in my love life. 'Well, it started with the flowers – a beautiful bunch of twelve gerberas that were waiting on my desk a couple of weeks ago when I got back from lunch. After that came the chocolates, a box of twenty of those tiny Belgian white ones, which weirdly hardly anyone knows are my particular favourites, and then—'

'Oh my God, you really *haven't* inherited anything from your mother, have you? I don't want an inventory, I want a story. Who's sending you this stuff?'

I thought about making her wait for my answer, because her comment about my mother had stung a little. But what was the point in having news if you weren't going to share it? 'Well, that's just it. To begin with I truly had no idea. There was no card with either of the first two deliveries.'

'Then how did they get to your desk?'

'I guess someone from the post room must have brought them up,' I hazarded.

'Maybe Paul?' said Karen hopefully, still clearly fixated on the mail delivery guy.

I gave a small secretive smile, as I leant a little closer towards her. 'I actually had a sneaking suspicion who they might be from, but it wasn't until the third delivery arrived last week that I was almost certain.'

'What was the third delivery?'

'A litre bottle of Evian with a gift tag attached saying *Drink me.*'

'God, I hope you didn't,' Karen interjected. 'Who knows what could have been put in it.'

'Why would anyone do that?'

'Honestly, do you really not read *anything* apart from the FT?' was her head-shaking reply.

I leant back in my chair and frowned, still disappointed with my friend's reaction. 'The water hadn't been tampered with, and nor had the chocolates. And anyway, by the time the theatre tickets arrived, I was confident I knew who was sending them.'

'Please tell me you didn't go to the theatre to meet some random secret admirer, who could have been an axe murderer, for all you knew.'

'What *is it* with you and axe murderers?'

Karen shook her head, making her look a little like a dishevelled dog with a troublesome ear. 'Suzanne, if you don't tell me who this mystery man is, there's a good chance you won't live long enough to be wooed or rude.'

'It's Darrell,' I said simply, and although I tried really hard to stop it, somehow a huge grin spread itself across my face.

'Who is Darrell?'

'The guy I met when I went to that conference three weeks ago.'

'The bloke you took up to your room? The one who could have been a sex offender?' she asked, her voice unfortunately loud enough to carry to the people working on the next bank of desks. A few of them looked up, and I felt a hot blush colour my cheeks.

'The guy who was actually a perfect gentleman, who bought me drinks and then escorted me safely to the door of my room,' I corrected firmly. There must have been something in my voice that alerted my old friend that this particular running gag was now long past its expiry date.

'Sorry,' she said, sounding contrite, and yet somehow still quite concerned.

'So the man you met in the bar has somehow tracked down where you work – and we'll ignore for now how borderline stalker-ish that is; he's bombarded you with presents and arranged for you to meet him at the theatre? It's all a little intense, don't you think?'

For someone who'd been quite happy to see me paired up with the mailman a few minutes ago, I was a little disappointed by her lack of enthusiasm, and I couldn't help wondering if she wasn't just a tiny bit jealous. I'd certainly heard her complain more than once about the lack of romance or spontaneity in her own long-term relationship.

'It wasn't intense. It was actually rather lovely. We went out last night and had a really amazing evening.'

It was impossible to stay mad at Karen; we'd been friends for far too long. Although I was still bristling a little when Eric appeared to reclaim his chair a few moments later.

'Let's talk some more about this over lunch,' Karen had suggested, returning her attention reluctantly to her screen.

I nodded and slipped away, already knowing that the steaks in the restaurant where we'd chosen to meet wouldn't be the only thing to receive a grilling that lunchtime.

It had taken quite a few double dates, and interrogations worthy of a Spanish inquisitor, before Karen had given Darrell her seal of approval. To be fair, no one could have tried harder than he did whenever we'd gone out together as a foursome. Darrell was charming, funny and always first at the bar to buy a round of drinks, or trying to discreetly settle the bill without splitting it. But none of that impressed Karen. What swung it in the end was something far simpler. 'It's the way he looks at you,' she had admitted, as we wandered around the shops together one lunchtime. 'The expression in his eyes when you walk towards him. The way he stares intently at your face whenever you speak. And how he laughs at your jokes, even when you screw up the punchline – which you do quite a lot, by the way.'

I had smiled, while absent-mindedly fingering the price tag of some silky lingerie, trying to decide if Darrell would like me in – or out – of it.

Karen had looked at me, at the vaguely dreamy expression in my eyes and then at the garment swinging on its tiny hanger from my finger. 'You're really starting to fall for him, aren't you?'

I felt my cheeks flush, like a teenager, as I nodded. 'I think I might be,' I confessed.

'Even though it's all been so fast, and there's still so much about him you don't know?'

'I know all that I need to. I know how he makes me feel.'

Karen shook her head as she followed me to the queue at the till. 'What about that crazy ex-girlfriend of his, the one he never wants to talk about?'

I handed over my card and waited as the shop assistant folded the silken garment and began wrapping it in crimson-coloured tissue paper. 'So he doesn't want to talk about her. So what? You can hardly blame him for that. It was obviously a pretty ugly and traumatic break-up. Of all people, I can respect his right not to want to share every last detail of his past with the rest of the world.'

Karen made a small sound of disapproval, which may or may not have been because she'd just seen how much I'd paid for a tiny scrap of lace frippery. 'Having a famous author for a mother doesn't exactly count as having a dark and mysterious past – which, incidentally, I *still* don't know why you insist on keeping secret. If she was *my* mum, I'd be shouting it from the rooftops.'

She bit her lip, as though tasting the words she was about to deliver next, already knowing how unpalatable I was going to find them. 'If you and Darrell are serious, if this thing is *really* going somewhere, those are questions you have a right to ask. You know there are two sides to any relationship break-up. Darrell could be at least partly responsible for things ending so toxically.' She said the last hesitantly, already knowing it would put a grim and determined set on my lips. She was absolutely right, it did.

'I just don't want you to end up being the next Mrs Bluebeard,' Karen had muttered as we emerged from the shop and began to head back towards our office building. 'I know Darrell seems like the perfect boyfriend right now – and hell, what do I know, maybe he is every bit as wonderful as he seems – but I bet you anything his old girlfriend has a completely different take on whatever happened between them.'

I pressed the button on the pedestrian crossing, and frowned at the little red man who was telling me to stay put, because I really wanted to keep walking and leave Karen's voice of reason back on the pavement behind me.

'Sometimes in life you just have to trust your instincts,' I said firmly, making it clear that the mysterious girlfriend in Darrell's past was a subject that was no longer up for discussion. 'Right now I'm happier than I've been in years. Can't you just share that with me?'

Karen looked torn, but in the end, what bound her to me was stronger than all of her doubts or suspicions. She linked her arm through mine as the green man appeared. 'Of course I can, hon.'

My mother was an altogether harder nut to crack. More of a resilient Brazil than a pliable pecan. Even now, on the day she had totally surprised me by paying the balance on my wedding dress, the light of doubt was still in her eyes. She might have dialled down the dimmer, but I could still see it glimmering in the darkness in the small bistro where we'd gone for lunch.

'Perhaps I should just have something light,' she said, perusing the menu, 'as we're going out for dinner tonight.'

'I think the place Darrell's chosen is all about artfully

garnished plates and minute portions,' I said, trying not to notice the thought bubble that had popped up above my mother's head with the word *pretentious* floating in it. 'It's the kind of place where you pop into McDonald's on the way home because you're still absolutely starving.' My mother's eyes met and held mine. 'He's just trying to impress you,' I added hopefully.

'I stopped being impressed by any man's over-the-top flamboyant gestures a great many years ago,' my mother said. I already knew exactly where this sentence was heading. 'Your father saw to that.'

Thankfully, we were interrupted by a young, fresh-faced waitress, who popped up enthusiastically beside our table, wielding her small order pad like a radar speed gun. 'Have you ladies decided yet, or do you need a little longer?'

'I'd like the pasta, please,' I said, passing the waitress my menu.

'And I'll have the chicken salad,' my mother declared, after running a quick eye down the list of options.

I thought of the dress I'd left behind at Fleurs, the one I wouldn't be seeing again until the day of my wedding, and wondered if I should change my order. The dress had fitted me perfectly, leaving no margin to either gain or lose weight. I shook my head and allowed the tiny concern to tumble back behind far larger and more troubling ones. The dress was practically the only thing about the wedding that wasn't bothering me.

'So, you do know that Dad is arriving back in the country at the end of the week?'

My mother's smile, which was still sitting on her lips for the waitress, froze slowly by degrees. It was like watching a barometer drop. 'I suppose that means you haven't had a last-minute change of heart about inviting him?'

It was, almost word for word, exactly the same question Darrell had asked several weeks earlier. Ironically, on this one aspect of the wedding, my mother and fiancé were in total agreement.

'Whatever has happened in the past, he is still my father. I know he's missed many milestones in my life, and I'm not saying that I can ever totally forgive him for that, but not inviting him to my wedding, not even giving him a chance to be part of the day, would just feel... wrong. I want *both* of my parents to be there.'

Of course, the moment I'd said those words to Darrell, I instantly wanted to rewind time and take them back. My thoughtlessness made me feel absolutely terrible. Because of that stupid and mysterious feud he'd had with his parents, hardly anyone from Darrell's family was planning on attending our wedding. Even worse, practically all of his old friends were apparently still in contact with his ex, so they weren't coming either, out of loyalty to her.

'Don't you think, if you reached out to your parents, this would be a perfect time to heal the old wounds and put all of this behind you?' I had suggested gently, working largely in the dark, because I still had no idea what on earth could have happened to cause such a seemingly unbridgeable rift. But whenever I brought up the topic, Darrell's shoulders would stiffen and a lockjaw expression would immobilise his face. There was so much anger and pain in whatever had happened between them that I always stepped rapidly back from it, as though I was teetering on the edge of a chasm I could easily fall into.

There was no pain in my mother's expression at the mention of her former husband, just the kind of bristling irritation you might feel towards a wasp that keeps endlessly circling your outdoor picnic, threatening to ruin everything.

Despite adopting an air of nonchalance when telling Karen I'd been seeing someone, my entire relationship with Darrell had been one huge leap of faith. And in a way it still was. That first headlong jump into the unknown had been taken when I'd removed the single theatre ticket from its envelope and decided to meet the mystery man who'd been secretly pursuing me.

Like many single women, I'd been on my fair share of blind dates, yet this one felt different – perhaps a little more partially sighted than totally blind. Not unsurprisingly for me, I got to the theatre far too early. Darrell (or possibly, *not Darrell* at all) had scribbled a suggested meeting time on a small yellow Post-it note, stuck to the ticket: *Meet me at 7.15 by the Box Office*. There was nothing alarming about his handwriting; no red flags were raised by the steep backward slant of his letters, or the way his pen sliced boldly through the letter T. And yet every time I looked at the note, I felt a shiver of something I couldn't quite name run down my spine.

There were plenty of people milling around the entrance to the theatre, couples and larger groups, but no single men. No Darrell. Would anyone go to the trouble of seeking out where I worked, sending me gifts, and then not show up? Rather than wait around to find out, I decided to go for a brisk ten-minute walk around the block. Flashback memories of being stood up at seventeen hadn't faded with time, even though roughly fifteen years had passed since the night I'd been left standing alone outside the cinema, long after the film had begun. The experience had stayed with me far longer than the face or the name of the boy who'd changed his mind.

Only Darrell hadn't stood me up.

By the time I once again approached the theatre, my pulse was racing, as though I'd sprinted around the block – which, in the heels I was wearing, would have been physically impossible. My nerves felt like violin strings, one peg-turn away from violently snapping. I could see someone standing there, waiting. A man. They had their back to me, and in the unnatural glare of the sodium street lights, it was impossible to see if his hair was the same shade as the man from the hotel. The man who'd bought me drinks, who'd made me feel amusing, interesting and – for the first time in quite a while – just a little bit sexy.

I felt sick and excited in equal measure. My footsteps slowed and then faltered to a stop. Even though I knew he couldn't have heard the clip of my heels on the pavement, he suddenly straightened and spun towards me, as though I'd called his name. His smile was on maximum wattage even before he'd completed the 180-degree turn. His eyes were warm, and crinkling at the edges like sweet wrappers. He smiled with his entire face, and it was so open and genuine that every last nervous thought I'd been harbouring simply evaporated away.

'You came,' he said delightedly, holding out his hand, palm side up. It seemed the most natural thing in the world to place my own hand in his. It was the middle of October and the evenings were rapidly growing colder, but all I could feel was the warmth of his fingers curled around mine. He inclined his head in the direction of the theatre. 'We should probably go in and find our seats.'

I smiled and nodded, and allowed him to lead me up the three shallow marble steps to the theatre's entrance. He held my hand all the way to our seats, and kept hold of it through the first half of the show. The gentle stroke of his thumb on the sensitive skin of my palm made it hard to concentrate on the performance, made even breathing naturally a new and interesting challenge.

Darrell was clearly a very tactile man; that much was obvious from the guiding hand resting in the small of my back as we climbed the stairs at the intermission and headed towards the bar. Once there, he again reached for my hand and wove us through the jostling crowds to a quiet corner where an ice bucket holding a bottle of champagne sat waiting. I looked at the small card with his name printed on it beside the two glass flutes.

'You must have been fairly confident I was going to come,' I said. There was something in his smile that made the breath catch in my throat. Several heads had turned our way at the sound of the popping cork, but suddenly it felt as if the bar was empty of everyone except the two of us.

'Not at all,' he confessed, pouring the champagne into the glasses without ever taking his eyes off my face. I knew without a doubt that if I'd done that, our shoes would now be splattered with alcohol, but he didn't spill a single drop. He passed me a glass, and his voice was low and doing something really unexpected deep within my stomach. 'I just knew that if you came, I'd want us to celebrate the moment, because it would be the night when something important had first begun.'

'And if I hadn't come?' My voice was practically a whisper.

Darrell gave a small, sad shrug. 'Then I'd definitely have needed this to console me for being the idiot who'd let you slip through his fingers.'

Those fingers were still holding mine that night, as we travelled in the taxi towards the restaurant to meet my mother. She'd politely declined our offer to pick her up, preferring to arrange her own transport. 'She probably just wanted to terrorise another cabbie,' I told Darrell jokingly, hoping the real reason wasn't that she was trying to minimise the time she had to spend in the company of the man who was soon to become her son-in-law.

My anxiety levels weren't being helped by either the rush-hour traffic or the fact that by the time we'd flagged down a cab on the busy road outside my flat, we were almost half an hour late.

'I'm so sorry, my meeting overran,' Darrell apologised, letting himself into my flat with the key I'd had cut for him several months earlier. 'Then by the time I'd gone back to my place and showered and changed, the traffic had already built up.'

Acid irritation burnt in my throat, the kind that didn't respond to Rennies and had a tendency to end up with someone saying *I told you so*. I swallowed down both the words and the emotion, because I wanted – no, *needed* – tonight to go as smoothly as possible. Things were going to get prickly enough once my father returned to the UK, so getting my mum's albeit late-in-the-day approval of our marriage seemed doubly important.

'So how did the dress fitting go today? Were you pleased with how it looked?'

I turned my head away from the side window, where I'd been busily glaring at every car that cut into our lane, making us even moments later than we already were. For the first time that evening, I could feel a genuine smile of complete happiness creep over my face.

'It was absolutely beautiful. Even better than how I remembered it. And what's more incredible is that both Karen and my mother really loved it too. It got everyone's seal of approval.'

Darrell reached for my hand and kissed my knuckles, just below the large diamond he'd placed on my ring finger. 'I really wish I could have been there. You know, I half thought about secretly following you and peering in through the window.'

I sat up a little straighter on the worn leather bench seat of the taxi. Darrell did this sometimes; he'd say something totally unexpected, and it almost always threw me off balance. 'Well, I'm very glad you didn't,' I said, aware that my voice sounded a little like a slightly irritated school teacher. I took a breath and softened my words with a smile. 'And anyway, don't you know that it's bad luck for you to see the bride in her dress before the ceremony?'

He kissed my hand again, and chuckled. 'Don't panic. I had back-to-back meetings all day that I couldn't get out of. I'm just going to have to wait another three weeks for the big reveal.' My eyes were still a little watchful, wondering if he had genuinely considered gatecrashing my fitting. 'But, just for the record, I don't believe in that old superstitious nonsense. I *already* have all the good luck in the world. I'm getting married to you, aren't I?'

And just like that, I was reeled right back in all over again. His arms wound around me as he pulled me towards him and kissed me with a passion that made my cheeks glow hot, right there in the back of the taxi. After a minute or two I called a halt to our passionate embrace, just in case the driver's eyes had been tempted to stray from the road to the action taking place directly behind him.

Darrell's eyes twinkled mischievously, but he allowed himself to be gently but firmly pushed back.

'Talking of people following people,' I began artlessly, dropping my voice so that the driver couldn't hear us, 'I decided not to mention anything to Mum about what's been going on recently. She doesn't need another reason to raise objections.'

The twinkle died in Darrell's eyes and was replaced with an expression of pain. 'I didn't realise she still wasn't on board.'

I bit my lip, and thought yet again that I would make an absolutely appalling spy. I was rubbish at keeping anything from anyone.

'It's not that she's not on board… per se,' I said, trying to soften my words by gently running my hand down the length of his arm. I could feel the muscles, bunched and tense, beneath the expensive fabric of his Italian suit. 'I just think it's a combination of things. It's how she feels about marriage, it's how quickly we made up our minds – but most of it is probably down to my father coming back.'

Darrell's eyes said *I told you so*, but fortunately his lips knew better. But he wasn't wrong; my mother would have been far easier to win over if I wasn't forcing her to play happy families with the man she once claimed she never wanted to see again – well, at least not until Hell had begun offering ice-skating sessions.

'Anyway, I just wanted to warn you not to mention anything about... you know... any of the stuff that's been going on.'

Darrell nodded, and there was a tension in his jaw that hadn't been there before. 'Don't worry. That's the *very* last thing I'm likely to mention tonight.'

It was exactly one week after we posted out the first wedding invitations when it started.

Weddings take a lot of organising, and the more I tried to keep on top of things, the more I could see why people hired a professional planner. When Darrell offered to help by writing out the invitations to his own guests on the list, I silenced my inner control freak and happily passed him a small bundle of engraved invitations from the box I'd collected from the printers. His pile was considerably smaller than mine, and I felt guilty that while my list kept growing like an out-of-control amoeba, his just kept depleting. 'It's because of my job,' he had explained, gently smoothing away the frown lines between my brows with a tender finger. 'I travel so much it's hard to make new friendships or hold on to old ones.' I opened my mouth to say something, but he silenced me with a kiss, resuming our conversation while my eyes were still fluttery and half-closed and my lips were still parted, waiting for more.

'I have loads of acquaintances, both here and abroad, but nobody I care enough about to ask to our wedding. There's only *one* person who *has* to be there, and as long as *she* turns up on the day, I don't need anybody else.'

'Oh, she'll be there,' I said, confirming my answer with a long kiss, which I broke off to teasingly question: 'It was *me* you were talking about, right?'

His laughter had filled the room, and we were both still smiling as he pushed me gently back against the settee cushions, our plans of invitation-writing suddenly abandoned for an altogether more interesting pastime.

I rarely spent the night at Darrell's flat. To be honest, I found his one-bedroom apartment rather cold and impersonal, like a second-rate hotel room. It was a sentiment he seemed to understand and completely agree with. 'Its only merit is that it's convenient and practically on the airport's doorstep, so it's ideal for when I've an early morning flight to catch,' he'd explained the first time he'd taken me back to the grey concrete block, which externally had all the charm of a municipal car park.

The flat was a colour palette that went from grey to grey, and had obviously been decorated with practicality rather than style in mind, by someone with zero interest in making it homely or welcoming. 'That's why I prefer spending the night at yours,' Darrell had said, coming up behind me and winding his arms around my waist as I stared in despair into his practically empty fridge.

'Why? Because I actually have a kitchen full of luxury goods, like milk for tea or coffee?' I said, only half teasing as I looked down at the empty fridge door.

'I don't starve when I'm here alone,' Darrell said, nibbling my ear, as though to prove it by making me his next meal. 'Although I admit my appetite is far better satisfied at your place.' Darrell did that a lot, turn an ordinary conversation like asking whether he had milk for our coffee into something just a little bit risqué, a little bit provocative. And the more I blushed whenever he spoke that way, the more he did it.

'Well, I definitely won't miss anything about this place when you give up the tenancy,' I said, pushing the fridge door to a close.

Darrell had his back to me and was pouring hot water into our coffee mugs. Something a little like a summer heat haze shimmered over him as he froze mid-stir at my words. Very carefully – too carefully – he replaced the kettle on its base before slowly turning around.

'Suzanne, I thought you realised... I'm not giving this place up. It's just too useful for my business trips.'

'But... but...' I shook my head as though I was a stuck needle that couldn't get past that small three-letter word. In a way, I couldn't. 'But why? What's the point of keeping it? It makes no sense, especially not financially.' There she was again, my inner accountant, screaming out to make her point.

Darrell's eyes met and challenged mine, and for just a moment I thought I saw a flicker of irritation dance within them. We'd been together, and practically inseparable, for months, yet suddenly, without any warning, we were here, teetering on the edge of our very first disagreement. *Ever.* When the ink was hardly dry on our wedding invitations, our timing couldn't have been worse.

Suddenly, Karen's words whispered in my head, like an annoying ghost. She and Tom had only been to Darrell's flat once, and her verdict the following day had hardly been complimentary. 'A mirror on the ceiling and black satin sheets? His place looks like an archetypical bachelor pad from the seventies, or the set of a porno movie.' I had bristled angrily, mainly because I privately agreed with her, though now I would never be able to admit it.

'I wouldn't say that,' I'd said obstinately, jabbing at the button to call the lift for our floor as we waited in our building's reception.

'Well, I'm sorry, Suze, but I would. It looks like the kind of place you take random girls back to after picking them up in a sleazy bar somewhere.'

I had turned to her, swivelling on my heel just in time to see her clap her hand to her mouth, remembering – just one sentence too late – how Darrell and I had first met.

'Not that I meant that Darrell still does that – or that he's *ever* done that,' she said, stumbling over the apology in her haste to get it out of her mouth past her own foot. 'I just meant his flat has a tacky retro kind of look to it. Oh God, just forget I ever said anything,' she pleaded.

And I thought I had done, until right now, when Darrell was looking at me and I was trying not to let myself ask if there was any other reason, apart from its proximity to the airport, why a man would want to keep a bachelor pad after he was married. Admittedly, Darrell's job involved a huge amount of international travel, but was that a valid enough reason not to let the flat go? Who started a marriage with 'his and hers' homes? More worrying than those questions was the one I was deliberately avoiding: *I loved Darrell, but how well did I actually know him? Enough to trust him?* It would have been a hell of a lot easier to answer that if the question wasn't ricocheting around my head in my mother's voice.

'If it's just about the money, then don't worry. I can afford this.'

I shook my head. We were both on very good salaries, and I knew he could easily cover his rent and still contribute to the mortgage on my place. What worried me most was what I now saw as a reluctance to let go of life as a single man. Did it reflect a lack of commitment to our marriage... to us?

I could feel the prickle of tears smarting like soap suds in my eyes. The invitations had been sent, the venue was booked, the flowers were chosen, and my dress had been ordered. Everything was almost ready, except, perhaps, the groom. The kitchen suddenly seemed suffocating, as though there wasn't enough air in the room for both of us. Through a threatening shimmer of tears, I looked for an escape. 'I... I just need to go down and get something that I've left in my car.'

Darrell abandoned the coffee-making and crossed the small room, his arms outstretched. 'Suzanne, you're upset.'

No kidding, Sherlock, I thought, even while I was shaking my head in denial. 'No, no, really I'm not,' I said, wiping the back of my hand beneath my eyes, making sure no escaping tears dared make me a liar.

'Let's sit down and talk this through, sensibly,' he said, his voice softly cajoling as his arms wound around my waist.

I took a single step backwards, which I think surprised him as much as it did me. His arms fell away and swung uselessly at his side, as though he'd suddenly forgotten how to work them. 'You really *are* upset, aren't you?' There was an expression on his face that vaguely resembled a wounded puppy. He looked so hurt that I almost caved; I almost said he could have a whole string of properties, as long as he still wanted to live with me in one of them. My mother was practically screaming in dismay in my head.

I shook my head so vigorously that my ponytail slapped me, first on one cheek and then the other, as though I was hysterical and needed a sharp wake-up call. Did I?

'I really have left something in my car, Darrell,' I pleaded, hoping he could see that I wanted – no, needed – a few minutes away from him to compose myself. 'Let me go down and get it, and then we can talk,' I said, already plucking my bag from the kitchen worktop.

We did talk when I got back from the underground car park – but it certainly wasn't about whether or not he should keep his flat.

Darrell had two allocated parking bays. His car was in one, and mine sat beside it, parked slightly at a skew, because I was always worried about hitting one of the concrete pillars. I don't care much for underground car parks. Well, not the car parks themselves; what I mean is that I don't much care for them when I'm alone, at night, when the overhead lights begin to flicker in the way they were doing now. Suddenly, every scary movie I'd ever seen, where someone in a hood or a mask pounces on a defenceless woman on her way back to her car, was replaying right there in the front of my mind.

The argument – if that's what it was – with Darrell had already set my nerves on edge. The car park setting pushed them a little closer to the precipice. But it was the thing sitting on my windshield that tipped me over the chasm.

At first, I thought the item pinioned to the glass beneath my wiper blade was an advertising flyer, until I glanced around at the other parked cars and realised mine was the only one to have one. Without even knowing why, the small white envelope filled me with trepidation. I reached for the wiper to release it, holding it gingerly by the corner as the words scrawled on it came into focus. The writing was messy and smudged in places, as though written in a hurry. It was addressed to 'The Bride', which made no sense at all. I knew no one in this building, except Darrell, so how did anyone know this was my car? Even more worrying, how had they accessed a secure underground car park to put the envelope on my screen? If whoever had left it was a resident of the building, if Darrell had inexplicably decided to invite one of the neighbours he scarcely knew to our wedding, why hadn't they just posted their reply through his letter box?

My fingers were trembling as they broke the seal on the envelope. More scrawled writing covered the pre-printed reply. It was a standard acceptance card, the kind they sell at newsagents and stationers everywhere. It wasn't one of the engraved personalised printed cards that I'd slipped into every invitation sent out to our family and friends. But something told me this reply hadn't been sent by anyone who fell into either of those categories.

Ignoring the spaces where you were meant to confirm or decline the invitation, the author of this message had written across the entire face of the card. Their disregard for the dotted lines offended me, but nowhere near as much as their words:

I will <u>NOT</u> be attending your wedding... and if you've got any sense, you won't either.

I didn't wait for the lift, but took the stairs, all five flights of them, which meant that by the time I hammered on Darrell's door I was breathless and trembling and could no longer tell whether it was from anxiety or my exertions.

'What? What is it? What's wrong?' Darrell asked when he opened his door and I practically fell into his arms. He looked past me into the deserted hallway as though expecting to see... I don't know what. Perhaps that man with the axe Karen spent so much time going on about.

He kicked the door shut and led me into the lounge, one arm circled around my waist, supporting me, because suddenly my legs couldn't remember how to do it. Still too shocked to speak, I handed him the envelope first, and saw his brows furrow to meet in the middle in confusion, and then inch even closer together when I passed him the card. I was watching him carefully, but I could decipher none of the expressions that flitted across his familiar features, because they dissolved and changed into the next one too quickly.

The final expression, the one he decided to stick with, was one of ironic and slightly irritated amusement. Holding one corner of the reply card, he tapped it against his outstretched palm. 'Is *this* what got you so scared? I thought someone had attacked you or something.'

I shook my head, and tried to regain control of my breathing, which proved if nothing else that I really ought to exercise more, because the climb up the stairs had totally winded me.

'What does it mean? Why would someone leave it on my car? And why does it sound so threatening?'

Of my three questions, the second one seemed to bother him most. 'This was on your car?'

I nodded, wiping my damp palms on the legs of my jeans. Beneath the denim I could feel the muscles of my thighs still trembling, as though electrically charged.

For a moment I thought I saw a glimpse of anger on Darrell's face, and then it was gone and his mouth twisted into a wry grin. 'Well, obviously, it's somebody's idea of a joke.'

'Who? Why would anyone do that? And if it's a joke, it isn't a very funny one.'

'Agreed,' said Darrell, turning to a small cabinet and pulling out a bottle of amber-coloured liquid. I don't drink whisky, but this didn't seem the right moment to remind him of that. There was a generous double shot in the glass he passed me.

'Drink,' he ordered, standing over me like a scary nurse dispensing medicine. 'It'll make you feel better.'

The alcohol burnt like fire all the way down to my stomach. 'So who do you think left it?' I asked, trying hard not to cough like a teenager who's just raided her parents' alcohol stash.

Darrell sighed and then shrugged. 'If I had to take a guess, then my money's on one of the guys from the gym. It's their kind of prank – stupid and immature.'

Darrell was one of the minority; he was someone who actually made full use of his gym membership. The evidence of it was there, every time he unbuttoned his shirt. But this was the first time he'd ever mentioned interacting with any of the other members.

'You've never talked about anyone from there before. Are these people friends of yours?' I could hear the note of censure in my voice, the unspoken criticism that said I didn't like his friends. I'd met and been introduced to so few people from his world, it was unfortunate to take an instant dislike to some of the first people he'd chosen to mention.

For just a moment I thought I saw irritation on his face, but then he sat down beside me and pulled me against him. I went willingly into his arms, feeling instantly safe and also a little foolish. Had I really just massively overreacted to a rather pathetic practical joke?

'They're more acquaintances than friends,' he admitted. 'But a couple of them live in this building, so I'm pretty sure it must have been them.' He had his arms tightly secured around me and murmured into my hair, which meant I couldn't see his face or his expression as he spoke. 'I'm sure they thought they were being hilarious,' he said, his words fanning my forehead. 'I mentioned the wedding in passing the other day, so I guess that's what inspired this wind-up. I'm sure they didn't intend to frighten you.'

'Well, they kind of did,' I said, still decompressing from panic to foolishness.

'Then I'll definitely speak to them about it,' he said, sounding grim. 'They took it too far.' I wondered if he realised his hold on me had suddenly tightened to such a degree that it was just this side of uncomfortable. 'No one is *ever* going to hurt or scare you. Not without having to go through me first.'

3

I stood fidgeting on the pavement, shifting my weight from one foot to the other, while Darrell paid the taxi driver. Through the large glass frontage behind me, I could see my mother in the restaurant, sitting alone at the bar. Darrell's intention to make this a memorable evening hadn't exactly got off to a good start.

He slipped an arm around my shoulders as the taxi sped away. It must have felt like cuddling up to a statue. 'You're so tense,' he declared, giving my arm an affectionate squeeze and lightly kissing my cheek. 'Relax, babe. It's all going to be fine.'

I tried to smile, but my lips were reluctant to comply. 'It's just that I hate being late, you know that. And I really wanted tonight to go well, and now I feel all jangly and on edge.'

'Well, we could have gone for that tried and trusted way of getting you to chill out – but if we'd done *that*, we'd have been even later.' For once, his risqué humour failed to make me smile.

'Jeez, you *are* nervous,' he said, dropping his arm and reaching for my hand. 'Come on then,' he said, tugging me towards the entrance. 'Let's go and prove to your mum that the best love stories aren't only to be found in books.'

There were two empty martini glasses on the bar beside my mother's designer handbag. That wasn't an encouraging sign, because it meant that she, at least, had managed to get there early. It was a trait we shared, and one she'd probably passed on to me in the first place, right along with my bright blue eyes. But, to be fair, she neither glanced at her watch nor made any comment about our punctuality as we crossed the room to greet her. I was still apologising into a waft of hairspray and perfume as she hugged me. My explanation about traffic jams and road closures was swept aside by an elegant manicured hand.

'I told her not to worry,' said Darrell smoothly, bending down and lightly touching his lips to my mother's cheek. I watched as he pulled back and then looked momentarily confused as she proffered the second cheek. I'm sure she didn't do it deliberately. I knew very well it was the customary way people in her industry greeted each other. But if she'd been looking for a means of momentarily wrong-footing her future son-in-law, she couldn't have chosen better.

'Can I get you both a drink?' Darrell asked, already making eye contact with the waiter behind the bar.

'Two's usually my limit,' said my mother with a smile that, if you didn't know her as well as I did, you might mistakenly think was genuine. *Touché, Mum. You got in the first jab.*

'Of course,' Darrell said, subtly shaking his head at the approaching barman. 'I'll just go and check us in with the maître d'',' he added, heading off towards the podium in the plush reception area.

'Give him a chance, Mum, please. He's trying so hard to make you like him.'

The red lipstick of her smile didn't exactly soften her reply. 'He's certainly trying.'

I ignored the double meaning. There was no point at all in getting into a battle of words with a bestselling novelist. She was always going to win. I wouldn't come into my own until it came time to work out the percentage for the tip.

Darrell seemed to be taking longer than expected confirming our table was ready. He was half a room away from us, facing in the opposite direction, so I could neither see nor hear him, but his body language was positively screaming out to me across the bar. Something was wrong. I slipped off my stool and laid a hand lightly on my mother's forearm. 'Wait here a minute, Mum, I'm just going to see if he needs a hand.'

Elegantly plucked eyebrows arched slightly, but I didn't hang around long enough to wait for her comment. Instead, I crossed to the podium, where a smooth-faced head waiter was talking in measured and controlled tones. Darrell's hands were resting on the man's podium, his arms braced, like a preacher about to give an inspiring sermon. The maître d' kept glancing down at those hands, as though he'd really like to flick them off.

'What's up?' I asked, my glance switching between the two men. One looked impassive; the other looked ready to explode.

'I'm afraid, madam, there has been some sort of confusion.'

'There was no confusion,' retorted Darrell tightly. I glanced at his face. He should take up ventriloquism, I found myself thinking randomly, because he'd said that almost without moving his lips. 'This table has been booked for weeks. I have the confirmation right here,' he said, pulling his phone from his pocket and rapidly scrolling through his emails. He laid the phone upside down on the podium, like a Vegas gambler putting down the winning card.

The maître d's eyes flicked briefly down to the screen and then back up to us. A couple came into the restaurant behind me. Silently, using just his eyebrows and a discreet hand gesture, a second waiter was summoned to deal with the new arrivals, who were quickly shown to their table. Forestalling the comment he must have known Darrell was going to make, the waiter said pointedly, 'They had a reservation.'

'*I* had a reservation – *have* a reservation,' Darrell countered, his voice just a decibel or two louder than socially acceptable.

'And it was cancelled,' replied the head waiter.

'What?' said Darrell. 'No it wasn't. I didn't cancel it.'

The maître d' looked down at a leather-bound book on the podium before him. He ran a long, elegant finger down a page of neatly written notes, and then looked up, his eyes momentarily flicking towards me. 'A young lady cancelled the booking.'

Darrell turned to me, his voice suddenly uncertain. 'Did you cancel the reservation?'

'No. Of course not. It must be a mistake.'

The maître d' gave a small Gallic shrug, despite the fact that his accent was pure Home Counties. He bent down and peered more closely at the written note. 'It says here that the booking was cancelled two days ago by a Mrs Suzanne Kingston.'

'That's *my* name,' I cried, shaking my head in confusion. 'Or at least it will be in three weeks' time. Until then I'm still Suzanne Walters. But I certainly never phoned the restaurant, or cancelled the booking.'

The maître d' didn't care. His only concern was in calming the situation. 'I'm terribly sorry, sir, but as I'm sure you can appreciate, the restaurant is extremely popular and is always booked to capacity several weeks in advance. Regretfully we have no availability for walk-ins.'

'We're not walk-ins,' said Darrell doggedly, but the fight had gone out of his voice. He lifted his head, and we exchanged a meaningful look. Despite all his assurances that he had taken care of things, it had happened again.

'Is something wrong?' All three of us jumped at the sound of my mother's voice.

'There's just been a bit of a muddle with the reservation,' I explained. It seemed to be the safest party line to adopt.

'I asked my secretary to confirm the booking a couple of days ago, but somehow the wires got crossed and it ended up being cancelled.' *Wow.* I turned to Darrell, quietly awed by the ease with which the lie had slipped from his lips. I was incapable of telling an untruth without blushing, stammering or over-embellishing. Everyone always saw straight through me. But Darrell had sounded so incredibly convincing that even *I* was prepared to believe him, despite knowing perfectly well that he had no secretary.

'Aw, what a shame,' said my mother, and I thought I could see a glimmer of relief in her eyes.

The head waiter was looking at her curiously, and I could almost read his mind. My mother's face was well known. You don't write that many books or give that many interviews without people recognising you now and again. I glanced at Darrell and could see a possible solution pop into his head like a light bulb. I shook my head, shooting down the idea before it took flight. No way would my mother ever ask for, or accept, preferential treatment in a restaurant. If Darrell even thought of saying *Do you know who this is?*, we might just as well call off the wedding here and now.

The evening *was* salvaged by my mother, not by playing the celebrity card, but by suggesting that we ate at the restaurant in her hotel. We did, and we had a perfectly pleasant time, with good food of sufficient portion size that no fast-food restaurants were required on the way home. But behind the polite conversation, the banter and repartee, in the moments when my mother's attention was elsewhere, Darrell and I kept exchanging meaningful glances. It really wasn't over, and I was beginning to worry that it never would be.

Having to wait several hours to say your piece is frustrating. The spark that lit your fury has a habit of flickering out, meaning that when the topic is eventually raised, your words are already filled with a dull resignation, and your anger has gone cold. It's the most dangerous kind.

'How the hell did your ex know we were going to be at that restaurant tonight? Did *you* tell her?'

Darrell looked at me carefully, and I could see him still trying to gauge just how bad this conversation was likely to get. 'Of course not. And before we start jumping to conclusions, we have no way of knowing it was definitely her.'

Words weren't required for my reply. Raising my eyebrows was every bit as eloquent. Darrell shook his head, still not prepared to concede any ground. 'We *don't* know, Suzanne, not for certain. Stop and think about it for a minute; it makes no sense. For a start, how would *anyone* know which restaurant we'd booked for this evening?'

He made a valid point, but I was about three hours beyond reasonable. 'Perhaps your "secretary" told her,' I said, air-quoting the word, despite the fact that doing so always made me feel theatrical and a little bit foolish. 'Or maybe she knows your password and hacked into your emails.' His brow furrowed, and I could tell he hadn't even considered that possibility. 'You promised me you were going to speak to her, that you wouldn't just leave it to your friends to tell her to back off.' I could hear the anger rising in my voice, and from the concern in his eyes, so could Darrell. 'You told me it was over, that nothing else was going to happen, and yet here we are again. This *has* to stop.'

Darrell's eyes flickered and in the dim interior of the taxi it was impossible to look into them, to read if he was telling me the truth. 'I *did* speak to her, and she denied it all. I know you're upset, but I really don't think what happened this evening was anything more than a genuine mistake.'

I swivelled on the cab seat, looking at the kaleidoscope of street lights and neon shop signs flashing past my window. They blurred and merged, as though I was watching the kind of technique they use in films to indicate the passage of time. Within the cab, the exact opposite was happening. We weren't hurtling further forwards, we were stuck in neutral, wheels spinning, but getting absolutely nowhere. Exactly where we'd been since Darrell's former girlfriend had first begun her campaign to jeopardise our wedding.

I took a couple of deep breaths, determined to feign a composure that I certainly wasn't feeling. 'Well, *if* you spoke to her,' – my tone made it clear that I no longer totally believed that he'd done so – 'and she's still pulling this kind of stunt, then I think it's now time we involved the police.'

He laughed, but when he saw the deadly serious expression on my face the sound died in his throat. 'The police? *Really*, Suze? Have you thought how that conversation might go?' His eyebrows rose almost as effectively as mine had done, as he pantomimed holding a telephone to his ear. 'Hello officer, yes, I'd like to report a crime. My dinner reservation got maliciously cancelled tonight, and someone needs to be arrested. I think it should be my ex-girlfriend. No officer, I don't have any proof. None at all.'

I sighed, because I supposed he could be right. This *could* just have been an innocent misunderstanding. And we still didn't know for certain who was behind the chain of unsettling incidents that had begun all those weeks ago with the note on my windscreen.

We sat in silence for the remainder of the journey, and it wasn't until the cab driver flicked on his indicator and pulled up at the kerb outside my building that Darrell reached for my hand.

'Do you still want me to stay over tonight?' His voice was hesitant and when I looked into his eyes I was surprised to see genuine apprehension that I might say *No*. There was a young boy's vulnerability in his expression, and it tugged at my heart in a way I hadn't been expecting.

I gripped his hand tightly. 'Of course I do. We're in this together.'

It took me a great deal longer to fall asleep that night than it did Darrell, despite the fact it was *my* bed we were sharing, rather than his. It was the bed we'd be sharing permanently in just three weeks' time. Well, as permanently as his frequent business trips would permit.

He was snoring, ever so lightly, and I was still at that stage in our relationship where I found it cute and endearing. 'Really? Most nights I'd happily smother Tom with his own pillow,' Karen had said when I'd told her this. 'And I bet a jury of women would let me walk,' she'd added with a knowing nod.

'Well, I kind of like it,' I'd told her. 'I don't even mind when he talks in his sleep.'

'Darrell sleep-talks?' Karen had pounced on this delightedly, lowering the fork that was halfway to her lips, letting the salad on it fall back on her plate. 'What does he say?'

I'd suddenly felt uncomfortable, as though I was betraying Darrell and disclosing his secrets. 'Nothing much. Nothing that makes sense, anyway. Mostly he just says my name.' Karen feigned a tiny gagging motion, and we both laughed.

'Don't mind me,' she said eventually. 'I'm probably just jealous. You're still at that starry-eyed stage, whereas Tom and I are like an old married couple. Without the proposal, or the ring, or the wedding, of course.' There was just a hint of bitterness in her voice. She looked down at the table, shook her head and made a small dissatisfied sound, which could have been directed at either her low-calorie lunch or her relationship, it was difficult to tell.

'So what else does Darrell say? Anything juicy?'

My laugh had sounded embarrassed. 'No, of course not. You really *do* have a one-track mind sometimes.'

Karen had given an evil grin, which faded when she saw I was no longer smiling. 'Sometimes he has nightmares, and calls out in his sleep.'

'What does he say?'

I shrugged, feeling disloyal to have parted the bedroom curtains on our private relationship. 'Nothing. Well, nothing that makes any sense. I guess he must be worrying about something. Work, perhaps?'

'Don't take this the wrong way, but you don't think he's getting cold feet, do you? Wedding jitters?' she'd suggested. I tried to tell myself her question hadn't sounded just a little bit hopeful.

'No,' I said, shaking my head positively. 'Anyway, aren't those meant to be a bride's thing?'

'Anyone can change their mind at any time. It's never too late, hon,' Karen had replied, almost as though she was holding open a door, in case I wanted to walk through it. Which I did not. But it did tell me that Karen still had her doubts about my forthcoming marriage.

'Well, I don't want to change my mind, and Darrell definitely doesn't. I don't think I've ever heard of a groom so excited about the big day as he is.'

★ ★ ★

59

Now, with less than twenty-one days until we became husband and wife, I should be lying there worrying about table decorations, wedding favours and whether my dress would look better if I invested in a pair of magic knickers. Or whether my warring parents could actually make it through an entire day without killing each other. But instead I was lying in the dark beside my softly snoring fiancé, mentally running through the list of acts, ranging from mischievous to malicious, that we'd been on the receiving end of. Acts that – until we proved otherwise – we could only say had been perpetrated by person or persons unknown. Acts that Darrell assured me would now stop.

As though compiling a list for a complaint to the police, something Darrell categorically refused to consider, I began to catalogue them in the darkness of my insomnia.

After the card on my windscreen, nothing else had happened for a while, and I had happily accepted Darrell's explanation. His muscle-head friends at the gym had been spoken to, and according to Darrell they had apologised profusely. 'They looked like big school kids caught out in a prank,' I remember him telling me a couple of nights later. 'They had no idea you'd get so freaked out. Too much testosterone – or too many steroids,' he'd quipped, drawing a very firm and final line under the incident. A line I had every reason to trust, until about three weeks later.

I was sitting at my desk, grappling with a set of figures that refused to add up to the same amount twice. Deciding what I really needed was a coffee break, I reached for the phone to see if Karen was free. Just seconds before my hand touched the receiver, it began to ring.

'Hello,' I answered, frowning distractedly as I finally spotted the mistake on the sheet of figures that had been defeating me.

'Is that Suzanne? Suzanne Walters?'

I didn't recognise the voice. I picked up a pen and ringed the incorrect numbers on the spreadsheet. 'Yes. That's me. Can I help you?'

I knew from the ringtone that it was an internal call, but the number flashing up on the display meant nothing to me.

'It's Paul here. From downstairs.' I frowned, wondering why the name sounded familiar, and then felt a stupid blush flood my cheeks as he added, 'From the post room.' This was the guy Karen kept going on about. The one she reckoned should be working as an Abercrombie model, rather than a mailman.

'Oh, hello,' I said, extremely glad he didn't know I was now picturing a model on a black-and-white photo shoot, on a windswept beach, with a half undone shirt. 'What can I do for you?'

'Erm,' he began hesitantly, almost as though he too felt awkward. Perhaps he was a mind reader, in which case I was probably about to be hauled in to Human Resources on some kind of sexual harassment complaint. 'I was wondering if you're busy right now?'

It was such a peculiar and unexpected thing to be asked that the red pen I'd been toying with slipped from my fingers and rolled off the desk. 'You see, I have a delivery for you down in the post room. And I was wondering if you'd be able to come down to collect it.'

I frowned as I bent to retrieve the pen. 'Not really,' I said, eyeing the figures I was keen to return to. 'I'm kind of busy at the moment. Can't you just bring it up, as usual?'

He was quiet for a long moment, as though there was something he really wanted to say, but couldn't quite work out how. 'Well, it's not quite that simple. It would be so much easier if you could just pop down for it.'

I looked at my desk, my eyes settling on the small framed photograph of Darrell and me. We'd asked a passer-by to take it on a sunny Sunday afternoon in the summer. We were sitting on the grass in Hyde Park. Darrell's arm was thrown casually around my shoulders, and we were both laughing. Whatever the mysterious delivery was, down in the post room, I was pretty certain it would be from him. Even though the early days of our courtship were long behind us, Darrell still sent me thoughtful gifts for no reason whatsoever. Bouquets of flowers weren't just for birthdays or anniversaries, at least not in Darrell's book. I smiled at the image in the frame grinning back at me. I really was incredibly lucky.

'You're sure you can't bring whatever it is up here?' I asked Paul one more time.

'I'd really rather not,' he said, sounding apologetic but strangely unbending.

'Okay then. I'll come down. You're in the basement, right?'

'I'll meet you by the lifts,' he said, sounding curiously relieved, and then hung up without another word.

★ ★ ★

I had to take two lifts: the one down to reception had thick carpets, mirrored walls and piped music, while the service one, tucked away behind a marble pillar, was far more utilitarian. I was the only occupant of the second lift, which took me down into the bowels of the building far less smoothly than my first ride. It was quite a relief when the carriage juddered to a halt and the display lit up to announce we'd reached Level B1.

I stepped out into a concrete corridor, which seemed to belong to an entirely different building. Fluorescent strip lights illuminated a long grey passageway, which held all the charm of one of Her Majesty's prisons.

'Suzanne – I mean Miss Walters,' said a deep voice from somewhere behind me. I spun around, already correcting him as I turned. 'Suzanne, please,' I said, smiling a little dazedly in the fluorescent glare. Surely no one should look that good under this type of colour-draining artificial light? Wasn't it, in fact, illegal to look like anything except a cholera victim on a particularly bad day? That memo had clearly never made it to the post room. The man standing before me was washed in colour, from the auburn highlights in his thick, slightly over-long hair, to the brilliant green of his eyes, the colour of jewellery-shop-window emeralds. His skin was lightly bronzed, as though the memory and the tan of a foreign sun upon it had no intention of fading just yet.

He was tall, well over six foot, and even though I was wearing my work stilettos, the ones with the heels just this side of impossible-to-run-in, he still dwarfed me.

He rubbed one palm against the leg of his faded denim jeans, before extending it to me in greeting. I was a few seconds too slow in raising mine in response. My cheeks felt a little warm as we bizarrely shook hands in the corridor. If Paul noticed my clumsy embarrassment, he was too polite to comment on it, while I was too busy feeling annoyed with myself for being surprised by his greeting. Why *shouldn't* someone who pushed a mail cart for a living have impeccable manners?

'I'm sorry for dragging you away from your desk,' he said, beginning to walk towards a pair of swing doors at the end of the corridor. I fell into step beside him, unconsciously lengthening my stride to keep up with him.

'That's all right,' I said, even though my in tray was so full, I was probably going to have to stay late again that night to catch up. 'I must admit I was a little intrigued by your call.' I must have sounded excited about whatever was waiting for me beyond the swing doors: the parcel with my name on its label.

Paul frowned and paused with his hand flat against one half of the swing doors. 'I just didn't feel... comfortable... delivering this up to your desk.'

This time it was my turn to frown. It sounded like asking me to come down to collect the item was intended to spare me in some way. For the first time it occurred to me that perhaps this might not be something I actually *wanted* to receive.

'What exactly is it? What have I been sent?'

In answer, Paul pushed open the door and courteously stood back to allow me to walk through it first. The post room was larger than I had imagined it would be. One wall was lined with pigeonholes and there were two enormous metal desks sitting in the centre of the room. Both were currently unoccupied.

Around the perimeter of the room, a collection of mail carts were lined up, looking exactly like the ones the seven dwarfs had used in the diamond mine. Some were empty; some had parcels and hessian sacks filled with post, waiting for the next delivery round. Paul kept walking, stopping just short of the final cart. Within it I could see an easily recognisable cellophane-wrapped package. Darrell had sent flowers to me at work many times, although perhaps none of the arrangements had been quite this large before. The bouquet was facing away from me, so I couldn't see the flowers within it. Paul took a discreet step to one side, turning to study a noticeboard, which largely seemed to have several-months-out-of-date memos pinned to it.

I reached out for one corner of the cellophane bouquet and turned it around. For one crazy moment I thought the florist had mistakenly put the flowers in upside down. All I could see at the top of the arrangement were woody green stems, covered in thorns; I looked down to where the bouquet was bundled and tied together with ribbon, and saw the heads of the roses. Only they hadn't accidentally been inverted in the packaging. Every single one of the rose blooms had been severed from its stem. They sat pooled at the bottom of the cellophane like tiny red decapitated heads. I pulled the bouquet from the cart.

'Did they get crushed, or damaged after they were delivered? Is that what happened?'

Paul turned back from the noticeboard, shaking his head regretfully. 'No. That's how they were when they arrived.'

'Then... then there must have been some mix-up at the shop,' I said, still trying to find a logical explanation. But from the quickened beat of my heart, and the sticky, sweaty film on my palms, I already knew what this was.

'All deliveries to the building come in to the main reception,' Paul said. His voice was kind, measured and sympathetic, and it made me feel like crying. And I really didn't want to do that; not yet, not here. That was what the Ladies' room was for. I wanted to be angry. I *deserved* to be angry, because it had happened again. That much I already understood. What I didn't know, was why.

'Reception then phone down here,' Paul continued to explain, as though it was somehow important that I understood the protocols and procedures, 'and I go up to collect the delivery.' I nodded, unable to tear my eyes away from the mutilated flowers. 'When I saw what had happened to these, when I saw the—' He broke off, as though suddenly changing his mind about what he'd been about to say.

'I went back up to check. But all they could tell me was that the flowers hadn't been delivered in the usual way. No one had signed for them. They'd arrived during a busy period when the reception was crowded. When everyone had gone, they found your bouquet propped up against the counter.' Paul got to his feet and crossed to one of the desks, pulling open a metal drawer. 'With this.'

The card wasn't in an envelope this time. It was edged by a thick black border, and was instantly recognisable as the type usually found attached to funeral flowers. As before, it was addressed to 'The Bride'. I'm no expert on calligraphy, but the handwriting looked the same as the message on the acceptance card left on my windscreen. *Condolences on your forthcoming wedding.*

I swallowed noisily, and for a dreadful moment thought I might be inexcusably sick all over the post-room floor.

'Sit down,' ordered Paul, pushing me gently on to a nearby threadbare office chair. His brilliant green gaze went from me, to the card, and then back to the flowers, rapidly assessing. 'I take it this is a little darker than just someone's idea of a practical joke?'

I gave a shrug, which in my head wanted to appear nonchalant, but in reality probably looked beaten and pathetic. Without bothering to ask if I wanted a drink, Paul crossed over to a small kitchen area and switched on the kettle. I have no idea how many teaspoons of sugar he put in that tea, but it was enough for the spoon to practically stand up unaided.

'Better?' he asked, after I'd taken a couple of sips and set the mug back down on the desk, before cavities the size of potholes started appearing in my teeth.

'Yes,' I said, shaking my head slightly, looking for my composure, and realising I must have left it up by my desk on the tenth floor, because it certainly wasn't anywhere to be found down here.

Paul sat down on the desk opposite me, his long legs swinging slowly backwards and forwards. 'So, congratulations are in order, then? I take it you're getting married?'

I knew he was trying to infuse some normality into the situation, but I was still struggling to get past the nasty message on the card. Someone clearly hated me, and I had no idea why. I had no enemies – well, none that I was aware of. Was this to do with me, or Darrell? Or was it somehow connected to my mother? Some of her early fan correspondence had been a little scary and intense. Had someone discovered I was her daughter, and was so tangled up in the mystical world she'd created that they were muddling fact with macabre fiction?

I shook my head. That made no sense. I never used her surname and very few people even knew we were related. And mostly her fans were lovely. They were far more likely to send teddy bears and cuddly toys than two dozen decapitated roses.

The phone on the desk rang, making me jump as though the sender of the flowers had somehow found me here. Paul saw my reaction and gave a sympathetic smile as he lifted the receiver and dealt with the call, all the time glancing over at me in concern. I took a couple of deep breaths and tried to pull myself together.

'Sorry about that,' he apologised as he hung up.

I started to get to my feet. 'Look, I really should go. I'm keeping you from your work.'

He gave a casual shrug, as if to say the wheels of industry would probably keep turning just fine, even if the mail was a few minutes late. He was probably right.

'Why don't you stay here for a little longer, until you've calmed down properly,' he suggested. 'You're still rather white.'

I nodded and sank back gratefully into his chair, while he wheeled out the one from the neighbouring desk and dropped on to it.

'So I take it you don't know who sent them to you?' I shook my head. 'Or why?'

'I have no idea.'

'Maybe a distraught and heartbroken ex-boyfriend?' he

suggested, his lips twisting slightly, trying to judge if it was still a little too early for humour.

I gave a tentative smile and it felt good, like pouring alkali on acid. 'No exes in recent history, not heartbroken or otherwise. Not for a very long time, actually,' I added, wondering why I was suddenly baring my past to a total stranger in this way.

His grin grew broader. 'Well, that just can't be true,' he said, his green eyes twinkling.

'Seriously, are you flirting with me? Now? Because that's all kinds of wrong. Besides which, how old are you anyway? Eighteen? Twenty?'

He laughed then, and the sound filled the room, the way music does in a chapel. 'Hardly. Although thank you for that. Actually, I'm twenty-seven.' I raised my eyebrows and he shrugged. 'Yeah, I still get asked for ID wherever I go,' he added ruefully.

'I'm not surprised.' He was only a few years younger than me, but looked a decade less. He leant forward, his elbows resting on his knees, and his work ID pass swung forward on its lanyard. It was impossible not to read the name printed on it: *Paul Winterscotch*. It was a very unusual name, yet one I knew well. It was etched in stone above the entrance to this building; it was written in script across the top of every piece of letterhead or stationery I pulled from my desk drawer.

'Winterscotch?' I queried. He gave a shrug. 'Are you related to...?' I lifted one finger and pointed it straight up.

'To God, no,' he quipped. 'But to Donald Winterscotch up on the twentieth floor, then yes, guilty as charged. He's my father.'

'But... but you work in the post room,' I said, instantly blushing, because I knew I must have sounded like the worst kind of snob.

'I do,' he declared. 'And very nice it is too, because it gives me the chance to meet lots of lovely people, like you, and make tea for them.'

I blushed again. For goodness sake, what was wrong with me today?

'This is a bit of a family tradition,' Paul explained, sweeping his arm out to encompass his surroundings. I tried very hard not to stare at the particularly well-toned bicep visible beneath his short-sleeved T-shirt. 'Both my grandfather and father started in the company at the bottom, and worked their way up. I'm just doing it a little later in life. I spent several years travelling after getting my Business Master's.'

I looked down at my feet, knowing I should probably apologise for the implied insult, but wasn't sure if that would just make things worse.

'Most of the time people don't even notice the name, even though I'm hardly going incognito with this thing hanging round my neck,' he said, tapping the plastic badge with the very attractive photograph on it. I looked like a startled convict in mine – it was even worse than my passport photo. Randomly, I wondered what Darrell's passport photograph looked like. I couldn't remember ever having seen it.

'I don't exactly advertise the family connection,' admitted Paul.

'I can totally understand that,' I said. And then, quite bizarrely, I found myself telling him who my mother was

– something that usually took many years for me to reveal to new acquaintances.

'Your secret's safe with me,' he assured, glancing discreetly down at the watch on one tanned wrist. Despite the fact I now knew he could easily have afforded a Rolex, I caught a glimpse of the figure on the watch's face, which, unless I was mistaken, was Mickey Mouse. I smiled and realised that even though I'd only known him for less than half an hour, I already liked and trusted him.

'So what do you want to do about those?' Paul asked, getting to his feet and nodding towards the flowers.

'Bin them,' I said decisively.

He nodded. 'Okay. I'll take care of it for you. But first, do you have a phone on you?'

I reached into my jacket pocket and drew out my mobile, vaguely shocked when I saw the time. I'd been away from my desk for ages.

'Photograph them. Just in case you need... I don't know, evidence or anything. And hang on to this,' he said, picking up the black-edged card that I'd thrown down on his desk.

I took it, holding it by just one corner, as though the poisonous words scrawled upon it might contaminate my fingers.

'Someone out there has a nasty little mind. But don't let them ruin your excitement about your big day. When is it, by the way?'

'Soon,' I replied. But instead of sounding happy, my voice sounded as grim as my mother's had done when I told her I was engaged.

★ ★ ★

Darrell was sitting in my lounge, on my settee, watching my television, drinking coffee from one of my mugs, when I let myself into my flat that evening. None of that should have annoyed me, because I was the one who'd phoned and asked him to meet me here, even though we hadn't planned to see each other that night.

But I couldn't stop the frisson of irritation that ran through me. He was sitting there, totally oblivious to everything. And again, he could hardly be blamed for that, because I'd chosen not to tell him anything about the dead flower bouquet over the phone. I wanted to be standing right in front of him, looking into his eyes, when he tried to tell me it was once again probably one of his bench-pressing pals, just having a laugh. Because, frankly, this time that excuse wasn't going to fly. For a start, how would any of them have known where I worked?

I shrugged out of my jacket, lobbing it over the back of a chair, and walked towards the settee. Darrell had his back to me, transfixed by whatever he was watching on the screen. I knew he'd heard my key in the lock, but apart from shouting out a greeting, he had yet to turn around.

'Darrell—' I began, only to be silenced by his upraised hand.

'Have you seen this?' he asked, his eyes still on the television.

My glance flicked from the hand, still lifted above his head, as though holding back traffic, to the screen. There was a small box in the lower corner of the picture with the word 'LIVE' in it, and beyond that a confusion of emergency vehicles, crowds of onlookers and, bizarrely, a very large crane.

'No, I haven't, I—'

He talked right over me. 'There's been an awful accident at that theme park near here. Some of the carriages on one of the big roller-coasters have collided. The casualties have been horrific, and there are still people trapped on the ride.'

I felt a momentary spasm of sympathy for the victims, mixed with guilt that I was prioritising my own personal drama over theirs. 'That's terrible,' I said. I paused, waiting for him to turn around, expecting him to be sufficiently in tune with my emotions to realise something was troubling me. Something far closer to home.

A rescue helicopter swept into view on the screen and Darrell's attention was sucked back to the enfolding drama at the theme park.

'Would you please turn that off for a moment?' I asked, my voice tight and controlled.

For the first time he must have heard something in it, or seen a shadow in my eyes when he finally turned to face me. His hand reached immediately for the remote control, but he didn't switch off the set, he just muted the sound, and that annoyed me long after the conversation that followed was over and done with.

'It's happened again,' I said, without preamble.

'What's happened again?' Darrell asked, looking genuinely bewildered. For just a fleeting second I saw his gaze return to the television; the arrival of the helicopter was clearly more diverting than whatever was bothering me.

I reached into my handbag, plucked out the card with the black border and dropped it over his shoulder. *Incoming*: just like a small but deadly explosive. It landed face up on the cushion beside him. He didn't reach for it or pick it up, but instead read it from the place where it had fallen. His eyes looked dark and turbulent, like storm clouds, as they met mine.

'Tell me everything,' he said.

There was very little consolation in knowing that my story was finally of greater importance to him than the roller-coaster tragedy.

'Where are these flowers now?' was his first question.

'Paul threw them away for me.'

'Paul? Who's he? One of your colleagues?'

'He's the guy who works in the post room.' Darrell nodded, and I knew the man who'd kindly sat comforting me that day had already been dismissed as an unimportant walk-on in this play. It was a trait of Darrell's I'd noticed before, his inclination to judge a person's importance by how they earned their living. My mother, *New York Times* bestselling author: very important. The man who delivered the post... considerably less so. I wondered what he'd say if I bothered adding that one day Paul Winterscotch would most likely own the company I worked for. It wasn't relevant, so I said nothing.

'I really don't think your gym buddies were behind this one, do you? In fact, the more I think about it, why would grown men get involved in such an infantile prank? It seems highly improbable to me that they were *ever* involved.'

'But they apologised for it,' Darrell reasoned. 'Why would they confess to something they didn't do?' He made a good point. 'Anyway, there's no reason to believe these incidents are related in any way.'

I sat down heavily on the armchair opposite him, ignoring the fact that there was plenty of room beside him on the settee. 'Are you kidding me? You can't possibly think they're not connected. Even the handwriting looks the same.'

Darrell picked up the card, and spent a long time studying the formation of the letters. 'Actually, it looks quite different to me.'

I sighed deeply. 'What did you do with the first card? We should compare them.'

'I burnt it,' he answered, leaning back and folding his arms in an oddly defensive pose. Darrell didn't smoke. His flat was totally electric and had no fireplace. If I ever wanted to light candles at his place, I had to bring my own matches, because he never had any. So burning the card seemed an odd and strangely overdramatic method of disposal.

'Well, I'm sorry, but I think you're wrong. I think they were sent by the same person. For a start, they were both addressed to me as *The Bride*.'

'You *are* the bride. Well, you're going to be soon,' he said, chancing a small smile, which was way too early to introduce.

'Well, clearly someone isn't happy about that,' I said. It was something even he couldn't refute. 'Paul suggested it might be a disgruntled ex?'

'Paul the postman? He seems to have got very involved in this whole thing, if you don't mind me saying.'

Actually, I found I *did* mind, but I really didn't know why, except it felt as though Darrell's objection to Paul might possibly be a smokescreen, thrown up to obscure the real issues here.

'There's certainly no one in *my* past who has any reason to be anything but delighted that we're getting married,' I said, my eyes searching his face, ready to spot a betraying lie. 'Can you honestly say the same thing?'

Darrell rarely spoke about his previous relationships, and I'd never pushed him to reveal more than he was willing to offer. Prying felt wrong, and looking forward was always preferable to looking back. But this was different. And so, for the first time, Darrell reluctantly lifted up one corner of the veil he'd thrown over his recent failed relationship, just enough to convince me of something he so clearly believed. Whoever was trying to sabotage our impending wedding, it definitely wasn't his ex.

In the weeks that followed, it was a line Darrell held and maintained like a defending infantryman, I recalled as I rolled on to my side, watching as the bedside clock clicked over into yet another hour. I had work in the morning, and was going to be completely wrecked if I didn't get some sleep soon. And this was old ground, which we'd both walked backwards and forwards over many times before, looking for answers we never found.

Eventually, I fell asleep with a carousel of memories spinning in my head, memories that were guaranteed to ensure my sleep was not peaceful: anonymous notes, mutilated flowers, callers who hung up when the phone was answered, a slashed tyre on my car, and a long, raking scratch down one side of his. Nothing dangerous, admittedly, and while they *could* be unconnected, it still felt as if someone was so opposed to our wedding they'd resorted to cheap scare tactics lifted straight out of a thriller.

That night I dreamt I was standing in a church, wearing

my beautiful Fleurs wedding dress. Darrell was smiling beside me, his eyes glowing with love, and in that peculiar way that dreams have, it didn't seem at all odd to find the ceremony being conducted by the maître d' of the restaurant. We'd just reached the point in the proceedings when the congregation was asked if anyone had any objections, and if so, to speak now. For a moment there was the breathtaking relief of silence, but then a voice, which I almost recognised, called out from behind me. 'Yes. I do.' I turned, in what felt like slow motion, but before I could see their face, the church bells began to clang and chime.

My hand shot out from beneath the duvet to silence the alarm. It was time to get up.

4

'I thought you said it was this way?' Darrell shot me a quick meaningful glance, which I probably deserved. I'd been snapping at him all morning, and that just wasn't like me, or fair to him.

I linked my arm through his, and turned us both around to study the illustrated floor plan of the airport, fixed to a nearby wall. I squeezed his arm gently, and he looked down at me, clearly waiting for the next volcanic eruption. There'd been several over the last twenty-four hours, so I could hardly blame him. Luckily, I managed to remember where I'd last left my smile, and pulled it quickly into place.

'Sorry. I don't mean to take it out on you. I'm just incredibly nervous about this reunion.'

'Really?' he questioned, gently tipping the end of my nose with his finger, before bending down and giving it a quick kiss. 'I'd never have guessed.'

'It really hasn't helped that Mum has been sliding in the dagger of doubt at every opportunity,' I said, frowning as

I studied the complex diagram, still trying to find a helpful 'You Are Here' marker.

'Dagger of doubt?' said Darrell, with a teasing chuckle. 'That's a very evocative description for a cold-hearted accountant to come up with. Perhaps you're more like your mother than you realise?'

'I certainly hope not,' I declared, leaning closer to the map and finally finding a tiny red arrow to indicate our location. 'Because if I am, I'd probably be ramming that dagger straight through my father's heart the moment he walks into Arrivals.'

'She *does* still seem very bitter, even after all these years,' Darrell agreed. 'Just remind me never to get on the wrong side of her.'

I smiled weakly, thankful he obviously still didn't realise that, actually, he was already practically there. I'd hoped the last week would have helped a little in getting them to bond. We'd seen Mum practically every evening, and Darrell was doing everything in the 'How to be a perfect son-in-law manual'. Maybe that was the problem. Maybe he was still trying too hard?

Only two nights ago I'd emerged from the shower to find he was already in bed, a copy of one of my mother's earliest books in his hands.

'I don't know how come I never read these as a kid,' he'd said, looking up briefly from his place with a slightly shamefaced expression. 'I always thought they'd be a bit girly and sissy-ish, but actually they're bloody good.'

I smiled, my heart suddenly full of love for a man in his thirties who chose a story of wizards and dragons as his bedtime reading... just for me. How could you not melt at that?

Perhaps Mum would never love him. Perhaps she'd never understand that his awkward laugh and the jokes and quips and bluster were only because he wanted everything to be perfect. And having a mother-in-law who approved of her daughter's choice would have gone a long way towards that.

Not that she'd said anything negative to me about Darrell over the past week; but she hadn't actually said anything positive either. The same could not be said about her former husband. She had *plenty* to say about him, except none of it was good.

'I really hope he's not intending to bring that blonde bimbo with him. Because there's no way you're going to want her leering back at the camera in your wedding photographs. What's her name? Cindy, Barbie... some sort of plastic doll's name, isn't it?'

I'd only just managed to squash my smile down. 'Candy,' I said, keeping my head down so she wouldn't see the mischief dancing in my eyes. 'Her name was Candy, but actually I believe they broke up a couple of years ago. He's been single ever since.'

I risked a quick glance. My mother was flicking through the photographs of the floral arrangements I'd chosen for the reception tables. 'Well, he probably drove her just as crazy as he did me,' she said, passing the enormous wedding portfolio back across the table to me. 'I like the flowers you've picked, by the way.'

This time I let my smile show, because it was a small and encouraging thaw in her icy disapproval of anything at all to do with my wedding, or getting married in general.

I slid the bulging folder back into the large tote bag I carried with me wherever I went. My mother's comments revealed far more than she realised. Because I'd never told her anything about the woman who'd moved into my father's apartment above the bar, around the time I graduated from university. The only way she could have known either her name or what she looked like was if she'd done some surreptitious Facebook stalking. If she had, I was quietly impressed, because she usually left anything to do with social media down to her publishers. If Darrell had had a Facebook page, I would definitely have done the same, to try to learn more about the woman who was clinging like a barnacle to the remnants of her relationship with the man I was soon to marry. But Darrell claimed social media was one of the most pointless advances in technology. 'All everyone does is post photographs of their dinner or their cat,' he'd once scathingly declared.

Darrell was studying the Arrivals board above my head, and I felt my stomach collide uncomfortably with several nearby organs when he announced, 'His plane's landed. Come on then, let's go and find him.'

I'd been surprised Darrell didn't appear to have a better working knowledge of the airport. We'd got in the wrong lane for the short-stay car park, meaning we'd had to circle the entire complex before eventually finding the correct place to park. We were early (way too early, but of course that was to be expected), but when I'd asked him which was the best restaurant for grabbing a late breakfast, he didn't seem sure. Nor did he know the quickest way to the Arrivals hall.

'It's because I usually come by taxi, I rarely eat at the airport, and when *I'm* here I'm obviously heading for Departures,' he reasoned, when I'd challenged why he seemed more lost than the tourists milling around us. It was a reasonable explanation, and the fact that I was seizing on the smallest thing to be angry about was more a measure of my own anxiety than his inability as a guide.

It had been over four years since I'd last been to Spain; since I'd last seen my father. As a child, I'd dutifully visited him for four weeks every summer after the divorce. I have vivid memories of being put on a plane in London by one parent, and being met at the gate in Malaga by the other. They weren't great holidays. He was busy building up the bar, and I was lonely, missing home, Mum and my friends. When I was thirteen years old, after a particularly bad stay, I screwed up the courage to tell him at the airport that I didn't want to come back the following year. The look of pain in his eyes still haunts me to this day.

Of course, when I turned eighteen, having a father who owned a bar in Spain made me almost as popular as having a bestselling children's author for a mother had done as a child. There'd been several holidays with school and university friends around to dilute the awkwardness, as we both sadly realised that somehow, in the intervening years, we'd practically forgotten how to be father and daughter.

The first thing that shocked me about my dad, as he walked with a crowd of sun-bronzed holidaymakers into the Arrivals hall, was that I almost didn't recognise him. I hadn't seen him for years, and the last time I did, he'd had that worrying look of a man who probably spent as much time drinking in his bar as he did working behind it. Back then, his thinning hair was still being worn swept over a hairline that was creeping ever higher. And the buttons on the colourful floral shirts he'd taken to wearing were stretched and gaping over a stomach that had enjoyed many pints and paellas with equal gusto.

So, not surprisingly, the middle-aged man with the closely cropped hair and the trim waistline who smiled and waved his arm through the air when he saw me was a bit of a shock.

We walked towards each other through the crowds, Darrell steering me out of the path of numerous small wheeled suitcases, which I would certainly have tripped over. My whole body was thrumming, like electricity humming through a cable. Darrell could feel it, and squeezed my hand so hard the diamond of my engagement ring must have dug painfully into his palm.

My father and I came to an awkward halt in front of each other, neither of us sure what the appropriate greeting should be. To hug, or not to hug? That was the question. Sensing an awkward gap that needed to be bridged, Darrell extended his hand.

'Hello, Mr Walters. I'm Darrell, Suzanne's fiancé.'

Their handshake seemed to unlock the rigor mortis of the moment, and when it was over I leant towards my father and his arms went around me. 'It's so good to see you again, Suzy,' he said into my hair, his voice gruff. It was the closest I had come to crying in front of him for a very long time.

★ ★ ★

Over the years, my parents had perfected the art of yin and yang parenting. If he zigged, she zagged. If he went left, she went right. If he blew hot, she was guaranteed to be glacier cold. So it was surprising to discover that on this one hugely important and significant detail, they appeared to be in total agreement. My father didn't seem to like Darrell either.

It took me a while to realise this. It certainly wasn't obvious on the drive from the airport to the hotel I had booked for him. Not the same one my mother was staying in – I'm not *that* stupid. The afternoon traffic was heavy, absorbing most of Darrell's concentration, so most of the journey was devoted to politely skirting over superficial details – mostly about the wedding, as though he was just a distant relative we'd invited to make up the numbers, rather than Father of the Bride, and the man whose arm I would be leaning on as I walked up the aisle in less than two weeks.

We had arranged a quiet dinner for just the three of us. It should have been a perfect time to segue him into the plans for the next fortnight, but right from the moment we met him in the hotel foyer I could sense a growing tension between the two men, which was so palpable it almost felt like we should pull out the fourth chair at the table and invite it to sit down and join us.

Initially, my father spent a considerable amount of time glancing from that spare seat to the door of the restaurant. It took me longer than it should have done to realise what – or rather who – he was waiting for.

'Mum's not coming this evening,' I told him eventually, as I poured water from a jug into our glasses. My father's eyes were cast down, focused only on the passage of the ice cubes tumbling out of the pitcher and crashing into the waiting glasses. For a man who'd spent the last twenty years of his life working in a bar, he seemed to find it singularly absorbing.

'I imagine she wants to spend as little time in my company as possible,' he said carefully, fingering and rearranging the cutlery beside his plate.

'No. It's not that. I think her publishers were planning on taking her out for dinner tonight,' I said, blushing like a teenager caught out in a lie.

His hand went from the cutlery to briefly cover mine. I glanced down and saw he also had brown age spots on skin that was no longer smooth and taut across his knuckles, the way it had been when we'd stopped holding hands. *See, you and Mum* have *got something in common after all.* The thought almost made me laugh explosively, but the sad look in my dad's eyes defused it.

'You don't have to cover up for her, Suzy. I didn't expect anything different.'

'Suzanne's been pretty anxious about how everyone would get along after such a long time,' divulged Darrell, reaching for my other hand. To the other diners it probably looked like we were about to conduct a séance.

'Not really,' I said, lying for the second time in as many minutes and shooting Darrell a warning glance, which he totally failed to pick up on.

'We just don't want there to be any awkwardness to spoil anyone's enjoyment of the day,' continued Darrell blithely.

My father's eyes flickered for a moment and my hand felt cold when he removed his. That was the first moment

I realised he didn't like Darrell. 'The last thing I've come all this way to do is cause trouble at your wedding,' he reassured me gently.

I don't know what made me do it. Having not breathed a word of anything to my mother all week, I was astonished at how easily the truth spewed out of me, as though it was something bad I'd ingested that my body could no longer tolerate.

I turned to Darrell. 'I think if our day is going to be spoiled in any way, it's more likely to be your malicious ex-girlfriend rather than my parents who is the cause.'

Darrell's eyes expressed his hurt and disbelief that I'd upended the bag and spilled out our secrets all over the table. I instantly wanted to turn back time and un-say it. His face, the look in his eyes... oh God, it was worse than kicking a puppy. Utterly inexcusable. Why had I done it?

'What's this all about?' my father inevitably asked.

I sighed and shook my head, knowing it had been too much to hope for that he wouldn't have heard or picked up on my comment. I downplayed it. I made it sound irritating but unimportant, and not something that kept me awake at nights, worrying about what was coming next. I believe I might even have laughed a couple of times, as though having someone trying to sabotage your wedding was actually amusing. *Hey, do you remember the time your crazy ex turned up at the church, darling?*

My attempts to make light of the situation were totally ineffective.

'What do the police have to say about all this? Have they—?'

'We've decided not to involve them,' interrupted Darrell.

I saw a long-forgotten expression on my father's face. It was a steely look, usually reserved for those who'd consumed too many sangrias and whose judgement was impaired. 'That's your first mistake,' he countered, sitting up a little straighter in his chair, unconsciously squaring his shoulders as he faced his son-in-law-to-be. Oh crap – this evening wasn't going to plan at all. 'This person, this woman, is guilty of – at best – harassment. That's a crime, and the police need to be called in to stop her from causing any more mischief.'

'Well, we can't say for sure that it is—' I began, loyally cleaving to the man who was going to spend the rest of his life with me, rather than the one who'd chosen to spend *his* half a continent away.

Darrell's voice was dull and flat, practically a monotone. 'She's not well... mentally. She's sick. Unbalanced. And I won't call the police, because doing so would almost certainly destroy whatever stability she's still holding on to.'

My eyes were large, my mouth was probably hanging open as I turned in my chair. I knew none of this. Darrell had never so much as hinted that she might be suffering from a genuine mental illness. Suddenly I felt frightened, not of the woman or what she could do to me – *that* thought would probably come creeping up on me unpleasantly later, I was sure. No, what scared me was that this was one huge ground-breaking disclosure to suddenly drop on me from a great height. How, and more importantly *why*, had he never mentioned this to me before?

'And you knew all about this, Suzy?' My face was still turned towards Darrell, so my father couldn't see the questions in my eyes, the shock still parting my lips, as though this new truth was just too big to swallow down all at once.

Very carefully I took back control of my features, and turned to face my dad. The sound of torn loyalty filled my head like separating Velcro. 'Yes, Dad, I did. She's not been well. She needs to be treated with sympathy and compassion. I'm sure once we're actually married, when the wedding is over and done with, she'll be far better able to move on, and let go.'

I could see Darrell nodding gratefully in my peripheral vision. He reached for my hand, and because my father's eyes were still on us, I had no choice but to let his fingers wind through mine.

'I know we've been calling her Darrell's crazy ex, but I didn't think she was actually, you know… properly crazy.'

I'd persuaded Karen to meet me in a small park just around the corner from our office block. I had a tendency always to get to work early, but Karen was habitually late. Getting her to meet me half an hour before work began was a big ask. I came prepared with the right currency to buy her good humour: a caramel cappuccino and a double chocolate muffin.

'I don't think "crazy" is an official diagnosis – it's not very PC for a start, but basically I think that's about the gist of it.'

Karen sunk her teeth deep into the sponge of the muffin. 'What did Darrell say when you challenged him about it?' I closed my eyes, trying to shut out the memory of our late-into-the-night conversation, as well as a light shower of muffin crumbs. 'You *did* call him on it, I hope. Why on earth was he keeping it a secret from you?'

The traces of the night were still lingering within my eyes, and in the shadowy circles beneath them. 'Probably because he still doesn't believe she's behind any of it,' I said.

'Well, if he's *that* convinced, why won't he let you call the police?' I loved the way she cut straight through to the important question.

'He says he doesn't even want them questioning her. That she's not strong enough.'

'Because... he still cares about her?' *This* was why I'd called Karen today. This was why I needed to speak to her, because I knew she wouldn't be afraid to ask the questions I was too scared to voice.

'Maybe,' I said quietly, staring deep into my cappuccino, as though the answers were all there, lying just below the froth.

'He's protecting the wrong woman,' she said darkly. 'You're the one he should be looking out for.'

I gave a tired shrug, fighting the urge to say 'I know'. 'All he keeps saying is that we just have to ignore it, and that everything will stop after the wedding.'

'How can he be so sure, when he claims he doesn't know who's doing it?' Karen was wasted in accountancy. She thought like a prosecutor during a quick-fire cross-examination, and that was just what I needed right then. 'Unless he already suspects who it might be?'

I shifted uncomfortably on the wooden bench, looking into the distance at the grey ribbon of path that wound through the park. There was a continual flow of early-morning joggers, providing a soundtrack of trainers slapping against tarmac.

I didn't want to risk Karen accidentally reading the memory of Darrell's final words on my face. *You're so sure the person behind all of this is connected to me. But remember, there are people close to you who've been opposed to our wedding too.*

He'd refused to say anything else. He'd just left the ugly thought hanging in the air, like a dirty bomb. There were only two people he could possibly be thinking of, and the idea that either of them was involved in any way was totally ridiculous. Neither Karen nor my mother would ever resort to anything this spiteful or vicious. And the fact that Darrell could even hint that it might be them made me question how little he knew about me or the people I cared about.

We didn't speak much after that. We balanced on either edge of the mattress all night, leaving enough space for at least two more people to sleep between us. He'd apologised in the morning, pulling me into his arms and murmuring that he'd only said it because he was overwrought, and that he hadn't really meant it. Of course it wasn't them. It was a stranger. A jealous, petty, nasty-minded stranger. He'd kissed me on the mouth, and I could taste toothpaste and coffee on his lips, and the lingering sour trace of a lie. He still thought the perpetrator was someone close to me, and I was a long way from being able to either forget or forgive his words.

It was thirteen days until our wedding.

★ ★ ★

'Hey, that's your new friend down there, isn't it?' Karen asked, balling up her muffin wrapper and lobbing it into a nearby bin.

I squinted into the morning sunshine, shielding my eyes with my hand like a visor. 'I wouldn't exactly call him that,' I said, allowing my eyes to travel along the jogging path until they settled on Paul Winterscotch, who was just approaching a bend. He slowed down to take the corner, looked up and saw us. His pace slowed from a jog to a trot, as he raised one arm and waved. Feeling a little self-conscious, I raised my own arm and did the same.

'Ooh, I think he's heading this way,' commented Karen unnecessarily, as Paul veered off the path and on to the grass and began to make his way up the slope towards us. 'Want me to leave?' she asked wickedly, which earned her a quick sideways glare.

'Not as much as I want you to stop being ridiculous,' I hissed back, through the smile I had ready and waiting for the very attractive man whose pace had now slowed down to a walk as he approached us.

Karen was humming something under her breath, which sounded suspiciously like an off-key version of the theme from the Diet Coke advert. Not that I couldn't appreciate what had prompted it. It was a warm summer morning, and Paul was wearing a standard jogger's uniform of shorts and T-shirt, which clung interestingly to his body in a way that no woman – not even one less than two weeks away from her wedding – could fail to notice.

'I thought it was you,' he said, smiling easily to include both of us in his greeting.

'It is,' I said stupidly. Karen gave a burble of laughter into her coffee. I shot her a look that said, *If you start choking now, there's no way you're getting a Heimlich from me, my friend.*

'You've been jogging?' I asked ludicrously. Karen coughed. I shot her another glance.

Paul either didn't notice or was too polite to comment on my obvious awkwardness. 'I try to get a few miles in each morning, whenever I can,' he said, lifting a water bottle to his lips. I deliberately focused my attention on a particularly interesting bush rather than watch him swallow the refreshing liquid. That was one cliché too far, even for me.

He lowered the bottle, his bright green eyes darkening a little in concern as he clocked the panda-like circles beneath my blue ones. 'Is everything okay?' he asked, his gaze darting briefly to Karen before settling once again on me.

'Yes, everything is absolutely fine,' I said, a lie I don't think any of us believed.

'Okay then,' Paul said slowly. 'Well, I should probably be heading back before I'm caught sneaking into the executive shower room again.' His grin was more dazzling than the sun climbing the sky above us. 'See you on the eleven o'clock collection,' he called back over his shoulder as he jogged away.

Karen waited until he was safely out of earshot. 'There's not one thing about him I don't like,' she said.

'There's not one thing about him that you actually know,' I countered, bending to retrieve my empty coffee cup.

'Not true,' she argued. 'I know he's kind, considerate, drop-dead gorgeous, delivers the mail on time, and is heir to a very successful company. And if I'm not mistaken, he is also a little bit smitten with you,' she added, winking comically. 'Shame you're already taken.'

It wasn't a conscious decision, but I'd found myself listening out for the rumble of the mail cart each day. More than once my eyes would stray to the clock, and if I had to do anything that would take me away from my desk, I tended to do it *after* the eleven o'clock collection and delivery. Not that we spoke every time he dropped mail into my in tray. Sometimes I would be on the phone, or in conversation with a colleague, but even then our eyes would meet, and there would be something warm and friendly in them that I came to look forward to seeing each morning.

About a week after the decapitated bouquet had been delivered, Paul dropped something on my desk, besides the mail. It was a small bunch of bright yellow gerberas, loosely wrapped in paper.

I'd put down my pen, swivelling my chair slowly around to face him.

'They were selling them off at half price on that market stall on the corner. I saw them when I went out to pick up a sandwich for lunch. I thought you might like them. They have heads,' he added with a smile. For a moment I could think of nothing to say, and during my silence Paul began to look unsure, as though he'd just noticed an invisible line he probably shouldn't have crossed.

'When you buy a girl flowers, you're not meant to tell her you got them cheap,' I advised with a smile, as I bent my head to the blooms. 'Girlfriends in particular don't like that.'

'I'll bear that in mind,' he replied easily, picking up a pile of letters from the out tray and dropping them into the cart, 'when I next have one.'

My eyes mutinously refused to leave his, however hard I tried to tug them away. 'Thank you for the flowers, Paul. It was a really thoughtful gesture.'

I'd kept them on my desk long past the time when their heads had grown droopy and they were ready for the bin. And I never once mentioned them to Darrell.

5

The ringtone was unfamiliar. Mine was 'La Bamba', which amused me every time it rang, except when I forgot to put it on 'silent' in meetings. Darrell's had the far more generic tone that had come with the phone. But this was different; it sounded like a wind chime caught in a gentle breeze, which quickly rose through the Beaufort scale. It had easily escalated to a hurricane by the time we were both awake.

'What *is* that? What's ringing?' I asked, squinting in the dawn light slicing through a gap in his curtains.

'Ugh,' grunted Darrell inarticulately beside me.

'Is it an alarm… or a phone?' I questioned, struggling up on to one elbow.

The bed suddenly bounced, as Darrell leapt from it faster than someone performing a seat drop on a trampoline. He hurried across his bedroom floor, still naked. 'Go back to sleep,' he urged, throwing a quick glance over his shoulder. I was already sitting up by then, the duvet dropping around my waist. For the first time ever, he didn't so much as glance at my breasts.

The chiming had reached an impossible crescendo. No way was anyone going back to sleep now. Darrell yanked open the top drawer of his dresser and groped around in its shadowy depths. I caught a glimpse of something slim and black in his hand before he hurried from the room towards the lounge. He paused briefly to shut the bedroom door behind him. Another first, in less than twenty seconds. I shivered, and it had nothing to do with the temperature of the room.

I always felt a little displaced when I spent the night at Darrell's flat. Although I kept a small capsule collection of necessities in his bathroom, and clothes in his wardrobe, we were both more comfortable at my place. A sizeable section of my wardrobe was already taken up with Darrell's clothes.

We hadn't intended to spend the night here. We'd had a final meeting with the caterers, which had overrun massively. We'd only swung past his flat so he could pick up a clean shirt for the morning, but when we'd returned to my car just ten minutes later it had refused to start.

'Damn it,' I muttered, as the turn of the key produced only a dull clicking noise. Darrell got me to spring open the bonnet and spent the requisite amount of time fiddling with things he probably shouldn't touch, and jiggling wires that were best left alone.

'You have no idea what you're doing, do you?' I asked, coming up behind him and winding my arms around his waist. He stopped studying the engine as though it was an alien spacecraft and turned to look at me with a boyish grin.

'Haven't got a clue.' We both laughed, and I remembered all over again why I loved him. It shocked me a little that recently I'd started to forget.

'I'll call the AA in the morning,' I said sleepily, speaking into the breadth of his back. 'Why don't we just stay here tonight?'

Perhaps he did look a little reluctant, but I think that was probably because he hated disappointing me in any way. 'Really? I don't have a single thing in the fridge for the morning.'

'That's okay. I picked up some bread and milk earlier,' I said, reaching for the supermarket bag on my back seat. 'Come on. If we hurry you can have me in your bed in ten minutes.'

We got there in eight.

Darrell's voice wasn't raised, but he wasn't exactly whispering either. Not that it made much difference either way. The closed bedroom door effectively stopped any intention I might have had of eavesdropping. Of course, I could always go and press my ear against the door, the way you see people do in films, but I already had a horrible vision of Darrell suddenly bursting back through it and catching me in the act. And also I didn't want it to look as though I didn't trust him, because of course I did. I was going to marry him, wasn't I? And yet... whose phone was that? Why was it hidden away in the back of a drawer, and why was he taking the call privately in the other room, instead of in here with me?

The bedroom door bounced violently open. Just as well

I *hadn't* been standing behind it, I thought, or else I'd be splattered against the wall like roadkill by now.

'Whose phone is that?' I asked, watching him slide it once more back into the dresser and firmly shunting the drawer to a close.

'It's mine,' Darrell replied succinctly.

I turned my head to his bedside table where his phone, his *real* phone, sat, hooked up to the mains and charging, as though on life support. 'I thought *that* was your phone.'

He shook his head, as though I was being difficult, and yet I really didn't think that I was. 'They're both mine. The one in the drawer is my work mobile.' It was a perfectly reasonable explanation. Lots of companies provide their employees with a phone for business use. But I distinctly remember asking once if he had one, and Darrell very clearly replying that he did not.

'They changed their policy a little while ago,' he said easily, sliding back into bed and pulling me against him. His limbs were cold from the five minutes he'd spent in the lounge, chatting on the phone I hadn't known he had.

'So, can I have the number?'

'What number?'

I didn't count to ten, because I wasn't exactly angry, but I did pause because I was more than a little irritated. He must have known perfectly well what I meant. 'The number of your work phone. Can I have it?'

'Why would you want it?'

'To call you, or text, or send a message. You know, the usual reasons someone wants their husband's phone number.'

He smiled slowly. 'Husband. You called me your husband.'

'I did,' I said, realising that what I had intended as a tool of persuasion, he had interpreted as a loving endearment. 'Well, you will be soon.' Darrell smiled and began to dip his head to kiss me, stopping only when I spoke before his lips touched mine. 'So I should have that number.'

He straightened slightly and I knew he was now doubly irritated: first by the call that had woken us, and now by me.

'You can reach me on my regular phone. The same way you always do.'

'But what if I can't get hold of you? What if you lose your phone, or it gets stolen? Surely it makes sense for me to have *both* numbers?'

He shook his head. 'That one gets turned off when I'm in meetings, or ignored if it's not convenient to talk. I don't want to ever risk missing you because you were trying to reach me on that number. And also the company are really weird about us using the work mobiles for anything other than business. It's probably best not to piss them off.' I heard what he said perfectly well, and heard just as clearly what he *didn't* say. *Don't piss* me *off.*

'Now, come here, woman,' he said, his voice a low growl. 'We might as well take advantage of this unexpectedly early start to the day.'

We made love, and it was good; it was *always* good. Darrell was an attentive lover, always making it much more about me than him, and yet the whole way through it, even when I was holding on to his sweat-damp shoulders and softly moaning his name, I couldn't help but think this was just a hugely effective diversionary tactic, to stop me asking any more questions about the phone.

A little later, when I emerged from the shower, Darrell was already dressed. I could hear the sound of the kettle boiling and the distant clink of crockery in the kitchen. I looked around for something to wear, and reached for the shirt he'd worn the night before, still draped over a chair. As I buttoned it up over my still-damp body, I couldn't stop my gaze from wandering to the top drawer of the dresser. It held my attention as I dragged a comb through my hair, slipped my feet into a pair of flip-flops I'd left beneath Darrell's bed, and slid my engagement ring back on my finger. Perhaps it was the ring that did it. Perhaps I managed to convince myself that this close to our wedding, there should be no secret mysteries between us. And despite the very enjoyable method he'd chosen to shake me off the trail, something about that phone didn't quite add up.

Am I really going to be one of those wives who goes through her husband's pockets and checks his emails? I asked myself, almost horrified as I felt myself gripping the drawer knobs firmly with both hands. Yes, it appeared that was *exactly* the kind of wife I was going to be.

The drawer didn't squeak on its runners. It opened smoothly, allowing me to see the neatly folded boxers Darrell preferred, and a veritable mountain of black socks. What it *didn't* reveal was the phone, because obviously he'd already moved it by then.

He'd lied to me, and there was no point pretending I was okay about that. I was still bristling when I joined

Darrell in the kitchen, unable to shake the feeling that life was starting to seem unnecessarily complicated. Even hunting for the loaf we'd brought in the night before felt like a challenge. It wasn't in the bread bin, nor on any of the clinically bare kitchen worktops. Darrell was busily scrolling through various internet pages on his iPhone – the phone I *had* known about – as I continued to search for the bread.

'Did we bring that supermarket bag up from my car last night?'

'Yes,' Darrell said, distracted by whatever he was reading on his screen.

'Where's the bread then?'

'Same place as always – in the fridge,' he replied, his attention still entirely on his phone.

'We *never* keep the bread in there,' I said, crossing to the tall white appliance, as if to prove him wrong. 'It gets too cold to make good toast, remember?' I pulled open the door and stared at the loaf of bread, sitting in splendid isolation on the top shelf, almost as though it was mocking me.

Darrell looked up from his phone, his attention suddenly all on me. 'Of course we don't. I must have stuck it in there when I was putting the milk away. Do you fancy some toast?'

I shook my head. 'Actually, I'm not really that hungry after all. I'll just have some coffee.'

'Probably just as well,' Darrell said, his voice strangely guarded. 'Because I don't think I have time for breakfast. I'm so sorry, hon, but I'm going to have to go away for a few days. That was what that phone call this morning was all about.'

'But you promised there'd be no more trips now until after the wedding,' I said, feeling weirdly betrayed. 'There are still a thousand things to organise, and you promised me you'd help.'

He crossed the kitchen and wound his arms around my waist. 'I want to be here, sweetheart, I really do. And I know what I promised, but there's been an emergency and I now have to cover someone else's trip.' He pulled me closer and I felt something flat and hard bang against my hip bone through the thin fabric of his shirt. I'd found where he'd put the second phone.

'The guy who was meant to be going on the trip is at the hospital right now. His little girl has been rushed in with appendicitis, so obviously he's not able to go. Someone has to take his place.'

'But why does that someone have to be you? Isn't there anyone else who could do it? Someone who *isn't* in the middle of planning a wedding, perhaps?'

Darrell bent his head and kissed me gently. 'This wedding has been planned more thoroughly than a military manoeuvre.' His eyes went to the tote bag sitting on a chair, holding my bulging wedding planning portfolio. 'You are the most organised woman in the entire world. You don't need me for this bit. All *I* need to do is show up in a fancy suit on the day. Anyway, it might actually be nice for you to spend a bit of time with both of your parents when I'm not around. Who knows, you might even be able to persuade one of them to actually like me.' I stiffened in his arms and he felt it. 'Did you think I hadn't noticed?'

I burrowed my face into the front of his shirt. 'I was kind of hoping you hadn't.'

He kissed the top of my head, inhaling the scent of my hair, as though storing away a memory. 'As long as *you* like me, as long as *you* love me, I don't give a toss about what anyone else thinks. My own family have turned their back on me. If yours do the same I'll be disappointed, sure, but I'll get by. Just as long as I have you, just as long as we're together, nothing else matters.'

He threw clothes for his trip into a small suitcase with astonishing speed. 'You learn to pack fast when you're always travelling. It's a good trick – I'll teach it to you,' he promised. He zipped up the hard shell case with a flourish. 'How long did the AA say they'd be?'

I glanced at my watch. 'They won't be here for at least another forty-five minutes.' Darrell frowned. 'Damn it. I can't wait that long. I'm going to miss my flight.'

'That's fine. Don't worry about me. I'll lock up here after they've sorted out my car.'

Darrell looked worried. 'I don't like leaving you here alone. Not after what was left on your windscreen...'

I glanced up at him in surprise. It was rare for him to ever bring up the topic of our ongoing harassment. That was always far more likely to come from me. 'But that first note was a practical joke from the guys at the gym, wasn't it?'

He studied me for a long moment and I could see him trying to work out if I was being deliberately disingenuous or cleverly devious. To be honest, I wasn't quite sure myself. 'Yes. Of course. That one *was* down to them.'

★ ★ ★

It was a faulty alternator. I didn't know what one of those was, or how it had somehow managed to take out my car's battery, but fortunately the mechanic who turned up a short while later appeared to.

'It'll take about half an hour to fit you a new one,' he advised from the depths of his van. 'If you want to wait upstairs, that's fine. I'll give you a shout when I'm done.'

Back in Darrell's kitchen, I washed up our breakfast things and ran a cloth over the already spotless worktops. It was only when I replaced the sliced loaf into the bread bin that my brow furrowed and a niggling feeling of unease settled somewhere between my shoulder blades.

It felt weird being in Darrell's home without him, almost as though I was trespassing, which was crazy because he was frequently alone in my flat. I keyed in a message to my line manager explaining I was going to be late, and then spent several minutes roaming the flat, trying to pick up a phone signal. My hunt for the elusive little bars led me from room to room, until eventually I found just enough strength to send the message in the bedroom. Frankly, I was amazed Darrell ever got *either* of his phones to work in this place, I thought as I turned away from the window. Perhaps it was because I was remembering Darrell's odd caginess about his work mobile, perhaps the drawer had been left slightly ajar, or perhaps something somewhere was leading me inexorably along a path I wasn't sure I wanted to go down. Whatever it was, as I approached the dresser drawer – *to firmly close it, not to pry*, I told myself – I caught sight of a familiar dark maroon object just visible beneath the displaced pile of socks. I pulled the drawer open wide enough to slip my hand in and extract the slim document. I'd guessed what it was from the moment I'd spotted its distinctive colour. I turned it over in my hand, looking for a snipped-off corner to indicate it was no longer valid, but all four edges were intact. It was Darrell's passport.

I opened it up and saw the man I loved staring back at me. No one looks good in their passport photograph. I'm cadaver pale in mine, and frankly look way too sick to travel anywhere. Perhaps it was his unsmiling image that bothered me. In every single photo of the two of us, Darrell was always beaming widely. It seemed strange to see him looking so stern and serious, staring directly into the camera. He looked like someone I didn't know, and for a moment – just a fleeting one – I thought there was something in his face that I didn't like. I shook the notion away. This was the face of the man I was going to be waking up beside for the rest of my life. This was the face of the man who'd passionately made love to me only a few hours earlier. My fingers tightened on the open passport in my hands. This was the face of the man who was not going to be able to get on his flight, because in his rush to leave that morning, he'd left his passport behind.

I hurried to the window to pick up a phone signal, already trying to calculate how long it would take me to drive to the airport after my car was fixed. I had no idea what flight he was on, or even which airline. In fact, I *never* knew. That hadn't ever occurred to me before, but now it seemed peculiar. Shouldn't he give me that information? Shouldn't I ask for it?

Just when I was certain his phone was about to go to voicemail, Darrell picked up. It wasn't a clear line, and there was a roar of background noise, which meant he had to raise his voice just so I could hear him.

'Sorry, Suzanne. Say that again. I left what?'

'Your passport, you nutter. You've left it behind. Are you at the airport yet?'

Before he had a chance to answer I heard an easily recognisable tannoy message, announcing a flight's final call in the background.

'I'm not sure how long it'll take me to get there,' I said. 'The guy is still working on my car. I suppose I could call a cab.'

'Don't worry. I've already checked in and am on my way to the gate.'

'But how? I have your passport here,' I said, holding it up in my hand, as though presenting it as evidence in a trial.

'Yes, that's okay. I have two,' he said hurriedly, the words getting lost in another booming announcement. 'I have to run, my gate's about to close. I'll phone you later. Love you,' he said, all on one breath. And then he was gone.

I lowered myself on to the edge of the bed, still frowning as I flicked through Darrell's passport. How could he have two passports? Was that even legal? The one in my hand looked pristine, even though I saw it had been issued some time ago. I fanned through the pages, looking for a stamp, or a visa, or an *anything* to indicate that the passport had ever been used, but I could find none.

The back page of the passport was possibly the most illuminating. I stared at my own name and contact details listed under 'next of kin'. Surely his own parents should have been named, and not me? Even if they were temporarily estranged, they were still his next of kin until we were married. Perhaps he too didn't know where they currently lived. Because as hard as I'd tried, I certainly hadn't been able to locate them on social media. Not that Darrell even knew that I'd been looking for them, of course, much less why. My plan to track them down and invite them to our wedding was a secret I'd shared with no one. It was to be my surprise gift to him.

The ringing of the doorbell made me jump guiltily. The whole flat seemed suddenly far too full of secrets and mysteries. I thrust the passport back into the dresser and hurried to the door, where the mechanic stood grinning broadly. 'All done, love,' he declared, passing me back my keys. I found myself quietly envying the simplicity of having a problem that could be so easily and quickly fixed. I was growing tired of every question I asked spiralling into yet another one.

I was still preoccupied when I summoned the lift to take me down to the underground car park ten minutes later. My head was buzzing, and I had the first telling strains of a really bad headache, just waiting to clamp my skull in a vice. The lift doors slid open and I stepped into the carriage, giving its solitary occupant a cursory nod, the way people do.

'G'day,' the young man said, his greeting more of a giveaway to his nationality than his sing-song Australian accent.

'Hello,' I replied, sounding terribly British and a little unapproachable. I wasn't being rude, but I didn't feel like making idle lift conversation. I looked down at my feet, as though the study of my court shoes was suddenly very important. It was impossible not to catch a peripheral glimpse of his own feet. They were large, encased in what looked like very expensive trainers. It wasn't a particularly warm morning, yet the man was wearing shorts. His thick muscular legs were covered in ginger hair, which I was inadvertently staring at in a rather disturbing perverted way. My eyes did a sidelong reconnoitre and travelled up his body to a thin grey sweatshirt with the logo of a university on it. A large sports bag was slung over one shoulder, and peeking out from within it I could see a rolled-up towel.

I glanced at the floor indicator. We were almost at ground level. I turned to the man, knowing I was about to do something either very sensible or incredibly foolish. I just wished I knew which one it was.

'Excuse me.' Again I sounded horribly British. He didn't seem to notice. 'I know this might sound a little odd, but you wouldn't by any chance be going to the gym right now, would you?'

You have to love the Australians and their friendly, approachable, laid-back attitude. He didn't seem at all put out by the curious question from a total stranger. He nodded down at his attire and the huge bag he was carrying, and grinned. 'What gave it away?'

I smiled hesitantly, unsure how on earth I was going to proceed. 'You live in this building, don't you?' He smiled back and gave an almost imperceptible wink. Oh God, now he thought I was hitting on him, and nothing could be further from the truth.

'Are you a member of the gym on Barrack Road?' I asked, all on a rush.

'I am,' he answered, leaning back against the wall of the carriage, still clearly believing he was being flirted with.

'I see,' I said falteringly. I took a deep breath and just decided to go for it. I held out my hand – might as well make the formal British thing a total cliché. 'I'm "The Bride".'

He looked momentarily confused, before placing his own huge hand in mine and shaking it warmly. 'And I'm the groom?' he said hesitantly, as though we were playing some sort of intriguing word association dating game.

I shook my head. 'No. I'm "The Bride". As in, I'm Darrell's fiancée. I believe you left something for me on my car?'

The smile was growing weaker. Well, I suppose that wasn't unexpected. He had the look of a man who has just realised the woman he's stuck in a small metal box with might possibly not be in full possession of her marbles.

'I'm sorry, love. I'm not getting you.'

'Darrell Kingston. Flat 5b. We're getting married in two weeks.'

His smile was practically non-existent and unsure now. 'Er... congratulations?' he said, hoping he'd somehow plucked the right response. He hadn't.

'Darrell. Tall. Chestnut-coloured hair. Fairly well-built. He goes to the Barrack Street gym.'

'It's a good gym,' my Antipodean companion agreed.

'You and Darrell are friends? You hang out together at the gym?'

The man was shaking his head and looked immensely grateful when the lift pinged softly to announce we were now at ground level.

'I'm sorry, love. I don't know anyone called Darrell.'

He must have seen the confusion, doubt and God only knows what else on my face, for he added consolingly: 'But I'm sure he's a great guy.'

Only a short while ago it would have been very easy to agree with him on that one. Now I wasn't so sure.

Clearly anxious to make his getaway – and who could blame him – my Australian lift companion strode into the underground car park. He pulled his car keys from the pocket of his shorts, which probably triggered his next question.

'What else was that you asked? Something about leaving something on your boyfriend's car?'

I shook my head sadly. 'No. Not his car. My car. But don't worry. I must have been mistaken.'

'You've travelled a fair bit, haven't you?'

Paul dropped a cluster of manila envelopes into a wire tray, and neatly manoeuvred his mail cart into a gap beside my desk. I'd been back at work for just fifteen minutes, and I'd spent most of those waiting for the eleven o'clock postal collection. There were at least half a dozen phone messages, scribbled on Post-it notes, decorating my computer screen like misshapen bunting at a fete. I should have peeled them off, turned on my computer and at least pretended to be working, but I was still processing everything I'd discovered in the five hours since I'd been woken up by Darrell's hidden mobile.

'I suppose you could say that,' Paul answered, giving a slow, lazy grin that made his single status a complete mystery. 'Why? Are you in need of travel advice? Where *is* it you're going for your honeymoon, anyway?'

'I have no idea. It's a surprise,' I said, not sounding in the least bit excited. That's what happens when you've accidentally overdosed on mystery and secrets.

'Oh,' Paul replied, managing to inject quite a lot of meaning into such a small two-letter word.

'During your travels, have you ever heard of anyone holding multiple passports for the same country?'

It was easy to see that I'd piqued his interest. He leant back against a filing cabinet, resting one elbow upon it, causing his T-shirt to separate from the waistband of his jeans. At any other time I'm sure that thin sliver of tanned torso would have been a major distraction, but this morning... not so much.

'Yeah, several people,' Paul answered easily. He lifted one hand and began counting names on his fingers: 'Jason Bourne, James Bond, Ethan Hunt—'

'How about *real* people?' I interrupted, storing away his choice of books and films as interesting trivia.

'Not unless they're involved in espionage,' he said, still not realising I was serious. 'Are they?'

'Darrell has two UK passports,' I said flatly. 'Well, two that I know about. Who knows how many more there are.'

Paul looked momentarily floored. 'Why?'

'Good question. I have absolutely no idea.'

'Well, what did he say when you asked him?' It was the most logical question in the world, and I felt pretty stupid when I had to admit that, actually, I hadn't done so yet. 'There was no time. He was running to catch a plane.'

'Presumably using one of his many passports,' said Paul lightly, surprisingly coaxing a smile from me. I really hadn't expected to find any of this amusing.

'I guess so. Just ignore me, I'm probably overreacting. It's just been a weird morning. There've been lots of things that haven't added up.'

'That has to be an accountant's worst nightmare,' he teased, which managed to draw out a second smile. He paused for a moment, looking quietly pleased, before continuing. 'As far as the passport thing goes, are you absolutely sure your fiancé doesn't work for the intelligence service?'

I laughed, but there was a brittleness to the sound. 'I don't think I'm sure about *anything* today.'

He nodded slowly, as though carefully considering the best path to walk through a minefield. 'Have you checked on the internet about owning more than one passport?'

I didn't actually slap my forehead at my own stupidity, but I certainly felt like doing so. I leant forward to switch on my computer, peeling off the collection of Post-its while I waited for it to fire up. Paul moved to stand behind my chair, placing me in the downdraught of whatever gel or soap he'd used in the executive bathroom. Darrell favoured the type with heavy spice overtones, but Paul smelled of the ocean, conjuring up images of breaking surf and long sandy beaches.

I clicked impatiently on the mouse, suddenly regretting inviting Paul to join in my search for answers. Having him stand this close and feeling his breath fan my hair as he spoke was promoting an inexplicably dangerous reaction within me. Thankfully, he seemed totally oblivious of this.

'There you go,' he announced, reading from the screen. 'It's called a "concurrent passport" and it's common among frequent business travellers.'

'Darrell certainly travels a lot,' I agreed.

'Mystery solved then,' Paul said happily, moving back to his mail cart once more. I wanted to ask him to stay; I wanted to tell him about all the other things that were suddenly bothering me. But it wasn't his job to be my sounding board, it wasn't his job to sort out my confusion, or help me figure out why everything suddenly felt as though it was riddled with cracks and could shatter or implode at any moment. None of that was his job. It wasn't even his job to be my friend and confidant, except I seemed to have appointed him to that role. I wondered if he even knew.

'He looks thin, don't you think?'

I lifted my head and my eyes followed the retreating figure of my father as he headed for the Gents' cloakroom.

'Actually, I think he looks pretty good. He's lost some weight, but it suits him. He looks really healthy.'

My mother lifted her gin and tonic and took a slow, careful sip. 'I suppose he told you all about the scare he had last year?'

'No. What sort of a scare?' I sat up straighter, instantly alarmed.

My mother rarely made a gaffe. Faux pas didn't seem to plague her the way they did me. I was forever putting my foot in my mouth. So it was both unusual and unsettling to see her momentarily discomforted.

'He probably didn't want to worry you.'

'Perhaps not, but you've just done that for him,' I said, sounding genuinely concerned. 'What kind of scare?'

'A heart attack,' she said succinctly. Her lips were tight, as though she was clamping them shut in case they betrayed any further secrets. 'Only a small one – or so he said.'

I shook my head in disbelief. 'And you knew about this and never told me?'

She looked shocked at the sharpness in my voice. 'Of course not. He only told me at lunch yesterday, and now I'm telling you. Full disclosure all round.'

I leant back against the red velvet of the restaurant chair. The surprises kept coming, like repeated blows in a boxing round. 'You and Dad had lunch yesterday? Without me? Without even *telling* me?'

Perhaps that came out a little more plaintive and forlorn than it had sounded in my head, for my mother's eyebrows rose elegantly. 'You were at work,' she reasoned. 'And I thought it best for your father and me to clear the air in private before all the frenzy of the wedding truly begins. Also, I needed to see just how badly I still wanted to kill him.'

She delivered the last without so much as a glimmer of a smile. Some people didn't 'get' her sense of humour. Fortunately, I wasn't one of them.

'And did your thoughts turn murderous?'

'Surprisingly, no, they didn't.' She turned to look out of a nearby window, effectively hiding her very expressive eyes from me. 'He's changed.'

The object of our discussion pulled out his chair and rejoined the table.

'Mum said you had a heart attack,' I accused, jumping straight in before he even had a chance to settle in his seat. 'Why didn't you tell me?'

He gave me an 'it was nothing' shrug, and my mother a sharp glare. 'It was more of a wake-up call than anything major,' he replied, reaching for his glass of soda water and ice. That was another surprise; apparently, he was no longer drinking. But the biggest shock of all, the one that was still making my head spin like that girl in *The Exorcist*, was that my parents were doing a very passable impression of an extremely civilised divorced couple.

'But are you all right now? Are you fully recovered? Do you have to take things easy? Oh God, perhaps I shouldn't have asked you to come over for the wedding. It's too much stress.'

'I'm not stressed,' he replied calmly, and it was true, he certainly didn't appear to be. 'Except perhaps with your mother, who doesn't know how to keep a secret.'

'There are more than enough of those flying around as it is,' I said unthinkingly. 'We certainly don't need any more.'

As if they'd practised it, they turned to look at me with perfect synchronicity. I hadn't been the subject of that degree of combined parental scrutiny for more years than I could remember.

'Is something wrong?'

'What's happened now?'

I wasn't used to them being on the same page about anything. Hell, I wasn't used to them even reading the same book, so this felt really weird and unfamiliar. I almost crumbled under the combined weight of their concern. But whatever I said next was going to paint Darrell in an unfavourable light, and their opinion of him was already unfairly discoloured, so this close to the wedding was definitely not the right time to bring it up.

'Has this got something to do with his deranged ex-girlfriend persecuting you?' questioned my mother.

I turned to my father, who had dropped his eyes to the menu, as though hoping to escape my anger by losing himself somewhere between the starters and the mains.

'*Now* who can't keep anything to themselves?' I said, not sure if the situation was better or worse now the cat was well and truly out of the bag.

'Well, I'm very glad he told me,' my mother cut in smoothly. 'Frankly, Suzanne, I'm more than a little disappointed that you didn't trust me enough to do so yourself.'

'It wasn't that,' I said, feeling guilty in a way I hadn't done for years, probably not since all those disappointing English exam results. 'Darrell and I decided that the best course of action was *not* to react. Whoever is doing this obviously wants to see us upset and irate, and so ignoring it is probably annoying the hell out of them.'

'And that seems wise to you, does it? Pissing off a potential psychopath? Great plan, if you don't mind me saying.'

'It's easy to see who's the author with the overactive imagination in *this* family,' I said wryly. 'You went straight from minor prankster to *Fatal Attraction* bunny-boiler in just one leap.'

'Your mother is absolutely right,' said my father, laying down his menu beside his plate. They were words I truly don't think I'd ever heard – or had expected to hear – from him, and I took a moment to savour them. From the look in my mum's eyes, so did she.

'Don't underestimate the potential seriousness of this. I can't understand why that fiancé of yours is so bloody calm about the whole thing. If someone was threatening the woman I loved, there'd be hell to pay.' There was an awkward little moment when he looked across at my mother and their eyes met and held. I blinked in total disbelief as a small flush coloured my mother's perfectly powdered cheeks.

'You know, it might not be the worst idea in the world to consider postponing the wedding for a while, just until all this unpleasantness has died down.'

I turned to my father angrily. 'No one is postponing anything. Everything is booked, the guests are coming, my dress is waiting to be delivered. We are all systems go.' I took a slow, cleansing breath and softened my tone. 'I know you're only saying this because you're worried about me, but honestly we have everything under control and the wedding is most definitely going ahead. Cancelling isn't even a consideration.'

There was a long moment of silence, where no one met anyone else's eyes. I'd thought my role here today would be to act as referee between my two warring parents. What I'd never expected was for them to be suddenly and crazily united in their opposition to the marriage of their only daughter.

Hot tears distorted my vision as I grabbed the menu, totally incapable of reading the rows of blurred and dancing words. 'I know neither of you particularly like Darrell,' I said quietly.

We went through the requisite awkward silence, which eventually my mother broke. 'It's more that I feel there's so much about him I still don't know. Even *you* have to admit there are aspects about him that are puzzling. Not to mention that it is extremely odd, never having met his family.'

I opened my mouth to explain, yet again, about the estrangement with his parents, but Mum just held up one perfectly manicured hand. 'Yes, I know. They don't talk to each other and they won't be at the wedding. Perhaps if we knew *why* that was, we might understand it a little better.'

'I've always considered myself a pretty good judge of character – you have to be when you run a bar like mine,' said my father. 'You develop an eye for trouble before it even starts; you sniff out the punters who're going to get lairy and ruin the evening for everyone else. Sometimes you hear more by what someone *doesn't* say than what they do.'

My voice was tight as I ran my fingers below my eyes. The lashes felt wet and spiky. 'I'm afraid this time your senses are all way off the mark, Dad. I'm sorry that neither of you approve of my choice, but that's what Darrell is: *my choice*. And now you're both just going to have to trust me enough to know I've made the right one.'

It was five days until our wedding.

6

It was my last morning at work before the wedding, and I was frantically trying to clear all my outstanding jobs so I could go off on honeymoon without worrying. Between tasks I eyed the phone on my desk warily, jumping each time it rang. There'd been calls in the middle of the night on the last three evenings. The kind of calls that when you 1471'd them, all it said was 'The caller withheld their number'. But of course they had. They'd also withheld from speaking. It made no difference whether I remained silent, or repeatedly asked 'Who *is* this?' into the receiver. They never said a word. My landline wasn't ex-directory. But as soon as we came back from our honeymoon it would be, and the number would be changed.

Darrell had snatched the phone from my hand the last time, swinging his legs out of bed and muttering into the receiver, 'Catherine?' The hairs on the back of my neck had risen. He'd never mentioned her name to me. He'd told me she was his past and had no place in our lives; that was the reason he'd never identified her.

'It's more likely he doesn't want you tracking her down on Facebook and confronting her,' guessed Karen. It was hard to argue with her, especially when she was one hundred per cent right. 'You know, instead of wasting all your time trying to find Darrell's parents, you should have been trying to track down his psychotic ex. Then we could go round and… and…'

'And what?' I'd asked. 'Threaten her? Bully her? Intimidate her? Kind of like she's been doing to me, you mean?'

'Point taken,' grumbled Karen. 'How *are* you getting on with tracking down his family, then? Have you found anything yet?'

'Not a damn thing. What started out as a great idea for a surprise wedding gift has so far turned into a wild goose chase. Every lead I follow up is just another dead end, both in the UK and Australia. It's like they disappeared, or something.'

I knew the line I was crossing by digging into Darrell's past was smudged and thin, and I was straddling it as cautiously as a nervous tightrope walker in slippery shoes. But I *was* doing it with the best of intentions. And it was only going to be a short-term secret. Eventually I'd come clean, and he would thank me for doing this. *Wouldn't he?*

In my head I could see it so clearly, playing out like a movie on the Lifetime channel. Darrell would arrive at the wedding, and there would be his parents, waiting. He'd be shocked at first, maybe even a little angry. But then someone's arms would open, and someone else would start crying. And then there'd be apologies and explanations, followed by forgiveness and tears…

Only it didn't look as if it was going to work out like that.
I stared at the picture of Darrell on my desk. *What happened
between you and your parents? What was so terrible that you
don't even know which country they now live in?* Even if by
some miracle I *did* manage to find Darrell's missing parents,
there wasn't enough time left now to fly them back for the
wedding – even assuming they were willing to come.

'So you're hanging up your gumshoe hat, are you?'

'You do realise no one actually calls them that? No one
has probably *ever* called them that.'

Karen took a mouthful of her lunchtime salad and
chewed despondently. 'I'm not sure why I'm still dieting.
Your wedding's in less than forty-eight hours; it's too late
now to look skinny in my bridesmaid's dress.'

'You're going to look absolutely gorgeous,' I assured her,
trying to ignore the alien-in-my-stomach spasm I'd felt when
I realised the time until I became Mrs Darrell Kingston was
now measurable in hours.

'No one's going to be looking at me anyway,' continued
Karen. 'All eyes will be on you in your amazing wedding
dress.'

'Talking of which, I spoke to Gwendoline from Fleurs
this morning, and she's going to personally bring the dress
to the hotel on the morning of the wedding.'

'Great. At least that's one less thing for you to worry
about,' Karen said, unashamedly stealing a chip from my
plate.

★ ★ ★

The hotel was a beautiful converted eighteenth-century manor house. There was a long sweeping gravel drive that wound through the trees, teasing you with tiny glimpses of the main building, until it opened out into a huge circular forecourt. I followed a succession of small, discreetly positioned white wooden arrows to an area designated for guest parking. Karen was already there, leaning up against her car and rattling off a message into her phone.

The deep gravel crunched beneath her sandals as she made her way over to me.

'You're early,' I cried, pulling her into a hug, which left me feeling oddly choked and emotional. 'I can't believe it. You're *never* early.'

'And you *always* are,' she said, nodding wisely, as though I might be thinking of contradicting her. 'So I thought my first chief bridesmaid duty would be to make sure I got here first to greet you.'

'Can you be "chief" if you're the only one?' I asked, pulling my overnight bag from the back of my car. Darrell had carried it down for me that morning, before he'd left for the day with a long 'to-do' list of chores in hand.

'Just leave it in the boot, don't worry about locking the car,' I'd said, kissing him goodbye at my open front door. 'I'll be heading off myself in about fifteen minutes.'

Darrell had pulled me slowly against him, and out into the corridor, stealing one final kiss. I'd glanced beyond him down the empty hallway. It was early and none of my neighbours were around, and yet it still felt inappropriate to be outside of my flat wearing only a short silky gown that did a very poor job of concealing the outline of my breasts.

'Darrell, no. Someone might see,' I'd said, sounding like a nervous Quaker as his hand slid down over one breast and found the nipple through the satin fabric. He lifted his mouth from mine, but the hand stayed where it was.

'There's no one here,' he'd said, his voice dipping into the kind of huskiness that told me exactly what was on his mind.

I'd placed both my hands on his chest and pushed him back. 'Enough,' I'd said, softening the word with a smile. 'You have a long list of things to do, and I have to go and get pampered all day.'

Darrell had smiled, and released my boob after one final tweak of the nipple. I'd stepped back into the sanctuary of my own flat. 'I'll see you tonight at seven, at the rehearsal dinner,' I'd said, primly gripping the two sides of my gown together. I don't know why I bothered; my body's reaction to his touch was still clearly showing through the revealing material.

An odd feeling of unreality settled over me as Karen and I walked towards the hotel's main entrance. Through the trees I caught a glimpse of the lake, beside which workmen were already starting to erect the canopy beneath which Darrell and I would stand tomorrow to exchange our vows. And tonight, in one of the small private dining rooms, we would host a small rehearsal dinner for twenty people.

Then tomorrow at eleven o'clock... From out of nowhere my subconscious conjured up the sound of a mail cart trundling down a carpeted corridor. The brain is funny like that. While you're busy thinking about one thing, it throws another thought into the mix, out of pure mischief, just to see what happens. I shook my head to dislodge the inappropriate image. It was an unfortunate coincidence that the time I was scheduled to become one man's wife was already associated with an entirely different man in my head. Clearly I'd spent far too long watching the clock and waiting for Paul, and now I was paying the price. Well, I could do nothing to change the time of my wedding, but I could certainly put a stop to my daily conversations with Paul. After the wedding, things would be different.

I shouldn't even be *thinking* about Paul today, I acknowledged, as I walked up the stone steps to the hotel entrance. There was no excuse; it wasn't even as if I'd seen him recently. Not for almost a week, I realised. The mail cart had been pushed by one of his colleagues all week, and on the third day – when I'd casually enquired where Paul was – I was told he was taking some time off. There was no explanation for the weird disappointment I'd felt that he hadn't mentioned it to me himself. Obviously he was free to do exactly as he pleased – particularly as he practically owned the company, or would do one day. But a tiny voice kept asking why he'd not said anything to me. Perhaps it was time to finally acknowledge that one of us had possibly been reading a great deal more into our eleven o'clock chats than they should have been.

We had just enough time to check into our rooms before our first treatments in the hotel spa.

'See you in five,' Karen said, disappearing down the corridor to her own room.

My room was lovely, all chintz fabrics and reproduction furniture. It even had a four-poster bed, which made me stupidly excited for absolutely no reason at all. I threw my overnight case on to the bed and ran open the zipper, wanting to grab my toiletry bag for the spa. I noticed 'it' immediately, because it was right there on the top, where it definitely did not belong.

Unlike the previous messages, this wasn't on a card, nor was it addressed specifically to me. But as it was sitting *inside* my case, right on top of my underwear in fact, I didn't think there could be any question about the intended recipient. I didn't even want to touch it. It had no place being there among my things. It was a single sheet of lined paper, which appeared to have been roughly torn from a notebook. Even the handwriting looked rushed and hurried, as though the author had scribbled it quickly, before they were caught. I swept the paper off my clothes, as though it was contaminating them. It fell on to the deep pink pile of the carpet, an ugly intrusion in my beautiful hotel room.

Have you no shame? read the message, in huge untidy letters. *His hands were all over you.*

She had been there. Somewhere in the corridor she had been there, watching as Darrell had touched my body. My stomach reacted instinctively, in exactly the way you would expect on encountering poison. I ran into the adjacent bathroom, my hand clamped over my mouth, only just managing to make it to the toilet before losing my breakfast.

After that she was everywhere. And nowhere. She was the woman in the jacuzzi, who looked at me with mean, narrowed eyes when I got to my feet and stepped out of the bubbling tub. She was the manicurist with the surly expression, who nicked my cuticle when filing my nails and mumbled only an insincere apology. She was the woman in the restaurant, sitting alone in a corner table for one, whose eyes raked the other diners in our matching white waffle gowns.

'Are you *sure* you're all right? You still don't seem to be in a very relaxed, chilled-out kind of mood,' observed Karen in concern, after the waitress had finished refilling our coffee cups. *Yeah, because that's just what I needed, more caffeine. Like I wasn't jumpy enough already.* But of course I'd been trying to hide that fact from Karen all day. Although apparently, without much success.

'I *am* relaxed,' I insisted, my spoon clattering noisily against the china cup as I stirred my coffee far more vigorously than required. 'It's just pre-wedding jitters. It's a big step, getting married, you know,' I added unnecessarily.

Karen looked at me carefully, and I could almost hear her inner debate. Speak now, or forever hold her peace. She chose to speak. 'It's a step you don't *have* to take tomorrow, you know. If you've got any doubts at all, or have last-minute cold feet, no one is going to blame you for deciding to call things off or postponing them.'

It's not the kind of thing you expect your bridesmaid to say to you on the day before you get married. Although I could hardly blame her for putting two and two together and coming up with five, because I'd chosen not to tell her about that vile note, or how it had come to be in my luggage. There was only one person I wanted to discuss that with, and I wouldn't be seeing him for another six hours. It would have to wait.

'These feet are perfectly toasty,' I said, extending one towelling-slippered foot from beneath the table. The newly painted bright pink nails looked outrageously cheerful, mocking my inner mood. 'And with seventy friends and family already on their way here, or heading this way in the morning, I think it actually *is* too late to be rethinking anything.'

'Until you actually say "I do", there's all the time in the world,' Karen reassured, nodding her head encouragingly. That's when I realised she might actually be hoping that I *was* going to cancel everything. But why? I thought she'd got past her misgivings about Darrell. Was he right? Did she resent the fact I was going to be heading up the aisle before her? The thought shouldn't even have been able to creep into my head, and yet suddenly I found myself thinking the unthinkable: could Karen have been the one who'd silently crept up to my unlocked car and left that note in my suitcase?

I got quickly to my feet, desperate to leave the ugly seed of an idea behind before it took root. 'I'm fine. Everything is fine. Except that we now have only four minutes to get to the treatment room for our hot stone massage.'

Karen fell asleep during hers, but although the warmed oil and strategically placed stones were relaxing, I couldn't turn down the dial on my anxiety. It was firmly settled in the red zone, where it was destined to stay until Darrell slipped the thin platinum band on my finger, hopefully without anyone leaping to their feet during the ceremony, screaming out their objection.

★ ★ ★

Darrell wasn't spending the night at the hotel. We'd decided to stick to that one piece of propriety at least, and not see each other tomorrow until the actual ceremony. He'd be returning to his own flat tonight after the rehearsal dinner. But I'd left word at Reception, asking them to direct him to my room as soon as he arrived that evening.

I was just finishing my make-up when a soft knock sounded on the door, followed by his familiar voice, calling out in a sing-song tone: 'Room service.'

Despite the jittery herd of elephants that appeared to have taken up residence in my stomach, I smiled. I went to the door and checked through the peephole before unlatching it. The fisheye lens distorted the image of the man I was marrying, making him momentarily a crazy hall-of-mirrors stranger, then he shifted a little closer to the door, and he was Darrell again. I opened the door, grabbed his hand and practically dragged him across the threshold into my room.

'Hey, hang on a minute,' he said, still playing off a totally different page than me. 'I'm a soon-to-be married man, and this *definitely* isn't covered by room service. In fact—' He broke off suddenly, reading the expression on my face. No words were required.

'What's happened now?'

I crossed over to a reproduction armoire and pulled open the bottom drawer. It held two objects: a Bible, courtesy of the Gideons; and the note, courtesy of person or persons unknown. If I'd hoped the good in one might cancel out the evil in the other, I was mistaken. The scrawled words still had the power to hit me in the stomach like a mule kick.

Darrell's face turned pale, then ashen as he read the note and heard where I'd found it. *There literally isn't any shade lighter he could turn*, I thought in concern, as I watched a waxy sheen glisten over his skin. He walked woodenly to the edge of the four-poster and sat down heavily. He leant forward, his hands in his hair, his elbows on his knees. His head was almost imperceptibly moving from side to side, as though he was listening to some inner voice that was disagreeing with him.

I said nothing for several minutes, allowing him to process what had happened. I expected him to eventually lift his head and give me the usual *This is nothing to worry about* or *We should just ignore it* response. I was even prepared for yet another round of *We still don't know it's her*. What I wasn't ready for, what I hadn't even for one single moment considered, were the words that came from him in a crushed tone, as though something deep inside was broken.

'I think we should cancel the wedding.'

I don't remember crossing the room. One minute I was over by the dressing table, the next I could feel the pile of the carpet beneath my bare knees as I looked up at him in distress.

'What? No. We can't.'

He reached for my hand, missing it on the first pass, because suddenly his eyes were full of tears. I was more shocked by that than I think I'd been by the note. It was the first time I'd ever seen him cry, and for a moment I felt thrown. I had no idea how to react. Perhaps I did hesitate for a moment, just a fleeting one, imagining a world where I just said *Okay then, let's do that*, before the sensible side of me kicked in. The side that had carried a wedding planning portfolio around with her for the last six months, who knew exactly what every last minute of the next twenty-four hours was meant to look like. And cancelling the wedding now, because of... because of her... just wasn't in the script.

'Maybe that was it,' I said desperately, gripping his hands so tightly the skin of his fingers turned almost as pale as his face. 'Maybe that was their last-ditch attempt to ruin the day for us. And if we cancel the wedding, then they'll have won, won't they? They'll have driven a wedge through us, through you and me, and we might never get over it.'

He released one hand and wiped it across his eyes, looking almost surprised to see the dampness on his fingertips. My heart broke a little when I realised he hadn't even known he'd been crying. 'Then what do you want to do?' he asked, his eyes staring so deeply into mine, my soul felt bare and exposed. 'Whatever you want to do, Suzanne, I'll go along with it.'

I closed my eyes to shut out the expression in his. I saw myself as though in a corridor that branched off in two different directions. Take one, and I would become Mrs Darrell Kingston, take the other and I'd go back to being a single woman, because there would be no 'us' after this if I cancelled the wedding. I knew that, even if Darrell didn't. One path led to a life as a married woman, the other left me free to see and do whatever I wanted: date, don't date; live alone, live with someone else; watch the clock each day, waiting for something I had no right to want as much as I did, or move forward.

'No one is going to stop me marrying you,' I said definitively. 'No one. Whoever is doing this, whether it's Catherine—' I heard Darrell's sudden indrawn hiss of breath, shocked that I had remembered her name – as if I was *ever* likely to have forgotten it. 'Whether it is her, or someone completely different, it doesn't matter. They have no way of knowing where we are, or how to find us here. They won't know the name of the hotel, or that tomorrow is our wedding day. And by the time we go back to our normal life, it will be done. We'll be married, and then all of this will finally stop.'

The private dining room looked elegant and very British, making me feel like a *Downton Abbey* extra who'd been sent the wrong dress code memo. My short red cocktail dress with matching strappy heels was sexy and a little daring and chosen deliberately because of its contrast to the classically beautiful gown I'd be wearing the following day. Darrell had met me in the hotel lobby. He'd said he wanted to take a walk in the grounds to calm down and clear his head before meeting our guests – practically all of whom were either my family or my friends. Unsurprisingly, the guests *he'd* asked had politely declined the invitation.

Darrell held out his hand to me as I stepped off the sweeping staircase, and if it weren't for our modern outfits, we could have been transported back to a time when people 'dressed for dinner'.

His eyes appraised me with obvious appreciation. It was that kind of dress. 'I've not seen that one before,' he whispered into the fall of my hair, as he leant forward to kiss me.

Tomorrow my hair would be worn in a loose topknot, and decorated with tiny fresh flowers, but tonight it was softly curled and falling freely over my shoulders. I smelled the hint of alcohol on his breath, even before I caught its lingering taste on his lips. I guess Darrell had found an alternative method to calm down, rather than taking a walk.

'I think everyone's here now,' he said, guiding me towards the private room. I felt a moment of guilt that I hadn't been here to greet them, but like Darrell I had needed time to decompress from the anxiety we were both determined to hide from our guests.

'I wouldn't worry,' Darrell replied, when I commented on how rude we must seem. 'Your parents seem to be enjoying the opportunity to play host.'

'What? Together? No arguments or disagreements?'

'Not a one, as far as I can see,' confirmed Darrell, his hand reaching for the ornate brass door handle that led to our private dining room. 'In fact, they even arrived together in the same taxi.' I turned to him, my face a picture of amazement. 'It wouldn't surprise me one little bit if there's not another wedding in the Walters family before too long,' he said with a small wink.

I was still trying to get my head around that fact, and how it made me feel, when he threw open the door and we entered the room, to a chorus of delighted cries and – embarrassingly – even a small round of applause.

The wedding festivities had begun.

Given the whirlwind nature of our courtship and engagement, this was actually the first time that many members of my family had even met Darrell. It could have felt awkward and uncomfortable introducing him to strangers who he'd be related to the following day. But Darrell was on a major charm offensive. Both of my young teenage cousins clearly thought I'd won the fiancé lottery and giggled and blushed prettily whenever he spoke to them. Even my usually prickly elderly aunt took me to one side and murmured that it looked like I'd found a 'good 'un'. I smiled weakly as she continued with her usual lack of filter: 'At least you picked more carefully than your mother did.'

Both of us looked across the room. My father was in the middle of telling a story to a group of family members he'd probably not seen in years. My mother was part of that group and, astonishingly, when the entire circle erupted into gales of laughter, she not only joined in, but also briefly laid one hand on his arm. I caught the look he fleetingly gave her, and turned away, as though I'd intruded on something intimate. Could Darrell be right? They did appear to be getting on unaccountably well for a couple whose divorce was neither amicable nor civilised.

By the time we'd taken our places at the table, two glasses of Prosecco had filed the rough edges off my jangly mood. Everything was going to be fine; the wedding was going to go without a hitch, I vowed, smiling around at the room full of people. Everyone here was important to me in some way, and just having them there empowered me. I felt stronger and braver knowing they were on my side. All of them – even my outspoken aunt – wanted only what was best for me. I glanced over at Darrell sitting beside me and felt suddenly sad that in a room full of people, he had no one. Except me, of course. He had me.

I wondered if, beneath the charm, he felt isolated. He might be able to fool the giggly cousins and my aunt, but I could see he was still on edge. I knew that even before one of the waitresses dropped a tray of cutlery on to the parquet floor. As the clatter of falling silverware ricocheted around the room, Darrell had half leapt from his chair as though someone had launched a grenade through the open French windows. His eyes darted between them and the door to the room.

'Hey, you're jumpy,' Karen's boyfriend, Tom, observed. They were sitting diagonally opposite us and must have seen the way Darrell's eyes had flown from window to door, as though at any moment he expected a crack SAS squad to come crashing into the room... or someone equally dangerous.

'You look like a man planning a hasty getaway,' Tom joked, unfortunately. A comment that earned him a sharp kick beneath the table from his girlfriend. 'Ow! What did you do that for?' he asked, turning to Karen with a hurt expression on his face.

'My foot slipped,' she replied sweetly, before turning to me and mouthing *Sorry*.

All things considered, the meal was progressing exactly the way I had planned. The conversation was flowing, the food was delicious and I was finally starting to relax, until the moment when everything changed. I felt it first in the bones of my ankle, where my black beaded evening bag was propped up against my foot. I'd almost left my phone in the hotel room, purely because everyone I knew was either going to be at the rehearsal dinner or would know that I was, so wouldn't be trying to call me.

At the last moment I switched off the ringer and dropped the mobile into my bag, where it landed on top of my comb and lipstick. And now it was ringing, silently ringing. Very subtly, as though retrieving a dropped serviette, I leant down and popped open the bag's clasp. An insistent buzzing sounded from within, as though I'd accidentally trapped an exceedingly pissed-off bee inside it. My hand hovered over the phone and then hesitated.

'What is it?' asked Darrell, drawing his chair a little closer to mine. I looked up, caught my mother's far too perceptive eyes watching me from across the room, and tried to summon up the most natural smile I could find to plaster across my face.

'Someone's phoning me.'

It's weird how instantly we were on exactly the same page. Did that signify how compatible we were, or just that we were both trapped in the same nightmare? 'Don't answer it,' Darrell said sharply.

I didn't even bother to ask him why. We both knew why. She'd already found out so much about me: where I worked; where I lived; the car I drove. Tracking down my mobile number was yet another trump card she'd managed to score.

'It's probably just some random PPI call,' said Darrell, but I could tell from the tone of his voice that he didn't really believe it was.

'I don't think so.'

'Did you see the number?' he asked, speaking out of one side of his mouth. The other half was still smiling at the room in general.

I looked down into my bag at my now silent phone. The last thing I intended to do was to start scrolling through my call log with my entire family watching on.

'Well, they've gone now,' Darrell declared, reaching for his glass of wine and taking a generous swallow. He hadn't even replaced the glass on the white-linen-covered table before my phone began to ring once more.

I didn't stop to think, I just jumped to my feet and bundled my bag beneath my arm, as though trying to stifle its soundless cry.

'Suzanne—' began Darrell, his hand reaching out to me, but he touched nothing except the space where I had been sitting. I was already halfway across the floor, heading towards the discreetly illuminated Exit sign.

As soon as I was clear of the room, my hand dived into the bag and plucked out my phone, like a furious kingfisher swooping for a minnow. There was a number on the screen that I didn't recognise. My heart was pounding as I side-swiped to accept the call.

'Who is this?' It wasn't the way I usually answered the phone, and clearly it surprised the caller, for there was a moment of stunned silence before I heard my own name being posed as a question.

'Suzanne?' So much for the PPI theory, I thought, leaning heavily against a large marble column in the reception area. Thankfully, the foyer was empty except for the two members of staff behind the desk, who were busily absorbed in their own conversation.

The voice in my ear repeated their question. 'Suzanne? Is that you?'

I opened my mouth to confirm my identity, but never got the chance to speak, for the phone was suddenly whisked out of my hand. Darrell's eyes were glittering with anger, directed not at me, but at my caller.

'This has to stop,' he said tersely into the phone. 'Right now. Right this moment. It all has to stop.'

I was watching his face anxiously. The emotions passed over it, like clouds scudding over the moon. His expression was unreadable as he listened to the person at the end of the phone for a moment, before slowly withdrawing the mobile from his ear and handing it out to me. There was a new look on his face, and frankly I didn't like it much better than the one that had come before it.

'It's for you,' he said darkly.

'Yes, well, it would be, seeing as it's my phone.' Suddenly I was annoyed, and embarrassed, dreadfully, awfully, scarlet-faced embarrassed.

'I thought—' he began, and then broke off.

'Yes, I thought so too.' I looked pointedly at the door to the private dining room. 'I think one of us had better go back to our guests.' Darrell waited for a moment, as though there might follow a discussion as to which one of us that should be. I didn't move.

'Yeah, well. I'll go back in then, shall I?'

I waited until he'd taken half a dozen steps before slowly lifting my phone once again to my ear. 'I am *so* sorry about that.'

'No problem.' Paul's voice was calm, as though being yelled at by two different people within as many seconds happened every time he made a call. 'Is everything okay over there?'

I gave a sound that I truly thought was going to be a laugh. No one could have been more surprised than me when it turned into a sob. 'Yes. No. Not really.'

'Okaaaay,' said Paul, clearly at a loss to know what to say. And who could blame him?

'Things have been a bit... fraught... tonight,' I began, and then realised I had no reason to be dragging Paul into our horrible, ugly situation. Another thought suddenly occurred to me.

'How did you get this number? I've never given it to you.'

This time *he* was the one who sounded awkward. 'Ah well, that's a case of total abuse of privilege. I shamelessly exploited the fact that my father's elderly secretary has a soft spot for me, and I got her to pull your personnel file.'

I may have gasped a little, but it was a nice kind of gasp, not the kind you make when someone is stalking or threatening you. I now knew the difference.

'I know,' Paul replied solemnly. 'Shocking misuse of power, isn't it? I'll probably have to spend the next five years of my life working in the post room as a penance.'

Amazingly, I laughed, and it felt so good that I still remembered how to do it.

'So what turned you to the dark side?' I asked, still smiling, and wondering if he could tell that I was from my voice. 'Why did you want my number?'

'Because I've been off all week, and I got my dates mixed up and thought your wedding wasn't for another fortnight. I came by your desk this morning at—'

'Eleven o'clock,' I interrupted, with another smile.

'Yes, at eleven o'clock, and saw everything tidied up and squared away. And then your colleague – the one with the glasses – said you were getting married *tomorrow*.'

'I was. I mean, I am,' I corrected, wondering what that very telling Freudian slip might have revealed.

'Yeah, well, I know that now. And there was something important I wanted to say to you, before you got yourself hitched.'

Everything around me suddenly went very quiet. The women behind reception were still talking, I could tell that from their moving lips; a concierge wheeled a luggage trolley across the marble tiled floor, and yet it made no noise at all. The only sound I could hear was my own heartbeat.

'What? What was it you wanted to say to me?' That surely couldn't be my voice. It sounded nothing like me.

'I… I just wanted to say… to say…' This was very unlike him. I might not know Paul well, but eloquence was never something he'd struggled with. He knew all the words, only for some strange reason he appeared to be having trouble finding the right ones tonight.

'I just wanted to say… good luck. I hope everything goes well tomorrow. I wish you all the happiness in the world.'

A single tear formed at the corner of my eye. I tried to blink it back, but it was determined, and slid slowly down my cheek. I tasted its saltiness as it grazed against my lips. No more followed it. I wasn't crying. I had no reason to cry. It was a perfectly nice message from someone I hardly knew, not really.

The man I loved was sitting in a room full of my family

and friends, doing his best to make them see why he was the person I wanted to spend the rest of my life with. And I had no business being out here talking on the phone to another man.

'I have to go,' I said hurriedly.

'Of course,' Paul responded, and I could tell he was both annoyed and embarrassed.

'Goodbye, Paul,' I said softly, and then broke the connection before he could reply.

'Well, that was awkward,' said Darrell under his breath, as I slid back on to my seat beside him. 'The post room certainly works late at your office, doesn't it?' he added.

He was half turned in his chair, his body language an open challenge. Okay, he had a right to be annoyed. Your fiancée is not meant to be taking telephone calls from other men on the night before your wedding. But then she's not meant to be the target of a hate campaign from your deranged ex-girlfriend either. We were both guilty. We were both innocent.

'He just wanted to wish us well,' I said, subtly altering Paul's message.

'That was nice of him,' Darrell said. Even a deaf man could have heard that he didn't mean it.

'Paul is just a friend,' I said, annoyed with myself for having to justify one tiny secret, while Darrell was holding on to so many more.

'Is he coming to the wedding tomorrow?'

I sat up sharply in my seat, genuinely shocked. 'No. Of course he isn't.'

Something seemed to relax in Darrell then, and for the first time since taking the phone call, he reached for my hand and laced his fingers through mine.

'Sorry. I overreacted. I guess even tonight, with our wedding in the morning, I still can't believe how lucky I am to be marrying you.'

I smiled, or at least I tried to. I think I did okay.

7

The make-up artist packed away the collection of products it had taken to effect my transformation, while I stared at the stranger in the mirror, who looked a little bit like me and an awful lot like someone far more polished and glamorous. At least I'd look good in the wedding photos, I thought. I'll probably be glad of that over the next fifty years or so. I gulped, and saw the woman in the glass do likewise. Fifty years of marriage… what would that feel like? I had no point of reference, no compass locator to guide me. My own parents had barely even managed three. Had my mother felt like this on *her* wedding day? I could have asked her, I suppose; she was only three doors down the corridor right now, already getting dressed in her mother-of-the-bride outfit.

I cinched the silk robe a little more securely around my waist and thanked both the hairdresser and the beautician for their work. As soon as they left I went straight to the large Georgian windows and threw them open, letting out the lingering aroma of hairspray (my hair was going *nowhere* today) and cosmetics. I breathed in deeply, waiting for the feeling that I was slowly suffocating to fade. Perhaps breathing into a brown paper bag would have been more beneficial than inhaling a lungful of country air? That was the recommended treatment for anxiety attacks, wasn't it? I felt my lips twist into a smile as I visualised walking down the petal-strewn aisle in my flowing wedding dress, a bouquet in one hand and a brown paper sack in the other. *That*'d be a good photo for the album.

A deep-cushioned window seat was set beneath the casement, and I sank down on to it, curling my legs up beneath me like a child. If I leant out and craned my neck to the right, I could see the ornamental lake, and beside it the decorated wedding canopy. I could also see the neatly lined-up rows of chairs, each tied with a red satin bow, and beside them a long linen-covered table, already set up with champagne glasses. I leant out further and stared at the red-carpet aisle that I would walk down as a single woman, and walk back up as someone's wife. A light knock on the door, and I drew my head rapidly back inside, like a startled tortoise.

'Suzanne, open up, it's me,' hissed my bridesmaid, as my fingers fumbled awkwardly with the door catch. It was strange how even the simplest of motor skills were a struggle for me this morning. It was probably just as well that hands other than mine had been responsible for my hair and make-up.

I eventually pulled open the door to find Karen standing in the public corridor wearing only an incredibly short towelling robe. She dived into my room, just as a young family emerged from a door opposite. 'Definitely a bad idea to stand in a corridor semi-naked,' she said, pulling ineffectually on the hem of her robe.

'Tell me about it,' I replied, without thinking.

Karen's neatly plucked eyebrows rose slightly, but I shook my head and changed the subject. 'If that's what you're wearing to walk down the aisle behind me, you're going to totally upstage my lovely dress.'

She smiled. 'Even if I dropped the robe, all eyes would *still* be on you,' she said loyally. 'Your hair and make-up look amazing, by the way.'

'Thank you,' I said, claiming credit I hadn't earned. All I'd had to do was sit there.

'Have you heard from Darrell this morning?' asked Karen, bending down and lifting the silver lids off a largely untouched selection of breakfast plates on my room service tray. She selected a soft buttery croissant from one and flopped down on to a wing chair to eat it. 'My diet's officially over, by the way,' she said, sinking her teeth deep into the golden flakes of pastry.

'Help yourself,' I said, indicating the bowls of fresh fruit, cereals and jams also on the tray. 'I couldn't face eating anything,' I confided.

'If you swoon going up the aisle, don't expect me to catch you.'

'Do people still swoon these days?' I asked, sitting down opposite her and glancing at the time on my phone. 'In answer to your question, I haven't spoken to Darrell today, but he *did* message me.'

I swivelled the device around so she could read the screen. 'Good morning, wife. Tomorrow I'll whisper that to you as you lie beside me.'

'Aw, sweet,' declared Karen. 'He's quite the romantic, isn't he? Tom would *never* send me a message like that in a million years.'

I smiled and nodded, feeling disloyal that sometimes – just sometimes – I found it all a little too much. How ungrateful would that have made me sound? I didn't show her the second message, the one he'd sent a short while ago, which asked: 'Is everything still quiet at your end?' It was. But the fact that both of us were still anticipating some last-minute attempt to derail our day was hardly comforting.

'It'll soon be over,' he had whispered as he folded me into his arms and kissed me goodnight after the rehearsal dinner. The taxi he'd ordered was waiting at the bottom of the hotel steps, but Darrell had seemed in no hurry to leave me. 'We'll soon be married and then there'll be nothing anyone can do to keep us apart,' he vowed. The love on his face jarred slightly with the steel in his voice.

'Tomorrow,' he had said, making the word sound like a promise as he kissed me one last time before running lightly down the steps to the waiting cab.

'Tomorrow,' I had repeated softly in the empty foyer.

'So what time is the florist coming? Is it before scary Gwendoline arrives with your dress?'

I smiled because I knew exactly what she meant about the owner of Fleurs Wedding Gowns. 'I just *knew* she didn't trust that I was listening properly when she was showing me how to lace up your dress. Still, I'm glad you booked their "Dress the Bride" service, even if it does mean I now won't be able to claim my Good Bridesmaid badge.'

I got to my feet and squeezed Karen's shoulder. 'Oh, you'll still get it,' I said warmly, not knowing how true those words were soon going to be.

My mother arrived shortly before the flowers. I wished she could have been just a few minutes later. It was hard to disguise my instinctive panic as I opened the delivery of cardboard boxes and peeled back the layers of tissue paper. My fingers were trembling as I tore away the final one, as though this was suddenly a high-stakes game of pass the parcel.

The tissue paper floated to the floor as the boxes revealed nothing more than the bouquet, buttonholes and corsages we had ordered. Even so, my fingers rummaged beneath the flowers, looking for a hidden card covered with writing I would instantly recognise. There was none.

'Have you lost something?' asked my mother, looking on curiously as I slowly withdrew my hands from beneath the blooms. I felt a small embarrassed flush warm my cheeks.

'I just wanted to make sure everything was here,' I said, lying very badly indeed.

Karen returned to her own room to slip into her bridesmaid's dress, leaving my mother and me alone for the first time in days.

'If you're sure you don't need me to help you into your dress, I think I'll take the buttonholes down and wait in Reception with your father. I do believe he's rather nervous about his role today,' she confided, revealing so much more than she realised by the softening in her cornflower-blue eyes and the curve of her lips.

'You and Daddy seem to be getting on very well,' I commented, wondering where the childlike title had suddenly sprung from, after decades of absence.

'We do seem to be,' she admitted. She reached for the box of buttonholes, her gaze fixed on them as she added quietly, 'I know I was initially opposed to it, but actually I'm glad you asked him to give you away today. It means a great deal to him.'

I looked up and was surprised to see her eyes were full of tears. She never cried, and the fact that she was doing so now, on my wedding day – a day she had never wanted to see – was even more astounding. 'I love you, Suzy, and I am proud to call you my daughter. Whatever happens today, I want you to always remember that.'

It wasn't until she had disappeared, with the box of buttonholes tucked securely beneath her arm, that it occurred to me what a peculiar remark that was.

'Stand perfectly still now,' commanded Gwendoline, her hands poised above the satin ribbons and loops, like a concert pianist about to perform a concerto. There was certainly rhythm and fluidity in her movements as her fingers flew with lightning speed, threading, looping and tightening as she went. In less than half the time it would have taken Karen to accomplish, my dress was snugly laced against my body.

'I'm kind of disappointed you didn't do the knee-in-the-middle-of-the-back thing,' said Karen, which made us both smile. Gwendoline did not join in.

'No one needs to do that with a Fleurs gown,' she

declared, before allowing one small smile to escape. 'They fit the bride far too well for that.'

With my dress fully fastened, all that remained was to step into the white satin shoes with their tiny sparkling embellishments, which stood side by side next to the bed.

'Just like Cinderella,' Karen said, her voice choked as my feet slipped into the shoes. We hugged, and I saw the small wince that Gwendoline couldn't quite suppress.

There was only one thing left to complete my look. I crossed over to the dressing table and reached for the small black velvet box that Darrell had given me the previous night, just before he left. I had taken the box carefully from his outstretched hand. It looked old, possibly even antique. The velvet pile was worn smooth in places, as though it had been opened by the fingers of many generations before mine. Almost reverently, I had lifted the lid and stared down at the white satin interior, where a pair of antique diamond drop earrings had twinkled back up at me. I didn't need to ask if they were real. Cubic zirconia is good, but it doesn't sparkle like that.

'Oh Darrell, these are absolutely exquisite,' I had breathed, my fingers grazing gently across the surface of the glittering stones.

'They were my great-grandmother's,' he'd said quietly.

I'm sure my surprise must have been written all over my face, but he never saw it, for his attention was only on the family heirloom. 'They've been passed down through my family, and every Kingston bride has worn them. Will you wear them tomorrow?' he had asked, his voice oddly unsure and emotional.

'I would be honoured to,' I had answered truthfully.

His family should be here to see this, I thought, as I stood before the mirror and threaded the beautiful earrings through my ears. Whatever has happened, the fact that he'd given me the earrings to wear meant that family was still important to him.

'That just leaves the veil to secure in place and then I will take my leave,' began Gwendoline, reaching for the garment bag that contained the last accessory to turn me into a fairy-tale bride. Her fingers were scooping the soft folds of fabric from the bag when the telephone beside the four-poster bed rang.

I stared at it for two rings before taking a step towards the bed. I think Karen asked if she should get it, but her voice sounded far away and distant, as though she was talking to me from another dimension. All I could hear was the ringing of the phone and the resulting thud of my heart. I shouldn't know what this was. And yet I did. I shouldn't be fearful; it could be something entirely innocent. And yet I already knew it wasn't.

My palm felt damp as I reached for the receiver, but I didn't drop it. My answer was already on my lips, even before the receptionist in the hotel foyer had finished speaking.

'Send her up,' I said, with a dull feeling of inevitability.

Not surprisingly, Karen initially refused to leave. 'Please just go and wait back in your room,' I implored, half pushing her towards the door. She was surprisingly sturdy and immovable, digging her kitten-heeled bridesmaid sandals into the pile of the carpet, like a stubborn seaside donkey.

'No way. This woman is a bona fide nut job. This is *exactly* the sort of person who turns up wielding an axe.' She nodded emphatically, as though a lifetime of prophecies were about to come shockingly true.

'Tell you what, if she's carrying one, I just won't let her in,' I said, my fingers firmly fastened on the flesh of her upper arm as I continued to attempt to propel her from my hotel room.

'This isn't something to joke about,' Karen said, her voice dire.

'I'm not laughing,' I replied, with unnatural calm. For hadn't I always known that this – or something very like it – was coming? Hadn't I known it, in fact, from that very first moment when I'd found the card on my windscreen?

'Would one of you two young ladies please explain to me exactly what is going on here?' enquired Gwendoline, a little surprised by the turn of events, but largely unfazed. My veil was still draped reverently over her extended arms, like a beloved pet serpent.

'Suzanne is about to do something extremely foolish, and I'm trying to stop her,' declared Karen, her voice beginning to crack from both fear and frustration. Gwendoline's pencilled eyebrows rose with perfect synchronicity. 'She's going to invite a crazy woman into her hotel room.'

The eyebrows managed, incredibly, to rise even higher. Gwendoline eyed first Karen and then me, and I could almost hear her thinking that the room might already have its full quota of those.

'We don't know that she's crazy,' I countered, directing my comment to the owner of the bridal shop. Aside from an almost imperceptible flare of her nostrils, Gwendoline still appeared remarkably unperturbed by Karen's dramatic statement. *Did this sort of thing actually happen more than the bridal magazines I'd read would have you believe?* I wondered.

'This woman, is she one of your guests?'

'Hardly,' muttered Karen, before I had a chance to reply. 'She's the groom's ex-girlfriend.'

'Ahh, I see,' said Gwendoline on a sigh. Very carefully, she began folding the veil back into its garment bag. Perhaps after a lifetime in this profession, she really *had* seen it all before.

I stopped trying to manhandle my friend like an over-enthusiastic bouncer, and went instead to the door. I might have looked calm, but my heart was beating fast as I swung it open. I'd been half expecting to find her there already, the woman who'd haunted my life like a living ghost for the last few months. But the corridor was still empty.

'Please, Karen. Just take Gwendoline with you and wait in your room. I need to do this alone.'

Karen hesitated, hearing something in my voice that said more than words could ever convey. Very reluctantly, she took a step towards the hallway.

'Don't shut the door,' she instructed. 'Don't turn your back on her. Don't—'

'She's probably just going to yell at me,' I said, my eyes widening in alarm as Karen turned on her heel, strode back into the room, and headed for the breakfast tray. With a meaningful look she bent down and gathered up every single piece of gleaming silver cutlery.

'Let's not take any unnecessary chances, eh?' she said, with an armful of flatware clasped against her chest. At any other time I would have laughed, but not just then.

'Please be careful,' urged Gwendoline, as she followed a reluctant Karen into the hallway. 'And I don't just mean of the dress,' she added. *That* was the closest I came to smiling. My own well-being was clearly not Gwendoline's major concern here.

I watched them all the way down the corridor until they reached Karen's room. There was an unnatural stillness to the hallway after my friend's door had clicked to a close. The only sound I could hear was my own ragged breathing. All I could do now was wait.

From somewhere unseen, around a bend in the corridor, I heard the subtle ping of a lift reaching my floor.

'There's a woman here in reception who says she has to speak to you urgently before your wedding,' the receptionist had said, with an obvious apology in her voice. Had the hotel employee looked at her watch before making the call up to my room? Yes, I imagined she had. She would know our ceremony was due to begin in a little over half an hour. Had she glanced across at my father, who was probably pacing the foyer, rehearsing his speech one last time as he waited for me? Undoubtedly. 'She says you'll know who she is. And that you'll want to see her,' the receptionist had added uncertainly.

That last comment was curiously both right and wrong.

Her identity wasn't in question. It was finally time for me to meet Catherine, the woman who'd shared Darrell's life before me. But did I want to see her? No. Absolutely not. And yet I knew that if this was ever to be over, I *had* to.

I waited for her knock on my door. Three sharp raps, neither timorous nor bold, but somewhere in between. I walked jerkily towards the door, as though my knees had forgotten that they knew how to bend. I'm not sure which one of us gasped first. Perhaps we did it simultaneously? After all, we had so much else in common, why not our reactions? She seemed genuinely shocked to see me in my wedding dress. What on earth had she expected? I was due to get married in thirty minutes, what else would I be wearing?

The reason for my own gasp was harder to pin down. Some of it came from fear, I'm sure, but the rest of it was from a vague feeling of déjà vu or recognition. I *knew* this woman, didn't I? I took two steps backwards into my room and she countered them by taking two across the threshold.

She was a fraction taller than me, and perhaps a year or two older. That surprised me. By her actions, by the childish campaign she had waged, I'd always imagined that she'd be much younger, in her early twenties perhaps. This woman in her thirties looked outwardly respectable and sensible, and somehow that made her even more dangerous. She cleared the edge of the door and pushed it shut behind her. So much for Karen's advice about keeping it open.

I continued to stare at the woman, even as her large brown eyes did the same to me. There was something so very familiar about her, as though I had seen her many times before, but in a different setting. It was that unsettling feeling you get when you encounter someone out of context: the shop assistant you pass in the park; the doctor's receptionist pushing a trolley in the supermarket.

'You're prettier than I thought. Up close, you're much prettier.'

This was not the time to thank her for the compliment, and I truly didn't think she'd intended her words to be one anyway.

'What are you doing here?' It was a good opener for me to begin with, but she stared at me as though I might be pretty, but I was also incredibly dumb.

'I came for your wedding, of course,' she said, giving a brittle laugh, as though something inside her was broken.

'You're not welcome here,' I said, hearing the tremble in my voice and hoping that she could not. 'I don't want you here, and Darrell *certainly* doesn't want you here.'

She laughed again, and I wondered if Karen had been right. Was she actually insane?

'Oh, I'm certain Darrell doesn't want me *anywhere* near here. Or near you. And yet he must have known I would come, that I *had* to come,' she said, sounding almost as though the decision to be here, in my hotel room, on the morning of my wedding, had been forced upon her.

'Listen, Catherine, I know—'

She gasped and took a half-step backwards, as though I'd struck her. 'You know who I am then? You know who I am, and yet you're still going through with it? You're still going to marry him?' Her voice was incredulous, as though I was the one in the wrong here.

'I realise you're very upset. I know that for you to be here today, you must once have loved Darrell very much.'

'Of course I love him. I'll *always* love him. That's the deal though, isn't it? You're never allowed to stop. Even if you hate them, even if you hate what they're doing, you still can't stop loving them.'

'You have to realise that it's over between you and Darrell. I'm sorry, but you have to accept that and leave us both alone. *I'm* the one he's marrying.'

'Not if I can help it.'

Suddenly I was very glad that Karen had removed the sharp implements from the room, because that had sounded very much like a threat.

'You can't force him to go back to you,' I said, inching slightly backwards. Perhaps if I could just get to the phone beside the bed, I'd be able to call down to Reception, to summon help. I glanced over at my mobile, which was sitting uselessly on the other side of the room.

Catherine was speaking, but I was too preoccupied with trying to reach the hotel phone to take in what she said. She took a step towards me, her hands reaching out and grasping my shoulders, hard enough to leave marks.

'What did you say?'

With difficulty, I shrugged off her hands; they felt like claws. Ten red circles stood out like measles spots on my bare skin, showing how hard she had grabbed me.

'I... I...'

'You said something about me getting Darrell back? As if we were a couple? Is that what you meant?'

I nodded, my throat too constricted with fear of this wild-eyed woman to articulate a reply.

'God. You really don't know a fucking thing, do you? Darrell isn't my lover.' She gave a small sound of disgust. 'He's my brother.'

★ ★ ★

I don't remember moving to the chair, but suddenly it was there, right behind me. I sank on to it, and after a moment Catherine crossed to the one on the opposite side of the coffee table and did the same.

'Darrell doesn't have a sister,' I said dumbly, even as my eyes were running over her face. Those eyes. The shape of the nose, the fullness of her mouth. No wonder she had looked familiar.

'We're twins,' Catherine added without expression. She gave a laugh that held no humour at all. 'Lovely to know that he's still pretending I don't exist. Sometimes I wonder why I even bother trying to save him.'

'Save him?' I asked, feeling like I was on a carousel that was spinning as fast as a centrifuge. 'Save him from what? From whom?'

There was pity on her face then, only I didn't know who it was for: her, me or Darrell.

'From himself. I'm here to save him from himself... *again*.'

She paused, and I wondered if she was waiting for me to say something, but I had so much to say, so many questions to ask, they were bottlenecked in my throat, choking me. At last, one managed to squeeze through.

'Has this got anything to do with the feud he has with his – with your – parents?'

Her eyes, Darrell's eyes, opened wider. 'Oh, so you know about that, do you?'

There was a bitterness in her voice that scored me like acid. 'I only know that he doesn't speak to them any more.

That there was a serious falling-out. And that they moved to Australia.'

Catherine laughed then, and for a moment I wondered if she really might be unstable after all. Was *that* why Darrell had never told me about her? 'Australia? Oh my God, if this wasn't all so dangerous, it really would be funny. They've never been any further than Calais in their entire lives. They live in Wales. Not in the same town where we grew up. Obviously. And we all use my mother's maiden name these days. Except for Darrell, of course. He's still a Kingston.'

'Are you in some sort of witness protection scheme?' I hazarded uncertainly. 'I tried to find your family. I wanted to invite his parents – your parents – to our wedding, but I couldn't track them down.'

'Well, wouldn't that have been fun?' Catherine replied bitterly. 'I doubt they'd have said yes though, even if you'd found them. You see, we've already been to Darrell's wedding.'

My heart began hammering against the wall of my chest, as though it was trying to get out of here before the woman sitting opposite me totally destroyed it. Too late. There was nowhere for it to go.

'You're so stupid. You're *all* so stupid. Darrell is *already* married – and has been for the last seven years.'

There was a glass of iced water in my hand. I had no idea how it got there. It was almost a shock to see Catherine replace the glass jug on the tray. 'You should drink that. You've gone a funny colour,' she observed.

'Darrell was married for seven years? He's divorced?' My voice was tentative, as though I already knew the answer to those questions. I just wasn't ready to hear them.

'*Is* married. Not divorced. Not separated. He'll never leave Alice. And she'll keep taking him back and forgiving him, time after time.'

'What? Alice? He has a wife called Alice? But he can't have,' I said, getting shakily to my feet. 'Because we're getting married. We're getting married *today*,' I said stupidly, indicating my long white bridal gown, as though she might possibly have forgotten the occasion I was dressed for.

'Not if I can help it, you're not. Not unless you deliberately want to enter into a bigamous marriage. Oh, and by the way, those are my great-grandmother's earrings. I'll have them back, please.' She held out her hand for the diamonds. I tore them from my ears so roughly I actually made them bleed and never even noticed. Catherine dropped them into the pocket of her jacket.

'This isn't the first time he's done this, you know,' she said, pulling a packet of cigarettes from her bag and lighting one. In view of the larger issues, it seemed ridiculous to point out that this was a 'no smoking' room. 'I have to admit, I'm surprised it went this far. I thought he'd have stopped it long before now, once he realised that I'd found out what he was doing again.'

'How many times has this happened? How many other women has he done this to?' That voice wasn't mine. It was the voice of a victim; a victim who'd just crawled away from the wreckage of an almost fatal accident.

'This is the second time,' Catherine admitted, destroying the structure of my future with her words. 'After the first time, it all got very ugly. That was why we had to move and change our name. That was what Darrell's feud with the family was about. But Alice... well, she loves him. She stayed with him. He persuaded her he'd get counselling, he told her he would never, ever do it again. And yet...' She stopped and swept her hand around the room, full of wedding paraphernalia.

I made a low noise, which sounded like an animal in pain. I'd been so stupid, so trusting and so very, very stupid. How could I not have seen through all the lies? The constant business trips; the second phone; the two passports?

'If it's any consolation, he probably loves you very much,' observed Catherine drily, drawing heavily on her cigarette.

That was the moment when finally – thankfully – I got angry. Blood-red, boiling angry. 'Love?' I shrieked. 'He doesn't even know the meaning of the word. How can you love someone and do this to them? To me? To the woman who came before me, *and* to his goddamn wife?'

Catherine looked at me through a long exhaled plume of cigarette smoke. 'You think you know Darrell, but you don't. Not the *real* Darrell, not the boy I grew up with. He was the golden child. He always had everything. He had the looks, the intelligence and the ability to do or be anything he damn well wanted. And he wanted it all. You think it's an accident that he has the kind of job he's got, the type that allows him to lead two entirely separate lives? Of course it's no fucking accident. Darrell's greedy—' She spat out the word nastily, and it was only then that I realised that as much as she might love him, she really didn't like her brother very much. 'He's always had everything, and he just doesn't see any reason why that shouldn't continue. I've no doubt he wants very much to be your husband. But he also still wants to be Alice's.'

I felt sick, actually physically sick. I wanted this woman out of there, but she looked almost comfortable now. The power in the room was all hers.

'Why... why hasn't he been arrested? You say he's done this before? Then why haven't the police arrested him? He should be in prison.'

Catherine's eyes flickered, and just like that the power shifted, and suddenly it was all mine. 'Because, so far, I've been able to stop him. The other woman was so humiliated by what had happened, she refused to press charges, and anyway I managed to stop it far sooner than this time.' She looked at me with something that in another time and place might actually be admiration. 'You don't scare off easily, do you? Whatever I did, I couldn't seem to drive the two of you apart. You must love him very much.'

'The man I thought I loved doesn't even exist.'

Catherine nodded, and there was actually sympathy on her face. 'He needs help,' she said solemnly. 'Proper help this time.'

'He needs to be behind bars,' I countered, my voice as hard as the diamonds in the earrings he'd given me to wear.

'Well, technically he hasn't actually committed a crime yet. It's only bigamy if you go through with the ceremony. He refuses to listen to me, and he knows me too well, that's the trouble with being a twin. He knows I'll never report him, whatever he does. He really believes that once the two of you are married, I'll disappear back into the shadows and say nothing.'

'Would you?' I asked, horrified.

She was quiet for a long time, considering her answer. 'Probably. If he went to prison it would destroy my parents.

I couldn't do that, not to them, or to Alice. I really like my sister-in-law.'

It was as if she'd taken a knife, sliced it through my beautiful white dress, and plunged it straight into my heart. 'Okay,' I said, getting to my feet. 'You can leave now. You've said what you came here to say.'

'So you'll call it off? You'll just walk away?' she said hopefully, reaching for yet another cigarette from the packet. Her fingers were trembling as she extracted one.

'Or maybe I'll just walk down those stairs in the next fifteen minutes and marry him after all,' I said, throwing open the door. 'And then, right after, I'll phone the police to make sure that this never happens to another dumb bride. Ever again.'

'Fuck me.'

'You said that already.'

'I'm probably going to continue saying it for some time to come,' said Karen. 'Get used to it. I always *knew* there was something fishy about him. I just *knew* it.'

I looked at her through narrowed eyes. 'I think this goes way beyond "fishy", don't you? This is criminal.'

There was a knock on the door and Karen leapt up to get it. Gwendoline came into the room carrying a silver tray with three large brandies on it, and a bottle ready for refills.

'I told them you might be a little late down, that there was a small problem with the dress and we were waiting for a seamstress.' She gave a small sound to indicate just how unlikely that lie had been.

'It's probably bought you a little more time, but if you don't do something soon, both of your parents are going to get suspicious. Your mother is a very perceptive and determined woman,' Gwendoline added.

'What are you going to do?' asked Karen.

'I know what I *want* to do,' I said darkly, feeling the fire of the brandy score a path down my throat. 'I want to kill him.'

'Ditto that.'

'I want them to lock him up and throw away the bloody key.'

'Perfectly understandable,' Karen conceded. 'But to do that, he actually has to *commit* a crime. He actually has to marry you. Is that really what you want to do?'

I shook my head miserably. 'I just feel so stupid. So gullible and dumb. I feel like the biggest idiot that ever walked the face of the earth.'

'You're not the idiot. He is,' said Karen. 'But as ugly as all this is now, if you go through with the ceremony just to bring him down, what will that do to you?'

I went to the window. Over the noise of the chirping birds I could hear the vague strains of the string quartet, who were filling in time while they waited for the bride to put in her appearance. Brides were traditionally late. It was what everyone expected. But not me. I was never late. Not for anything. A sob tore from me, as I thought of everyone down by the lake, waiting for me.

Suddenly I couldn't breathe.

I hurled the empty brandy glass across the room, not even noticing when it shattered against the wall.

'Get me out of this dress,' I cried, pulling frantically at

the boned neckline, as though it was crushing my chest. 'Get this bloody thing off me.' My hands were scrabbling at the ribbons, which had laced me in as tight as a straitjacket.

Both women flew across the room to reach me. Karen was crying along with me, but Gwendoline was amazing, all calm voice and soothing arms. 'Hush now, it's coming off, it's coming off. Stand still, sweetheart, you'll soon be free of it.'

And when the final ribbon was pulled out of its loop, when the dress fell around my feet like a pool of white lava, I breathed easily and felt it then, the cool breeze of freedom, soothing my panic.

Karen gave me her hand, and I stepped out of the fallen white folds as though escaping from quicksand. I looked back once over my shoulder and saw Gwendoline crouched down, picking the dress up from the floor. 'Get rid of it for me, please. I never want to see it again.' She nodded sadly.

I felt better when I was back in jeans and a T-shirt. I felt like me again, or as much like me as I was going to be for a while.

'Are you sure about this?' I asked.

Karen nodded solemnly. 'It will be the pinnacle of my career as your bridesmaid.'

'As my *chief* bridesmaid,' I corrected, tears slowly falling down my cheeks. They'd been doing that for a while now, totally ruining the beautician's hard work.

'They still probably think you're just going to be late,' she added. 'But if you want to get away without facing anyone, you're going to have to do it right now.'

I nodded slowly. 'Tell my parents I'll call them later. Make sure they know that I'm okay.'

'Consider it done,' assured Karen.

'Tell everyone else that I changed my mind.'

'And Darrell?' Karen prompted hesitantly. 'What do you want me to tell him?'

I gave a small bitter laugh. 'Tell him I met his sister. That should do it.'

Karen smiled in a way that told me that of all the tasks I was asking of her, that one would be her favourite.

'Do you want me to call you a cab so you can be gone before I go down?' she asked, reaching in her bag for her phone.

I shook my head and instead picked up my own. 'It's okay. I'll do it.'

Things happen for a reason. Good things and bad things. Sometimes you need distance to work out which is which. Sometimes, you just know.

The number was in my call log. It was answered on the second ring. I glanced at my watch. It was exactly the time I was supposed to be walking down the aisle.

'I don't suppose you're available for an emergency eleven o'clock collection, are you?'

'I'll be right there,' said Paul.

8

Six Months Later

The first flakes of snow started to fall just as we pulled up outside the church. They swirled lazily down, settling on my hair and bare shoulders like confetti. I resisted a childish urge to stick out my tongue to taste the icy crystals, which would probably have earned me a disapproving look from my mother, who'd emerged from the limo right behind me. Or maybe not. She'd changed recently. We all had. I imagined there was very little I'd ever thank Darrell for, but the events of last summer *had* brought about a new closeness between Mum and me. She was softer now, less judgemental, except on those occasions when Darrell's name was mentioned. Then she morphed into a Fury-like creature, with a murderous gleam in her eyes. 'I could happily kill him,' she'd said at least a hundred times, which was better than the '*I told you so*'s I'd been expecting. Strangely, she'd never said those words, not even once. 'If you want to kill that little toerag, take a number and get in line,' my dad had growled.

He'd hugged me fiercely at the airport before flying back to Spain one week later. It had felt odd having Mum beside me to wave him off. That *definitely* wouldn't have happened before Darrell and the wedding-that-never-was.

'I might actually miss your father a little, now that he's gone,' Mum had confessed, as we'd stood at the huge plate-glass windows watching his plane take to the sky.

Somehow I'd managed to hide my smile and I'd reached for her hand, surprised at how comforting it felt to have it wrapped around mine once more. 'Spain's not so very far away. Perhaps—' She'd shot me down with a single look. Yes, she'd changed... but not quite *that* much.

And now my father was back again. To attend a wedding that everyone hoped would be a great deal more successful than the last one I'd planned. It was already off to a good start, I thought with a smile. At least this time the groom wasn't already married.

The chiming of the church bells beckoned us towards the oak doors, which were flung open in welcome. Waiting inside the familiar parish church of my childhood were my family, friends and – of course – the man I loved. I wondered how many guests on the left-hand side of the church, the bride's side, were thinking back to the much grander affair they'd attended last summer. At least those on the groom's side didn't have those memories to taint today.

The limo driver, who was holding an enormous golf umbrella above our heads, waited patiently as I picked up my bouquet of yellow gerberas. They were an unconventional choice for a wedding, but they were the first flowers Paul had ever given me and had become our 'thing'. Roses, for obvious reasons, would always hold far less pleasant memories.

Paul had even produced a bunch of the cheery yellow blooms from the boot of his car when we'd gone away for a recent trip to the coast. It had been our first holiday together and the beachside property he'd found couldn't have been more perfect. The quaint clapboard cottage was set almost directly on the sand at the end of a long, twisty lane and was an idyllic spot for a romantic getaway. And we clearly weren't the only people to have thought so, for the guest book was filled with the names of couples who'd celebrated landmark moments in their relationship by staying there. Among the *'Perfect spot for our anniversary'* and *'We got engaged!!!'* comments were two particularly intriguing entries.

'What do you think happened here?' I asked, swivelling the guest book towards Paul and running my finger beneath the names of a Sophie and Ben, who in a previous February had written *'So happy he brought me here'*. Then, I flicked forward to six months later where I'd spotted the same distinctive penmanship beside another entry that read *'We came back'*, but oddly this time the only name beside it was Sophie's.

Paul had smiled and gently lifted the book from my hands. 'Who knows? Maybe they split up.' I'd shaken my head, my interest still piqued, but then all thoughts of previous guests disappeared as Paul reached for my hands. 'I'd like to see your name and mine together in that book for many years to come,' he'd said, his voice suddenly husky. We were careful never to talk about the future, although increasingly it was becoming harder and harder for me to imagine one without him in it. 'I know you want to take this thing slowly,' he said, his green eyes holding mine captive, 'and I understand why, I really do. But I want to make sure you know that I'm all in. I'm done. This is it for me.'

'Me too,' I whispered.

'Good,' he said, his breath mingling with mine in the gentlest of kisses. 'The future will find a way of sorting itself out,' he promised. 'It always does.'

It was warm sitting beside the cottage's inglenook fireplace, but it wasn't flames that melted my heart, it was the look in his eyes. 'I don't care if some people say it's too soon – I knew you were the one from that very first day, when you sat in my post room, trying so hard not to cry.'

'*Your* post room?' I asked, my voice caught somewhere between a laugh and a sob. 'And there I was thinking you were just the guy who delivered the post.'

He grinned. 'Ah, didn't I tell you? My father owns the company.'

I grinned right back at him. 'My mother's a famous novelist.'

'You win,' Paul said, bending down and kissing me in a way that made all further conversation redundant.

It wouldn't have surprised me if some of the guests in the church today thought this wedding was a little hasty; rushed even. I'd heard it referred to as a whirlwind courtship by more than one person. And in a way they were right, because it had swept through our lives like a gust of exhilarating fresh air. The only thing that really mattered was that the people I loved, the people I *truly* cared about, all knew differently.

Today's celebration would be nothing like the wedding Darrell and I had planned to have. And that was no happy accident; it was one hundred per cent deliberate. From the time of year – winter rather than summer – to the flowers, and the cake, *everything* was completely different. And that included the dress. This gown hadn't come from Fleurs and was a world away from the dress I'd chosen from there. This one was a sophisticated slim sheath in champagne-coloured satin. It was a Grace Kelly meets Audrey Hepburn kind of gown, and when I saw the price tag I felt a wave of guilt that my mother had now bought *two* extremely expensive gowns in a little over six months.

She'd shrugged, this new *laissez faire* mother of mine. 'It's only money, Suzy. What's the point of having it if you can't enjoy it?'

I looked at her now as we drew to a halt at the entrance to the church. Karen was waiting just inside the doors, in case of any last-minute wardrobe malfunctions, but happily there were none that needed her attention.

The difference that made *this* wedding day even more special was that today my mother and I would walk side by side up the aisle to the altar. My father had happily agreed to this slightly unconventional arrangement, and I loved him for allowing Mum and I to have this last precious moment together.

'Is everyone here?' I whispered to Karen, as she brushed a few lingering snowflakes from my hair and shoulders.

'If you mean Paul, then yes, of course he's here,' Karen replied, giving my hand a friendly squeeze. She smiled warmly, her gaze encompassing both my mother and me. 'You both look absolutely lovely.'

'So do you,' my mother said, her eyes going down to the exceedingly large bump straining at the fabric of my best friend's dress. 'Blooming, in fact.'

'Too blooming big to have squeezed into a bridesmaid's dress,' Karen quipped back, but there was a radiance on her face that was almost always present these days. 'Well, if you're both ready, I'll nip back in and tell the organist he can do this thing, shall I?'

Before we walked in tandem into the candlelit church, I turned to my mother in the tiny vestibule, wanting to freeze this moment in my memory for all time.

'I love you, Mum.'

'I love you too, sweetheart.' Her hand was still squeezing mine as the first notes from the organ swelled to fill the church. We turned as one and began to walk up the aisle.

My eyes went to him first, the way I suspected they always would. In his dark suit, Paul looked beyond handsome as he stood at the end of a pew watching our approach. The pride on his face was a snapshot I would cherish forever.

My father was wearing a remarkably similar expression, except – if I wasn't mistaken – there were tears glinting brightly in his eyes as we covered the last few metres. It was the first time I'd ever seen him cry, and it was almost my undoing.

'Dearly beloved, we are gathered here today to celebrate

a particularly joyous union,' began the vicar, looking fondly at the people assembled before him. 'Who giveth this woman to be married?'

My throat was clear, and my voice rang out loudly in the hushed silence of the church. 'I do,' I said, lifting my mother's hand and placing it gently into my father's waiting one. Smiling and crying at the same time, I took a small step backwards and slipped into my allocated seat in the front pew. Paul's arm snaked around my waist and pulled me closer to his side, to the place I never wanted to leave.

Hours later, when she stood on the balcony of the house I'd grown up in, my mother turned her back on her assembled guests and with a joyful laugh threw her bouquet over her shoulder to the hallway far below. I caught it. Naturally.

PART TWO

Bella

9

This was wrong. So very, very wrong. The day wasn't meant to end like this. *I* wasn't meant to end like this. I was only twenty-eight years old. I still had my whole life ahead of me. It wasn't meant to be over in this way, in fear and confusion; in a carnage of twisted metal, staring into the eyes of a stranger.

It was oddly quiet, as though the world had suddenly been put on 'mute'. The sirens that would soon split the air had not yet been summoned. Above me, swooping through a clear and cloudless blue sky, I could just make out the call of startled gulls, their cries mimicking those that were beginning to rise from the onlookers on the ground far below us.

Low key, she'd said. *I don't want a big fuss*, she'd said. *And I certainly don't want it to be tacky.* So I was understandably surprised when the Barbie-pink limousine turned up at my door that morning to collect me. The windows were blacked out, but when the uniformed chauffeur deferentially held open the door for me, my preconceptions about my best friend's hen party flew past me in an air-conditioned gust from the limo's interior. Sasha, the bride, was beaming broadly from the crimson padded bench seat, a half-empty glass of Prosecco in one hand and a full one for me in the other.

'It's eight o'clock in the morning,' I said, shaking my head in amused disbelief as I took the proffered drink.

Sasha's neatly threaded brows rose a centimetre or so. 'And your point is?'

'I don't normally have alcohol with my cornflakes,' I said with a smile, taking a sip from the perfectly chilled wine.

'This is a special day. Absolutely nothing about it should feel normal, or boring. It's my hen do.'

'I think everyone can see that,' I teased, taking in the satin 'Bride-To-Be' sash that was looped over her shoulder. It was an interesting addition to her skimpy denim shorts and vest top outfit.

'Don't worry, Bella,' said Mel, from the opposite bench seat. 'She's not forgotten us.' She pointed to the pink sashes emblazoned with the word 'Bridesmaid' that she, Jessica and Louise, the other members of the bridal party, were currently modelling.

I slid on to the seat and gave a good-humoured shrug. Personally, I'd have chosen to spend my hen 'do' at an exclusive spa, being pampered and polished for the big day, but this wasn't my wedding. Nor was there likely to be one in my foreseeable future, an ugly niggling voice in the back of my head took pleasure in reminding me. I was the only member of the bridal party with a commitment-phobic partner who'd recently taken to speed-walking past every jewellery shop window. After two years together, Aaron seemed perfectly happy to *never* upgrade his title from 'boyfriend' to 'fiancé'.

In consequence, I spent a lot of time telling people I was far too focused on the dog-grooming business I'd set up eighteen months ago with Wayne, my poodle-loving, hilariously camp business partner, to be worried about getting married. But those who knew me well saw through the lie, just as I saw through theirs. As much as they tried to hide it, my close girlfriends thought I could do better than Aaron. Much, much better.

'Getting engaged isn't everything,' Sasha had declared loyally. 'It's not like there's a race to see which one of us is going to be first to the altar, is there?' Which was easy for her to say when she was blatantly about to win that particular event. 'Just give it a couple of years, after Bella's won *The Apprentice* and set up her global dog-grooming franchise... or something.' My lips curled at the memory as I looked warmly over at her now. The glass-beaded tiara had slipped slightly on her long blonde curls, and even with hardly any make-up on, she was still the most beautiful girl in the car. She winked, and I winked back, our secret signal, born what seemed like a thousand years ago. She had my back, and I had hers. That's the way it had always been, right from the very first time she'd linked her arm through mine in the school playground and declared that we ought to be best friends, because neither of us had one of those yet. It might not have been the best reason for a lifelong friendship to be forged, but five-year-old Sasha had known a thing or two, even back then, because we'd been inseparable ever since.

Therefore, if she wanted me to look like a total idiot in a pink sash at the theme park today, or like a large, peach-coloured meringue in my bridesmaid's dress in three weeks' time, well, that was fine with me. That's what friends do for each other.

'Should we take our bags in with us?' I asked, eyeing the five holdalls packed with our change of clothes for the evening activities, although I still had no idea if I'd be awake enough for the fancy restaurant, much less the planned visit to a club afterwards.

'No, we can leave them in the car,' Sasha advised, scooting lithely over the bench seat and emerging into the already hot day. The weather had certainly warmed up over the two-hour drive to reach our destination, and all five of us were sporting a pleasant rosy glow to our cheeks, although that might have something to do with the three empty bottles of Prosecco that now stood inverted in the ice bucket in the back of the limo.

We all reached in our bags for sunglasses as we emerged like skydivers from the depths of the pink vehicle. I took a moment to rummage in my tote for an old scrunchie that I used when working, and twisted it around my straight chestnut-coloured hair, fashioning a long swinging ponytail to keep it off my neck.

'That's right isn't it, Derek? You're staying here all day, aren't you?'

The grey-liveried driver nodded. 'I am. I'll be here waiting for you ladies, whenever you're ready to leave.'

I gave him a small apologetic smile. That couldn't be much fun, hanging around and waiting for a group of largely overexcited twenty-somethings to realise they were actually far too old to spend their day on hair-raising roller-coaster rides, like octane-fuelled teenagers. 'I hope it won't be too boring for you,' I said, giving our driver a cheerful wave. 'See you later.'

I never saw him again.

We had a great morning, despite literally losing Mel in the crowds, not just once but *twice*, and then losing Louise – metaphorically – after a particularly violent spin on the teacups. She came off with legs that looked as solid as al dente spaghetti strands, and a complexion that was practically the same shade of green as my eyes.

'That should be banned,' she said, pointing an accusatory finger at the ride, which five-year-olds were gleefully leaping from with no apparent ill effects. 'Don't *you* feel sick?' she cried, looking almost disappointed when I shook my head.

'But then I've always liked fast rides,' I conceded.

Louise shuddered dramatically and I sensed that she might be done for the day, apart from attractions designed for pre-school-age children.

'I'm guessing you *won't* want to go on The Hybrid with me, then?' I teased, pulling the folded park map from the back pocket of my jeans. Sasha came up behind me and rested her chin on my shoulder as she studied the brief description of the park's newest attraction, an eight-loop roller-coaster.

'Well, I don't think Mel will make the height criteria,' she said, softening her words with a warm smile directed at our diminutive red-headed friend.

'Haha,' said Mel, who, despite her fondness for heels and platforms, only came up to our shoulders. 'Actually, I think I'd better go with Louise to the Ladies',' she said, slipping an arm around the waist of our motion-sick friend, who was still looking decidedly pasty.

'Bridesmaid down,' murmured Jessica, falling into place on Louise's other side. 'And we haven't even *started* on the tequilas yet.'

'Looks like it's just you and me,' I said, turning my head and staring into Sasha's twinkling blue eyes. 'If you're up for the challenge.'

'Always,' she said, with a fleeting grin.

'Stay by the loos and we'll come and find you when we're done. It's only a ninety-second ride, we won't be long.'

'No way. No sodding way.'

'Is that "no" to the ride itself, or just the length of the queue?' I asked, feeling childishly disappointed as I studied the wait time indicator, which was currently predicting a delay of fifty minutes before it would be our turn to experience the park's newest attraction.

Sasha stepped back from the bustling crowds and lifted one hand above her eyes to form a visor, following the progress of a single carriage as it careened at a seemingly impossible speed from one gravity-defying loop to the next.

'A bit of both, I think,' she said. 'I don't want to spend ages waiting for something that'll be over in ninety seconds.'

'Nah, far better to leave that for your honeymoon,' I quipped.

Sasha's chuckle sounded both sexy and smutty. 'Seriously, Bella. Do you really think it's worth it? We could probably do three other rides in the time it would take to do just this one.'

She made a good point, I thought, as my eyes travelled the length of the long snaking line of would-be riders, which folded back on itself like a compressed concertina. A sudden roar from overhead made the entire crowd jump, as an enormous animatronic dragon's head belched out a sheet of flames from behind the ride's castle facade. Some people cheered, while others laughed nervously and tried to pretend they weren't jumpy at all.

The theming, it had to be said, was particularly impressive. 'It looks just like those books we used to read when we were kids,' Sasha said nostalgically. 'You remember the ones? The stories with the wizards and the lava-spewing dragons?'

I smiled, knowing exactly the series she was talking about, because they were still sitting on the shelf of my bedroom in my old family home. Like so much of the house, my room was frozen in the past, locked into a 2006 time warp. It was as though Dad had been scared to change a single thing after Mum died. Perhaps he thought it made it easier for me. Maybe it did in a way, but losing your mum at fourteen leaves a scar that no amount of time will ever erase.

My thoughts had taken a distracting detour into the past, to a place far too dark to belong to this day of celebration. I was still trying to shake them from my head when I was rocked backwards on my heels as I collided with a tall figure, who I'd somehow failed to notice was in my path. Strong fingers reached out to grab and steady me, leaving me nose-to-chest with what appeared to be a wall of solid muscle. I instinctively stepped out of his hold, weirdly rattled by the touch of a stranger's hands on my bare arms. Although the impact hadn't been particularly painful, it had stopped us both in our tracks.

'I'm sorry,' he apologised, even though I was pretty certain the fault had been entirely mine.

'No. It wasn't you, it was me,' I corrected, my words sounding more like a break-up line than an apology. It was the phrase Aaron had used when he'd suggested we 'take a breather' from our relationship last summer. Even though we'd got back together after only six weeks, those words had done something to the foundations of us. It had made me realise that what I'd thought was made of granite might possibly be constructed of something far less durable. I scowled at the memory, and unfortunately the tall, dark-haired man I'd barrelled into thought it was directed at him.

'Okay then,' he muttered, with a shrug that seemed to imply a great many things about my manners. He strode away before I could say anything else, and that bothered me, although I had no idea why.

'Let's go and find the others,' I suggested, taking hold of Sasha's arm to steer a pathway through the park-goers who *were* prepared to queue in the sun for the ride.

'No, hang on,' Sasha insisted.

Life is much like a roller-coaster, twisting and turning, spiralling out of control just when you think you know where it's going. And the pivotal moments, when everything is about to change, come with no warning sign or klaxon. They just creep silently up on you.

I know Sasha blamed herself for the longest time for what happened next. It's possible she still does. But the fault wasn't hers. It could just as easily have been *me* who insisted we went on the ride.

'Let's queue,' she declared, slipping into line behind a group of girls who looked certain to fail the height criteria.

'But you don't want to ride it.'

Sasha gave a pretty shrug and the tiara slid to an even jauntier angle on her head. 'And *you* don't want to look like a peach-coloured cupcake at my wedding, but if you're willing to do that for me for an entire day, I'm sure I can last a minute and a half on a roller-coaster for you.'

I squeezed her arm, and she smiled at me, and yet a thread of trepidation remained in her voice as she added, 'Just don't blame me if I throw up all over you.'

10

The wait was actually less than the board had predicted. Even so, I was growing hot and thirsty as we shuffled towards the head of the queue in the summer sunshine. I was on the point of suggesting we duck out and go for an early lunch instead when I had the unmistakable, goose-walking-over-my-grave feeling of being watched. I turned around, my eyes immediately locking on those of the man I'd collided with. *Boy, some people really know how to bear a grudge*, I thought, pointedly turning my back to him. Even so, I could feel the burn of his stare from where he stood in the single rider queue.

'Sorry girls, you're not tall enough.' The ride attendant had the look of a prison warder and I felt like telling the disappointed teenagers there was no point in arguing with her. But they did anyway, moving quickly from pleading to pissed-off, without success. Sasha and I exchanged a secret smile. They sounded *exactly* like us at their age. The girls stomped off, disappointment exuding from them like a vapour.

'I suppose there's no chance of *me* not being tall enough?'
said Sasha hopefully to the woman, who looked as happy as
a traffic warden who'd just slapped a fine on a windscreen.
'No, you're good,' said the woman, ushering us through the
metal turnstile.

'Sasha, you really don't have to do this if you don't want
to,' I offered. It was impossible not to notice that she'd gone
a shade paler under her summer tan.

'No. It was my idea,' she maintained. 'And *you* want to
do it.'

I looked at the carriages and felt a small thrill stir in the
pit of my stomach. She was right. I did.

'You're in luck, ladies. The front carriage is all yours,'
declared a ride attendant decked out in an outfit that was
supposed to look like chain mail and was probably just as
uncomfortable.

'Yay,' said Sasha, as though we were off to the gallows.

I climbed into the small metal carriage, stowing my bag
and sunglasses in the mesh holdall by my feet. Sasha slid in
beside me and immediately tried to pull down the padded
safety bar.

'They don't engage those until everyone is on,' I said,
placing my hand over hers on the bar. I was shocked to
discover she was actually shaking. 'You're really scared,
aren't you?'

A blush came into her cheeks, which helped dispel a little
of the pallor The Hybrid had painted on them.

'I'm just being daft,' she said, twisting in her seat and
watching as the carriages behind us began to fill. She
swivelled back to face the front and I could see her eyes
following the track where it fell away a short distance in

front of us, and then rose up again towards the sky in a gravity-defying ascent.

'So, tell me about your final fitting yesterday. I bet your dress looked totally amazing,' I prompted, because if there was one topic guaranteed to take Sasha's mind off the ride, then it was her spectacular wedding dress. But today even the designer gown from the exclusive bridal shop couldn't distract her. She leapt suddenly to her feet and snatched up her bag.

'I'm sorry, Bella, I can't do this. It's scaring the crap out of me.'

She was already clambering over me to step out of the carriage, but when I went to follow her, she pressed her hand firmly on my shoulder. Afterwards she told me that every nightmare she ever has of that day features that moment: when she'd pushed me back down on to the ride.

'Stay,' she urged, looking much happier now that she'd made up her mind not to. 'You know you want to see what it's like.' That's the thing about friends who've known you for over twenty years: there's absolutely no point in lying to them.

'I do,' I admitted.

'Don't feel bad about chickening out, you're not the first,' assured the ride attendant, as he directed Sasha towards the exit sign. 'You can wait for your friend at the bottom.'

I waggled my fingers at Sasha as she was ushered from the ride; in the distance I heard a voice calling out: 'Single rider for carriage number one.'

The seat beside me was once again filled, but when I turned towards the new arrival, my smile of greeting faltered on my lips. Of all the thousands of people in the park that day, why did it have to be the *one person* I'd decided I didn't like?

The Hybrid hadn't been built for someone that tall, and all at once the compact carriage seemed full of long denim-clad thighs and feet that barely fitted into the well designed for them. I squeezed myself as far to the right as I could, painfully knocking my ankle against a metal bolt as I did. For the second time that day, I was scowling when he spoke to me.

'Hello.' His voice was friendly enough to make me wonder if he hadn't realised I was the girl he'd been openly staring at in the queue. 'Again,' he added with a flash of a smile that revealed extremely white, even teeth.

I mumbled a greeting as I tried and failed not to acknowledge that he was very easy on the eye. When we'd bumped into each other, my only impression had been his height and breadth. Now, at close quarters, I could see that he was the classic cliché: tall, dark and handsome. The black hair and the cleanly shaven square-cut jaw reminded me of someone, but it was only when he readjusted the black-rimmed glasses on his nose that I made the connection. The man sitting beside me was a dead ringer for Clark Kent, Superman's alter ego.

'Did your friend change her mind?' His question confirmed he'd definitely been watching us, although weirdly he didn't appear to be trying to hide it. Wonderful. I was now incarcerated in a small metal vehicle for the next minute and a half with my very own stalker.

'Uh huh.' I hoped my monosyllabic answer would convey I had no desire to chat. The sooner we accelerated away at speed, the better.

'Ah, the famed roller-coaster walk of shame,' he said, with a smile that was so unexpectedly charismatic I felt momentarily disoriented, as though the ride had already begun and gravity could no longer be relied upon.

'You like roller-coasters?' The question surprised me, popping out almost of its own volition. But his answer surprised me even more.

'Not particularly.'

I looked up, trying to peer through the reflective surface of his glasses to see if he was joking, but they were coated with something that defied all intruders.

'Then why—?'

'It's my job.'

'You ride roller-coasters for a living?' Who had a career like that, and why had no one told me about that profession when I'd been trying to work out what to do with my life?

'I write travel guides. Most specifically, guides about theme parks.'

It was an intriguing occupation and I regretted my earlier frosty attitude, because I really would have liked to hear more about it.

'Oh well, I bet you'll love this one.'

He shifted slightly in his seat, his hip bone momentarily coming into contact with mine. 'I doubt it,' he said, sounding a little resigned.

A bored-looking attendant began walking along the row of carriages, pushing each safety bar in place, as if on an assembly line. Ours came to a rest against my companion's abdomen rather than mine, leaving a gap of several centimetres between me and the restraint. I tugged down on the thickly padded bar, trying to inch it a little closer. I could sense the dark-haired man watching me.

'Ever been on one this fast before?' he asked conversationally.

I shook my head, pretty sure my ponytail must have struck him in the face with the action. Why on earth did they make these carriages so small? Despite scooting as far from him as I could, my left leg was still pinioned against the length of his; his denim fusing with mine, as though the two fabrics were loom-mates being drawn back together.

'Are there any?'

'There's one in Dubai, and Six Flags... oh, and then there's the one in Japan.' He knew roller-coasters the way I knew dog breeds. What a pair of nerds we were, I thought with a twisted smile.

The sound of raised voices distracted me and I glanced at the ride podium, where two teenage members of King Arthur's court had now been joined by a third. One was speaking animatedly into a walkie-talkie, while another was repeatedly jabbing at buttons on a huge aluminium panel, which looked like it belonged in a cockpit rather than an amusement park. Was there some sort of problem?

'They're taking their time to get going,' my companion observed mildly. I looked around and saw that several other riders in the surrounding carriages were clearly thinking the same thing. Heads were turning, and brows were furrowing. No one looked exactly worried (except possibly me) but the air of excitement that had been hanging over the ride was suddenly infiltrated by filaments of tension, like small arcs of electricity.

For no reason I could pinpoint, I suddenly wanted to get off the ride, *really* wanted to get off. The illuminated green exit sign that had led Sasha to safety beckoned to me like a beacon. I didn't care how stupid I looked; I'd say I was feeling sick, or something. The wine I'd drunk earlier was swirling unpleasantly in my stomach, so it wasn't even a lie.

But before I could attract anyone's attention, a switch was flicked and the *Excuse me* my lips were getting ready to form was blasted from them as the ride rocketed away from the platform. We shot away so fast my turbulent stomach felt as though it was surely travelling several carriages behind ours. The air stung my cheeks as they were pulled back in a look I'm sure was far from attractive. We plummeted down an incline, leaving even more internal organs momentarily displaced. And then the track rose up, almost vertically, like a mountain summit. The cry that escaped me was echoed like a Chinese whisper in every carriage behind us. I glanced to my left and caught my ride companion's quick flash of a smile. If my lips had been able to move, I might have attempted to smile back. But then we were shooting down the other side of the incline and angling around a bend so sharp my body slithered against his. Before I could apologise we'd tilted back the other way and were hurtling towards another peak in the track. We crested it, and I can still recall that one blissful moment when I remembered that this was actually great fun. I liked the speed, I liked the momentum, I liked looking down and seeing the ground whipping past in a multicoloured blur.

Except all at once it wasn't whipping or blurring at all, but coming sharply into focus as the ride jerked to an unexpected stop. Our carriage, which was already over the top of the pinnacle, came to a halt at a precarious angle, facing downwards. I tightened my vice-like grip on the bar and braced my feet against the inside of the carriage, wincing as my bruised ankle protested at the manoeuvre. Out of everything that came after, *that* was the thing that stuck in my head like a burr... the pain from my ankle.

'Is it meant to do this?' I asked, turning to the stranger beside me, my voice betraying the fact I already knew the answer to my question.

He didn't bother lying, although part of me really wished he had. 'I don't think so,' he replied, peering over the edge of the track at the ground, which suddenly seemed incredibly far below us. Perhaps he saw the rising panic in my eyes, for he immediately back-pedalled. 'But these things are always having technical glitches. They'll get it sorted out in a moment or two.'

'I don't think—' I began, but the sentence was torn from me, as without warning we shot off again. I waited for the relief to flow through me, but it never got a chance. I never saw the obstacle, the single, detached, riderless carriage from the previous ride, but the man beside me did. I heard him swear, and the fear in his voice shocked me far more than the profanity. His hand reached out and covered mine on the bar.

'Hang on,' he yelled. 'This is going to be bad.'

It was a very accurate prediction.

There was no time to scream, no time to do anything. I remember the feel of his fingers gripping mine, as if united we might somehow get through this unscathed. But of course, that was impossible. Still, I think I'll always be thankful that someone, even a stranger, was holding my hand at the moment when my life changed.

Our carriage hit the stationary vehicle with a metal-crunching jolt, which for a split second I feared would catapult us off the track and down a hundred metres to the ground below. But instead we crumpled around the halted machinery, like a crushed plastic drink cup. I felt the impact through every bone in my body. Some broke, some were crushed, but the itemisation of my injuries was lost under a wave of pain so intense I felt as if I was drowning in it.

11

There was a long jarring moment of silence before the screams began. Some came from the riders behind me; some rose up like vapour from the ground below us. Was one of those voices Sasha's? Had she been looking upward, smilingly following my thrill-seeking ride when we crashed?

Reality came back in tiny increments, as though waking from a dream. I could feel fingers touching my face, tentatively pushing back the hair that had been whipped free from my hairband. I tried to open my eyes, but something sticky and thick was steadily dripping on to the lids. I blinked, until my vision cleared from red to pink.

'Are you all right?'

I forgave the man whose blood was dripping on to me for the ridiculous question. An ugly jagged cut ran from somewhere unseen beneath his thick dark hair and emerged, like a wizard's brand, on his forehead.

'I'm not sure,' I said, my voice a terrified gasp. I could feel pain everywhere, each individual agony vying for supremacy. I tried to move, struggling as panic gripped me even more tightly than the twisted, crumpled metal that was imprisoning me. 'I don't think I can get out!'

The man pressed his hand with surprising firmness on my shoulder. 'Don't even try. You could make things worse.'

Worse than being trapped in an unstable roller-coaster carriage, God knows how many metres above ground? Wasn't that already as bad as it could get?

'What happened? Why was there another car on the track? Why didn't they stop us in time?' My voice was rising with each question. I'd never been hysterical before; I'd always believed I was a good-in-a-crisis kind of person. But then I'd never been in a situation this dire before. I suppose very few people ever had. Emotions were roiling through me, like lava looking for fissures in bedrock. An eruption felt inevitable, and I was pretty sure that once it started, stopping it would be beyond my control.

'You have to try and keep calm,' he urged. I nodded, imagining the tether on my control as if it were a dog's leash that had to be wound more securely around my hand. Strangely, the analogy to something that was so much a part of my everyday life *did* help. A little.

'Good,' he said in response, his tone calming. 'You're going to be okay.'

I considered challenging that statement, but there was something strange about his voice that worried me. He sounded suddenly weaker than he'd done only seconds before. 'They'll have help on the way up to us very soon. I'm sure they've already—'

The rest of his sentence was lost as he suddenly pitched forward, his upper body landing on me in a breath-stealing thump, as heavy and as immovable as a dropped sack of grain. The crash had crumpled our carriage in such a way that when the man slumped forward, he had nowhere to fall except on top of me. One moment I could breathe, and the next my face was lost beneath the breadth of his shoulder.

He was a dead weight, innocently suffocating me; taking my life and never even realising it. It took all my strength to push the flat of my hand against his shoulder. Even though he was unconscious, I could feel the solid wall of muscle beneath my palm. With each ineffectual shove I could feel my panic begin to rise. I could not, *would not*, survive this accident, only to die slowly and ignominiously beneath the weight of another casualty. I'd like to think it was my fighting spirit that found the strength to push him free of my face, but it was just as likely that he fortunately regained consciousness before inadvertently smothering me.

I gasped in a huge lungful of air, like a drowning person, shrieking at the pain of a thousand sharp shards that felt as though they were piercing me from the inside out. I had no need of an X-ray machine to confirm that some of my ribs were broken.

'Sorry,' my companion apologised, as though we were commuters who'd accidentally encroached on each other's personal space during the rush hour. I saw the effort it took him to brace his weight on one elbow to free me from his body. I looked up in concern. The small amount of colour he had left was fast disappearing from his skin even as I watched, as though the accident was gradually erasing him. Was that how I looked too?

'How badly are you hurt?' he asked, each word coming out in a husky rasp.

'I don't know,' I said, hearing the panic in my voice. 'My chest hurts when I breathe in, and my legs—' Panic rose in me like mercury in a barometer. 'I can't move my legs!'

He glanced down to where the lower half of our bodies disappeared in the convoluted remains of our carriage.

'That's hardly surprising. I think our car took the brunt of the impact.'

I nodded, my ears tuning in to the cries of passengers from the other carriages.

'Are there other people hurt?'

He lifted his head, and I saw his blood-streaked forehead crease in a frown.

'Maybe,' he said carefully, his eyes as inscrutable as a poker player's. What was he seeing? What wasn't he telling me?

He turned back to face me. 'Mostly I can just see a lot of very frightened people back there.'

'In here too,' I added, my voice wobbling on the tears I could no longer hold back.

His hands came up, gently cupping either side of my face. In other circumstances, it was probably the way he tenderly held a woman just before he kissed her.

'Don't be afraid. You're not alone. I'm right here with you.'

'I don't even know your name,' I said stupidly, as though that somehow mattered. And strangely it felt as though it did.

'My name is Will,' he said, his eyes even managing to crinkle at the edges in a smile.

And that was how I met the man who changed my life.

★ ★ ★

'How long do you think it will take before help arrives?'

Will paused in his attempts to lever up the safety bar. Beads of perspiration had broken out all over his face and his efforts had made the blood flow even faster from his head wound. The bar, not surprisingly, hadn't budged a centimetre.

'Soon,' he said. 'They'll be here soon...' He seemed to struggle for a moment to remember my name, even though I'd only told it to him a minute or two ago. People with a serious head injury were probably not meant to exert themselves the way he was doing. 'Bella!' he completed, conjuring up my name like a forgetful magician.

Of course, he had no way of knowing how quickly help was on the way, but I wanted so much to believe him that I didn't challenge his answer. Will returned his attention to the bar, this time attempting to use his shoulder to release the restraint. He grunted like a wounded animal, then swore using words I'm certain weren't in 'mild-mannered' Clark Kent's vocabulary. The bar stubbornly resisted all movement, confirming that his similarity to Superman really was only skin-deep.

'Fuck it!' he said, thumping angrily on the bar with his fist. 'It won't budge.' He glanced back along the length of wrecked carriages, shaking his head as he watched other trapped riders with the same idea reluctantly come to the same conclusion. 'No one is getting out of here by themselves.' He wiped his hand across what he probably imagined was a sweat-drenched brow and looked almost surprised when his palm came away scarlet.

'You're bleeding quite badly,' I told him, biting my lip in concern. 'Perhaps we should try to stop it?' The steady flow was continuing to drip on me, but that wasn't what was bothering me. What if he passed out again from loss of blood, what if he stopped breathing?

'My head is the least of our worries,' Will said, craning his neck and looking down at the figures on the ground, who were scurrying around like displaced ants.

'Can you see what's happening down there?'

He squinted, and repositioned his glasses a little higher on the bridge of his nose. I noticed for the first time that one of the lenses had cracked in the accident. It made him look strangely vulnerable.

'They're moving everyone away from the ride,' he said, his breath fanning my face as he leant over the edge of the carriage to get a better look. I could smell sweet aftershave and bitter perspiration, and a strange metallic odour that I'd read somewhere was the smell of blood. 'It's chaos down there,' he concluded, manoeuvring himself back as far as he could into his own space.

From one of the carriages down the ride a woman was screaming for help, her cries growing increasingly hysterical. Another voice angrily told her to *shut the hell up*. It was frightening to see how the veneer of civilised behaviour was so quickly stripped away in a crisis.

'Once they figure out a way of getting us down, everything will be fine.' You had to admire a man who could lie with the skill of a second-hand car salesman, but he wasn't fooling me. Nothing about this was fine, and might possibly never be again. There was no way of telling how seriously either of us was injured, and the fact that I could no longer feel my legs was more terrifying than being in agony would have been.

'I think my ankle's probably broken,' Will admitted, almost reluctantly, when I pressed him for a summary of his injuries.

'Are you sure?'

'I broke it playing football years ago, and it felt pretty much like this, as I remember.'

'At least you can feel *something*,' I said, my words a terrified whisper. 'My legs are just numb.'

We both looked down at the twisted metal that held us in its jaws like a steel trap. Will's eyes – which I could now see were the same shade of blue as the summer sky – darkened as he turned to me. 'Still no feeling in either of them?'

I shook my head, and swallowed down the terror that was trying to claw its way out of my throat. 'No. But that must be because they're squashed up in there, right?'

'Yeah. I'm sure that's it.'

His hand moved along the padded bar and found mine, his long fingers sliding between my own. His hand was larger than Aaron's and his grip much firmer. It should have felt weird holding hands with a stranger like this, but I was already praying he'd not release me yet.

'So, a hen do, right?' Will's tone was light, and you didn't need to be a genius to work out he was trying to distract me. For just a moment, I was happy to let him.

'How did you guess?'

He smiled, his eyes dropping to the pink sash I was wearing.

'When's the big day?'

'In three weeks,' I said sadly, already certain I wasn't going to be there to see my best friend get married.

He smiled. 'The groom's a lucky guy.'

I'd spent most of my teenage years accepting that boys were always going to notice Sasha before they looked at me, and I thought I'd long since stopped feeling irritated whenever it happened. It was quite a surprise to find that I still minded.

'Phil definitely is,' I agreed.

The whirring sound of rotor blades filled the air and our heads jerked up in unison. A helicopter had arrived before the fire engines, and everyone trapped in the wreckage started to go a little crazy with excitement. There was shouting, and arms were waving, semaphoring like windmill sails, as though we were marooned on an island and the pilot might possibly fly past without seeing us.

Will had shielded his eyes with one hand, and I saw the moment when his smile changed into a frown. 'Vultures,' he muttered in disgust.

I squinted into the sky, half expecting to see a swooping bird of prey, but there was only a circling helicopter.

'It isn't a rescue helicopter,' he explained, his lips twisting as though he'd tasted something bitter. 'It's from a TV station. I guess we're breaking news.'

Dread filled me at his words. 'Oh no. My dad always has the news on in his workshop. He's going to be frantic when he hears about the accident.' I looked down in despair at the crumpled front of the carriage. Somewhere among the twisted metal and debris was my mobile phone, or what was left of it.

'Do you have a phone on you?' I asked Will desperately.

He read the panic on my face and immediately understood. 'Back pocket of my jeans. Right-hand side. But you're going to have to reach it, because I don't think I can.'

I slid my hand around his waist as far as I could reach, my palm moving from fabric to skin as it travelled beneath his ripped T-shirt. I grazed over his hip bone and the taut muscles of his back, pausing at his sudden indrawn breath.

'Sorry. Am I hurting you?' I asked, wondering if he'd played down the extent of his injuries, but Will just shook his head.

'It's just bruises,' he said, nodding for me to continue.

My fingers were slower now, more cautious about causing him pain. I found the band of leather of his belt and dipped lower, seeking his pocket. My search had brought us so close there was literally no space between us. I could feel my breasts crushed against his chest, the soft skin at my waist pressing into the buckle of his belt, and the zip of my jeans gnashing its teeth against his. But anything lower than that was felt only by Will. Below my hips I still had no sensation.

My fingers slid over a firm buttock and dived into his pocket. I wriggled them down in the impossibly small gap until they grazed against something flat and metallic, which I hooked out like a heron with a fish. But my victory was fleeting, because from the broken screen and dented casing I already knew his phone was broken beyond repair.

'Maybe your friend will let your dad know what's happened,' Will suggested, looking lost as fresh tears began to fill my eyes.

'She might. But she won't be able to tell him that I'm all right. Hell, even *I* couldn't have told him that... but at least he could have heard my voice.'

'She'll probably call Phil too,' Will added consolingly.

I nodded, wiping the back of my hand roughly across my eyes to brush away my tears. I couldn't lose control now. I had to keep my head together.

'I guess *you* have people you'd have wanted to call too? Parents, or a girlfriend?'

Will shook his head.

'A wife?'

That one brought a wry smile. 'No takers in that department, although I came pretty close last year.' His eyes flickered, and I guessed that whatever had happened was not a happy memory. 'And as for my parents, they've retired to the South of France. Hopefully we'll be out of here long before news of what's happened today travels that far.'

A muted cheer rose up from the ground below us, which was quickly drowned out by the sound we'd all been waiting to hear. Sirens. Lots of them. I reached instinctively for Will's hand, not even surprised to find it already outstretched and waiting for mine. Help was finally here.

12

'What's taking them so long?' Strand by strand, like a disintegrating rope, my control was slowly starting to shred.

'They're probably still trying to work out the safest way to reach us.'

For the last thirty minutes we'd been receiving snippets of information from someone several carriages back. Unlike ours, their mobile phone was still working, and they'd been receiving updates from friends on the ground, which they'd passed in relay along the line of carriages. The messages were delivered in a series of shouts, which the wind kept trying to whip away.

It was surprisingly breezy for such a hot day, and with every gust I panicked that the carriages might become uncoupled from the track and hurtle like lemmings off The Hybrid to the ground below.

'Another fire engine has just arrived,' a voice behind us shouted out. 'That makes six in total and twelve ambulances.'

Two helicopters were still swooping overhead, like buzzards circling roadkill. It was a horrible analogy, but one I couldn't seem to get out of my head. With the sun now high in the sky, the day had grown excruciatingly hot. The weathermen had promised the warmest day on record, and unfortunately it looked as though they were going to be proved right.

'I'm so thirsty,' I said, my lips as dry and parched as my throat. I thought longingly of the water bottle that had been in my bag, no doubt crushed like the rest of my belongings.

'Try not to think about it.' Will's face was also running with rivulets of sweat and yet his voice was cool and calming. I was beginning to realise that he wasn't just good in a crisis, he was *amazing*. His steady voice and unflappable attitude stayed my panic, in a way I'm not sure would have happened with anyone else. How would it have been if Sasha were beside me now? Or Aaron? As disloyal as it might be, I instinctively knew that my boyfriend wouldn't have handled things as well as Will was doing. Aaron wasn't good around illness, a fact he freely admitted. Even when his grandfather had been desperately ill in hospital, he'd had to steel himself to visit him. 'I just don't cope well around sick people,' he'd said at the time, wrapping his arms around me and kissing the side of my neck. 'So don't you go and get ill, hmm?'

'I'll do my best,' I'd told him. It had been in the early days of our relationship, when I was still falling too fast to see his attitude as anything to worry about.

'So,' Will prompted, snapping me out of my thoughts of Aaron. 'Tell me some more about yourself. Let's start with your job. What do you normally do when you're not skiving off on a hen party?'

'I own a dog-grooming business.' Will's eyes widened in surprise and he nodded encouragingly, clearly wanting more. 'It's called Doggy Divas, and we've been going for almost two years now. It's doing quite well, actually,' I admitted, unaware that a note of pride had crept into my voice. 'It's hard work, but I have the best partner in the world, who I love to bits.'

'Phil?' Will guessed.

I frowned, worrying all over again about his head injury. Why would he think I worked with Sasha's fiancé, or that I loved him for that matter?

'No, I'm talking about Wayne, my *business* partner.'

'Who you love?'

I smiled, visualising my uber camp, over-the-top friend. '*Everyone* loves Wayne.'

'Ahh... I thought you meant "partner" as in boyfriend.'

I shook my head, and then instantly regretted it. I was getting the most dreadful headache, which I suspected was caused by dehydration, and every movement seemed to make it worse.

'No. My boyfriend's name is Aaron.'

Will was now looking more than a little confused. 'I'm not sure I'm following this. You love your business partner Wayne; you've got a boyfriend called Aaron; and yet you're about to get married to Phil? And you said your life wasn't interesting!'

My laughter came from somewhere unexpected, given our current situation.

'I'm not marrying Phil – Sasha is. Why did you think it was me?'

In answer, Will looked down at the pink sash my friend had slipped over my head what felt like half a lifetime ago. It had slipped around my body, the only letters still visible spelling out the word 'Bride'. I tugged on the pink satin, and heard a ripping sound as it snagged on a jagged piece of metal and tore in two. The sash came free in my hands.

Will's eyes flickered over the letters that had been hidden: 'smaid'. For some reason, they made him smile.

Whatever he might have said next was lost – the sound of a heavy boot on metal made us both look up as the first rescuer to scale the hundred-metre climb to reach us finally arrived.

Over the next fifteen minutes, more firefighters climbed The Hybrid to join us, their faces unreadable masks as they surveyed the task ahead of them. It was more the things they *didn't* say than the things they did that worried me.

Miraculously, most of the other passengers had sustained only minor injuries, and were released carriage by carriage from the ride and then led to a platform, where a cherry picker would lower them to the ground. But our own release was considerably more complicated.

Until the arrival of the paramedics, Will had been holding my torn sash against his head as a makeshift dressing, and it was worrying to see that what began as tiny red rosebuds on the fabric had quickly blossomed into enormous scarlet flower heads. And yet from the moment the paramedics joined us, I felt we were in safe hands.

'Well, this is all a bit of a pickle, isn't it?' declared a female voice with a thick Yorkshire accent. As understatements go, that had to be right up there with the best of them. Cathy introduced herself as though we'd just met at a party, over cheap plonk and sausage rolls. 'You'll meet my partner, Vince, in a minute – if the daft sod hasn't had a coronary on the way up here. He's nowhere near as fit as he likes to make out.'

Her chatter was jovial and irreverent, and totally at odds with her professionalism as she pulled on surgical gloves and began to examine us both with skilled and gentle hands. She was probably only fifteen years or so older than me, but there was something reassuring and maternal about her. It was there in the way she lightly stroked my shoulder before running her hands down the bits of my body she could reach. It was so long since I'd felt anything like a mother's touch. I hadn't even realised I'd begun to cry again until Cathy pressed a tissue into my hand.

'Give your girlfriend a cuddle, Will. She needs one.'

I was about to explain that Will and I weren't a couple, but his arm was already around my shoulders, pulling me against him. It was so comforting I completely forgot about correcting her.

'Ah, Vince. So you decided to join us after all,' Cathy cried, turning with a smile to greet the paramedic, whose bright red face clashed alarmingly with his green jumpsuit.

'"Just a little bit of climb? More of a stroll, really?"' the new arrival gasped, no doubt quoting his colleague. She grinned and reached for the bag he'd been carrying, delving into its depths for supplies.

As the pair applied dressings to our wounds and assessed our injuries, the banter continued. It was a distraction I imagined they regularly employed to calm their patients, and I had to admit, it worked. Almost without me noticing it had happened, Cathy had rigged up a drip, which was now feeding into my arm. Their routine was so slick it felt almost rude to interrupt it with the question I could no longer stop myself from asking.

'Why can't I feel my legs?'

Cathy's eyes flickered, but it was Vince who answered.

'It could be any one of a multitude of reasons, Bella. The doctors are the only ones who'll be able to answer that properly, once we've got you out of here.'

Beneath my head, which was leaning on his chest, I felt the skip and subsequent increase in Will's heart rate. It was weird how neither of us seemed to have noticed his arm was still around me.

Vince, who was squatting low on Will's side of the carriage taking his blood pressure, looked up with eyes that promised nothing except straight talking.

'I know what you're thinking. You've gone straight up there to the worst-case scenario and there's probably nothing I can say that'll talk you down from there. So all I'm going to tell you is that it's far too soon to know anything for certain. Just hold on to your positive thoughts – and to each other. And don't go crossing any bridges until you absolutely have to.'

I nodded dumbly, seeing multiple versions of the paramedics as my eyes filled with frightened tears. It was impossible not to notice that they hadn't said I was being silly. They hadn't said, *of course you'll be able to walk*. They hadn't wanted to lie.

I looked up at Will and caught a moment I'm sure he never intended me to see, as he brushed a single tear from his eye.

It took them five hours to free us, far longer than I'd anticipated when that first red-faced, slightly out-of-breath firefighter had appeared beside us, and during that time Will and I fast-tracked from people who'd been strangers only hours earlier to ones who knew so much about each other we could probably have sat exams on the subject. I knew where he'd grown up – *Oxfordshire, posh private school*; that he was the middle of three sons – *didn't really get on with his oldest brother, who was a pompous idiot* – his words not mine; and that he'd got into journalism quite by accident at university – *after volunteering to write a review for the student newspaper*. I knew he visited his parents twice a year at their villa in Nice – *always on his mum's birthday and sometimes on Mother's Day too*. And that he'd lost his heart for the first time on his seventh birthday – *to a beagle pup called Lily*; the same beloved pet who was also responsible for breaking it some twelve years later when she passed away. He could *pretty much quote every line from the* Star Wars *movies* – which I hoped he'd never prove to me; and openly admitted that he *cried every single time* he watched *The Notebook* – a fact that impressed me a great deal more.

As the hours went past, I felt that I knew this man better

than many of my closest friends. I willingly admitted my initial assessment had been completely wrong. He was a good guy, a *great* guy; the kind of guy who'd make someone a wonderful boyfriend. Why he was single was a total mystery to me.

I surprised myself by telling him about my mother – something I rarely did when meeting someone for the first time.

'That must have been so tough to get through,' he'd said gently.

'I'll let you know when I'm there,' I replied soberly, which earned me a tender hug as he drew me even closer against him. His body was supporting almost all the weight of mine, which was just as well, for as the minutes ticked into hours, I could feel myself growing weaker and increasingly light-headed. I could tell from the muted conversations between Cathy and Vince that either my condition or Will's was beginning to cause them greater concern. They were huddled for a very long time with the chief fire officer, and finally, after a trio of gravely affirmative nods, they approached the carriage.

'Will, Bella,' the senior officer began, his chirpy voice not quite matching the look in his eyes. 'We're all ready now to start cutting you free. I just wanted to run through how things are going to go from here.'

Will reached for my free hand, and squeezed it encouragingly.

'Once we've cut the safety bar off, we'll begin slicing through the carriage. We're going to start on Will's side first, so you'll be getting the lucky first ticket out of here.'

'No.' There couldn't have been a single head that didn't

turn towards Will in astonishment. 'Get Bella out first. Once she's free then you can work on me.'

The fire officer shook his head slowly, with an 'I've-heard-it-all-before' kind of expression on his face.

'That's very noble of you, son, but that's not how things work around here. *We* get to decide the order of things, so we can keep everyone safe – my crew as well as you two.'

'I don't want to leave Bella alone,' Will said, shaking his head slowly as though politely refusing the dessert trolley.

'Hey. What are we? Chopped liver?' said Vince, resting his hand on Will's forearm. 'We're going to be right here with her all the time, mate. She won't be alone. You can trust us to take good care of her until you see her again.'

Will still looked as though he was about to refuse, but I saw the way Vince's fingers had tightened around the suntanned skin of Will's arm. The two men locked eyes, and a silent conversation took place. This was more than just reverse chivalry, or even expediency. There was a reason Will needed to be out of the way before they set me free. One of us was in a far more serious condition than we realised, and I saw in Will's eyes that he'd already worked out who it was.

'I promised I'd stay with you.'

'That's okay,' I whispered, feeling naked and vulnerable in front of the team of professionals listening in on our conversation. 'I'm going to be fine.'

As the firemen began getting their equipment into position, Cathy and Vince were busy doing the same with their own.

'It's impossible to know how the situation will change once you're both free,' Cathy explained, checking that the neck brace she'd slipped around me earlier was still secure. Will was also wearing one, and as they slid a long board beside the track in preparation for lifting him away, I felt panicked by our imminent separation. He said he didn't want to leave me, and more than anything I selfishly didn't want him to go.

The sun was much lower in the sky when they were ready to begin slicing through the carriage with hydraulic cutters and spreaders. A heavy canvas sheet had been draped in front of us, which I imagined was as much to prevent us from seeing our injuries as it was to protect us from loosely flying pieces of debris.

The first sparks of pain began to pierce the numbness almost as soon as the safety bar had been removed. I took a draught of the gas and air Cathy was holding in readiness, grateful for the woozy half-drunk feeling it gave me.

Even with their sophisticated extraction equipment, it still took time for the firemen to cut open the twisted metal, but eventually the front of the carriage was peeled back as effortlessly as a sardine can.

For all his earlier bravery, Will was clearly in a lot of pain as experienced hands slipped beneath him to slide him on to the waiting board. Even so, he still held on to my hand until the very last moment, when Vince gently disengaged our fingers. The rescuers worked with efficient urgency as they strapped the man who'd shared every moment of this terrible experience with me on to the board.

With his head securely fastened Will could no longer turn to look at me, so his parting words were addressed to the sky as they carried him on to the cherry picker's platform.

'Stay strong, Bella. I'll do everything I can to get a message to your dad when I'm down. I'll see you very soon.'

I wanted to thank him, not just for remembering how desperately worried I was about my father, but also for everything else he'd done for me over the last five hours. But I didn't have the words, and even if I'd miraculously found them, the pain that had started as an angry growl when they'd begun to free us had now become a ferocious roar. I sucked hungrily on the mouthpiece, gulping down enormous lungfuls of pain relief, as everything slowly swam out of focus.

13

Faces stared down at me; some I knew, some belonged to strangers. They floated on disembodied heads in and out of my field of vision. I struggled to move, but was powerless to do so, for I was still trapped. Only now it wasn't just my legs, it was my *whole body*. I strained against immovable straps. Someone had tied me down, but I had no idea why. The next time my eyes fluttered open, they didn't immediately close again. The faces were gone and I was alone.

Slowly, in sharp-edged fragments, the day began to return to me. The pink limousine... my first ride of the day, and the ambulance with the wailing sirens... my last one.

My eyes flitted from side to side, seeing the same blue fabric curtains to my left and right. From beyond them came a low drone of background noise and voices, which were occasionally punctuated by the squeak of rubber wheels on linoleum. I was in a cubicle, and logic told me it must be in a hospital, although I had no memory of being brought here.

A small oblong window set high in the wall revealed that what little light the day had left was fading fast, although I was sure the sun hadn't yet set when they'd begun to cut me from the crushed carriage. It had taken them longer than they were expecting to extricate me. Mercifully, most of what had happened existed on a different plane of consciousness to the one I'd been on. Although only loosely tethered to the present, there had been moments when fear or pain had tugged me right back down into the thick of things. I could remember hearing Vince urgently insisting that it was time to call for a surgeon, which had made no sense at all to me. It was the fire chief, whose name I'd never been told, who'd urged him to wait. 'Just give us ten more minutes. If we haven't got her out by then... you can make the call.'

It was only now that I understood why a surgeon would have been summoned to the accident site. Had those ten minutes been enough? My terrified gaze flashed to the foot of the bed. There was a huge frame holding the blankets away from my lower limbs. I had no idea what was beneath it... was it the outline of my lower legs, or a dreadful void where they should have been?

The cry that escaped my throat didn't sound entirely human, but there were people standing beyond the cubicle who recognised its timbre and inflection. They came running. The curtain rings screeched on the metal pole like angry barn owls as first my father and then my best friend surged into the tiny cubicle. As they approached, my first thought was that they both looked sick enough to warrant hospital beds of their own. I looked beyond the pair, searching for another face, but there was no one behind them.

My father has a ruddy complexion. Even in the depths of winter he still looks like he's spent his day under a blistering sun or on the bow of a ship. The only time I'd ever seen his face bleached of colour, as it was now, was on the day of Mum's funeral. It was a horrible thought to have lodged in my head as he reached for my hand, which was lying like a broken wing beside me. His thick fingers, bearing the cuts and scars of his work tools, were gentle as they expertly wove beneath the trailing wires and tubes, without once disturbing the canula embedded in the back of my hand. Even the skills you don't choose to remember are sometimes hard to forget.

'Daddy.' When had I last called him that? Not for a decade or more, I'm sure.

'I'm here, baby, I'm right here,' he replied. But he lied, for this hollowed-out shell of a man wasn't my bold, fearless father. This wasn't the man who'd vowed to slay the monsters living beneath my bed, or any boy who dared to break my heart. This man was fragile and afraid, and barely in control of the limbs that were trembling almost as much as his voice.

'I wasn't sure if you'd be here.' The words sounded thick and woolly in my mouth.

'I got here as fast as I could.'

Once again my eyes strayed to the curtains behind him.

'Your dad heard the news and came straight to the park.' I turned to Sasha on the other side of my hospital bed. Her hair was dishevelled and her make-up was streaked like dirt stains down her cheeks. It was the closest nature would allow her to look less than beautiful, with swollen eyelids and freckles that stood out like paint splatters across her nose. 'God knows how he got past the security cordon to find us in the crowd. But he did.'

'How bad is it, Dad? What's happened to my legs?' My eyes went fearfully to the frame that hid the truth beneath a canopy of blankets.

'You've got some pretty serious injuries to both of them.' His eyes skittered away from mine as though afraid of what I would read in them. 'They need to operate on them straight away.'

'Tonight?'

He nodded and glanced briefly at his wrist watch. 'Right now. They told us we could only see you for a moment before they take you up.'

'But they can fix me, right?'

Dad had the kind of eyes that were born to tell nothing but the truth, however hard it was to hear. What they told me now was that the damage was so much worse than a jumble of broken bones.

'They say the trauma surgeon here is one of the best in the country. He served in Afghanistan with the army. We're lucky to have him.'

I felt a great many things right then, but lucky wasn't one of them. And it wasn't a glowing résumé that I wanted, it was an assurance that everything was going to be all right. It was the one thing my father couldn't give me.

'Are there... are there any other people here?'

'We sent the girls home in the limo a couple of hours ago, if that's what you mean,' explained my father. 'Sasha here refused to go with them.'

Sasha's hand linked with mine, the way it had done a thousand times before. Her slim fingers squeezed lightly;

she understood it wasn't the missing bridesmaids I'd been asking about.

'I've left messages everywhere for Aaron, but so far he hasn't answered any of them. I'll keep trying to get hold of him while you're in surgery,' she promised. Her eyes were swimming with tears, and with a single blink one fell from her cheek on to mine. 'I'm so sorry, Bella. I never should have left you. I'm the worst friend in the entire world.'

There was no feigning my surprise at her remorse. It was completely genuine. 'What are you talking about? You did nothing wrong. If you hadn't got off when you did, then we'd *both* have been hurt, instead of just me.' Except of course it wasn't *just me*, was it? It never had been. Whatever I was going to say next was cut short as the cubicle curtains flew apart, like the opening of a stage show. A nurse and two orderlies stood in the entrance.

'It's time for you to go up,' the nurse informed us kindly. 'You need to say your goodbyes now.'

'Just one more moment,' I pleaded, my eyes darting from the nurse back to my friend. 'Have you heard anything about Will? How is he doing?'

'Who's Will?'

'He was the guy in the carriage with me. You got out... he got in.'

I could practically see the weight of even more guilt buckling Sasha's slender shoulders. 'I don't know how anyone else from the ride is doing. I'll try and find out for you.' She bent low and kissed my cheek and then practically ran from the cubicle. A muted sob, the kind that squeezes past the knuckles you're biting down on, followed behind her.

'Whatever happens, Bella, we're going to get through this,' vowed my father, gathering both of my hands within his bear-paw-sized ones. 'We're strong, you and me. We've been through worse than this.'

'We really *do* have to take her now,' reminded the nurse, with just a hint of an edge to her voice. Dad nodded, but held fast to my hand as they uncoupled the bed from the bay. He walked beside me the entire length of the corridor until we reached a bank of lifts.

'Can I go up with her?'

'I'm sorry, Mr Anderson, but it's not allowed,' replied the nurse, laying a hand on his shoulder, as though that would ever have stopped him. For the second time that day, I was about to be separated from someone I needed at my side. First it had been Will, and now it was Dad.

'Take care of my little girl,' he solemnly instructed as they wheeled me into the lift.

My eyes went to his face and stayed locked there until the very last moment, when the closing doors hid him from sight. My father came from a family who suppressed their tears. It took a lot to make him cry, and I'd only ever seen him do so twice in my entire life: on the night we lost Mum, and now again tonight.

An operation that lasts over seven hours is hard on a great many people: the surgeon; the anaesthetist and theatre staff; and of course on the friends and relatives who can do nothing except sit and wait for news. Ironically, the only person who *doesn't* suffer during that kind of marathon surgery is the patient themself. Their turn comes later.

I could hear snoring; deep stertorous snorts, that seemed to be reverberating around the room. Was that Aaron? The only time he ever snored like that was when he'd been drinking heavily, but I couldn't remember us going out the night before... or whose bed I was currently sleeping in, come to that, because it certainly didn't feel like mine. Panic brought me fully awake. Normally once you open your eyes the night terrors disappear, but for me that was when they started.

The light slicing through the window had a pink luminescent glow, and it took me several confusing moments to realise that what I was looking at was the dawn of a *new* day, rather than the fading stains of the old one. Like a scrolling slide show, yesterday's memories inserted themselves into the present, bringing with them a fear so immense I immediately began to shake.

My heart was thundering out of control as I lifted my head from the pillows and forced my eyes to focus on the foot of the bed. I have a strong stomach – it's pretty much essential when you work with animals – but seeing my legs encased in metal frames, with bolts and rods disappearing into the flesh, was almost too much to cope with. It looked like someone had gone to work with a Meccano set in an abattoir. My stomach, which fortunately was entirely empty, gave a token revolt and continued to roll mutinously until I dragged my eyes from the horror show of my lower limbs.

I flopped back against the starchy hospital pillows as hot salty tears escaped from my eyes and trickled lazily into my ears. He'd done it. The surgeon, who'd been just a kindly pair of dark brown eyes above a theatre mask, had kept his word. The last thing I remember hearing as I began counting back from a hundred was his promise that he'd do everything in his power to save my legs. At that moment I didn't care *how* grotesque they looked; at least they were still here.

'You're awake,' cried a familiar voice as the snoring came to an abrupt stop.

I smiled at my dad, who was slowly unfurling himself from the pretzel-like position he'd been sleeping in. He was way too tall to have slept in that uncomfortable bedside chair, although I doubt anyone would have been able to persuade him out of it. Something about seeing his legs cramped up like that tugged on a memory, but every time I tried to reach out and grab it, it slipped through my grasp like smoke. My gaze travelled around the room I'd been brought to, searching for someone.

'Where's Sasha?'

'I put her in a taxi a couple of hours ago and sent her home. She refused to leave until you were safely out of theatre, but she was absolutely exhausted.'

The smile I was aiming for twisted into a wince of pain as I turned too quickly towards him. Dad's face instantly darkened with concern. 'Steady, Bella. You need to lie completely still. You've been through quite an ordeal.'

I wasn't sure which one he was referring to: the crash, or the operation afterwards to fix me. As far as horrible experiences went, they felt pretty much on a par to me.

I'd never been a hospital patient before; I'd not broken a single bone in my childhood. Somehow I'd learnt to climb trees, ride a bicycle and bounce on trampolines without suffering any kind of mishap. But I was certainly making up for it now. The team of doctors surrounding my bed were looking down at me with the kind of interest zoo residents are probably familiar with. There were a great many young faces among the white-coated doctors, who I imagined were probably students. The fact that my injuries were of such interest and fascination to them could only be a bad thing, I concluded.

They answered the consultant's quick-fire questions, speaking in medicalese that no amount of *Grey's Anatomy* viewing could help me understand. Finally, the band of trainees were dismissed, leaving only the surgeon and his registrars at my bedside.

The first thing my father did was to thrust out a hand to shake those of the three men flanking my bed. 'I know I thanked you last night, but well, I was in a bit of a state then, what with everything...' His voice trailed off, and it was probably as obvious to the doctors as it was to me that he was still very traumatised by recent events.

'So, young lady. You set us quite a challenge last night.'

'Sorry,' I said, my voice a curious mixture of apology and concern.

'As we explained to your father last night, we're very pleased with how this first operation went.'

In my head it felt as though a heavy metal door was being slammed shut. Locked behind it was the life I had known before. Someone had to say it. In the end, my dad did.

'*First* operation?'

For the next twenty minutes we were tumbling in freefall, lurching from one piece of bad news to the next, as we learnt what my immediate future was going to look like. The very worst moment was probably when the surgeon reached for a chart and began listing the injuries I'd sustained – this time in layman's terms. He turned over two sheets of A4 paper in the file before he was through. There didn't seem to be a single bone that I hadn't crushed or broken in multiple places, or a muscle left un-torn, or ligament undamaged. I'd woken that morning feeling that keeping my legs had been the hurdle we'd had to overcome, so it was doubly devastating to learn that this was just phase one of the long process of putting me back together again.

'Exactly how many operations are we talking about?' That voice didn't sound like mine at all. Like everything else in my body, that too appeared to be broken.

'It's impossible for us to say at this point,' answered the surgeon, his face giving nothing away. 'But I think it's important for patients and their families to know from the very outset that we have a journey ahead of us, and some of it will be tough.'

My lower lip was trembling and I was very much afraid that I was going to start bawling soon, which I really didn't want to do in front of these strangers. Partly it was the realisation that my recovery was going to take so much longer than I'd imagined, and the rest was because the doctors seemed reluctant to forecast the eventual outcome.

'We simply don't know yet,' was the answer they gave to every one of my questions.

'But I *will* be able to walk?' I pressed on regardless, not liking the way the surgeon's brow had furrowed into lines, like a contour map. 'I mean, I've got feeling in both of my legs, so it's not as if I'm paralysed, or anything dreadful like that.'

The doctor shook his head slowly, wearing an expression that told me he had a far better idea of the outcome than he was letting on.

'Spinal injuries are sadly not the only reason patients find themselves confined to a wheelchair following an accident.'

My gasp was echoed by my dad's. His question beat mine to the punch, for my throat was suddenly too tight for speech.

'Are you saying that Bella is going to end up in a wheelchair? Nobody mentioned anything about that last night.' He sounded almost accusatory that such an important fact had been deliberately withheld from us.

'Last night we were all just grateful that we'd successfully managed to avoid an amputation,' the surgeon reminded us gravely. 'Now we have to concentrate on looking to the future and achieving the maximum level of mobility. Which, this early, is impossible to forecast.'

'But you have some sort of idea. You must have.'

Perhaps patients don't normally press him like that, or maybe he could see from my face that I needed to know what I was dealing with. His brown eyes softened and as he began to speak he took one of my hands in his. I saw that as a very bad sign.

'I don't think you'll ever run a marathon, or climb a mountain… or even be able to dance again.'

My eyes were awash with tears of self-pity, and it wasn't as if any of those things had been on my list of favourite activities. The trauma surgeon was quick to sweep in with more positive news.

'But your pelvis is undamaged, and miraculously there

were no internal injuries. I'm confident this won't affect your ability to have children in the future.'

Again, not something that was looming on my immediate horizon, but still good to know, I guessed.

'As far as walking – well, if all goes to plan we'll see you on your feet again one day, albeit with the help of a stick and very likely some sort of limp.'

The picture he was painting was growing darker with every sentence, and he wasn't done yet.

'At the other end of the spectrum, we're looking at being unable to strengthen and repair the legs enough to support you. And if that *is* the outcome, then obviously you will need to rely on the use of a wheelchair to get around.'

There was a long moment of silence as the bombs he had dropped on to our world exploded silently, destroying so many precious things I'd foolishly taken for granted.

'Your injuries were some of the most severe that I've seen in civilian life, Bella. But the human body is a remarkable thing. It finds ways to continually surprise and astound us. You've got the best orthopaedic team in the country right here, and any halfway decent doctor should be willing to admit that we don't know it all. We're not gods.' He gave a small ironic laugh. 'Although don't tell any of my colleagues I said that.'

He released my hand, which I had quite forgotten he was still holding. 'I don't want to set you any limitations today – it's far too early for that. We're going to take each surgery as it comes, and I have no intention of giving up, or giving in. I'm going to keep on fighting to get you the best possible outcome. All I ask of you is that you do the same.'

14

'Still nothing?'

I shook my head sadly, and passed the phone back to my father.

'What time did Sasha say she'd finally spoken to Aaron?'

'Just after six o'clock this morning.' I wondered if Dad was aware of that little scowl he gave whenever my boyfriend's name was mentioned. It was a poorly kept secret between us that his membership of the Aaron Weston fan club had lapsed recently. Aaron had fallen spectacularly out of favour with Dad after our temporary break-up last year. And while *I* might have forgiven that brief blip in judgement, Dad's memory was more elephantine.

'I imagine he's probably still driving. It'll take him quite a long time from Cumbria, won't it?'

Dad nodded, his expression still several degrees cooler than warm. 'You'd have thought the least he could do is answer his bloody phone, though.'

I shook my head, defending Aaron by instinct. 'He'll have it switched off if he's driving. Ever since he witnessed that accident when the van driver on his phone crashed into another car, he won't take a call – not even hands-free – when he's behind the wheel.'

Somehow even that admirable quality couldn't get Dad to like him more. 'That's all well and good, but given the circumstances, and knowing how badly you've been injured…' His voice trailed away. We both remembered only too vividly that when *Mum* had been in hospital, especially towards the end, Dad had to be practically pried from her side. He expected nothing less than that kind of devotion for me, but I knew Aaron better than that.

And yet, even though I knew he was still many miles away, *and* his peculiar aversion to hospitals, I couldn't stop myself from constantly checking the face of every new arrival on the ward.

'It was sheer bad luck the accident happened when Aaron was away on his company's team-building exercise thing.'

My dad gave an unimpressed harrumph. 'What a whole load of nonsense *that* is. A group of posh boys running around the countryside pretending they're Bear Grylls? What's that got to do with working in an office?'

I gave a tired shrug, unwilling to travel down this road again, mainly because I largely agreed with my dad's point of view.

'And making them surrender their mobiles and not being able to contact them in an emergency. What kind of idiot idea is that?'

'I *did* have an emergency contact number,' I said. 'It was keyed into my mobile.' We exchanged a rueful look, knowing my iPhone had been crushed even more catastrophically than I'd been in the accident.

'I'm sure he'll be here soon,' I said, with a small wince. The last round of painkillers I'd been given had worn off about thirty minutes ago and I still had another hour left before the next ones. Perhaps I could just sleep away the time until both the analgesics and my boyfriend arrived.

'You should go home for a while, Dad. Catch a few hours' sleep in a proper bed; have a shower and a hot meal.' He'd existed on nothing but coffee and unhealthy snacks scavenged from the vending machine, not willing to leave my side for even a quick trip to the hospital canteen.

'I'm fine right here,' he said mulishly, but in truth he didn't look great.

'If you went home you could collect some stuff from my flat for me and maybe swing by the shop to see Wayne.'

'Work is the *last* thing you should be worrying about,' he countered.

'I know. But I'm not sure what Sasha told him last night, and you know what a worrier he is. And what's happened to me affects him too.'

Dad gave a small nod, his lips relaxing into a smile. He had a lot of time for Wayne, both as my business partner and as my friend. His opinion of him was virtually polar opposite to his one of Aaron. 'Such a shame Wayne is… you know… not your type,' he'd said awkwardly after their first meeting.

'I think it's more a case of me not being *his* type,' I'd corrected laughingly.

'I suppose I *could* get back here for the early evening visiting,' Dad conceded.

I tried not to look as though I'd scored a victory, even though I knew I had. Feeling helpless was the thing that would tear my father down; he just needed to have something to do, something he could fix. I hurriedly concocted a list of items for him to bring, all of which I could probably do perfectly well without.

'You just worry about getting some rest,' said Dad, bending down low and kissing my cheek. His beard felt scratchy and the bags beneath his eyes looked hefty enough to use for carry-on luggage.

'You too,' I urged, taking his hand and squeezing it tightly. Now that he was about to leave I suddenly felt like an infant on their first day of school, afraid of being alone in a strange place.

'I'm really sorry, Dad.'

'What on earth for?' He looked genuinely puzzled.

'For giving you something new to worry about. For scaring you.' *For putting that look back into your eyes*, I added silently.

His hands felt hot as they squeezed mine back – the ward was now warm enough to grow orchids. I realised it was something I was going to have to get used to.

'You'll be all right until Aaron or Sasha gets here?'

I nodded vigorously, aware that my eyes were once again beginning to tingle. Another ten seconds and I'd be blubbing like a baby again.

'Go. I'll be absolutely fine.'

The bouquet was so big I couldn't initially see who was carrying it; and there was a box of chocolates, roughly the size of a paving slab, tucked beneath his arm. They were lovely gestures, but I'd gladly have sacrificed both in exchange for what I really wanted from Aaron. Where was the light in his eyes, which always ignited whenever he saw me? Or that slightly crooked smile, with the sexy undertones, that had the power to recalibrate even my very worst day? And as far as bad days went, this one was right up there in my all-time top five.

If he'd brought those things with him, they'd instantly evaporated when he walked into my hospital room. His gaze was fixed determinedly on my face as he approached the bed, as though driving past roadkill. The nurses had pulled back the blankets earlier, uncovering my legs in the overheated ward, but if Aaron's expression was anything to go by, perhaps I should keep them hidden from visitors.

He spent longer than necessary setting down the flowers and chocolates and had managed to get his features under some sort of control by the time he turned to face me.

'Oh my God, Bella. When Sasha told me that you'd been hurt, that you'd broken your legs, I had no idea they'd be so...' His words ran out, leaving an uncomfortable gap for me to insert my own: *Gross. Disgusting. Shattered.*

'I even bought a Sharpie at the petrol station, so I could write something funny on your plaster cast.'

He risked a quick sidelong glance at my legs, and caught a glimpse of a bolt and some kind of screw device disappearing into my thigh. There was an unhealthy pallor to his skin, the kind people get just before they faint. And for a moment Aaron's face seemed to disappear and in its place I saw Will's, right before he'd passed out on top of me. Despite asking several members of staff, so far no one had been able to give me any information about the man who'd been by my side throughout the accident. Will's parting words were that he'd *see me soon*, but I was beginning to wonder if we'd ever meet again.

'Is it okay to kiss you, or give you a hug?' I jumped guiltily at Aaron's question, as though he'd read my thoughts and known they'd been of another man. There was something quite touching about his hesitancy as he stood at my bedside, asking for permission to touch me.

'I thought you'd never ask,' I replied, opening my arms to him.

He held me weirdly, as though I was made of angles and spun sugar. The last time we'd seen each other was two mornings ago, when I'd climbed reluctantly from his bed, leaving him in a tangle of sweat-dampened sheets. Standing beneath the jets of his shower, my body had still been tingling from our lovemaking. There were things I'd quite like to change in our relationship, but our sex life *wasn't* one of them. Was that all over for us for now? It was a question for the doctors, although definitely not one to ask when my dad was in the room.

I lifted my face for Aaron's kiss but somehow his lips missed mine and grazed my cheek instead. But at least his hand was holding mine, our fingers entwined like vines.

'You can sit down, you know,' I said gently, trying not to think that he looked like a runner on the starting block, ready to bolt at the sound of a pistol.

'Perhaps I ought to see if someone has a vase for the flowers.' The words 'flight risk' flashed into my head and stubbornly refused to leave it.

'I'm sure they'll be all right until someone next comes in. They're in and out of here all the time.'

Aaron nodded and pulled the visitor's chair closer to the bed, perching uncomfortably on the edge of its seat.

'Are you in a lot of pain? You must be.'

I pushed the hair back from my forehead, letting it fall in a chestnut-coloured fan across the pillow. 'I'm on pretty strong meds most of the time. They make me kind of dopey.'

Regular Aaron would have made a quip then, asking how I could possibly tell the difference, but Hospital Visitor Aaron had a different reply. 'Maybe I should leave, and let you get some rest?'

'You've only just got here,' I protested, knowing even this early that I was glimpsing a peek into the future, and not liking what I saw. Was it really a surprise that Aaron looked like he'd rather be anywhere else in the world right now? I'd known how weird he was about illness and hospitals, and yet I'd always believed that if the patient was *me* he'd be able to overcome that phobia.

'The accident is all over the media,' he told me, while his right leg jiggled up and down in what could only be anxiety. 'It felt pretty surreal hearing it on the radio as I was driving back down.'

'How *was* your team-building exercise thing?' I asked, more to take his mind off his surroundings than anything else.

'Excruciating. Bloody torture, in fact. I don't think I've ever been so uncomfortable in my entire life.' I tried very hard to keep my features neutral, wondering if yomping over the hills of Cumbria was anywhere near as painful as being crushed on a roller-coaster.

'Have the doctors given you any idea yet of how long you're likely to be stuck in here?'

I chewed nervously on my lower lip, realising Aaron still wasn't fully aware of how severe my injuries were. This was probably the time when I should tell him; he deserved to know. And yet as my lips parted to reveal the truth, a lie slipped past them instead. 'They're not sure. There's a slim chance I might need another operation.' I glanced around the room, guiltily imagining what the doctors would say if they heard my watered-down prognosis.

Aaron's eyes flickered, but I wasn't quick enough to read the look behind their blue depths. 'I saw on the internet that some people on the ride had to wait hours to be freed from the wreckage.'

Once again, the memory of a tall, good-looking man filled my head. Will was starting to haunt my thoughts like a living ghost.

'It *did* take hours. We were the people they were talking about.'

'We? I thought Sasha hadn't been on the ride?'

My cheeks suddenly felt hot. Had someone turned up the thermostat even higher on the ward? 'Not Sasha,' I corrected. 'She changed her mind at the last moment. A boy from the single rider queue took her place. We kind of helped each other get through it.'

Why had I done that? Why had I referred to Will as a 'boy' when I knew perfectly well he was the same age as Aaron, or even older?

'Well, I'm glad you had someone with you. I would probably have been useless in that situation.'

Yes, you would have been. The thought popped into my head with such crystal clarity that for an awful moment I thought I might have said those words out loud.

★ ★ ★

Knowing how uncomfortable hospitals made him, I was quietly impressed with how Aaron was coping on this first visit. I told myself his feelings for me must be strong enough to outweigh his reluctance to be there. It was almost heroic... if you chose to look at it that way, which I decided I would. Although when a nurse trundling a medication trolley entered my room, he *did* leap to his feet as though spying an open cell door. 'I really ought to top up the car park ticket. I only had enough coins for an hour. Don't want to get clamped.'

'But you're coming back?'

'Of course,' he replied, easing past the nurse who was handing me a small paper beaker full of pills. 'I just need to pop into one of the shops and get some more change for the meter.' He was like a man in a sauna who'd just reached his upper tolerance of steam and sweat. 'I won't be long.'

I watched him go with a feeling of inevitability and then turned my head to focus on the blue, cloud-scattered sky, perfectly framed in the window beside my bed. In less time than it would surely have taken for the lift to reach the ground floor, I heard the sound of footsteps approaching my bed once more and a male voice clearing his throat.

'Did you forget to kiss me goodbye?' I asked with a smile, turning away from the window to face the man standing beside my bed.

'Well, they had me strapped to a stretcher at the time, so it would have been kind of tricky,' said Will, looking far better than a man with a great big bandage around his head had a right to. 'I could kiss you *hello*, if you like?' he volunteered with a grin, perfectly aware that my comment must have been intended for someone else.

Hopefully the Barbie-pink hue on my cheeks could be attributed to the warmth of the sun lasering in through the glass beside me, rather than embarrassment.

'Will. How *are* you?' I tried to dial down the pleasure in my voice at seeing him again, but I'm pretty sure my delight was plastered all over my face.

I lifted a hand and used it as a visor, as my eyes travelled down from the bandaged head to the stark white cast on his lower right leg. He was supporting his weight with the aid of crutches, which gave him a distinctly piratical appearance – in a world where pirates favoured black T-shirts and cargo shorts, that is. His smile was warm, but sobered dramatically as he looked down at my own injuries.

'Well, you flat out beat me on the broken bones contest, my friend,' he observed, his face not showing the same horror at my wounds that Aaron's had done. 'That's quite a piece of reconstruction they had to do there, Miss Dumpty,' he teased. Yet even while he was joking I could see the concern in his eyes. 'How long were you in surgery?'

'Seven hours,' I replied.

Without asking, he reached for the chair Aaron had so recently vacated and lowered himself on to it. 'Makes my own trip to the operating theatre more like a visit to a drive-through,' he said with a smile.

He fumbled a bit with the crutches as he settled himself down. 'I need to get better with these, or I'll end up breaking the other ankle,' he observed ruefully. And then, while I was still smiling, he leant over and *did* kiss me, on the cheek. 'It's very good to see you again, Bella Anderson. When they carted me off yesterday, I was pretty worried about leaving you behind.'

'"*We're survivors. We're going to get out of here,*"' I said, quoting the mantra he'd repeated to me not just once, but many times over the hours we'd been trapped.

'I'm really sorry I never got to speak to your dad like I promised,' Will apologised, looking around the room as though my missing parent might be hidden somewhere nearby. 'Is he here now?'

'He was until a couple of hours ago, but I sent him home to rest. Aaron's here, though.'

Once again, Will scoped the room as though an invisible boyfriend was about to magically appear.

'He'll be back in a minute.'

'Oh well, I won't stay long, then,' Will said, already looking as though he was about to leave. What was it about my visitors that made them want to head for the exit like Usain Bolt? 'I really just wanted to check in on you, like I promised.'

'I'm very glad you did.' My eyes went to the clock on the wall, as I wondered if it might actually be better if Will *wasn't* here when Aaron came back, seeing as he wasn't actually thirteen years old, as I'd implied. And then I noticed the time. It was, almost to the second, twenty-four hours since the moment of impact on The Hybrid.

'It was this time yesterday—' I began, my voice thick with memories I knew would feature in my nightmares forever.

'—that we each made a new friend,' Will completed, reaching for my hand and squeezing it warmly. 'That's the way we should mark the moment: when something good came out of something dreadful.'

15

In a romcom or a cheesy Hollywood movie, that would definitely have been the moment when Aaron walked in, when my hand was being tightly held by a handsome stranger. But real life isn't like a film script, and by the time Aaron returned some ten minutes later Will was already on his feet – or foot, in the singular, to be accurate – and getting ready to leave.

Admittedly, Aaron's eyes *did* flare slightly when he realised the person I'd been trapped on the ride with was a couple of feet taller and several decades older than I'd led him to believe. Thankfully he said nothing as I formally introduced them, as though we were all in a boardroom. In a manoeuvre that could easily have ended badly, Will juggled his crutches in order to extend his hand to Aaron.

As the two shook hands, I could see Aaron quietly assessing the other man. I held my breath, not even sure why. 'Bella told me you really helped her get through the ordeal yesterday,' Aaron said, his voice grateful.

'I think she helped *me* just as much,' Will replied, smiling down at me. Their hands were linked across my body and I couldn't help noticing how much paler Aaron's looked compared to Will's more suntanned one. I suppose it was hardly surprising, when one of them spent their days in an air-conditioned office, while the other travelled the world reviewing theme park rides. And really, what kind of a job was that for a man in his thirties? For the first time I wondered if what had happened on The Hybrid would make Will rethink his choice of career. Because I couldn't imagine a time when I'd *ever* want to ride on a roller-coaster again... I looked down at my shattered legs... *even if I could.*

'I'll try and look in on you again when I have my next appointment at the fracture clinic,' Will said with an easy smile.

'That would be great,' I replied, feeling my heart thumping forcefully in my chest as he swung himself closer to my bed.

Please do not *kiss me goodbye*, requested my eyes, or at least that's what I hoped they were saying. Aaron wasn't the kind of a boyfriend to get jealous or possessive and had always been perfectly comfortable with the time I spent with my male friends. It was something that Sasha mislabelled as complacency, but which I called trust. However, I wasn't sure if even *he'd* understand the strange way the accident had catapulted Will and me to a level of friendship it would otherwise have taken us months to achieve.

Will bent lower and whether I liked it or not, it looked as though that kiss was going to happen. I could smell a woodsy fragrance from his shower gel as he approached. Maybe a fleeting peck on the cheek would be okay?

Surely that wouldn't be misconstrued? I could feel my face unconsciously tilting towards him as he swept down lower... and then retrieved his hoodie which had slipped off the back of the chair. Relief swept through me first, and then embarrassment, followed by a niggling disappointment I refused to acknowledge.

'He seems like a nice guy,' Aaron said, glancing towards the door that Will had just exited through.

'It's hard to say, really. We didn't exactly meet under normal circumstances. We probably have nothing in common in real life.'

Aaron looked at me for a long moment, his expression thoughtful. 'No, you probably don't,' he concluded.

Sasha arrived with armfuls of the kind of things that only your best friend would know to bring. I peered into a bulging Boots carrier bag, which was like a lucky dip of all my favourite products. The face creams alone must have cost her a fortune. There was everything in there, from emery boards to tampons. 'I didn't know how long you were going to be in here,' she said by way of explanation. My eyes flashed over to Aaron, and she'd been catching and interpreting my glances for enough years to know that I was shooting down that topic before it took flight.

'Aaron, you don't happen to know if they've got a coffee shop down in the foyer, do you?'

'There's a Costa, I think.'

Sasha gave that smile that had been twisting men around her little finger for as long as I could remember.

'Two double caramel lattes?' he guessed with a smile.

'And something sticky to eat, with nothing less than a thousand calories in it,' Sasha added. 'Sod the skin-tight wedding dress.'

The everything-is-absolutely-fine-here mask on my best friend's face began to slide as soon as Aaron left the room, and then slipped off entirely when she lifted the sheet I'd asked the nurses to pull over my damaged legs. It looked bad, I knew that, but just *how* awful only hit home when Sasha stifled a gasp and her lower lip began to tremble. She started to cry, and it took only a moment or two before I joined in.

Her slender arms went around me and we rocked together as we sobbed. Sasha smelled of sunshine and Tresemmé shampoo, mixed with an indefinable sweet aroma, which I swear exuded from her pores like a pheromone.

'And there goes the make-up,' she said eventually, peeling away from me to grab us a handful of tissues from a nearby box. We wiped our eyes and blew our noses almost in unison, the way we'd done in the past when the older kids had picked on us in primary school; or when Sasha's beloved old spaniel, Jack, had passed away; or when neither of us had got the grades we'd wanted for our GCSEs. I had so many memories with this girl, and even though the good ones were what we chose to remember, it was the bad ones that bound us to each other. They always would.

★ ★ ★

Sasha had claimed the seat closest to the bed, while Aaron was looking out of the window, nursing his takeaway coffee and trying very hard not to get caught up in the crossfire. The disagreement was rapidly spiralling into an argument, but he knew better than to intervene.

'Absolutely not. No. It's not going to happen.'

'I think you'll find that as it's *my* wedding, that's my decision to make, and not yours.'

I glared at my best friend, marshalling my arguments, knowing as I did that she'd have an answer ready and waiting for every single one of them.

'Everything is booked and paid for. You've got guests and family coming from all over the country – and abroad. You can't just go pulling the plug on all those arrangements on a whim.'

'It's not a whim. I've given it a lot of thought.'

'Sasha, at most you've had twenty-four hours to think about this. You've been planning your wedding for the best part of *two years*. Do the maths – it doesn't add up.'

'I'm not getting married without the most important person in my life there with me.'

I gave a small snort, even though my heart was suddenly feeling a little too snug in my chest. 'I think you'll find the *groom*'s the one you can't manage without. We bridesmaids are kind of expendable.'

Sasha's eyes were awash with emotion. 'You're not expendable. You're my best friend, you always have been, and yesterday I could have lost you forever. The stupid theme park was my idea for a hen party, and so *I'm* the reason you're there in that hospital bed with your legs all beaten up and shattered. And who knows when you'll be—'

I cut her off like a striking cobra.

'Sasha, *none* of this is your fault. It was just a stupid accident – wrong place, wrong time. It doesn't trace back to you.' I sighed sadly, because I knew her decision was coming from a place of love, but I couldn't allow her to sabotage her wedding plans because of me. 'And what does Phil say about all this?'

Sasha leant forward, unconsciously fiddling with the solitaire diamond on her left hand. 'He understands how important you are to me. He'll be okay with this.'

You didn't need to be an archaeologist to brush the dirt off the lie and realise that her fiancé was less than happy with calling off the wedding because of my accident. I closed my eyes and tried to find the right words to fix this.

'Please, Sasha. Have you thought how dreadful it will make me feel if you cancel your wedding because of me?'

'It's not cancelling, it's postponing,' Sasha replied mulishly, but I could see that something of what I'd just said had hit home. 'When you're better, we'll reschedule it.'

My eyes met hers and I let my guard drop, revealing the truth as clearly as if I'd spoken the words out loud. Sasha's eyes widened and stayed that way as her lips began to tremble, but I shook my head and threw a warning glance across the room at Aaron, whose back was still turned from us as he stared out of the window, pretending he was Switzerland.

'I *will* be at your wedding,' I promised, aware that Aaron had spun around with a hopeful look on his face. 'In spirit,' I added firmly, 'I'll be there in spirit. Remember, I know every last detail about this whole crazy shindig,' I continued, remembering how I'd regaled most of them to Will on The Hybrid as we waited to be rescued. 'I'll be with you every single step of the way, but I'll just be doing it from here,' I said, forcing a smile up from an almost empty barrel. 'And the upside is that I won't have to wear that perfectly hideous dress you picked for us.'

Sasha's chin lifted in a challenge, but then I saw the smallest flicker of a smile at the edge of her mouth, and knew that I'd got this.

'I still can't believe you won't see me get married.' Fat salty tears were rolling down her cheeks. Even when she cried, Sasha looked pretty; that girl simply didn't know how to do ugly. She was going to make a gorgeous bride, but we both knew I wasn't going to be there to see it happen.

'I'll see the photos, and maybe someone could Skype the ceremony for me? It'll be like I was there.'

'I could do that,' suggested Aaron tentatively, as though walking cautiously across a frozen pond and wondering whether the ice would crack. For just a moment I felt a frisson of something I wasn't entirely proud of. The idea of Aaron going to my best friend's wedding without me simply hadn't occurred to me. It felt like a well-placed dagger sliding between my ribs. I hadn't even begun to catalogue all the things I'd probably never be able to do because of the accident, but I already knew that missing Sasha become Mrs Phillip Walker would always be one of the hardest to accept.

'Why does everyone bring grapes? Why not bananas? Or mangos?'

Wayne looked up from reading my hospital chart – which I'm sure he wasn't meant to be doing – with his cheeks bulging like a gerbil's, having scoffed half of the bunch he'd brought me, something else he probably shouldn't be doing.

'I've no idea,' he mumbled, swallowing rapidly to get rid of the evidence and then starting to cough alarmingly.

'If you're choking over there, you'll have to count me out for the Heimlich,' I said, only half joking as he looked up with streaming eyes and reached for the covered jug of water on my bedside unit.

'May I?' he wheezed.

I shrugged. 'You might as well, you've already eaten most of my fruit.'

This was Wayne's fifth visit in the two weeks I'd been in hospital. Half of me was always delighted to see him, while the other half was busy worrying about who was looking after our business while he was visiting me.

'Have you brought it?' I asked, once Wayne's colour had reverted to its normal degree of pallor rather than the vivid red of someone gasping their last breath. Wayne looked over his shoulder, giving a very poor imitation of someone in an old spy film.

'Where's your father?' he asked, looking decidedly shady as he reached for the large leather bag he'd brought with him.

'He had to meet a client this afternoon.' I watched Wayne relax as though someone had let the air out of a balloon. 'You aren't seriously scared of my dad, are you? You two have always got on so well.'

'When I'm not doing something he *expressly* told me not to do, we get along just fine,' Wayne clarified. He drew a familiar black case from his leather bag. 'And I'm not scared exactly... more extremely anxious not to make him mad at me.'

'Yep. That's the definition of scared, my friend,' I said, holding out a hand for my laptop, the illegal contraband I'd persuaded him to bring to the hospital. I slid open the zip and surveyed my link with the outside world like a long-lost friend.

'So it wasn't "missing" then, as Dad claimed,' I said wryly, as I turned on the laptop.

'It was where you said it would be in your flat. But you shouldn't be angry with him. He's only trying to stop you from worrying about anything except getting better.'

'I don't think how many screen hours I've clocked up is going to affect how well my bones fuse together, one way or the other.' There was an edge to my voice that I really didn't like the sound of. I sighed sadly. 'What Dad doesn't seem to grasp is that feeling out of the loop just makes everything worse.' The screen blinked into life with one of my favourite photographs of Sasha and me. It wasn't new, I must have seen it a thousand times, but never before had it made me feel like crying. But these days, almost everything did.

Wayne looked fake offended. 'I shall try not to take umbrage that you clearly have very little confidence that I won't run our business into the ground before you get back.'

'*If* I come back,' I said morosely. 'Until the next operation, they're not certain about anything.'

Wayne's pale-blue eyes blinked a little more rapidly than usual. Terrific. Now I was making my visitors cry too. His

Adam's apple was bobbing up and down like a float on a pond. *Enough of this*, I told myself fiercely.

'*Umbrage*, eh? Now there's a word you rarely hear outside the 1950s.'

Wayne looked instantly relieved to be drawn back into bantering territory. 'You know me, full of surprises.' He perched his small behind, much neater and more pert than mine, on the edge of the bed and gave my arm a gentle squeeze.

'Seriously, Bella, I don't want you worrying at all about Doggy Divas. Our Saturday girl – Sally – is going to work through the summer, and if we need to get someone in when she goes off to uni, then that's what we'll do.'

I nodded and hoped Wayne couldn't see behind my watery smile how much I missed making those kinds of decisions with him. But we'd been friends and partners for too long for him not to see it went deeper than that.

'It's just...' I began, knowing even before I completed this sentence that I wasn't going to be able to find the right words to make him fully understand. 'I feel like I've lost something, something important.' For a moment I thought he'd go for the easy quip, but thankfully he didn't. He just nodded his head and urged me to continue. 'I don't feel like "me" any more. With Dad I put on this big brave act, and yet he still looks like someone who's been sucked back into an old nightmare. Sasha is so overcome with guilt that I have to paste an idiotic happy face on whenever she visits, because I'm terrified she'll see how devastated I am about missing her wedding and call the whole thing off. And then there's Aaron...'

My voice trailed away, and I looked up and met Wayne's

concerned gaze. 'You've still not told him everything the doctors have said?'

I shook my head sadly. 'I keep hanging on, hoping for more positive news, but what if there isn't any?' I don't think my voice had ever sounded so forlorn.

Wayne trapped my hands within his long-fingered ones. 'If that man loves you the way he damn well ought to, it shouldn't make any difference.'

I sighed, knowing it wasn't as simple as that, but suddenly overcome with the kind of weariness that no amount of sleep could cure. 'I just want to feel like the old Bella again,' I said. 'Most of the time I don't even know where she's gone.'

We were interrupted before Wayne could reply by the arrival of Rosie, my favourite of all the nurses on the ward. She grinned and apologised for interrupting us, and said she'd be as quick as possible. 'Don't rush on my account,' assured Wayne, and there was something in his voice that I don't think I'd ever heard before. I thought he was just being his usual funny and charming self, although if I didn't know better I would have sworn he was flirting with the pretty young nurse. Rosie had certainly turned a very becoming shade of pink by the time she'd finished taking my 'obs' and had left the room.

It was only when I saw my old friend's eyes following her back into the corridor that it dawned on me that maybe I *hadn't* been barking up the wrong tree after all. I waited until I was certain Rosie was out of earshot before turning to him. Now I thought about it, Wayne had been quite smartly dressed on his last few visits, which I'd thought had been for me. Now I wasn't so sure. I said nothing, but allowed my raised eyebrows to ask the question for me. For a moment he hesitated, and then grinned and patted the back of my hand like an elderly maiden aunt.

'Just when you think you know all the answers, life has a funny way of surprising you, Bella.'

'It's just that I'd always thought... you know, that maybe you...' I was in danger of digging the world's biggest hole and burying myself deeply inside it if I chose to finish that sentence.

Wayne was looking through the window into the corridor where Rosie had disappeared with an almost sheepish look on his face. 'I've always thought that dogs have the right idea, you know. They're not hung up on gender the way people are.'

'True. Boy dog, girl dog, leg of a table. Pretty much anything goes in canine dating.'

Wayne's laughter was infectious, and after a moment I found myself joining in just as heartily. It was a release, probably out of proportion to the situation, but it felt so damn good. By the time we were done there were tears streaming down both our faces, but for once they weren't ones of sadness.

'There you go. You made a funny,' Wayne said, smiling down at me like the world's proudest parent.

I still wasn't entirely sure what had just happened, but all I knew was that I suddenly felt better than I had in days. 'Yeah, I guess I did.'

He bent low and gently kissed my forehead. 'That's my girl. That's my Bella. You're still here. You're still you.'

And for the first time since the day of the accident, I actually felt like me again.

16

When I'd told Wayne how each of my hospital visitors made me feel, there was one name I'd omitted from the list. *Because technically he wasn't a visitor*, I told myself. If a person was already in the hospital, and just *happened* to casually pop in to say hi, then that didn't count as a bona fide visitor. Did it? My omission certainly had nothing to do with the way I found myself expectantly watching the door of my room, or the curious lightness I felt whenever I heard the sound of crutches squeaking across the linoleum floor.

The nursing staff seemed happy to waive the strict hospital visiting hours where Will was concerned. I wasn't sure if that was down to his undeniable charm (even the frosty ward sister had succumbed), or because of our new-found minor celebrity status. It was something we'd discussed on his second visit, two days after the accident.

'There are so many other reasons I'd rather see my mug plastered all over the papers,' he'd said, unfolding the newspaper he'd bought in the hospital foyer and laying it down on my bed. On the second page were two large grainy photographs, positioned side by side. Mine was dreadful; three years out of date, and taken at a time when I'd been sporting a particularly unfortunate fringe. If I'd known that photo was going to be in virtually every national newspaper, I would *definitely* have deleted it from my Facebook page. Will's photo was a professional studio one, which he said he used for work.

'What kind of reasons?' I asked, closing the paper with a wince after seeing the third photograph in the article, showing the twisted remains of The Hybrid. Dad had been protectively shielding me from online photos, so this was actually the first time I'd seen the wreckage we'd been cut free from.

'Why else would I like to be famous?' he asked, his brow furrowing slightly. More of it was visible now that the wide crepe bandage had been replaced by a rectangular plaster. 'For rescuing someone from a burning building. For winning the lottery. Or better yet, for getting a Pulitzer for something I've written.'

It seemed rude to question whether books reviewing theme parks were that critically acclaimed, so I opted for a safer alternative.

'You'd have made a good fireman. You were certainly very calming when things were really bad after the crash.'

Will gave a crooked grin. '*Really?* Then I'm a much better actor than I realised, because most of the time I was shit scared. I was more than relieved when the real-life heroes arrived to take over.'

'You *were* my hero that day. I don't think I could have

got through any of what happened if you hadn't been there. I'll never forget what you did to help me, Will.'

He blushed, and for some reason I found that both touching and unexpected. 'I don't think I'll ever forget you either.' That wasn't quite what I'd meant, but to correct him would cause an awkward moment between us.

To be fair, for people who'd met in such a dramatic way, we had settled into an easy and comfortable friendship, which grew a little more familiar with every visit. I had no idea why the fracture clinic were keeping such a close eye on his broken ankle, but I was very grateful that his injury provided him with plenty of opportunities to visit me after his appointments.

Hospital days are long and quite frankly more than a little boring. So I told myself the delight I felt whenever Will unexpectedly appeared at my doorway was a natural antidote to the tedium experienced by every long-stay hospital patient.

Will had grown used to me greeting him with a happy smile, so the day he turned up and found me in floods of tears threw him off balance. Almost literally, in fact, as he hurriedly swung his crutches towards the bed.

'What is it, Bella? What's wrong? Have the doctors said something?'

It was a fairly intuitive guess. I'd shared the grim prognosis from the medical team with Will. Why it had been easier to do so with someone I'd only just met, when I *still* hadn't found the courage to tell my own boyfriend, was something I chose not to examine too closely.

'No. It's nothing like that,' I said, looking up, uncaring that my eyes were bloodshot to a vampire red and my nose was running. I had no vanity with this man, who could look unflinchingly at my mutilated legs in a way that even my dad found almost impossible.

Will plucked a box of tissues from the bedside cabinet and kept pulling them out and passing them to me until I'd finally mopped up the worst of the flow.

'So you've not had bad news?' he probed, when I could eventually talk past the lingering hiccupping sobs.

'No, it's not that. It's just me... being stupid.'

'You're not stupid,' he defended in a loyal knee-jerk response.

Somehow I managed to summon up a small laugh. 'Spoken as only someone who's never seen my school exam results could do.'

He smiled. 'They're not how you judge how smart a person is.'

I gave a wry smile, knowing without having to ask that he'd been a 'straight-A' boy.

'Then what is it? What's wrong?'

'Sasha's wedding is tomorrow and we were all meant to be together today, having facials and getting our nails done. Just silly girly stuff.' I looked up as though this explained everything, only to find him looking at me, wanting more. 'And my feet are all bruised and battered and I'll probably never have another pedicure again, because, well... who would want to go anywhere near my legs? They're a freak show.'

Of all the things I thought Will might do next – laugh, politely disagree, or try to cheer me up – the one thing I never expected was for him to reach over and whip off the sheet covering my legs, like a magician performing the famous tablecloth trick.

'Don't you dare say that,' he said, sounding angry, which was an emotion I'd never heard before from him. 'Your legs are the mark of a survivor. Okay, so they might not work well at the moment, and yes, there's a chance they might *never* work properly again.' Our eyes met at those words. 'But do you know what I see when I look at them? Because it sure as hell isn't the long puckered scars or the stitches and the metal pins and bolts. I see a badge of honour: they're a medal that only a survivor who's shown true bravery deserves to wear. I see someone who has the courage to get past all of this.'

I looked down at the legs I'd once been quite proud of. They used to look pretty good in shorts, I remembered, as though reminiscing about a long-lost friend. But Will's words were too powerful to ignore. I should be grateful, not wallowing in self-pity.

'I'm sorry. I guess I'm more upset than I expected about missing the wedding.'

'That's only natural. Is your boyfriend still going?'

I nodded, and tried to keep in mind that Aaron was only doing so as a favour to me. Thanks to him, I'd at least be able to watch everything as it happened on my laptop.

I thought I was done with tears for one day. I'd certainly cried enough of them, but when Rosie popped into my room at the end of her shift and pulled up a chair beside my bed, I had no idea that she was about to set me off again.

She was carrying a small chemist's bag, which she upended, catching the bright red nail varnish as it fell into her palm. Without saying a word, she turned back the bed sheet to expose my feet.

'What are you doing?' I asked, aware my question was ridiculous, as it was pretty obvious what she was up to as she shook the bottle and carefully unscrewed the lid.

'A little birdie suggested that this might possibly cheer you up.'

The tears felt very close as I asked: 'By any chance was that "little birdie" extremely tall, with dark hair, bright blue eyes, and hobbling around on crutches?'

'I couldn't possibly say,' Rosie replied, her lips curving in a smile as she bent and began to paint my toenails.

The laptop was set up and ready, with the familiar Skype logo filling the screen. The wedding was due to start in less than ten minutes and in my heart I was right there with them. Jessica had been in charge of linking me in to the bridal party preparations that morning, so I'd kind of been there with them as my friends had their hair and make-up done. Thanks to modern technology it almost felt as though I was in the room with them, smelling the clashing aromas of perfume and hairspray. Almost. The most poignant moment had been when Sasha finally slipped into her wedding gown. When you put a beautiful girl in a gorgeous gown she's always going to look spectacular, but Sasha took perfection to a whole new level. The bridesmaids with her in the hotel room cried when they saw her, and in the privacy of my hospital room, so did I.

And now they were all at the church, and Aaron was in the Skype driving seat, with his phone directed towards the altar where Phil was waiting to change my best friend's last name to his.

'Can you see all right?' whispered Aaron, redirecting the phone so I could see his face. I had to admit he was looking incredibly handsome for someone who'd once claimed he didn't want to attend this wedding. He'd made a big effort, and while I knew the new shirt and the smart haircut had been done for me, they still felt like an uncomfortable stone lodged in my shoe.

'Yes. I can see just fine. Thanks again for doing this for me, Aaron.'

He gave that smile, the one I'd fallen in love with. 'No probs, babe. Oh, I'd better shut up now. Looks like it's all about to kick off,' he said, switching the camera view to the church doors.

This was the worst moment, waiting for it all to begin. This was never the way Sasha and I had planned it when we'd played dress-up brides when we were kids. For a moment I felt like an outsider with my nose pressed up against a windowpane. I was alone… and then suddenly, incredibly, I wasn't. I heard the opening of a door; not the church one, but the one to my room. Will hobbled in, wearing not the jeans or shorts I was used to seeing, but an immaculate dark suit. He even had a perfect white carnation in his buttonhole. His smile was full of apology.

'Sorry I'm late. It took me longer to get dressed than I'd calculated.' His smile should have felt unfamiliar, but in that moment I felt as if I'd known it for a hundred years. 'I thought you might appreciate some company today.'

He manoeuvred his crutches and was beside my bed in two steps. In one hand he held a small corsage tied together with tendrils of curling white ribbon.

'I didn't know what the other bridesmaids were carrying, but as the chief one, I thought you needed flowers.'

He must have been bored. It couldn't possibly have been interesting watching people he'd never met, and was never likely to, get married and then celebrate for hours afterwards. And yet Will never once complained. When Aaron filmed the wedding speeches, Will produced a bottle of champagne and two plastic flutes. 'Don't let Nurse Ratched catch us,' Will teased, crossing to the venetian blinds and twisting them to a close, shutting off my room from view of the corridor. 'I've a feeling you're probably not allowed to get the patients drunk.'

I grinned as I watched him attempt to silently pop the cork, and then pour out two generous glasses of champagne. When Phil's best man toasted 'The Bride and Groom', fifty miles away from the wedding reception, in a shadowy NHS hospital room, two survivors from a theme park tragedy did exactly the same.

The irony of it only occurred to me much later. On the day that Sasha's relationship was being celebrated and secured for the future, my own was beginning to disintegrate. Not that I realised it at the time, of course.

After the speeches, I told Aaron he could shut down the Skype call. Was I expecting him to leave the reception at that point, now that his task was done? If I'm being honest, maybe I was. But perhaps he didn't want to appear rude. *I can hardly just eat and run, can I, babe?* Or perhaps he was just enjoying himself too much. Was it fair of me to begrudge him having fun? Of course it wasn't, but I did anyway.

After Will had been evicted at the end of visiting hours by a grumpy nurse who appeared immune to his charms, I was left with confused feelings. I'd been incredibly touched by what he'd done for me that day; it went beyond just an act of kindness, and that bothered me more than a little. Was I guilty of encouraging him? I rewound every one of our interactions, looking for any sign where I might unwittingly have led him on. I truly couldn't think of a single one. With my lower limbs looking like something out of a Frankenstein film, I had certainly never felt less alluring. Not that I *wanted* to look appealing to anyone except Aaron. It's not as if I was looking for an upgrade. The thought jolted through me like an electric current. Was that how I thought of Will? As though he was somehow better than the man I'd been dating for the last two years? The man who'd given up his Saturday to attend my friend's wedding, just to make me happy?

What kind of ungrateful girlfriend would study the posted Facebook photos of Aaron on the dance floor, glass in hand, laughing with a group of people I didn't know, and compare him unfavourably to the man who'd dressed up in a suit on a boiling hot day to be a 'virtual guest' at a stranger's wedding?

I fell asleep that night watching a video someone had posted of Aaron jiving enthusiastically with a girl I didn't recognise, just some random wedding guest, and tried not to feel bitter that even on my very best day before the accident, I'd never have been able to match her moves. Aaron loved to dance. It was his thing. It always had been. Had he realised that my days of joining him on the floor were definitely over? It should be irrelevant; it shouldn't matter one little bit… and yet I was really afraid that it would. It was time to tell him the truth.

'In a wheelchair? What… like forever?'

I shook my head sadly because he sounded so horrified, while in my head I heard a distant hammering. I was pretty sure it was the first nail being driven into the coffin of our relationship.

'I don't know yet. *They* don't know yet. But yes, it's a possibility.'

'And how come they didn't tell you this straight away? Why did they let you carry on thinking you were going to make a full recovery?'

I couldn't meet his eyes, and a hot flush was starting at my throat and creeping steadily northwards.

'You knew this? You knew this, Bella, and you never told me? Why didn't you say anything? We're meant to be a team, you and me.'

'I wanted to have more information. I kept hoping they'd be able to give me something more positive to go on. I hoped that after the next operation—'

'The one next week?'

I nodded. '—I'd be able to give you a clearer picture of what we could expect.'

'So it wasn't that you didn't trust me enough not to do a runner when I was told how bad it was?'

'Of course it wasn't,' I lied.

'Because it doesn't make any difference to the way I feel about you,' Aaron lied right back.

17

'We're so sorry, Bella.'

Do not cry. Do not cry, commanded a voice in my head. Unfortunately, the message didn't appear to be getting through to my eyes. I nodded blindly as my hand reached out towards my dad. His was outstretched, waiting for me. The surgeon gave us a moment to paint a new picture of our future before continuing.

'Even though the operation wasn't as successful as we had hoped, this is *not* the end of the road. We're not there yet.'

'More operations?' I asked dully, every part of me still aching and sore from the effects of the last one, even though it had been over two weeks earlier. They'd warned me about the after-effects, they'd told me to prepare for the pain, and naively I'd told them to bring it on, I could handle it. I was astounded by my own stupidity.

'In the future, yes. But first we need to give you time to recover from the last one.'

'Before you open up the scars and do it all over again? How many more times? Two? Three? More?'

The doctor's eyes flickered. 'It's impossible to say at this point. But yes, it could be that many...' He paused, before completing solemnly, 'Or more. We will keep going until one of two things happen...' My father and I sat up a little straighter, as though good posture would earn us a better outcome. 'We'll carry on until we feel that surgically there is no benefit in continuing to put you through this, or...'

His eyes were kind, even if his words weren't. I helped him out, because I already knew what he was going to say. 'Or until I say "when". Until I say I've had enough.'

'Precisely.'

Sasha had the kind of tan you can only achieve from an extended holiday in the sun. Honeymoon, not holiday, I mentally corrected. This was the first time I'd seen her after her five-week tour of southern Italy. Both she and Phil were teachers and had taken advantage of the long summer break to have the kind of extended honeymoon most nine-to-fivers can only dream about.

I could read her face as though it was a book. She was shocked to find me still in hospital, recovering from another surgery that had achieved next to nothing. It's fair to say that I was pretty much exactly where I'd been after the last operation. And while I was gradually learning to come to terms with the way things were, Sasha was still hoping for the miracle I no longer believed was coming.

'How is Aaron dealing with it?'

That's my girl; straight in there with the hard questions, I thought, looking at my friend with the kind of love I used to think only sisters could share.

'You know Aaron.'

Her glossed lips tightened into a line of disapproval in her sun-bronzed face. 'I do.' The last time I'd heard her say those words, she'd been pledging her love to her husband. They sounded considerably less warm this time around.

If I'd ever given any thought to how Aaron and I might break up, I'd imagined it would be amid an explosion of emotions; there'd be passion-fuelled arguments and blameful recriminations. We would combust, and then watch aghast as our relationship went down in a blaze of flames. The reality was so much less, and so much worse than that. My accident was the catalyst, but our ending began like a tiny crack on a windscreen, small and containable – not that bad really – until it began to spread out like a spider's web. Suddenly the damage wasn't minor and inconsequential any more as it encroached into every area of us.

It began so slowly that it was only later, with the benefit of hindsight, that the picture became clearer. His kisses became shorter, frequently landing on my cheek instead of my lips, a location they'd never aimed for in the past. And the hands I locked behind his neck to draw him closer were gently disentangled. *If I were to start kissing you properly, Bella, I hate to think of the trouble we could get into.* His words were delivered with his old sexy smile, but I couldn't shake the feeling that he was reading them off a script for a film we'd auditioned for a long time ago.

Sometime between operations number two and three, Aaron stopped waiting for the bell to signal the end of visiting hours. It was such a small thing, too insignificant to call him on it, but every time he glanced at his watch and got to his feet it felt like a tiny stab of a knife. And he'd started arriving late, always with a plausible explanation: the motorway hold-up Google Maps hadn't predicted, or the shortage of spaces in the car park.

I realised long before he did that Aaron was pulling away from me. I genuinely believe he didn't see what was happening, even though the writing was on the wall, graffitied there in large neon letters. I'm not sure how much longer we could have continued to ignore it, if I hadn't decided to intervene shortly after my third operation. Aaron had grown too good at hiding his emotions when I gave him an updated prognosis. His face was a blank mask, and only his eyes flickered when I told him that the odds of me ever being able to walk unaided were now reduced. He nodded, but said nothing, which in itself spoke volumes.

'Aaron, could you call one of the nurses for me?' I asked, the smile I'd forced on to my lips only just managing not to dissolve. 'I need a wee.'

He did as I asked, but I saw the way his eyes fixed on the wheelchair as Rosie helped me into it. Was he wondering how he'd cope when this was *his* task after I was discharged from hospital? Rosie had wheeled me halfway down the corridor towards the bathroom when I suddenly asked her to take me back. My resolve could easily have weakened, even then, if I hadn't looked through the window into my room where Aaron sat, believing he was unobserved. He was hunched forward, elbows on knees, his body language screaming defeat. His trademark perfectly styled hair was in disarray, as though despairing fingers had just raked through it.

He heard the squeak of the wheelchair tyres and lifted his head, a microsecond too slow to hide the look in his eyes. It was the one he'd done so well to keep hidden from me until now. He looked trapped, and in his eyes was the kind of look an animal gets right before it decides it has to chew its leg off in order to get free of the snare. Except Aaron wouldn't do that; he wouldn't let himself be *that guy*; the one who walked away from his injured girlfriend. He would never leave me, but he'd be staying for all the wrong reasons. There was only one person who could release him from me. Me.

'No. Of course that's not what I want.'

I'd expected nothing less than Aaron's knee-jerk refusal to my suggestion that we call time on our relationship. I wondered if he knew that even while his lips were saying 'no' to the prospect of release, his eyes had a kind of hope I hadn't seen in them for quite a long time.

'Aaron, it's okay. I understand. Things are different now. *I'm* different now.'

'That shouldn't matter. That *doesn't* matter,' he corrected rapidly, stumbling into a trap of his own making.

I smiled sadly and reached for his hand. 'This isn't fair on you.' In his eyes I could see how much he agreed with me, but even under torture he'd never admit it. Because to do that would be to admit to failure. And Aaron didn't do failure.

'I'm stuck in this chair for the foreseeable future, maybe forever.' There it was; that almost imperceptible shudder when he looked into our potential future and didn't like what he saw. It was all I needed to continue.

'I need to concentrate on getting better. That has to be my focus, and if I'm being perfectly honest here, I can't do that and worry about how you're coping with the situation. I've always known how you were about illness, and I can see how hard you've tried to get past that, but it's just not working any more. Not for either of us.' I never realised I had such a talent for lying, but once I started, the untruths were practically falling over themselves in their haste to get out. 'I need space – mental space – to concentrate on me for now. It's not fair holding you to a promise that we'd never even made to each other.'

His cheeks coloured slightly and I wondered if he recognised the subtle dig. Two years is a long time to be sitting on the dating fence, without ever discussing where we might be heading.

'This would have been a lot to take on, even if we *had* made some sort of commitment to the future,' I said, my arm sweeping over the injured legs he still couldn't bear to look at without wincing. 'We both know that everything we had will be different when I get out of here, so maybe now is the right time for us to take a break. We need to see how being apart makes us feel.'

The fraying edges of our relationship ripped even further apart as I watched him nod slowly in agreement. Was he agreeing because he thought this was what I wanted? Couldn't he see that I didn't mean a single word I was saying?

'I guess you're right. And if this is *really* what you want, what you *need*?'

I might have weakened then, if he hadn't already been getting to his feet, his hand unconsciously patting his pocket, ensuring his car keys were in place.

'It is. I think for now it would be easier if we cut all contact between us.'

Who was I kidding? Nothing about any of this was remotely easy. Even though this was all my doing, I'd still been hoping that Aaron would have fought a little harder for us. To be fair, he *did* look genuinely upset when he approached my wheelchair to say goodbye. He placed his hands on its arms, as though he needed steadying as he lowered his head to mine, possibly for the last time. His lips already felt like those of someone I used to love, as they brushed against mine.

Was I doing the right thing? As Aaron crossed to the door with slightly jerky steps, I still wasn't entirely sure. And yet he'd put up practically no resistance. Didn't that speak volumes? His heart wanted this, even if his conscience wasn't prepared to admit it. As hard as it was to acknowledge, this entire scene had played out almost exactly the way I'd anticipated. But everything changed with Aaron's parting words, delivered when he was on the point of walking away from everything we'd once had.

'I'd been looking at rings. Did you know that?'

For a moment my brain struggled to assimilate his words, as though he'd slipped into a language I couldn't speak. I shook my head slowly, truly shocked.

'I'd been thinking of asking you this summer, after Sasha's wedding. I didn't think you'd want to steal her thunder.' He gave a humourless laugh and feigned a shrug, as though he'd changed the meal he'd ordered from a menu rather than a decision that would have changed both of our lives. Just when you think your heart can take no more, along comes a sucker punch that knocks the air out of your lungs.

'I thought of maybe proposing when we went away to India.'

India. The holiday we'd spoken of, but never got around to booking. An almost proposal, on an almost holiday. I could see just enough pieces of the picture before they disappeared in a mist of memories I'd never get to make. Everything Aaron was saying was hypothetical, because Aaron *wasn't* actually proposing, he was just saying that once he had intended to. *Before.* That future had been written in the stars for the old Bella. The new version had an entirely different story ahead of her.

'You'll never know how much I wish things were different. We could have been so good together,' he said regretfully.

Leave. Please leave right now before you smash the bits of me The Hybrid hasn't already destroyed.

'I don't know how to stop being in love with you, Bella.'

It was a great exit line, even if it wasn't true.

Dad made a low growling noise when I told him that Aaron and I had decided to call it a day. It was the kind of sound I rarely heard outside of the grooming room. Even though he'd never actually warmed to my boyfriend, Dad was still furious that Aaron hadn't stuck by me after the accident.

Sasha's verdict was far more prosaic. 'What a total bellend,' she'd summed up succinctly, and then hugged me with a fierce protectiveness that made my ribs hurt. 'He didn't deserve you, he never ever did,' she whispered fiercely into my hair. For Aaron's sake I really hoped he didn't cross paths with Sasha until some of the fire and venom had left her system, because in the mood she was in she was likely to inflict lasting physical damage.

'Is this one of those things where I say how much I never really liked him, and then you go and get back together the following week and it all gets totally awks and we have to pretend I never said anything?'

I shook my head sadly at Wayne's question. 'I don't think my getting back with Aaron is at all likely.'

'Good. Because in that case it's safe to say the bloke is a total wanker.'

It was sobering to realise how little my nearest and dearest thought of the man who'd been in my life for the last two years. If the accident hadn't happened, if Aaron had gone ahead and bought me that ring, would any of them have ever said anything? I had a vivid image of a ceremony where not *one* voice but a whole chorus of them joined together to object when they were asked to 'speak now or forever hold their peace'.

18

'D o *you* think I made a mistake?'

Will took a long moment, his brow furrowing in concentration. The scar that had once been a vivid red exclamation mark descending from his hairline had long since faded to a faint pink legacy of the accident.

'Do *you* think you have?'

'That's not an answer, that's just another question.'

Will gave a crooked grin and settled himself a little more comfortably in the visitor's chair beside my bed. He fidgeted a little as he extended his leg, and I wondered if his ankle was troubling him again today. I'd watched him progress from plaster cast and crutches to a surgical walking boot and a stick, and now his ankle was finally unencumbered. The limp he carried would take a little longer to go, but it was less noticeable each time he visited.

'Break-ups are always tough,' Will declared. 'Even when you know without a shadow of a doubt they were the right thing to do, they still hurt.' There was something in his eyes, a flicker of a memory, and I knew in that moment he wasn't talking about my relationship, but his own broken one. We had probably covered every topic of conversation you could possibly imagine during his visits, but that one remained off limits. My natural feminine curiosity – which was a polite word for nosiness – was piqued, but I didn't feel I had the right to probe. We didn't have that kind of friendship. Although to be fair, if I was asked to categorise what type of connection we *did* have, I would have been at a loss for an answer.

'Will still visiting then?' Sasha had asked with a nonchalance I could see right through, as she spied the stack of new glossy magazines on my bedside table. Will rarely came empty-handed.

'Yeah. He still pops in whenever he has to visit outpatients, or more recently the physiotherapist.'

'Hmm,' Sasha said, with a knowing expression, as she idly flicked past page after page of adverts for designer watches. 'It must have been a really bad fracture he had, you know, to warrant that much aftercare.'

I'd frowned. 'I know what you're getting at,' I said, fighting an unexpected urge to blush. 'But it's not like that. Will is just being kind and polite.'

'Oh, Bella, "polite" expired a visit or two after the accident. And "kind" had probably run its course a month or so after that. Do you think that – just maybe – there might be some other reason he's still coming to see you?'

I'd shot her down and she'd given in with a pretty you-know-best shrug. But she'd planted a seed, which had unfortunately taken root. It was an unasked question that was there every time Will walked into my hospital room.

'To answer your question properly,' he began, jerking me back to the present with his words, 'I'd need to know Aaron better.' It was a politician's answer, but it was, I suspected, the only one I was likely to get. 'As I only met the guy once, it's not fair of me to judge him or your relationship. But I do know that going through something like we've experienced makes you reassess pretty much every area of your life. Did you know that eighty-five per cent of people who've been through our kind of trauma end up making major lifestyle changes?'

'Is that another of your made-up statistics?' It was an amusing habit of his, which never failed to make me smile.

'Maybe.' Will grinned, and then something unexpected happened. The laughter slid from his eyes, leaving something unfathomable in their bright blue depths. My stomach gave a little lurch, as though I'd stepped forward only to find the ground was no longer beneath my feet.

Flustered, I grappled to fill the silence. 'So are you one of the eighty-five per cent? Do you have big changes in mind?'

Instead of a smart wisecrack, Will kept his eyes fixed on mine as he nodded slowly. 'I'm giving up journalism.'

'You are? But I thought you loved writing.'

His smile released my gaze from his and I spent several unnecessary moments pouring a glass of water I had no desire to drink and then downing it in practically a single gulp.

'I didn't say I'm giving up writing, just the travel guides and theme park reviews. It's time to do the things in life I'm passionate about. Life's too short to keep putting them off.'

'And what is it that you want to do? What are your passions?'

His eyes were back on my face and it was a long uncomfortable moment before he replied. 'I'm going to write a novel. The idea has been bubbling away at the back of my head for a couple of years now, I just never let it push its way forward. But now... well, now it feels like it's the right time.'

'Well, good for you,' I said, genuinely pleased for him, even though I couldn't shake the feeling that there was a totally different conversation running like a subterranean stream beneath this one. 'What kind of book will it be? Crime? A thriller?'

'Actually, the book I *really* want to write is a love story.'

There was absolutely no reason to be embarrassed – I mean, it's not like he'd said he was going to write a male version of *Fifty Shades* – and yet I could feel myself growing warm as the blush crept over my cheeks. His eyes were on me, watching silently as I surfed the wave of embarrassment all the way to shore.

'I'd really like you to read it.'

I was flattered and a little confused. 'Unless it's about dogs, I'm not going to be much help to you. That's all I really know about.'

'You might surprise yourself,' Will replied enigmatically, and he steadfastly refused to reveal anything more about his project. 'You're just going to have to wait,' he said.

'I'm not going anywhere anytime soon.'

From my hospital bed, I watched the leaves turn brown and curl on the trees. I saw them flutter from their branches in slow, lazily falling flurries as the sky turned from summertime blue to the autumn grey of a dove's wing. I had been in hospital for over five months by then, and had undergone four fairly major surgeries with varying degrees of success, and endless hours of therapy, both physical and psychological. Somewhere along the line I'd reached a curious tipping point where my life within the hospital began to seem more real to me than the one I'd lived before. The new reality had superimposed itself over the old one.

I should have been ecstatic at the prospect of leaving hospital in a few days' time, but frankly the thought of doing so terrified me. An agreement had been reached with the surgical team that I should wait six months before deciding whether to have any further operations. 'Let's see how you cope outside of the hospital and how good a handle we have on your pain management before we make any further decisions,' my surgeon had advised. At the time I'd been thrilled at the prospect of finally leaving the hospital ward far behind me, but now the idea just sounded terrifying.

Dad, of course, had gone straight into practical mode. Finally, after months of feeling impotent and helpless, he at last had a chance to be useful. For the last three weeks he'd cancelled all his other jobs and spent his time modifying both my flat and Doggy Divas so that I could get around. Putting his carpentry skills to good use, surfaces had been lowered, doorways widened, and ramps installed wherever a step dared to rear its ugly head. 'You do realise there are probably all sorts of local authority departments that would have done this kind of stuff for us,' I said gently as he explained in detail about the handrail he'd installed by the loo so that I could manoeuvre myself on and off without help. Physical therapy had strengthened my core and upper body to a level it had never achieved before. I had biceps to rival Madonna's, and the larger dogs that previously only Wayne had been able to handle wouldn't stand a chance against my Superwoman-sized muscles. But it wasn't an across-the-board success story. I could stand – with support – for only a moment or two, and taking even a minute baby step was still beyond me. 'Plenty of time for all that,' assured Heidi, the chief physiotherapist, after yet another attempt to do so had resulted in me collapsing back in a sweat-drenched heap on to my wheelchair. 'Everyone progresses at different speeds. If I can get someone walking after a six-year coma, I'm certainly not giving up on you yet.' I admired her feisty optimism, although I wasn't sure I was ever destined to end up as one of her success stories.

'All I hope is that one day you can get me walking as well as Will does these days. He's got no trace of a limp any more.'

'Who?' asked Heidi distractedly, as she keyed information into her computer.

'Will. Will Carmichael. He's still one of your patients. He shattered his ankle in the same accident that I was injured in.'

The blonde cropped-haired physiotherapist shook her head slowly, before gearing up for yet another act of torture to put me through. 'Sorry. I don't recognise the name. Are you sure he's one of my patients?'

★ ★ ★

'I have something important to tell you.'

I looked at Sasha, who was fiddling with the long mohair scarf she'd just unwound from around her neck. She was plucking distractedly at the fibrous threads as though she was de-feathering a chicken.

'You're pregnant!' I guessed delightedly. 'I'm going to be a godmother.'

Sasha looked up from the mutilation of her scarf with horrified eyes. 'No! Give us a chance, Bells, we've only been married for thirty seconds.'

'Five months, three weeks and two days, actually,' I corrected. Long-term hospital incarceration makes you an excellent marker of time.

Sasha shook her head, still looking perturbed.

'So what's this news then?'

She looked down at her knees, as though the fabric of her denim jeans needed her full attention. 'I'm not sure I want to tell you.'

'Then why did you mention it?'

Sasha looked up with tortured eyes. 'Because I have to, even though I'm not sure I should.'

I repositioned my wheelchair, parking it even closer to the visitor's seat she was occupying. I was getting pretty nifty with it these days. 'You'd better spit it out before I throttle it out of you with just one arm.' I pulled back the sleeve of my T-shirt and flexed a pretty impressive bicep. 'I could do it now, you know.'

Even that barely elicited a smile. For the first time, I started to feel worried. 'Sasha, what is it? You're beginning to scare me.'

The fact that she took my hand in hers before speaking

didn't do much to calm me down. 'I saw Aaron the other day.'

My heart took a moment or two longer to deal with this news than my brain did. It skipped a beat and then overcompensated wildly as if I'd broken into a run, remembered from back in the day when running had been something I'd carelessly taken for granted.

'Oh.' One little word that hid a thousand confused emotions. 'Where?'

She named a popular bar that we used to frequent regularly. I steeled myself to hear about the girl he'd been there with. There *had* to be a girl. Aaron's life would have moved on, just as I'd known it surely would.

'To be honest, he didn't look great.'

That brought my head up sharply. 'How? In what way?'

'Just kind of... different, somehow. Diminished. He wasn't his usual over-the-top self at all. He looks like he's lost weight too – and not in a good way.' She paused as though reluctant to say more, yet knowing that she had to. 'He asked about you.'

That set the heart rate off again. In my head Aaron was in the past, but sometimes the rest of my body had an annoying habit of forgetting that. Sasha had no way of knowing how many times over the last five months I'd been just one number away from calling him. How my finger had hovered over the keypad on my phone, wondering what Pandora's box I'd be unlocking by making that call. Good sense had always stopped me.

'I told him you were getting out of here next week. I'm not sure whether I should have done that.' My old friend was biting her lip nervously.

I gave what I hoped was an unconcerned shrug. 'He'd probably have found out sooner or later anyway. It's not like it's a national secret or anything.'

Sasha nodded, still looking troubled. 'I think... I think he may still have feelings for you.'

I waited for my heart to pound, but it was under control now. 'I see.'

'Anyway, I just thought you should know.'

'Thanks for telling me, and also for not bludgeoning him to a pulp for not staying with me.'

'He came *this* close,' Sasha admitted, indicating a minute distance between her thumb and forefinger. 'But I guess you can't kick a man when he's down.'

Sasha was obviously looking for a subject to take us away from anything relating to Aaron, and she found it easily when she spotted the large manila envelope sitting on my bedside cabinet.

'What's that?'

I immediately had an irresistible urge to draw the envelope towards me in case she wanted to peek at its contents, which was something I'd not even done yet.

'It's Will's manuscript.'

Her eyebrows rose so high they practically disappeared beneath the wispy strands of her fringe. 'He gave it to you to read first?'

My cheeks were warming with a flush, which I hoped was counteracted by my casual shrug. 'I guess so.'

'Surely he has an agent or someone who reads things first?'

'I don't know. He just asked me to read it, and I said I would.'

There were so many questions I could see Sasha was dying to ask, and she was exerting an almost superhuman effort not to let any of them sneak past her guard.

'Is it any good?'

A pulse was beating revealingly at the base of my throat, which jarred with my casual reply. 'Dunno. Not got around to reading it yet. I haven't had time.'

Only a true friend would choose not to call a person out on such a blatant lie. I was awake practically eighteen hours a day, most of them spent alone in my hospital room. Of course I'd had time to read Will's manuscript in the five days since he'd given it to me.

'I'll get round to it in a day or two, I imagine.'

There had been time to read Will's novel four times over before I eventually grew a backbone and tore open the seal on the envelope. I had no idea why I was so hesitant about reading it. It was a real honour that he'd chosen me as his first reader, one I was in danger of throwing back in his face with my obvious reluctance.

'What if I don't like it?' I'd asked hesitantly as he pressed the weighty envelope into my hands.

'Then tell me.'

'What if I think it's the most brilliant piece of writing in the entire world?'

'Then definitely tell me,' he'd said, his eyes dancing with laughter.

I cleared my throat nervously and looked down at the brown package, the fruit of his labour for the last three months. 'What if I can't tell the difference?'

He'd laughed at that. 'Just read it, Bella. Tell me what you think. It's not a test, and even if you hate it, it won't change anything between us.'

'It won't ruin our friendship?' My tongue had tripped slightly over the last word. It had almost betrayed me by trying to substitute 'relationship' instead. But that would have been just as wrong as the word friendship had been. Will and I were more than one and less than the other. We walked a curious tightrope between the two existences, neither knowing exactly what would happen if either of us had ever demanded a definition.

I waited until the ward was quiet. The evening meal – which was always more of a late afternoon affair – had long been cleared away. The nurse pushing the medication trolley had distributed her pharmaceuticals, raising an eyebrow when I'd politely declined anything to help me sleep. I'd waited long enough to read this book, and I was determined now to do it in a single session, even if I had to stay up all night to do so. Somehow I'd instinctively known that once I turned the first page and entered the world where Will had lived for the last three months, I wouldn't want to leave it until I was done.

When the ward was finally silent, when the lights had been dimmed and voices were now speaking in hushed whispers, I switched on the bed's overhead light and slid the manuscript from the envelope.

The first draft of Will's novel was over three hundred pages in length, and I was lost after the first half dozen. I heard the distant bells of the nearby church chime every single hour, but aside from that reminder that the night was slipping silently into morning, I was transported from the world of the hospital to a place no book had ever taken me before. I smiled, I laughed out loud, and even cried a couple of times as the pile of read pages overtook those I had yet to turn.

The birds had already finished every chorus of their morning concert when I read the words THE END. I was completely lost in the story, still more connected with the characters Will had created than with reality. I was gathering up the pages, stacking them neatly so I could slide them back into the envelope, when I noticed that one appeared to be in the wrong place. Was it accident or design that the dedication sheet had been placed at the back of the manuscript instead of at the front?

My fingertips ran over the two words, understanding what they meant, and yet at the same time not understanding anything at all. *To Bella.*

***

We need to talk.

It was a terse text message, almost brutally curt after his one hundred thousand words of elegant prose. His reply was almost instantaneous, as though the phone had been in his hand, waiting for this very moment.

You've read it.

No question mark. It was a statement.

Yes

I'll be there soon.

***

I was nervous, which wasn't unexpected. The fact that he was too was somewhat of a surprise. With his usual disregard for visiting hours, Will must have driven straight to the hospital. The tips of his dark hair still looked damp from the shower he must have hastily taken.

He stood at the threshold of my room, for once looking unsure of his reception. And perhaps with good reason. I should have been exhausted from lack of sleep, and yet every nerve ending in my body was tingling as adrenaline pumped through me like high-octane fuel.

We stared at each other for what felt like forever. Will's eyes were speaking to mine, while our throats struggled to remember how to work. There were so many things I wanted to say and to ask, but as Will approached the bed, I could feel the speech I'd mentally prepared ripping to shreds.

'She's in a wheelchair.'

We were way past the point of him asking *Who?* or *What?* And yet I still clarified, as though he might have failed to notice this startlingly important detail. 'Emilia. The main character in your book. She's involved in a car accident, which leaves her in a wheelchair.' Will's eyes were still locked on mine, as though magnetically linked. He nodded slowly.

'She won't ever walk again?'

My words seemed to jab at him like a sword blade, for he flinched before sadly shaking his head. 'No, she won't.'

There were questions I had about the plot, but they were insignificant in the face of a much larger one. 'Am I Emilia? Is that what all this has been about?' Will's head shot up and I saw the shock register on his face. 'All these months of coming to visit me, was it all just research for your book?'

My voice sounded hurt; there was nothing I could do about that, because I *was* hurt. Something innocent and treasured had been sullied, and I was really afraid it was ruined now forever.

Will crossed to the edge of my bed, his steps jerky and clumsy, as though the many physiotherapy sessions had all been a total waste of time. 'Of course not. How can you even ask me that?'

I took a moment, making sure my voice was under control before replying. 'Because right now it's the only thing that makes any sense. All along, everyone has been wondering why you kept coming back. I guess now we know the answer.'

Will's head was shaking slowly from side to side. 'You've got this all completely back to front. My visits haven't been so I could use what happened to you for research for my book; visiting *you* was the inspiration for the story in the first place.'

'I guess it doesn't much matter which came first, though, does it? But you could have saved yourself a hell of a lot of time and effort. If all you wanted was to know what it's like to have your life destroyed in a senseless accident, to be told you'll probably never be able to walk again, you only had to ask. There was no need to spend all these months pretending you wanted to be my friend.'

'I *don't* want to be your friend,' Will replied, and then looked almost horrified at the confession, which sounded as though it had been ripped out of him. 'I mean, I do. Of course I do. But that's not what's happening here. What happened – at least for me – began months and months ago.'

'I... I don't understand what you're saying.'

Will's eyes looked sad, even though his tone was gentle. 'I think perhaps you do.'

Every hint or suggestion Sasha had ever made was suddenly hammering insistently on the door I'd resolutely shut them behind. There was no denying the irony in Will's voice, or the heightened colour on his cheeks, although bravely his eyes never strayed from mine. 'My ankle broke cleanly. It mended quickly. I had a couple of sessions of physio and then they signed me off. *Months and months ago*. I had no reason to keep coming back to the hospital time and time again.' His smile was rueful and crooked. 'Well, no medical reason, that is.'

My gaze involuntarily dropped to his manuscript, lying on the bed between us.

'And it wasn't for the damn book,' Will muttered, suddenly seizing up the bundle of pages and starting to tear them in half.

I gasped, my eyes wide and horrified as I watched the symbolic destruction of his work. At least, I hoped it was symbolic. This wasn't his only copy, was it?

Will was breathing heavily and looked set to destroy the remaining pages when I laid a restraining hand on his arm. His skin felt hot beneath my palm.

'Please tell me you've got this saved on a computer somewhere. Because it's actually pretty amazing.'

For a moment I thought my words didn't have the power to pull him back, but then his mouth relaxed and some of the tension began to slowly bleed out of him.

'Did you know that fifty-two per cent of authors fail to adequately back up their work?'

I felt a small responding smile start to tug at my lips. 'You made that up, didn't you?'

Will shrugged and then nudged the remainder of the manuscript aside, seemingly unconcerned when most of it slithered off the bed and scattered across the floor.

'I wrote this book *for* you, and *because* of you, but not *about* you. Does that make any sense?' He sounded curiously helpless for a man who'd demonstrated an enviable talent with words. 'But if you say you don't want it to be published, then it won't be. This book is my gift to you.'

My heart was pounding and for a moment I was scared of where we'd suddenly ended up. How had this happened? As always, in moments of uncertainty, I turned to humour.

'Oh no. I didn't get you anything.'

We needed that laughter and the release it instantly brought.

'I know this must seem like a bolt from the blue,' Will said, his eyes suddenly serious. 'But for me this has been coming for a very long time. Almost from that first day on The Hybrid, if I'm being completely honest.'

'It has?' My squeak could have rivalled Minnie Mouse. 'I always thought our connection was because of what we'd been through together. I thought that was why we were friends. I never thought that... I didn't realise...' My ability to finish a sentence was severely compromised. I was blushing a vivid tomato red. 'I didn't know that was how you felt. Given what's happened to me, I didn't think *anyone* would ever look at me that way again.'

Will shook his head as though I'd just said something incredibly stupid.

'Bella.' His voice was low and soft, like a confession in a church. 'If you could see you the way *I* see you... you'd be dazzled.'

My vision was no longer sharp; his words, and the sincerity in them, had blurred it. 'But you never said anything, not once. You never gave any hint of it.'

He reached for my hand, gently linking his fingers through mine. 'I couldn't. It wasn't the right time. To begin with there was Aaron, and I would never have tried to get between you. And then, when you broke up, I could see how much you still cared about him. The last thing you needed right then was some poor love-struck idiot declaring his feelings and confusing you even more. I decided I should wait until I was sure you were completely over him.'

There was a long pause. The longest one yet in our conversation. 'I'm still waiting.'

This was the moment I was meant to deny that anything was left of my feelings for the man I had loved for two years. Will's eyes were holding mine steadily, so that even blinking felt impossible. 'But I don't think it's happened yet, has it?'

I swallowed noisily in the sudden silence of my room. He'd been brave enough to bare his soul. I owed him the same honesty in my reply. 'I'm getting there, but it's been a lot to deal with.'

Will nodded, as though my answer wasn't what he wanted to hear, but it wasn't exactly a surprise.

'There's no hurry, Bella. There's no pressure, and there never will be. Getting well is all you need to worry about. But I had to let you know how I felt. I hated Aaron for walking away and yet I've spent so much time being grateful that he was too big a fool to realise what he was leaving behind.'

Will raised our joined hands to his mouth and gently grazed my knuckles with his lips. 'I won't ever do that.'

My smile was gentle but the look in his eyes was burning too brightly. It was like trying to stare directly at the sun. I wasn't ready. For distraction I glanced down at the pages of his book, littering the floor of my room. 'So Emilia falls in love with Sam, the driver of the car who hit her. How crazy is that?'

Will gave a shrug, and allowed himself to be diverted. 'Sixty-eight per cent of single people involved in a serious accident get married within a year. Sam and Emilia prove it.'

For a moment his eyes grew serious as the banter was discarded. 'Nothing has to change between you and me,' Will assured me gently. 'Not unless you want it to. I just want you to remember that if and when you do feel ready—'

The buzz of my phone was like an insistent hornet, cutting off his words. It was a catastrophic moment for an interruption. I glared down at my mobile, lying face up on the bed beside me. The screen was filled with a WhatsApp message, which I knew Will was close enough to read as easily as I could. I gasped softly as I read and then reread the words.

Bella, I've been such an idiot. A total fool. How can it have taken me this long to realise I don't ever want to be without you? Please call me, let me explain. I've changed, I really have. I love you, babe – I always have and always will. Aaron. xx

19

Six Months Later

They were like new parents, each wanting to push the pram. Except it wasn't a pram, it was a wheelchair, and I was perfectly capable of powering myself through the shop doorway. Sasha gave Wayne a 'now-look-what-you've-done' glare, which he pretended not to notice. Not for the first time I wondered if asking them both to accompany me today had been a huge mistake.

The thick pile carpet sucked at the wheels of my chair like quicksand, bringing me to a stop just inside the threshold of Fleurs Wedding Gowns. I glanced over my shoulder, fearful I'd see two black tramline stains from my wheels on the pale grey carpet. Thankfully, there were none.

The owner of the establishment was seated at an antique desk positioned to one side of the shop. She rose in a single fluid movement, like a black lily pushing up through the soil. Her dress was couture, I'd have bet Doggy Divas' last month's takings on it. I glanced nervously left to right at the wall-to-wall rails of wedding gowns. This was the bridal shop where Sasha and her mother had bought her own dress, and she'd been adamant that the search for my gown should begin here. 'It's the best place in town,' she'd extolled, which was probably true, but it still didn't feel very 'me'.

Gwendoline Flowers, the owner of Fleurs, seemed to glide across the room to greet us, rather than walk. She extended an elegant, slim-fingered hand to me. The nails were long and painted the same blood-red shade as her lipstick. They were the only splashes of colour in her otherwise black ensemble. I liked the way she automatically readjusted her line of sight to look me in the face as we shook hands. Not everyone did that. Many people found it difficult to make eye contact with someone in a wheelchair. Worse, some people seemed to confuse an inability to walk with a lack of intellect. Mostly I just found it funny when people spoke slower and louder, as though severe hearing loss was the reason I was in this chair.

'You must be my bride, Bella.' I only just managed not to smile at her greeting, which made it sound as though I was about to get hitched to Gwendoline rather than the man I loved. 'And of course Sasha I already know.' I could see my old friend unconsciously standing a little taller as she greeted the older woman. Gwendoline was the kind of person who made you regret that you'd given up trying to walk with a heavy book balanced on your head. Instinctively I found myself sitting up a little straighter in my chair.

The shop owner's eyes were gimlet sharp, like a raven's, and they slid over Sasha and me before settling on Wayne, who was flanking the other side of my chair. 'And is this our groom?'

All three of us laughed in that high, vaguely unnatural way people have a habit of doing when they're nervous.

'Noooo,' said Wayne, playing up the camp in case Gwendoline needed further clarification. 'I'm a very good friend of Bella's. She's asked me to come along today for my fashion sense.'

Gwendoline's eyes swept over him, travelling down in a single blink from his mousse-ruffled hair to his burgundy pointy-toed shoes. 'But of course,' she said smoothly. My lips were twitching as she ushered us towards a velvet-covered chaise longue. Despite my initial misgivings and her air of hauteur, I'd already decided that I really rather liked this woman.

'So tell me a little about your wedding. When is it to be, and how do you envisage looking on your big day?'

My fingers went to the exquisite princess-cut diamond on my left hand. It had sat on my finger for a little over two months, and I still couldn't look at it without grinning. At uncomfortable moments – usually those in hospital consulting rooms – it gave me strength and courage. Which were definitely needed now, as I spoke the words every bridal shop owner must dread hearing.

'That's what might be a problem. The wedding is very soon.'

A single swallow, and the warmth in her expression dropped infinitesimally as she asked, 'How soon exactly are we talking about?'

'Six weeks.' Strange how something I was so incredibly excited about suddenly sounded like an apology.

Sasha, as loyal as a Labrador and just as lovable, was quick to explain. 'Bella has another operation scheduled for the end of the summer, so they've had to bring the wedding forward.'

I flashed my friend a grateful smile. Not to be outdone, Wayne chipped in with the answer to Gwendoline's second question. 'And the way she wants to look, is beautiful.' He dropped me an enormous wink. 'Although frankly you could probably dress her in a bin bag and she'd still manage to do that.'

I had the best friends in the world, I truly did. They might squabble like siblings, but there were no two people on the planet who were better suited to accompanying me today. For just a moment I felt a knife-like stab of sadness for the loss of the woman who *should* also have been here with me. I missed Mum constantly, but most of the time it was with a low, dull, manageable ache. Today the pain was sharper, more acute. This was a mother and daughter thing, and as great as my friends were, there was a Mum-shaped hole in my day that no one could ever fill.

'My budget is rather low,' I said, thinking I might as well hit the consultant with all the negatives in one go. I named a figure, and I'm pretty sure her porcelain-white skin blanched a little. 'That's as much as I want to spend. We've had a lot of expenses modifying our new home to make it accessible, and I don't want to touch my compensation money for the wedding.'

Gwendoline smiled, and to be fair the expression on her face was more inspired than fazed. 'So we're tasked with finding a gown that fits your time frame, your budget, and works for someone in a wheelchair.'

A look flashed like a secret message between me and my friends. The shop owner's eyebrows rose expectantly.

'It also has to work when I'm walking,' I said nervously. Looking down, I noticed that I'd superstitiously crossed my fingers. 'I'm hoping to walk the twelve steps down the aisle.'

'Eleven,' corrected Sasha. 'I paced them again the other day. There are only eleven.'

'That's still six more than I can currently achieve,' I said worriedly.

'Plenty of time. Loads,' declared Wayne confidently.

Not for the first time, I was so glad I'd let my two friends in on my plan. Aside from my dad and my physical therapist, no one else knew. I fell asleep at night in the arms of the man I loved, dreaming of the expression on his face when I got out of the chair and walked up the aisle towards him.

'Well, it looks like we all have challenges to meet,' declared the owner of Fleurs gamely. Leaving Sasha and Wayne waiting on the chaise, I propelled my chair in Gwendoline's wake as we headed for the changing room. Once the door was closed behind us, she stood statue still for a long moment, running her eye appraisingly over me.

'Do you need to measure me or something? I can stand up for a minute if you do.'

Gwendoline shook her head. 'I know exactly what size you are *and* what will suit you. In fact, there is a particular dress I have in mind...' For a moment there was a flicker of indecision in her eyes; it was an emotion I was sure she rarely felt. 'It's from a cancelled order.'

'The bride changed her mind about the dress?'

'No. She changed her mind about the groom.'

'Oh,' I said, slightly shocked. 'Well, I *definitely* won't be doing that.'

Gwendoline gave a slow nod. 'As long as you're not superstitious and feel it might be bad luck to wear a dress with that history.'

I gave a rueful shrug and looked down at my legs. 'I'm pretty sure I've already had my share of bad luck. It's time for the good variety now.'

I'd wriggled myself out of my button-through dress by the time she returned with a satin garment bag draped over the crook of her arm. Suddenly and unexpectedly, I was so excited I could scarcely sit still. For the first time I understood why they made television programmes about this experience. It was actually tremendous fun.

Gwendoline teased down the zip on the garment bag and with each revealing centimetre I grew more and more certain that I was looking at the dress I was going to get married in. Perhaps, before the accident, I would have wanted a ball gown, a big poufy-skirted affair that made me look like a Disney princess. But those dreams were happily exchanged as Gwendoline shook the gown free from the bag and held it up for me.

'It's gorgeous,' I breathed, my fingers reaching out and gently tracing the fine silver-threaded embroidery. Under the artificial light, the gemstones scattered across the bodice twinkled invitingly.

'Are you ready to try on your wedding dress?'

'It might not even fit me.'

Gwendoline's eyebrows were extremely eloquent. They told me I was talking nonsense, and they were absolutely right. The dress could have been made for me. The unfortunate bride who'd ordered the gown and then cancelled her wedding could have been my body double.

I stood before the bank of mirrors in the changing room, one hand braced against the wall, the other supported in Gwendoline's firm grip. The bride staring back at me looked like she'd just stepped out of the pages of a magazine. Thanks to the cinched-in bodice, my waist appeared half its usual size and my boobs considerably larger. I looked down at a cleavage I swear I'd never seen before rising from the sweetheart neckline and shook my head in disbelief.

Almost afraid to ask, I turned to the bridal shop owner. 'Can I afford this? Is it within my budget?'

The moment of hesitation told me what I had already suspected. Beneath the ebony-covered exterior, this woman had the softest of hearts. 'It is,' she declared. We both knew she was lying.

Sasha cried. Wayne did too, which he made absolutely no apology for.

'You look like an angel,' he said, crossing over to my wheelchair, which I'd now returned to, and enveloping me in an enormous hug. 'If that man of yours changes his mind about marrying you, I'll do it myself.'

I smiled over his shoulder and winked at Sasha, who was working her way through her third tissue. 'No one is changing their mind about anything. This wedding is definitely happening.'

20

The church doors opened.

Everyone around me was nervous. I could feel their anxiety pulsing like waves, filtering through the air and mixing with the smell of the flowers in my hair, my bouquet and from the garlands looped along the pews. My dad was the worst. Three tiny nicks on his neck proved that even shaving had been a challenge that morning. I'd had to spend most of the fifteen-minute car journey to the church reassuring him that everything would be all right, which I'm sure was a strange reversal of roles.

'Do you know how amazed I am by you today, Bella?' he'd asked, his voice unusually gruff as the church spire came into view, silhouetted against a cloudless cerulean sky. If we'd dialled up the weather, we couldn't have asked for a better day. 'You are the bravest, most loving and caring daughter any parent could wish for. Your mum and I couldn't be any prouder of you.'

Behind the gossamer veil, I was suddenly in danger of ruining all of Sasha's best efforts with my make-up. The sun was streaming through the windows and while there might only be *two* shadows cast on the soft leather upholstery, it suddenly felt like a third presence was in the car with us.

'I'm really proud of you too, Dad,' I said, looking down at our joined hands; his work-worn and old, mine still waiting for time to leave their mark upon them. Life was full of changes, they were inevitable, but the closeness my father and I shared would endure. We'd make sure of it. And so too would the man who was about to become my husband. I smiled. It was something I'd been doing a lot of in the months since I'd left hospital; since the day I'd learnt what I meant to him.

How was it possible that everything you thought you knew and understood about someone could change so completely? His smile could alter my day. His kiss had the power to lift a mood from bleak to euphoric. I liked the 'me' I was with him; she was the best version of Bella I'd ever met.

The vintage Bentley purred up to the kerb and Sasha immediately emerged from the vestibule, looking amazing in a floor-length champagne silk dress. My bridal party was small and unconventional: a Bridesmaid-of-Honour and a Chief Bridesman. Frankly, Sasha and Wayne could have chosen whatever bizarre titles they wanted; all that mattered to me was that they were part of this special day.

The driver unloaded my wheelchair from the boot and Sasha positioned it beside the open car door. Decorated with gardenias and white ribbons, my friends had transformed the NHS-issue chair to a flower-covered throne. It looked beautiful, but I was still hoping to abandon it at the church doors. Eleven steps. My heart tripped and quickened as

I glanced through the lychgate. To date, the most I had managed to achieve was nine.

Dad pushed my chair across the uneven grass of the churchyard. I'm sure there must have been places close by with easier access, but this was the church where my parents had been married. We'd never considered looking anywhere else. Out of sight of our waiting guests, Sasha swept into action, straightening, smoothing and twitching my dress and veil in place. When she set the bouquet in my hands, I noticed her own were trembling.

'Remember, I'm going to be right behind you,' she whispered in my ear. 'If it gets too much, I'll be there with the chair, just in case—'

'Bella won't fall,' said my dad, with the confidence of someone who hadn't seen my latest efforts.

Sasha squeezed my hand one last time and then nodded to someone waiting just inside the entrance to the church. Seconds later, the opening strains of the song we'd chosen filtered out into the churchyard.

Every head turned as we moved from the shadowy vestibule into the church. But the only one I saw was his. I knew he'd look handsome in that dark suit and tie, but what overwhelmed me was the look on his face. It was joy, it was love, it was a promise that almost made the vows we were about to exchange redundant. No other man would ever look at me like he did, *love me* like he did. And I would never love anyone more than him if I lived to be a hundred.

Dad pushed my chair over the raised flagstone we knew we'd have to negotiate and then stepped out from behind it and into the aisle beside me. I lifted my bouquet and passed it over my shoulder to Sasha. Smoothly, just as we'd rehearsed, a figure rose from his seat at the end of the last pew in the church. The music was still playing as loudly as ever, but above it I could hear a ripple of hushed and curious whispers.

This was it. I was really doing this.

With almost balletic synchronicity, my father and Wayne presented their outstretched hands. There were gasps as I placed mine in theirs. Most of our guests knew I could stand, some of them had even seen me do it. But no one had seen me walk. Even the man whose name I was about to take thought two steps was all I could manage.

The hands supporting me were as steady as rocks, but I wasn't looking at Dad or Wayne as I took that first step. My gaze was locked on the person at the end of the aisle. Previously, I'd always looked down as I walked, watching each foot move forward, willing it not to fail. Today there was no need. I *knew* they wouldn't.

He was crying before I was halfway up the aisle, the tears coursing down his face. He made no effort to wipe them away. I saw him mouth *I love you*, not just once, but over and over again, like a chorus of a hymn you can't stop singing.

Nine steps easily became eleven. I swear I could have gone up and down that aisle all day long, powered by the love that surrounded me. When I reached the altar, his arms slid around me, and breaking with tradition the groom kissed the bride *before* the ceremony had even begun, and everybody cheered.

★ ★ ★

I clinked the back of my dessert spoon against my wine glass, hoping it wasn't about to shatter and spill shards all over the top table. Like a Mexican wave, silence settled across the room. Every eye was looking my way, every mouth was smiling. Using the arms of the velvet-covered chair, I pushed myself to my feet for the second time that day. To be fair, it got less of a reaction this time around.

'I know it's not usual for the bride to begin the speeches,' I began. Behind me, I could feel my husband's hand move to the small of my back, his touch a gentle caress.

'I promise I'll be brief. But before Dad embarrasses me with his speech and then the best man reveals all kinds of things someone really ought to have told me about my husband before today...' – I glanced down and caught his look of feigned horror – 'I wanted to say a few words. I think most of you know it's not been an easy year for me. And without the love and support of my family, my friends, but most of all of the man sitting beside me, well, I don't think I'd be standing here at all.'

The smile my words earned me almost made me give up on the rest of my speech and just kiss him instead. God knows it was what I wanted to do. I tore my eyes away from him and refocused. 'It's a little-known fact, but did you realise that eighteen per cent of people who meet on a roller-coaster end up getting married?'

Beside me, I heard Will laugh.

'So, to roller-coasters,' I said, raising my glass.

'To roller-coasters,' the room replied.

PART THREE

Mandy

21

She told me first.

It wasn't until much later, lying in my single bed listening to the sounds of the house settling for the night, that I realised what a big deal that was. She told *me* first.

Across the hallway, snoring loudly enough for the sound to travel through the closed bedroom door, was the man she should have spoken to. Beside him, probably curled against his back, was her second possible confidante. But she hadn't chosen to share her secret with either of my parents. She told me first.

It left me feeling humbled, overwhelmed and a little bit scared, to be perfectly honest. The one thing I *didn't* feel was surprise that she'd chosen me. We'd always been close, far closer than any of my friends were to their grandparents. For a start, I was named for her: Mandy for me, Amanda for her. But it wasn't just that. She'd passed on so much to me, things that went way deeper than just her rich auburn hair and brilliant green eyes. Hers had lost their lustre now, but when I looked at old photographs of when she was my age, we could have passed for sisters. But the greatest of all her legacies to me had been music. The love of it, the way it could change a mood, a day, even a life. My grandmother had been a piano teacher, until arthritis had robbed her of the ability to play. So I played for both of us now. And each time I sat down at the piano that had once been hers, I could feel her beside me, moving my fingers fluidly over the keys, making me sway as I played. It didn't matter if it was a Bach prelude or a Bruno Mars classic, she was always with me.

When Grandad passed away five years ago, there were members of our family – my dad included – who thought Gran wouldn't be capable of coping by herself. But not me. I knew better. My grandfather had always been a larger-than-life, take-charge kind of person, but Gran had never been in his shadow; she'd just chosen to walk in the shade. And after he passed away, she stepped out of it.

With very little fuss or outside assistance, she'd sold her far-too-big-for-one-person house and put down a deposit to secure a place in a newly built retirement complex on the other side of town. Dad, who was probably worried people would think he'd 'put her in a home', had been keen for her to move in with us, but Gran was having none of it.

'I know you have my best interests at heart, Gerald, and I love you for it, but for once *I* would like to be the one to decide the direction my life will take from now on. And my choice is to move to Sunnymede.'

Sometime over the last five years, and I really couldn't remember when it happened, Dad had developed selective amnesia and now seemed to think *he* was the one who had found Gran her new home. He liked nothing better than to show people the glossy Sunnymede brochure, declaring as he did, 'It's really a wonderful place. More like a five-star hotel than an old folks' home.'

Gran didn't care. She was happy there, really happy. Perhaps even more than she'd been when living with Grandad, I'd secretly thought more than once. Although Gran of course would never admit to any such thing; she was far too loyal to his memory. Or so I'd always thought... until today.

And now here I was, lying awake in the middle of the night, with a secret so huge it felt like a bomb ticking quietly away in my head. I couldn't defuse it, and it was far too big to ignore. The best I could hope for was that when this whole thing blew up, in the way I knew it surely would, we'd somehow be able to put the pieces of our family back together again.

What I liked most about Sunnymede, more than its luxuriously appointed suites (they didn't call them rooms), elegant communal lounges or rolling landscaped gardens, was that it was only a ten-minute bus ride from my school. I probably saw more of Gran now than I did when she'd lived in her own home. The rest of the family tended to visit her at weekends, when the home was bustling with relatives, but I preferred the less hectic atmosphere of the late afternoons or early evenings.

Not that Gran was the kind of person to sit around waiting for visitors. Since moving into Sunnymede, she'd made a whole new circle of friends. It was rare to find her sitting alone in her room. She was far more likely to be involved in one of the many activities on offer to the residents. Unsurprisingly, the ones she loved best were those that involved music.

There'd been one today. A string quartet from the nearby university had been invited to give a recital to the residents, and Gran had been keen for me to attend. She'd been my first music teacher, back when my legs were so short I'd needed her help to climb on to the piano stool, and she still liked nothing better than sharing her greatest passion with me. It was our *thing*.

The concert had already started by the time I'd hurriedly signed myself into the visitors' book at Reception and sped along the familiar corridors to reach the lounge, from where the sound of a Haydn sonata could already be heard. Gran's welcoming smile – the one I liked to think she kept just for me – had creased her face into accordion-like folds. As soon as there was a suitable break in the music she'd motioned me into the lounge, shuffling along the sofa she was sitting on to make room. She leant to her left and whispered something in the ear of an elderly woman seated beside her. Her companion turned and looked in my direction, smiling warmly as she did. It was Josie, one of Gran's closest friends at Sunnymede.

I apologised and '*excuse me*'d as I negotiated a pathway over an obstacle course of walking sticks, parked Zimmer frames, and swollen-ankled legs in thick surgical stockings. I sank down on the sofa just as the music began again. It was a snug fit, offering just enough room for an average-sized seventeen-year-old and two old ladies in their seventies.

Today's music wasn't really my kind of thing, but Gran was always telling me I should keep an open mind, particularly if I was serious about taking a degree in music when I left school. So I sat back and let the sonata wash over me, enjoying the performance because that's what the woman sitting beside me was doing. I loved the way Gran's gnarled fingers absently kept time with the music against her bony knees. She might not be able to play any more, but her timing and musicality were still far better than mine would ever be. Josie, bless her, was also tapping her hand to the music, except she was a million miles away from the beat the musicians were following. Very sweetly, Gran laid her hand over Josie's until she found the correct rhythm. I guess it didn't matter how old she was, Gran would always be a music teacher.

The concert ended with a mixed response. Many of the audience members clapped enthusiastically – I may even have given a small whoop or two, because actually it had been surprisingly good. Others got to their feet with vacant smiles and shuffled dreamily out of the room, off to who-knows-where. A few – who'd somehow managed to sleep through the entire performance – were jerked awake by the applause, and looked around in confusion at all the noise.

'Ah, that was so lovely,' sighed Josie, swaying slightly as she got to her feet. My hand shot out to steady her, but Gran got there first, her twisted fingers still plenty strong enough to grip hold of her friend's wrinkled hand to offer support.

'You know you're meant to use this to get up,' she chided gently, setting her friend's walking stick firmly beneath her hand. I breathed a little easier as a potential broken hip catastrophe was successfully averted.

Josie's smile was endearingly sweet as she looked over at me. 'That's your Gran for you, always worrying about everyone else. She needs to look after herself too, you tell her that.'

I nodded, feeling the first frisson of concern start somewhere at the base of my spine and steadily begin climbing up my vertebrae. Was there something wrong with Gran? Was that what Josie meant? I looked at the woman who I'd loved and admired for every single day of my life, and was suddenly overcome with fear for something I could neither change nor stop. In this place, death and ill health were frequent visitors. I still shuddered every time I walked down the corridor to see a room stripped bare, when only the day before it had been filled with personal possessions and furniture. There were armchairs that were kept forever empty in the recreation room, the presence of their former occupants too powerful to forget. Damn that concert, it had put me in a very strange mood.

'Well, I'll leave you two to have a nice little chat in peace,' said Josie, taking a cautious step, and when that one didn't end in disaster, following it with a second one. By the time she reached the door, I felt quite exhausted. Gran too had watched her friend's every step. Josie was right; she needed to relax more.

With considerably less effort, Gran got to her feet. Thankfully, the arthritis that had attacked her hands was taking a more leisurely journey to other regions. Nevertheless, I slowed my pace to hers as we walked side by side down the corridor and back to her suite. She had a lovely room, with a separate sitting area furnished with two comfy armchairs she'd brought with her from the home she'd shared with Grandad.

'Would you like something to drink, Mandy?' Gran asked, lowering herself on to one of the velvet-cushioned chairs. 'I'm sure one of the helpers could rustle us up a cuppa if I asked.'

'No, Gran, don't worry. I'm fine. I can't stay too long. I've a ton of coursework I need to do before—'

'—sneaking out to meet that young man of yours?'

Shock and surprise had a quick battle to see which expression would be reflected on my face. It was a tie.

'What?' chuckled Gran softly. 'Did you think I didn't know you were still seeing him?'

I blushed, turning my already pink face – they kept the home ridiculously warm – hot enough to make my foundation melt.

'I... I...' I had nothing to say. 'How did you know?'

'You were always a bad fibber, Mandy, even when you were a little girl.'

The blush was going nowhere, and I could feel myself squirming under Gran's surprisingly astute gaze. 'Besides, you're wearing a turtle neck on a warm spring day, so I imagine there's something beneath it you don't want everyone to see.'

My hand instinctively flew to the love bite I knew was safely hidden beneath the neck of my jumper.

'Ah, necking,' said Gran fondly, as though embarking on a jaunt down memory lane. As close as we were, I really hoped she wasn't about to share confidences with me about her and Grandad back in the day.

'I don't think they call it that any more, Gran,' I said, somehow managing to smile, even though I was still mightily embarrassed and also a little worried. 'You won't tell Mum and Dad, will you? You know how Dad feels about Jamie.'

Gran made a noise, which made me smile. 'Your dad needs to understand that it's not up to him to decide who you fall in love with.'

'Well, I'm not sure Jamie and I are actually *in love*, but...' My voice trailed away, momentarily lost in a daydream of a pair of bright blue eyes and a shock of hair, in a shade magazines call 'dirty blond', that fell floppily across his forehead no matter what he did to stop it. Without meaning to, I found myself smiling.

'I won't say anything to your dad. That will have to be your job, my girl.'

I swallowed nervously, remembering the rows we'd had when I'd told them the boy who'd asked me out had dropped out of school and had no intention of ever going back. Dad hadn't been happy, and that was *before* he'd even seen Jamie – or his tattoos.

'Just don't tell them, Gran. At least, not until after my exams.'

'Your secret is safe with me,' said Gran, pantomiming turning an invisible key against the softly puckered skin around her lips. 'But I would imagine your mum already knows. She's a smart cookie, and far less judgemental than your dad.'

It was strange to hear Gran say anything negative about Dad, even though she was absolutely right on this one. Dad was the kind of man who liked to keep everything in his life in neatly defined columns. It was probably the accountant in him. Having a straight-A daughter destined for a red-brick university falling for a tattooed apprentice mechanic... well, that simply didn't add up at all. Not in his books.

'Just follow your heart, Mandy. That's the best advice I can give you.'

Gran's hand reached out and straightened a vase of flowers that to me looked perfectly okay where it was, and then picked up and put down a magazine. She was definitely acting strangely.

'Gran, is anything wrong? You seem a bit, I don't know... distracted... today?'

She jolted guiltily, and was shaking her head long before the denial had left her lips.

'Do I? How strange. No, I'm fine. Absolutely fine.'

Except she wasn't. Anyone could see that, and somehow her anxiety was becoming contagious.

'Gran?'

For a long moment she looked at me, and I could almost see an inner war being waged in the faded green of her eyes. The decision to tell me flared as bright as a comet in their cloudy depths.

'What I just said, Mandy, about the heart...'

My blood turned to ice; I could feel it freezing in every vein and capillary. She had a heart condition, I thought, my panic already galloping off ahead of me. Angina, or maybe something even worse.

'Gran, are you ill? Is that what you're trying to tell me?'

Those eyes, so like mine, widened in response.

'No, my love. It's nothing like that.'

'Then, what is it?' I asked, leaning forward, my elbows

resting on my denim-clad thighs. 'Please tell me, because you're making me worried.'

Gran's smile was soft and full of love. 'That's the last thing I want to do. But yes, you're right, I *do* have something I want to tell you. It's something I've been wanting to tell you for quite a while now.'

She paused, and it took every ounce of my self-restraint to remain quiet as she worked out how to begin. Before speaking, she reached up to a shelf beside her chair, where a row of framed family photographs was kept. She took down one of my grandfather, staring fondly at it for several moments. It showed a man I had never known, with hair still full and dark, and skin unmarked by the passage of time. It made me realise how remarkably alike he was to my dad.

'I loved your grandfather. He was a good and decent man.' I nodded, somehow sensing that to speak now might derail her. 'My parents were delighted when we got engaged, did I ever tell you that?'

I shook my head, wondering why in all these years we'd never spoken about her life before she'd become a wife, a mother, and ultimately a grandparent.

'Your grandad was quite a catch. He could easily have had any girl he wanted in our town.'

'Well, he got the best one,' I declared loyally, a funny feeling beginning to grow deep in my stomach. This conversation was going somewhere I had never been before, and I wasn't entirely sure I was ready for the journey. 'He was lucky to have you.'

She smiled, more than a little lost in the past now, I think. One arthritic finger ran gently down the face of the man she had spent almost fifty years of her life with. Her eyes were a little misty as she looked up and met mine.

'I loved your grandad,' she repeated, as though I might be about to dispute that fact. 'But I was never *in love* with him.'

I went as still as a shop window mannequin, unsure what the appropriate response was here. My grandfather had been gone for five years, so it was a little late to suggest relationship counselling. I had no idea why, after all these years, this was something she'd felt the need to share.

There was a strange feeling of finality in the way Gran carefully replaced the photograph on the shelf.

'I have found someone, Mandy. Someone special.'

Okay, this time I *really* didn't know what to say. She was waiting for me to speak, and the silence was stretching on and on, soon to grow from awkward into uncomfortable. I must have considered and dismissed at least half a dozen comments, and still couldn't find the right one.

'Oh.' I imagine we were both disappointed that that was the best I'd been able to come up with. 'Do you mean you've found someone you like, in the same way you liked grandad?' I asked tentatively.

Gran's smile suddenly made her look at least twenty years younger, and I knew in that moment that the person she was thinking of was the one who'd put that look on her face. For a crazy split second, I felt jealous of losing her love to some unknown gentleman friend – 'boyfriend' was going to be too much of a stretch, even for me.

'No, sweetheart, not in the same way that I felt about your grandfather,' Gran corrected gently. 'About a thousand times more.'

I sat back in my chair, the air leaving my lungs in one long exhaled whoosh. This was big; it was a lot to take in. I could accept that maybe we'd all been wrong, and that my grandparents hadn't had the idyllic relationship we'd always thought they'd enjoyed. But it was much harder to get my head around the fact that at the grand old age of seventy-six my grandmother had fallen head over heels in love with someone else. It was the biggest revelation I'd ever had to deal with in all of my seventeen years. Or so I thought.

'So who *is* this person?' I asked. 'Have I met them? Do they live here in Sunnymede?' I was a frequent enough visitor to recognise practically all of the elderly residents. And one thing I knew for certain was that the women here outnumbered the men by about three to one. 'We're all tough old biddies,' Gran had once said, winking broadly. 'We've a longer sell-by than the men.'

I felt certain I'd already know Gran's new man friend, and began scrolling through the elderly gentlemen residents in my head. There were a few who Gran played cards with each week, whose names I was still struggling to remember, when unbelievably I saw my grandmother begin to blush.

'Josie,' she said, looking at that moment more like a teenager than I did. It was like one of those freaky Hollywood movies, where somehow two people switch bodies.

'Pardon?'

'It's Josie,' repeated Gran, and the curve of her bent spine seemed suddenly to straighten with those words. 'Josie is the one I'm in love with. And…' That blush was back now, at maximum wattage. '… and I'm very happy to say that she loves me too.'

★ ★ ★

I hit my pillow with a clenched fist, as though the feathers and down within were the reason I was still lying there, wide awake at two o'clock in the morning. I had to get some sleep. I had a history test in the morning, and coursework to hand in later; those were the kind of worries I was used to dealing with. But they'd been totally eclipsed by the revelation from my grandmother, who'd bravely come out to me that afternoon and entrusted me with the biggest secret I'd ever been told. The only problem was, I had absolutely no idea what to do with it.

22

'How did Gran seem to you yesterday?'

The spoonful of muesli I'd just popped into my mouth suddenly seemed to turn to sawdust, making swallowing virtually impossible. I reached for my glass of juice, buying myself a few extra seconds by taking an enormous gulp of Del Monte's finest.

'Same as normal, really. Why do you ask?'

I turned my head, addressing my question to the prime minister who was dominating the front cover of the newspaper, behind which my father sat. Mum had given up trying to get him to interact with his own family instead of a broadsheet columnist years ago. To be honest, mornings weren't his most approachable time, so it was odd that today – of all days – he'd decided to engage me in a conversation about Gran. Or perhaps it wasn't odd at all. Perhaps he already *knew*. I dismissed that thought almost as soon as it popped into my head. If my father knew what I knew, there was *no way* he'd be sitting there calmly munching his way through slices of toast and marmalade. I wasn't sure how he'd react when Gran eventually shared her secret with him. The only thing I *did* know was that it would be bad. Very, very bad.

The prime minister twitched and then folded in on himself as my father laid down the newspaper. 'Because she's my mother, and it's only natural to ask if she's okay.'

'She seemed fine, Dad,' I reassured him. 'Although obviously we weren't able to chat that much during the concert yesterday.' That wasn't quite a lie, but it was teetering dangerously on the edge of one. But at least I hadn't betrayed Gran's confidences.

'Hmm…' said my father as he drained his second black coffee of the morning. That was his limit. In a minute he'd get to his feet, look down at his watch – his father's, which he'd worn every day for the last five years – and declare he had to leave now to beat the traffic. He'd drop a couple of absent-minded kisses – one on my mother's cheek and the other on the top of my head – before disappearing off to do whatever it is that senior accountants do all day. My father was a creature of habit. But weirdly, this morning he was veering off piste. He paused after picking up his briefcase, his fingers restless as they clasped its leather handle. 'I've been a bit concerned about her recently. She's seemed kind of preoccupied on our last few visits. Not quite "with us", if you know what I mean.'

My mother was busy slotting dishes into the dishwasher, but she straightened up and turned to face her husband. 'Your mum *is* seventy-six, Gerald,' she said sympathetically. 'I know you hate thinking about her getting older, but it's not entirely unexpected for someone her age to start getting a little… forgetful.'

Mum had picked her words carefully. Dementia was my dad's greatest fear. It had stalked his own father from the shadows for the last few years of his life, and he was secretly convinced it was coming back to claim his mother too.

'I certainly hope it's not that,' he declared sorrowfully, his head shaking from side to side as though in time to a distant tolling bell.

I couldn't help it. The words seemed to burst from me of their own volition. 'Gran doesn't have dementia. There's absolutely nothing wrong with her mind. She's as sharp now as she ever was.'

My father crossed the kitchen and laid one big bear paw of a hand on my shoulder. 'I hope you're right, sweetheart. I know how fond you are of her.' He gave a small troubled sigh. 'But still, there's something about her lately that I can't quite put my finger on...'

'You're going to be late, Gerald,' warned my mother, even though he still had plenty of time to reach his office.

I waited until I heard the muted roar of his car starting up before turning to my mother, who'd been eyeing me perceptively since I'd jumped to the defence of my grandmother.

'Dad *does* love Gran, doesn't he? I mean, I know how close he was to Grandad, but he does love her too, doesn't he?'

A small furrow deepened between my mother's brows. She was doing her best to keep those lines at bay with a range of Boots' miracle creams, but they were still visible whenever she looked concerned. I could see them now.

'Of course he does. What a strange question, Mandy. Why do you ask?'

I fidgeted on my chair, already regretting that I'd mentioned anything. 'No reason.'

I got quickly to my feet, before I got tangled up in a lie I wouldn't be able to wriggle out of. I paused at the door, where I'd left my bulging tote bag. 'I might be a little late back this evening. I'm going to pop in and see Gran again.'

My comment set off a silent alarm in my mother's head, just as I'd feared it might.

'Again? But you were only there yesterday.'

'I know, but I think I must have left my history textbook in her room and I'm going to need it for my coursework.'

Mum was going to have to invest in a pot of even more potent cream to get rid of the lines my explanation had created. Her eyes dropped meaningfully down to my open bag, from which protruded a large hardback with Oliver Cromwell on the cover.

'Isn't that it, right there?'

I could feel a warmth creeping into my cheeks, and it was simply too much to hope that my observant mother didn't spot that too.

'Er no, it's another book – a *different* one – that I left at Sunnymede.'

She let it go. But that didn't mean she believed me. Gran was right. Not much gets past my mother.

I'd hoped that once I stepped through the school gates I'd be able to push thoughts of my grandmother from my mind, at least until later that day. But she was right there with me every minute of the morning, as I jostled through crowded corridors between lessons, and stared with unseeing eyes at the test paper in front of me. I wasn't pleased with the way I'd reacted yesterday. And the more I'd thought about it during the long, lonely, middle-of-the-night hours, the more convinced I became that I'd somehow let her down. Gran had taken a huge leap of faith in telling me about Josie, and I should have been far more supportive and far less shocked. That was why I needed to go back and see her again.

I don't remember filling in the answers on my history test, which meant I could very well be about to get my first ever F. Strangely, I didn't even care. At break I slipped quietly away from my usual group of friends, who were heading for the cafeteria, to find a quiet spot in the common room. Turning my back on the noisy ribaldry of the roomful of teenagers, I pulled out my phone and fired off a message. It was brief, and I had no idea if he'd even get a chance to read it until later.

Any chance of meeting up at lunchtime?

I must have timed it just right, for Jamie's response was practically instant. I'd flaked on our arrangements the night before because my head had been all over the place, so I imagine he thought I wanted to apologise in person. And I did. But surprisingly the *need* to see him outstripped my desire to do so. I wasn't *in love* with Jamie, or so I'd told my grandmother. I still believed I was much too young to understand what that emotion even felt like. And yet in a crisis he was the first person – the *only* person – I wanted to talk to.

Sure. Park gates at one o'clock?

He was there before me, leaning against the wrought-iron railings with two dripping ice cream cornets in hand. I leant up for a kiss before relieving him of one of the melting 99s. Being allowed off school premises during the lunch hour was a sixth-form perk, and yet whenever I signed out to meet Jamie it was hard to shake the feeling that I was doing something clandestine or illicit. It was as though we were having a secret affair, or something. Perhaps if I was bold enough to tell my parents that, despite their disapproval, we were still seeing each other, they might change their minds about the boy who treated me better than anyone had ever done. Was I just as guilty as Gran was of hiding important things from the people I loved? The thought made me uncomfortable, so I pushed it away.

What I liked best about Jamie, after the broad shoulders, beachy tousled hair, and his slightly dangerous 'edgy' look, was that he was a really *excellent* listener. The ice creams were long finished and we'd walked halfway around the park's boating lake before he spoke.

'Okaaaay,' he said, when I finally finished sharing my grandmother's revelation. At some point during our walk he'd reached for my hand and was still holding on to it tightly. '*Now* I understand why you bailed on me last night.'

'Sorry about that,' I said, leaning into his shoulder and welcoming its solid, rock-like quality beneath my cheek. He felt like an anchor in a sea full of shifting currents.

'It's kind of weird thinking of someone your gran's age getting together with *anyone* – either a man or a woman,'

Jamie said eventually. 'I guess you always think it's only people our age who fall madly in love.'

In the six months we'd been dating, this was the first time the L-word had entered our vocabulary, and I already knew I was going to spend a great deal of time later forensically deciphering that sentence to see if he was referring to our own feelings in any way. But for now my grandmother and *her* relationship was the priority.

'I just feel so bad for her, knowing that she hadn't been blissfully happy with my grandad for all those years, and not being able to tell anyone about it. *That's* more of a shock to me than how she feels about Josie, to be honest.'

'Hmm… somehow I don't think that's the way your dad's going to take it,' Jamie observed, his lips twisting wryly. As someone who'd already been on the receiving end of my father's disapproval, he probably knew – better than anyone – what he was talking about. 'For him it's going to be a double whammy. He won't like the idea of your gran being with anyone new. Perhaps it'll be *better* that she's fallen in love with a woman rather than replacing your grandfather with another man?'

I stopped on the path and stared up at my boyfriend, who was looking ridiculously attractive in the dappled lunchtime sunshine. 'Er, hello? Have you *met* my father?'

Jamie's laughter was so loud that several birds flew in a startled cloud of feathers from the surrounding trees. He had indeed met my dad, on two memorable and frankly quite disastrous occasions. It hadn't gone well, and I'd never shared with Jamie the conversations we'd had after he'd dropped me off from those dates. The words 'dropout' and 'tattooed petrol-head' had featured, and while all were technically accurate, they'd been used as weapons and not as adjectives. Suffice to say that shortly after that we'd taken our relationship 'underground', where it had happily flourished in its new subterranean environment. I only hoped that my dad would act in a more generous and liberal-minded way with his elderly mother. But I had my doubts.

'All you can do is be there for her,' Jamie advised reasonably. 'Your dad's old-fashioned, but he's not a bigot.' I bit my lip, and said nothing. 'He's probably just going to need some time adjusting to the idea that your gran has found someone else.'

I shook my head, trying and failing to imagine a time when my dad would *ever* be able to accept such a major change in my grandmother's life. 'Seriously, I'm worried Gran won't live long enough to see that kind of acceptance from my dad. It'll happen right after pigs start sprouting wings.'

Jamie laughed again, and then picked up my wrist to examine my watch. 'Sorry, babe, I have to go. They're going to let me change my first ever clutch this afternoon.' The dancing light in his eyes told me that for a boy who lived and breathed cars the way he did, this was indeed a big deal.

'Yay. You go... fit that clutch!' I said, welcoming the warmth of his lips on mine as they kissed me goodbye.

'And you go fix that gran,' he batted back in reply.

Gran had a mobile phone, albeit one that was practically out of the Dark Ages. I'd usually text her on it when I was planning on visiting after school, but today I sent no such message. It was only as I crunched my way up Sunnymede's deep gravelled driveway that it occurred to me she might actually be out on one of the many excursions the home regularly organised.

There was no one at the reception desk to ask, so I signed myself in and wandered down the familiar corridors looking for her. The lounge was empty apart from two elderly gentlemen residents who were snoring loudly from opposite ends of the room, apparently in some sort of competition with each other. My money was on the guy in the wheelchair.

There was no reply at Gran's suite, so I headed for her second favourite room, the conservatory. It was a large and airy addition to the main building, with oversized pots housing tall ferns and palms that provided many private nooks and crannies from which to admire the well-kept gardens.

I saw them straight away. They were sitting side by side on a chintz-covered two-seater, a depleted tea tray in front of them, happily watching the birds taking off and landing on a feeding table outside the French windows. Their heads were close together. Until yesterday, my only thought would have been that it helped them to hear each other better. Today I knew differently. Their obvious affection for each other made me smile, as I watched them unseen from the doorway. Josie's hair was a flyaway crown of steel grey curls, while Gran's was pure white and angora soft. As I child I'd loved to run my fingers through it, playing hairdresser and probably ruining a style she'd spent ages in a salon to achieve. And yet she'd never stopped me. An unexpected lump formed in my throat as I realised just how much I loved this woman, who'd shaped my life in so many ways.

Josie's hearing wasn't as sharp as Gran's. She jumped, obviously startled, as I called out a cheerful hello and walked towards them. Gran's smile was a mixture of warmth and surprise.

'Mandy,' she cried, and it was only as I bent down to kiss the velvet folds of her cheek that I noticed she and Josie had been holding hands as they watched the birds in the garden. Josie, looking embarrassed, had quickly pulled her hand away as though she'd been caught shoplifting. I felt an ache of sadness for the woman who'd stolen my grandmother's heart. I couldn't imagine how hard it must be, feeling guilty for something so natural, as though you'd done something wrong. I knew almost nothing about Josie's past – Gran had never mentioned it – but that one action told me more than a hundred conversations ever could.

'Well, this is a wonderful surprise, Mandy dear. I had no idea you were popping in again today.'

I dropped down on to a nearby wicker armchair and shrugged out of my jacket. 'I just wanted to see you again, Gran. Because, you know, we didn't really get to finish our chat properly yesterday.'

Gran's eyes might be slowly glazing with incipient cataracts, but they still saw so much more than I would ever be able to hide from her. Yesterday, just after she'd told me about Josie, our visit had been cut short by the ringing of the bell announcing the evening meal. If I'm honest, I'd been quite glad that it had given me a legitimate excuse to leave. I'd needed that time to fully take on board what she'd told me. But my head was straight now, and – more than anything – I needed to let her know how much I was on her side here.

'I'm just going to toddle off and leave you both to have a nice little chat,' announced Josie, her smile encompassing both Gran and me.

'Josie, you don't have to leave,' I insisted.

Using her walking stick for support, she took a few unsteady steps towards me, stopping beside my chair. 'Your gran is still your gran, sweetheart. I would never want to get in the way of your time with her.' Before either Gran or I could protest, she added, 'Besides, the mobile library is here, and I'm hoping they've got that new wartime saga I ordered.' She smiled down at her friend. 'You know how I love them.'

'Feisty heroines with pin-curled hair and bright red lipstick,' Gran said, nodding fondly at her companion. 'You were born in the wrong era, Josie.'

A fleeting wistfulness passed across Josie's wrinkled face, to be replaced by a sweet, self-deprecating smile. 'I'd never have been bold enough to pull off that look,' she said with a sigh. Her admission showed a glimpse of a woman who'd lived far more in the shadows than anyone ever should. But she was gone in an instant, dispelled by a little-old-lady chortle. 'My days of pillar-box-red lippy have been and gone, for sure.'

I waited until Josie had left the room before moving into the seat she'd just vacated. The afternoon sunlight slanting through the window caught the diamond in Gran's engagement ring, making it blaze like a miniature comet as I reached for her hand. 'It'll be yours one day,' she'd always told me, but even as a little girl I'd known there'd never be enough diamonds in the world to make up for losing this woman.

'So, Gran,' I began, lacing my unlined fingers between her gnarled ones. 'How are you today?'

She looked at me for a long moment, understanding that I wasn't enquiring about her physical health or making polite conversation.

'Very well,' she said at last, with just the hint of a curl to her lips. 'Relieved, actually, not only because I told you, but also that you've come back to see me again so soon.'

'Did you honestly think that I wouldn't?' My voice sounded genuinely horrified. 'You must have known that *nothing* could ever make the slightest difference between you and me.'

For the first time, Gran looked unsure and suddenly older. 'Well, I hoped it wouldn't, but it was a huge bombshell to drop. I couldn't be entirely sure how you'd take it.'

I squeezed her hand gently, mindful of the ever present pain in her arthritic fingers.

'You should know better than that, Gran. If you told me you'd murdered someone, my only question would be: *Where should we hide the body?*'

Gran chuckled softly and it felt incredibly good to hear that, as though a thousand-ton weight had been lifted from my shoulders. Beyond the window the robins were still pecking hopefully at the bird table, and the afternoon sun was bathing the grounds in an artist's palette of golds and bronze.

'Do you feel like going for a stroll in the gardens?' I asked on impulse. 'We can talk as we walk if you like.'

Gran *did* like, so I raced back to her room to grab the thick cardigan that was draped over the back of her armchair. As I plucked it up, I caught a glimpse of my grandfather staring down at me from the shelf of photographs. It was a more recent portrait, and in it I could see both the man I remembered and the man my dad would one day become. I stared into his eyes, before impulsively kissing my fingertips and pressing them against the face trapped behind the glass. 'I love you too, Grandad, but Gran deserves to be happy now that you're gone. I hope you feel that way too.'

I knew better than to offer any assistance as Gran's stiff fingers fumbled with the intricacies of the buttons on her thick cardigan. So I stood patiently waiting as she completed the task, understanding better than anyone that fierce streak of independence. It wasn't a long or hard search to see where my determined and headstrong nature had come from.

We slipped through the patio doors, scattering the robins who eyed us resentfully as we stepped from the path and on to the neatly manicured lawns. The gardens were well designed and ringed with wide concrete paths to accommodate the walkers and wheelchairs of the residents, but Gran always liked to go 'off-roading' on our walks through the grounds.

'I spent a long time last night thinking about what you told me yesterday,' I admitted, slipping my hand companionably into the crook of her arm. Gran patted it affectionately.

'I never meant to keep you from your beauty sleep, darling girl.'

'You didn't. Well, you did – but in a *good* way.' I snuggled a little closer to her arm, inhaling the familiar fragrance of the perfume she always wore. My grandfather used to give

her an enormous bottle of it every Christmas. Did it make
her think of him, I wondered, as she dabbed it on each day?

'I'm sorry, Gran.'

Gran turned to me, genuinely mystified. 'Whatever for?'

'For not knowing that you weren't living the life you
wanted.'

At first I thought the expression on her face was shock,
but I quickly realised it was actually much closer to anger.
And Gran hardly ever got cross with me. There was a bench
nearby and she led us to it, sitting at an angle so that she
could look me in the eyes as she spoke.

'I haven't lived an unhappy life, Mandy. Far from it. But
I have lived long enough to know that very few people are
deliriously happy all of the time. Your grandfather was
a fine man, a good husband and a wonderful provider,
but more than that he was an *exceptional* father to your
dad. Whatever might have been... deficient... in our
lives together was more than made up for by all of those
things.'

'Did you... did you always realise that you... that you
were...' Oh God. What was wrong with me? Who in
their right mind chooses to ask their seventy-six-year-old
grandmother about her sex life?

Gran's smile rescued me from the pit I was about to fall
into. 'That I might be... gay? That's the word people use
these days, isn't it? So much nicer than the terms they used
back in my day. To me, the word "gay" has always meant
happy and joyful. And that's *exactly* how Josie makes me
feel – so how clever of your generation to have found just
the right word to describe it.'

I nodded, as though I had personally chosen the term.

'For a very long time I did wonder what was wrong with me. I had everything that was meant to make me happy, and yet there was always the feeling that something was missing.'

'There is nothing "wrong" with you,' I declared hotly. 'You love who you love. That's how it's supposed to be, anyway.'

Gran reached up and tenderly cupped my cheek. 'So wise for one so young,' she said softly.

'Was Josie ever married?' I asked curiously, realising I couldn't remember whether I'd ever seen a ring on her finger. Gran shook her head gently. 'No. Josie said she knew when she was a young woman that she didn't have those sort of feelings about any of her would-be suitors. But in those days people hid that kind of admission. Josie has never had anyone special in her life, not in almost eighty years. Not until now.'

'Well, she hit the jackpot with you after all this time.'

'Bless you, sweetheart,' Gran said, her cheeks growing a little pink.

There was a question I'd been wanting to ask for the last twenty-four hours, and even now, as I voiced it, I wasn't sure if it was entirely appropriate.

'Did… did Grandad ever know?'

For the first time, my grandmother looked truly shocked.

'Oh my goodness, no. It would have broken his heart. You must remember what he was like? He was such a *manly* man; he'd have taken it as a personal slight. He was a fishing and football-loving and going-down-to-the-pub sort of man. He'd have been crushed to know I wasn't *comfortable* with that side of our relationship.'

I shook my head, realising with a kind of wonder how very far society had come in the span of her lifetime.

'I'm really sorry, Gran, that you weren't able to be with someone who made you truly happy years ago. I'm sorry you never found Josie until now.'

'Well, I'm not,' said Gran firmly, getting to her feet with a sprightliness that belied her age. 'If I hadn't met your grandad and married him, then there would have been no son for us to have, and ultimately no you either.'

She lifted both hands and cupped my face within them. 'And a world without Mandy Preston in it is far too gloomy and colourless to even think about.' She leant closer and kissed my forehead tenderly. 'You and your dad have been the greatest loves of my life. More than your grandfather, and more even than Josie. I regret nothing in my past, because it's given me both of you, and I wouldn't change that for the world.'

23

The music was loud. It was reverberating through the bricks of the house, making the windows rattle in their frames. Unless they were deaf or away on holiday, complaints from the neighbours were surely imminent.

'They've gone away with my parents for the weekend,' said Alex, whose house it was. He gave a cheeky shrug as though to say, what else is a seventeen-year-old boy meant to do in these circumstances *except* have a party. It would be practically unconstitutional not to.

We'd arrived late, and the party was already at the sticky-kitchen-floor stage by the time we eventually joined what alarmingly appeared to be my entire year group, crammed into one modest three-bedroom semi. I'd followed in Jamie's wake as he cut a swathe through the heaving throng of gyrating bodies as we headed for the kitchen, aware of the many admiring glances arrowing our way. Despite my new skinny jeans and black top, I knew perfectly well that none of them were directed at me.

There's a unique realisation that comes to you when

you know you're dating someone out of your league. I was batting. I knew it. My friends knew it. But curiously, Jamie continued to act as if it was the other way around entirely. My dad – if he knew we were still seeing each other – was the only other person on the planet likely to agree with him. Either Jamie's home held no mirrors, or he truly didn't understand the effect he had on pretty much every female who crossed his path.

Every school has one. That rock-star student with the brooding bad-boy good looks. The boy whose name is written inside hearts on the pencil cases of girls he's never even spoken to. Two years older than me, I was far beyond Jamie's radar range; I was just another girl who'd admired him from a distance. Until the day a carelessly tied shoelace changed all that.

As falls go, it had been pretty spectacular. People had been throwing themselves at Jamie McDonald for years, but I was the only one who'd done it literally. He'd caught hold of me as I careened past him on the Music Block staircase, my legs pinwheeling like crazy as I tried to gain purchase. If he hadn't caught me as he did, bones would surely have been broken. As it was, the only body part that risked breakage was my seriously infatuated fourteen-year-old heart.

To this day, Jamie claims to have been oblivious to the major crush I'd developed on him from the minute he'd steadied me on to my feet and stooped to pick up my scattered books, which had ended up all over the corridor.

'A musician,' he'd said with a smile, handing me back a book of piano concertos.

I'd blushed scarlet and mumbled something inarticulate, but from that day on, whenever we'd passed in the corridor, he'd always acknowledge me, jokingly calling me by the name of a different composer each time: *Hi Mozart; Hey Beethoven; How you doing, Handel.* Those random 'hellos' had earned me an elevated status among practically all the girls in my year. Of course, that all happened years before he ever asked me out, dropped out of school two weeks into the sixth form to work in a garage, and in consequence acquired a rebel status that was totally undeserved and yet somehow seemed only to add to his allure.

Jamie headed straight for the sink, which was already overflowing with empty cider bottles and beer cans. I hoped Alex had a good clean-up crew on standby, or he was likely to be grounded for the rest of his teenage years. I stood to one side as Jamie scrubbed away the fresh oil stains from his hands and forearms and pretended not to notice that half the girls in the kitchen were openly staring as he rolled up his shirt sleeves to reveal his not inconsiderable biceps.

'Sorry,' he murmured after several minutes of enthusiastic scrubbing, sliding his citrus-smelling arms around my waist. '*Now* I can finally do this without getting you dirty.' I would happily have run the risk of the smudgy fingerprints, especially as I knew how he'd got them.

I hadn't even noticed the stranded woman motorist on the side of the road. To be honest, I was far too preoccupied with what my parents had casually mentioned right after *Have a good time* and before *Be sure you're home by midnight.* It had left me in a decidedly reluctant-to-party mood.

Jamie had commented that I seemed distracted when we'd met at our usual street corner venue, just far enough away from my home that we wouldn't be spotted. I knew it must still sting that I wouldn't let him call for me, but there are only so many ways to dress up 'My dad doesn't think you're good enough for me' without causing offence.

Sensing my need for quiet, Jamie had taken my hand in his and pulled me against his side, giving us the appearance of conjoined twins as we walked through the darkened streets, slipping in and out of pockets of developing mist. I hadn't seen what he had as he drew us both to an abrupt halt. I squinted in the darkness, and could just about make out the shape of a car tilted at an odd angle on the other side of the road, almost lost in swirling clouds of mist coming off the common beside it. A woman suddenly emerged into a pool of light thrown by a solitary street lamp. She had something in her hand that she appeared to be swearing at.

'Hang on a second, babe. Let me just check that woman is okay.'

He released my hand and jogged lithely across the road to her, calling out as he did. Even so, I heard her instinctive gasp as he emerged from the shadows. Girls often gasped when they saw Jamie, although admittedly most of them didn't sound quite as fearful as this woman did.

'Are you okay? Do you need some help?'

'I've been trying to phone a garage, but I can't get any signal.'

Jamie dropped down to a crouch and examined the back of the woman's car.

'Flat tyre?'

'No thanks, I've already got one,' the woman fired back with the timing of a stand-up comedienne. She jumped slightly on hearing my footsteps, but relaxed visibly as I emerged from the darkness and stood beside Jamie, resting one hand on his shoulder.

'You can borrow one of our phones,' Jamie offered. 'Or I'm happy to change the tyre if you've got a spare and a jack.'

The woman hesitated for a moment. 'He's a really good mechanic. He knows what he's doing,' I said loyally, which earned me one of Jamie's heart-melting smiles that totally excused the small exaggeration. Well, he was on his way to being a qualified mechanic.

It wasn't quite pit-stop speed, but Jamie *did* make changing the tyre look remarkably easy. In a slick manoeuvre that comes when you're comfortable with tipping, the woman tried to get Jamie to accept a crisp twenty-pound note for his labour. He wouldn't even consider it.

'Make sure you get the puncture fixed,' he told the unknown woman as she slipped back into the driver's seat. She looked up at us with an expression of gratitude on her face. 'Thank you both for stopping to help me. Plenty of people wouldn't. If there's ever anything I can do for you, just let me know.' She pressed a small rectangular card into my hand. I glanced down at it in the dim sodium lighting as she pulled away.

'What did she give you?'

'A business card, I think,' I said, stuffing it into the back pocket of my jeans with only half a glance. I think it was for some place called 'Crazy Daisy'.

★ ★ ★

With two plastic cups of cider in hand, Jamie led me away from the main crowd of party-goers in the lounge and kitchen and into the hallway. The front door was wide open, which could well explain the extraordinary number of people I didn't recognise at the party. I wondered how many of the gatecrashers *Alex* actually knew. Despite the cool air gusting into the hallway, the heat from that many bodies was making the house uncommonly warm. We climbed the staircase, stopping by mutual consent halfway up the flight and sitting down. Jamie put a welcome arm around my shoulder and drew me against him.

'So what's up?'

'What makes you think anything is?'

Jamie's eyebrows rose into his hairline, giving him a momentary villainous look. It didn't mar his attractiveness. I'd yet to find anything that did. There was a scar bisecting his right eyebrow where the hair refused to grow. The school rumour mill claimed it was from a knife fight. He'd laughed hard enough to bring tears to his eyes when I'd told him that. 'It was from a fight... between me and a swing that I walked into when I was three years old,' he'd told me. It had taught me an early lesson that, with Jamie, what you saw wasn't *always* what you got. He continually surprised me, and the worried look on his face was doing exactly that right now.

'It's not... it's not about you and me, is it?' It was the first time I'd ever heard a note of vulnerability in his voice, and it made me want to either cry or cover his face with kisses. Possibly both. 'You're not about to say something that's going to break my heart, are you?'

I'm sure I must have looked every bit as astounded as

I suddenly felt. Did I *have* Jamie's heart to break? If I did, how come he'd never said anything about it until now?

'No. No, of course I'm not,' I said, dropping my head on to his shoulder as though it never wanted to be anywhere else.

'Phew,' he said, and I swear I could feel the relief as though it was a tremor, shuddering through him.

'Why would you even think that was what was wrong?'

Very tenderly, he turned to me and tilted my face so that our noses were practically tip to tip. It was hard to concentrate when his lips were that close to mine.

'Because I'm always afraid that one day you're going to get tired of having to hide me from everyone, or the grief you'd get from your family if they knew about me.'

This is what happens when you're a coward. This is what happens when you don't stand up for the people you – I stopped short of the word *love* – the people you care about. This is what happens when you're not brave. For a moment I envied my grandmother the courage to stand up for the person she was, and the person she loved. Which brought me right back to the source of my anxiety this evening.

'Oh God, Jamie. It's not you at all. It's Gran.'

How could you *not* love a boy who didn't dismiss your elderly grandmother as inconsequential? Who understood perfectly how precious that woman was to you? Who reached for your free hand, as Jamie now did for mine, and squeezed it warmly?

'What's happened now?'

'It's all going down tomorrow. The shit is about to hit the fan. Big time.'

'Oh.' It was a small word that encompassed a huge looming catastrophe.

'Mum and Dad think Gran's depressed and needs cheering up, so they're going to surprise her tomorrow by taking her out for Sunday lunch. Only I think *they're* the ones who are in for a surprise.'

'Do you think she'll tell them what she told you?'

I shook my head from side to side. 'I don't *think* she will. I *know* she will.'

There was a long moment of silence.

'Awks,' said Jamie, totally without irony.

'Awks indeed.'

I had my headphones on. They were the expensive noise-cancelling type, a gift from my parents for my last birthday, and yet I *still* heard the slamming of the front door and the raised voices in the hallway below. Tentatively, I pulled one of the pads away from my head, the history notes spread across my bed temporarily forgotten.

'Gerald, calm down.'

Something banged and then fell over, which was followed by a string of earthy expletives, half of which I wasn't aware my father even knew. Mum did not sound impressed.

'I really don't see how charging around and barging into things is going to help.'

I couldn't make out the exact words of my father's response, but I got the general gist of it. Oh, Gran. What *have* you done? I glanced back at my homework, which for the first time ever actually looked more appealing than slacking off. But I was only delaying the inevitable. With a sigh I pulled off my headphones and headed downstairs.

DANI ATKINS

My parents had moved from the hallway to the kitchen, but I could still hear them. I had a feeling that even our neighbours could tune in without too much difficulty. Mum was doing her best to placate Dad, which was a good idea, for his face and neck had turned the shade of pink it only did when he'd forgotten to apply sunscreen.

I padded into the kitchen, pulling the door to a close behind me. Dad's head shot up and for a moment concern for my gran was overshadowed by that for my parent. Dad looked completely lost and that really wasn't an expression I could ever remember seeing on his face before. He also looked angry – that one I *had* seen a couple of times, but never to this degree.

'Mandy,' he said, making my name sound more like an accusation than a greeting.

'I thought I heard a noise,' I said innocently, hoping to defuse the atmosphere with some gentle humour. From the flare of his nostrils, I suspected I was several weeks too early for that as far as Dad was concerned. From behind him I could see my mother shaking her head in warning. There was no need to ask how lunch with Gran had gone. The answer was obvious.

'Why didn't you tell us about your grandmother?'

My tongue was lodged somewhere at the back of my mouth, and seemed to have forgotten how to work. Not that it would have mattered either way. I could sense an unstoppable tirade was about to crash over us like a tsunami.

'Are you angry with me, or Gran?' I asked.

'Neither,' he said bitterly. 'It's those bloody idiots at Sunnymede I'm angry with.'

340

I must have looked as confused as I felt, for Mum added quietly, 'Your dad thinks Gran isn't very well.'

'What's the point of paying for a fancy home full of medical experts when they don't even recognise a clear-cut case of dementia when it's staring them in the face?' he thundered.

I glanced over at my mother, who was looking troubled as she poured hot water on to teabags. It was the British cure-all for any emergency, but somehow I didn't think PG Tips' finest was going to fix this situation.

'Gran isn't sick or suffering from dementia,' I defended loyally.

'Well, she's certainly not firing on all her cylinders at the moment. I take it she told you about this ridiculous notion of hers?'

'Gran told me how she felt about Josie, if that's what you mean.'

My father made the kind of noise I imagine a pressure cooker might do, right before it explodes all over your kitchen.

'Your grandmother has clearly lost her marbles.'

'Is that a new medical term for being gay?' I asked, unable to disguise the thread of anger in my voice.

My mother's eyes were flaring now. Do *not* make it worse, they were practically shrieking. But someone had to defend Gran, and I was the only one here to do that.

'Your grandmother is not gay,' Dad declared. Each word was sharply enunciated, as though severed with a knife. 'For God's sake, she was married to my father for almost fifty years. Does that sound like gay to you, because it certainly doesn't to me?'

'I don't think Gran realised the kind of feelings she was capable of having until she met Josie,' I said, trying to reach the reasonable part of him that was currently buried beneath an avalanche of distress. 'She's not saying this to upset you, Dad.'

'Well, I *am* upset. My mother is clearly not in her right mind, and this so-called friend of hers must have been – what's that phrase? – *grooming* her.'

I laughed then, which was a mistake, but what Dad was saying was so preposterous I couldn't take it seriously. The thought of sweet, frail Josie grooming anything other than a small Pekingese was utter nonsense.

'If my father knew about this, he'd be *spinning* in his grave,' Dad said brokenly, running a hand through his hair. 'This whole thing is just ludicrous.'

'You should have told me.'

The knock on my bedroom door had been light. The distant sounds of the lounge TV and my father's accompanying snores told me Mum had been biding her time to have a private word.

I sat up, and with feigned nonchalance pushed my mobile beneath the pile of colourful cushions at the end of my bed. I'd been messaging Jamie, keeping him up to date on how things had gone – badly – and telling him how much I wished he was here with me right now – also badly.

'It wasn't my news to tell, Mum,' I said sadly.

She sank down on to the edge of my double bed. 'I could have done with a timely heads-up though, sweetheart.'

'Was it very bad?'

Mum shut her eyes, as though the memory was still too painful to view again. 'It wasn't good,' she admitted. 'Although I'm sure the other diners in The Plough found it quite interesting.' She sighed. 'If I'd known what was coming, I'd probably have chosen somewhere less public.'

Okay. That one *was* down to me. 'Sorry, Mum.'

My mother shook her head sadly. 'It's really shaken your dad up, you know. He's very upset.'

'I bet Gran is too. Knowing Dad, I don't suppose he handled it very sensitively.'

'Your dad didn't handle it at all. He believes your gran is delusional. Weirdly, he'd rather accept she has Alzheimer's than consider she's fallen in love with someone.'

'Would it have made a difference if that someone had been a man rather than a woman?'

She considered my question with a thoughtful expression. 'It *might* have been easier, but he'd still have seen it as a betrayal of his father. He still misses your grandad very much, you know.'

'I do too. We all do. But that doesn't change what's happening now, does it? I just want Gran to be happy. Surely Dad should want that too?'

'He does, or he will do once the dust settles and he calms down.'

From beneath the pile of cushions, my phone pinged with an incoming message. We both turned towards the sound and I could feel a guilty flush warming my cheeks.

'Do *you* believe Gran is senile or has been brainwashed by Josie, Mum?'

Surprisingly, my mother actually laughed at that one. 'I can't imagine anyone *less likely* to be manipulated into doing something she doesn't want to do than your grandmother,' Mum said, reaching over and smoothing back a straying lock of hair from my face. 'That's where you get it from.'

I smiled, but even as I did a thought occurred to me, so startling that it wiped everything else from my head.

'Did you *know* about Gran? Before today, I mean?'

There was a tiny twitch at the corner of her eye that told me the answer before she spoke. 'I may have suspected something,' she admitted, as though giving incriminating evidence in a witness box.

'But you never said anything to Dad?'

'What do you think?' she asked with a wry smile, getting to her feet. She was halfway across my bedroom floor when she paused and looked back over her shoulder, her eyes travelling to the stack of multicoloured cushions at the foot of my bed. 'Don't stay up too late talking to your boyfriend,' she advised.

My mouth was still in a perfect circle of surprise long after she'd left my room.

24

'I think you've already got that one,' I said, looking down at the latest book Jamie had added to the growing pile of manuals in his arms.

'Different make of car, babe,' he said, dropping to a crouch to better examine the lower shelf of the bookcase in the charity shop. While he surveyed the books, I admired the view of his broad shoulders and the way his T-shirt separated enticingly from the waistband of his jeans. Admittedly, browsing through second-hand books wasn't the most thrilling way of spending a Saturday morning, but Jamie's excitement at finding a cache of car repair manuals was how I imagined mine would be on finding a first edition of the dragon books I'd loved as a child.

I wandered away from the bookcase and began idly flicking through a stack of old CDs. I tucked a couple of classical music ones that I thought Gran might appreciate under one arm. It had been two weeks since the unfortunate Sunday lunch with my parents, and although Gran had seemed remarkably okay with how things had gone, I couldn't help but worry about her.

'I always knew your dad would struggle to understand,' she had said, taking up a chair to one side of the baby grand piano in Sunnymede's lounge. I was busy adjusting the height of the stool, but paused to look over at my elderly grandmother. She was bathed in a nimbus of sunlight from the window behind her. It shone through her hair and gave her an almost ethereal appearance, like an angel emerging from a cloud.

To be honest, Gran didn't appear to be as troubled as I'd feared she might have been by my dad's reaction. 'Remember, I've known him longer than you have, my love,' she'd said, squeezing my hand warmly beneath hers. 'After forty-four years, there's very little about your dad that is likely to surprise me. I'd have been far *more* shocked if he'd simply accepted it.'

From my bag I pulled a sheaf of music that I'd been struggling with for weeks.

'Ah, Sibelius's Fifth,' Gran said softly, as though greeting an old friend. She waited as I set the music up on the piano stand and then inclined her head encouragingly as my fingers hovered above the polished ivory keys. This was where we connected better than anywhere else. This was the place where we spoke a secret language the rest of our family didn't understand. In the music we found a common harmony, but more important than that, we found each other. I gave her one last smile and began to play.

★ ★ ★

A noise from the pavement jerked me back to the present. The charity shop was particularly busy, so busy that perhaps I was the only person who'd noticed the young woman in the wheelchair outside, struggling to open the door. I rushed over to help her, holding it wide as she expertly lined up her chair to glide through the opening and into the shop.

'Thank you so much,' she said, smiling up at me as I squashed myself as flat as a cartoon character against the wall to get out of her way. There was something vaguely familiar about her face, something that rang a distant bell in my memory, but I couldn't quite place her.

'Yes, thank you,' echoed a deep voice from a tall attractive man wearing Clark Kent glasses, who'd come up behind the chair and guided it through the doorway with practised ease.

'I thought you were going to wait for me,' the man said, bending low and kissing the side of the woman's neck. It was a curiously intimate gesture, one that a stranger should probably not witness, but pinioned as I was behind the door I really had nowhere else to go.

Once the chair was clear of the door, I pushed it to a close, getting one more dazzling smile from the woman's companion. He had to be at least fifteen years older than me, but that didn't mean I couldn't appreciate the dark good looks that were every bit as arresting as Jamie's blond ones were. My eyes flitted between the two men. All we needed now was for George Clooney to put in an appearance and every demographic would be catered for.

I gave myself a sharp mental reprimand as I crossed the shop to rejoin Jamie. I was in danger of being just as bad as my father in judging people on their appearance rather than the way they behaved. But somehow I didn't think I'd been wrong about that man. I glanced back towards the counter, where the couple were patiently waiting to be served. They were holding hands, and he only released hers as he reached for a long oblong box, which he placed on the counter. I saw the flash of a ring on his left hand. Once again there was a peculiar feeling that I knew this couple from somewhere, but I just couldn't remember from where.

My interest in them had tipped over from idle curiosity to downright nosiness, and as Jamie was still immersed in diagrams of car engines, I kept watching as the man looked down at the woman, an easy-to-read question on his face. *Are you sure?* She looked up at him and nodded just once in confirmation. The man lifted the lid of the box, which infuriatingly was angled towards the woman behind the counter, giving me no clue as to what was inside it. The assistant reached into the container and something that looked a little like a billowing white cloud spilled out from one side. I caught a glimpse of a bodice scattered with sparkly beading and wisps of a flowing chiffon skirt.

'All done?' asked Jamie, nodding towards a second counter on this side of the shop. His books were already stacked up beside the till, and without a second thought he took the CDs for my grandmother from beneath my arm and added them to the pile. It was no surprise when he refused to let me pay for them.

'You can buy the popcorn at the cinema tonight,' he said by way of a compromise. I slipped my arm through his and reached up to deposit a thank-you kiss on his cheek, which already felt scratchy with stubble. As we left the shop to rejoin the Saturday morning crowds, I felt one final tug drawing my focus back towards the couple at the counter. I couldn't explain my fascination with them, and fortunately Jamie hadn't seemed to notice my rapt attention in two total strangers. As the door swung to a close behind me, I saw the shop assistant take the box they'd brought with them and place it beneath the counter. Even that felt important somehow, yet I had no idea why.

'Oh shit,' I muttered, glancing through the crowds and spotting a face I was more used to seeing peering over the back garden fence.

'What's wrong?' asked Jamie. His arm, which was looped around my shoulders, pulled me closer to his side. I stiffened, even though I knew I shouldn't, and of course he felt it. He looked up and followed the direction of my panicked gaze. 'Who is that?' he asked, his arm already falling away.

'That's our next-door neighbour, Mrs Blake. She's...' I felt a bit disloyal here, because there was no real malice in the woman who'd lived next door to my family for as long as I could remember. 'She's kind of a chatterbox,' I finished lamely.

Jamie understood, in a way that made me feel as though I was quite possibly the worst girlfriend in the entire world. Any girl – many girls – would be over the moon to be in my position, and yet here I was acting as though my relationship with Jamie was a grubby little secret that had to be hidden. All because of some outmoded idea my father had about who was, and who wasn't, good enough for me. Jamie had already taken a broad step to one side, his hands now thrust into the pockets of his jeans. He knew the drill.

Mrs Blake hadn't spotted me yet, so there was probably still time for us to duck into a nearby shop until she had passed. Jamie had slowed his pace and was now walking half a step behind me, a position where he could feasibly pass as just another shopper in the crowd.

It happened quite suddenly, with very little forethought or regard to the consequences of my actions. Afterwards, I liked to tell myself that I'd heard my grandmother's voice in my head, silently encouraging me, but in truth I could hear very little except the rush of blood in my ears caused by a surge of adrenaline. Fight or flight, wasn't that what that particular hormone was intended for? Who knew at the very last moment I would decide not to run, but to stand my ground?

Jamie's face was a picture of astonishment as I spun on my heel and placed my hands on his shoulders. It wasn't a passionate kiss, but our lips lingered long enough to ensure that anyone watching us couldn't mistake it for a casual greeting. Jamie was caught off balance in every sense of the word, and with his hands still buried in his pockets it's a wonder we didn't end up on the pavement being trampled underfoot by the Saturday morning shoppers.

We'd only just broken apart when a voice called out my name, just as I'd known it surely would.

'Mandy, what a surprise... seeing you here, I mean.'

I think we all knew Mrs Blake was probably more surprised by the kiss she'd just seen than by bumping into one of her neighbours in the high street, which – let's face it – was hardly surprising at all.

We exchanged the usual round of *'how are you?'*s and *'how are your parents?'*, and all the while we were speaking I kept my arm firmly hooked through Jamie's.

'And is this your young man?' Mrs Blake asked eventually.

Why had I waited so long to find this courage? Why hadn't I realised how wonderfully liberating it would be to look up at the tall handsome boy beside me and say with a proud smile: 'Yes. Yes it is. This is Jamie, my boyfriend.'

Sometime between my bold show of confidence in the high street and half past seven that evening, my fearlessness had begun to ebb away.

'Are you sure it's a good idea?' Jamie had asked, as we'd nibbled on paninis in our favourite café. 'Maybe we should ease your parents into the idea a little more gradually?'

I swallowed down a mouthful of practically molten cheese before answering him.

'No. We should definitely do this. I'm only suggesting that you knock on our front door and pick me up this evening – it's not like I'm asking them if you can move in.'

Jamie gave a shrug and a crooked half-smile, looking so much like he belonged in an indie rock band that the waitress walking by our table did a visible double take. Jamie didn't notice. He never did.

'If you're sure,' he said, his voice still weighty with doubt.

'I'm sure,' I declared, reaching for his hand across the tabletop and entwining my fingers with his.

And I *had* been sure: when we'd kissed goodbye on the street corner; when I'd watched him leave to spend the afternoon fixing a mate's car; even when I was meant to be thinking only about the machinations of Oliver Cromwell as I wrote an essay, I'd still been convinced my plan was sound.

The doubts started creeping in as I stood beneath the shower, with Molton Brown gel pooling in bright orange puddles at my feet. What would Dad say when he opened the door and saw Jamie standing on the doorstep? A horrible image of him simply shutting it in my boyfriend's face got caught in the loops of my imagination and refused to leave it. No. Dad wouldn't be rude, would he? Not to Jamie's face?

I glanced at the clock as I towelled myself dry. There was still time to call it off, to save this confrontation for a less turbulent period for my family. But as I was reaching for my mobile to change our plans, my grandmother's face seemed to materialise before me, like a senior citizen version of Jiminy Cricket. *Do the right thing*, it said. With a worried sigh, I laid down my phone.

All I'd told them was that a friend was calling for me on the way to the cinema. Not exactly a lie, but not entirely the truth either. All I had to do was make sure that I was still upstairs when the doorbell rang and that Dad answered it, and the rest... would hopefully fall into place. Admittedly, it wasn't a particularly well-thought-out plan, so it was hardly surprising that things didn't work out the way I'd hoped.

I was in my room, dressed and ready to go but pretending not to be, when Jamie messaged me with a prediction:

Your front doorbell is about to ring in ten seconds.

He was right, but what he didn't know was that so was the home telephone. I was peering through a crack in my bedroom door and heard Dad call out 'I'll get it', but I had no way of knowing if he meant the door or the phone.

Murphy's Law decreed that it was Mum who emerged from the kitchen to answer the front door. Given that she'd as good as admitted that she knew I was still seeing Jamie, his arrival had far less impact than I'd anticipated.

'Hello. It's... er, Jamie, isn't it? Why don't you come in for a moment? I don't think Mandy's quite ready yet.' She glanced up the staircase and caught me hanging over the banisters watching them.

'I'm on my way,' I called down, hopping around on one foot as I hurriedly fastened my sandals. I was already halfway down the staircase when Jamie stepped into the hallway.

'Thank you,' he replied, giving my mother his most charming smile. 'Jamie McDonald,' he introduced, going for an unexpected handshake. 'It's very nice to finally get to meet you properly, Mrs Preston.'

There was something wrong with the hand I saw him extend to my mother, and it took me several moments to realise what it was. It was red, or at least an exceedingly deep shade of pink, as though it had been scrubbed within an inch of its life to remove every trace of oil that it would have been covered with after working on his friend's car. He'd done that for me, I knew that, and all at once my heart seemed to need much more space in my chest cavity than it usually required. Jamie was also wearing a far more formal shirt than a trip to the cinema necessitated, and instead of being rolled up to reveal his forearms, it was securely buttoned at his wrists and almost up to his neck. There wasn't a single tattoo in sight. It was a strange moment to suddenly realise that I was in love with this boy, but then recently my life had been full of strange moments.

Something that *didn't* seem likely to happen, however, was the opportunity to reintroduce Jamie to my dad. The phone call was proving to be a lengthy one and didn't sound as though it was winding to a conclusion anytime soon. Dad had always been a phone pacer, and tonight was no exception. He was patrolling the kitchen as he spoke, glancing our way every time a circuit took him past the open doorway. The glimpses I caught were too fleeting to decipher. Perhaps that was just as well.

'It was very nice meeting you again, Jamie,' said my mother, surprisingly sounding quite sincere. She'd always been a sucker for good manners, and no one could deny that Jamie's had been impeccable. 'I hope we'll see you again soon.'

I waited until we were outside and the front door was securely shut behind us before letting out a long, low breath of relief.

'I think that went quite well.'

'At least your Dad wasn't sitting on the porch cleaning his shotgun,' Jamie said with a laugh. It was funny, but from the look in his eyes I suspected he was only half joking.

25

'**B**ravo!'
It was the second time in less than an hour that my grandmother had congratulated me. The first occasion had been in Sunnymede's lounge, as I finished playing her the last of the pieces for my forthcoming piano exam. On a nearby armchair, Josie was clapping with the kind of delighted enthusiasm that brought a genuine lump to my throat. And she wasn't alone, for the lounge had filled steadily with other residents, who'd happily settled down to enjoy the impromptu concert.

I beamed back at them as the applause travelled around the room like a Mexican wave. I knew every face and every name. Without intending for it to happen, I seemed to have been unofficially adopted as an 'honorary granddaughter' by many of Sunnymede's residents, bridging a gap left by family who lived too far away, or who didn't visit regularly.

'Play like that and you'll certainly impress the examiner,' Gran said, getting to her feet and laying a proud hand on my shoulder.

'She'll knock their bleeding socks off,' added Helena, an ever smiling octogenarian whose colourful language hinted at an interesting past, or a mild case of Tourette's. 'She's bloody amazing.'

Admittedly, my audience was biased, but the greatest approval, the *only one* that really mattered to me, had been warmly given and gratefully received. Back in Gran's suite, she insisted on opening a celebratory packet of bourbon biscuits – a sure sign she was delighted with the progress in my playing.

'It's all down to you, Gran,' I said, taking a biscuit from the willow-patterned plate she was holding out to me. 'I had the very best teacher.' I met her faded green eyes, which were a time-slip version of how mine would look in the future. 'And not just in music.'

Gran's virtually invisible eyebrows rose a little.

'I've learnt something even more important from you. I've learnt that nothing matters more than the people you care about, and how you have to stand up for them... and also for yourself.' I looked down at my hands, unaware I'd been quietly picking away at the edge of my thumbnail. I drew in a deep breath. 'So from now on I won't be hiding my relationship with Jamie from Mum and Dad.' I lifted my head up, almost surprised to hear my voice growing thick with tears. 'I'm very proud to be his girlfriend.'

Gran nodded gently in encouragement as I added, 'Dad's wrong about him, and if he can't see that, then I'm sorry for him, but I'm done with hiding someone who's that important to me.'

'Bravo, child, bravo! I'm very proud of you.'

'Dad isn't going to like it,' I predicted with an unladylike sniff.

'Your father will get over it,' Gran replied, passing me a perfectly laundered linen handkerchief. 'Beneath all that bluster and nonsense there's actually a gentle and sensitive man, who's just trying to protect his family, the only way he knows how.'

'Families,' I declared, in a *can't-live-with-them, can't-kill-them* kind of way, which made us both laugh. It also made me think of Josie, who had no family of her own, and who'd once again chosen to remain in the lounge rather than join us in Gran's suite. That was going to have to stop, I vowed.

In that weird, almost telepathic way that Gran and I had, she said then, 'I really hope I get an opportunity to meet this young man of yours, very soon.'

She did. But not in the way that any of us had planned.

I liked Thursday afternoons. There were blank spaces on my timetable with the words 'study period' on them, which every sixth-form student knows is simply a euphemism for 'go home early and do absolutely nothing'. I was probably breaking some sort of unwritten honour code by actually *studying* during my free hours that afternoon. But with both parents at work I had the house to myself, and was taking full advantage of the peace and quiet. The only sound in the kitchen was the quietly ticking clock on the wall, and the mouse-like scratching of pen on paper as I filled page after page of an exercise book with neatly written notes. I'd always been a hard worker, but right now it seemed even more important to prove that it was perfectly possible to date someone with totally different career and life goals, and still not let your grades slip.

I was humming to myself as I scanned through my work, when the muffled sound of my phone's ringtone interrupted me. Papers flew up and fluttered to the floor like autumn leaves as I rummaged hurriedly beneath the collection of books and sheaves of notes for my mobile. I found it one ring short of switching to voicemail.

It was a landline number, but one neither I nor my phone recognised. For a long moment there was silence on the line, and then the sound of breathing. Ragged breathing. I've seen enough *Scream* movies to know there were jokers in my year group who'd think this kind of prank was absolutely hilarious.

'Okay. I'm hanging up now,' I warned when the caller still hadn't spoken. I was two seconds from pressing the disconnect button when someone said my name; it was sandwiched between two long, raw-sounding gasps.

'Hello?' I said cautiously, bringing the phone closer to my ear. 'Who *is* this?'

There's that awful moment when, without visual confirmation, it's practically impossible to distinguish between laughter or tears. And then I felt my stomach take a lift-dropping plummet as I recognised her voice.

'Gran? Gran, is that you?'

A small hitching sound – was that a stifled sob? – and then a cough as she fought to regain control. 'Mandy, yes. It's me.' She sounded dreadful, worse even than when Grandad had died. Her voice was trembling, and sounded hollow and unsure. 'Mandy, something terrible has happened.'

My parents, I thought, feeling ice flood through my veins. *They've been in an accident.* I wasn't thinking straight, because the sane part of my brain knew they were both at work, but I was a child again. And whatever it was that was making my grandmother sound like this had to be bad. Very, very bad.

'Gran, what's the matter? What's happened?'

'It's Josie.'

A relief I vowed I would never, ever share with her washed over me, swiftly followed by a cresting wave of guilt.

'What's happened to Josie, Gran?' I asked urgently, already fearing I knew the answer to that question. *No, God. Don't you do that to those two sweet old ladies. You take it back right now.* Perhaps someone up there heard me.

'They had to call an ambulance for her. The paramedics took her away. They think she's had a heart attack.'

As devastated as I was to hear Gran's news, at that moment my concern was focused one hundred per cent on her.

'Oh Gran, I'm so sorry. What can I do to help?'

'I have to get to the hospital. There's no one with her and she'll be so scared. I've been waiting to see if someone from the home could take me, but they're all so busy. So I'm just going to go.'

'By yourself?' My voice went up several octaves in concern.

'I can't leave her there all alone.'

'No, of course not. But you shouldn't be going alone either.' By then I was already rummaging for my discarded shoes beneath the kitchen table. 'I'll come with you. I'll get a cab or an Uber and be with you as soon as I can.'

I doubt very much my Gran even knew what an Uber was, but the relief in her voice was so humbling that I could feel tears welling up in my eyes.

'Would you, Mandy? Could you do that?'

'Absolutely. Just hang on, Gran. I'm on my way.'

Afterwards, I wondered why I called him instead of phoning for a cab. But in a crisis you instinctively reach out for the person you need to get you through it. Gran reached out for me, and I reached out for Jamie.

I never phoned him at the garage – I wasn't even sure if he was allowed to keep his mobile on him in the workshop – so he must have realised something was up even before I began explaining what had happened.

He blew air from his lungs in a single long exhalation, as though about to give an expensive estimate for car repairs. 'Shit. That's scary. How's your Gran coping?'

'She sounded really shaky,' I admitted.

'She'll feel better once we get her to the hospital.'

I was so distracted that I didn't immediately pick up on his meaning. He was asking me for the name of the hospital when his choice of pronoun finally filtered through the haze.

'We?'

'Of course, "we",' he said, and just like that I fell a little bit more in love with this boy. 'I can be with you just as quickly as a cab could. I'll ask the boss if I can borrow one of the run-arounds.'

I wanted to thank him, to say that wasn't why I'd phoned him, that I'd called him because... I ran out of steam and answers to that one, but it didn't matter because Jamie was suddenly the sensible adult here, and I was happy for the moment to let him take over.

'Be with you very soon, babe.'

If the garage had been further away I might have debated for longer on whether or not to call my parents. As much as I felt they ought to know where we were, the fact remained that Gran had called *me* and not them. She'd trusted me with news about Josie, not just once but twice now, and I wasn't about to betray that. With Jamie's arrival imminent, I decided to compromise; I ripped a page from my exercise book and scribbled out a brief message.

Have taken Gran to the hospital. Will explain all later.

I propped the note up against the kettle, where it was sure to be seen by whoever walked through the door first. Two short blasts of a car horn from the street gave me no time to worry any further about my parents.

When he'd said 'run-around' I'd visualised an old banger with a different coloured paint job on every door and smoke belching out of its exhaust, so the gleaming, practically new vehicle waiting at the kerb was my first surprise. The second was slower to dawn on me as I jumped in and hurriedly clipped my seat belt in place. This was the first time I'd ever been in a car driven by Jamie. It was doubtless something else that my father wouldn't approve of, but there was no time to worry about that now.

I might have only eight driving lessons under my belt, but that didn't mean I couldn't recognise good driving when I saw it. The afternoon traffic was heavy, but Jamie wove expertly through the congestion as I directed him to Sunnymede.

'Does the garage know you've taken this car?' I asked, as Jamie fiddled with switches on the dashboard, which looked more like a plane's cockpit than the humble model I was learning on at the driving school.

He took his eyes off the road just long enough to flash me a smile. 'Why? Did you think I'd stolen it?'

Jamie was teasing me, I knew that, trying to smooth out the lines of anxiety I could feel my brow had furrowed into. He took one hand off the wheel long enough to squeeze mine reassuringly. 'Pete – the garage manager – was really good about it. I told him my girl's gran needed to get to the hospital and he didn't even hesitate, just threw me the keys. *Family comes first*, he said. He's a great bloke.'

An unfamiliar warmth had crept into my stomach, which I was pretty sure had come after hearing that Jamie had referred to me as 'his girl'. It had ignited all kind of fires within me that I never wanted to put out.

Gran was waiting outside the doors of Sunnymede. I spotted her long before we crunched to a stop at the end of the gravelled drive. Her anxiety not to waste a single second by waiting for us in the comfort of the foyer tugged at my heart. There's something very touching about the way the elderly dress, as though they're in a totally different climate from everybody else. Despite the warmth of the day, Gran was wearing a woollen coat, with every single button done up. She even had a patterned silk scarf knotted at her throat.

Far more concerning than simply wearing the wrong clothes was seeing the wrong expression on her face. The frail old lady waiting on the paving stones by the door wasn't the smiling, confident pensioner I was used to seeing. This woman was pale – worryingly so – and her cheeks looked pinched and as dry as parchment. She also looked at least ten years older than my grandmother had done the last time I'd seen her.

I was out of the car almost before it had drawn to a complete stop and ran towards her, my feet sending up tiny showers of gravel in my haste. I slipped an arm through hers, more for comfort than support, and led her towards the borrowed car. Jamie had also climbed out and was now holding open the rear passenger door. Gran needed help to fasten the seat belt, her fingers fumbling clumsily with the metal clasp. She'd never needed that kind of assistance before. *This is just temporary, it's because of the shock*, I told myself as I scooted around the back of the car to climb in the other side. *Gran will be back to her old self as soon as she knows Josie is okay. And if she* isn't *okay, what happens then?* questioned a troublesome voice that sounded so real I even glanced over my shoulder to see if someone had spoken those words out loud.

'I'm going to sit in the back with Gran,' I whispered to Jamie, 'if you don't mind?' He smiled and shook his head.

Gran was sitting bolt upright, as though good deportment might influence the outcome of the day. She was gripping the handles of her handbag with fierce pressure that was surely painful for her arthritic fingers. I laid my hand over hers, and gave them a reassuring squeeze.

After volunteering the name of the hospital, Gran hardly said a word during the twenty-minute journey. We drove in silence except for Jamie's running commentary of our ETA as the minutes counted down on the satnav screen. Five minutes from our destination Gran turned to me, her faded eyes flooded with tears that had yet to spill.

'I'm very scared, Mandy.'

'Oh Gran, I know you are. I am too, but they'll be taking really good care of her, I'm sure of that.'

With only two minutes left until our arrival, Gran finally let the thought that had been torturing her out of its cage. 'What if we're too late? What if she's already gone?'

I met Jamie's eyes in the rear-view mirror. Mine were frantic, because I was very much afraid that was *exactly* what we might find when we got there. I don't know what I'd have done if Jamie hadn't spoken up just then.

'They can work absolute miracles these days, Mrs Preston. You wouldn't believe it. My grandad had two heart attacks, but after his treatment and the pills they gave him, he bounced back as good as new.'

Gran looked at the blond-haired young man behind the wheel, realising – perhaps for the first time – that he wasn't just some random cab driver. She looked to me with an unasked question in her eyes. I nodded.

'Thank you very much, young man. That was very kind of you to tell me that. I'm glad your grandfather is doing so well.'

Jamie dropped us at the main entrance and then drove off to find a space in the hospital's multi-storey car park. As we walked arm in arm through the revolving doors, I could feel the tension thrumming through Gran like a pulse.

'Josephine Whittaker...' said the receptionist, drawing out the name as though it was a conundrum she hoped to solve soon. She'd been scrolling through screen after screen on her computer for so long I was starting to feel as though my nerves had been fed through a shredder.

'Ah, here she is,' she declared at last.

'Is she... is she okay?' Was the receptionist even allowed to tell me if she wasn't, I wondered?

'Are you a relative?' she asked, looking up from the computer. Gran, who'd lived an entire lifetime by the maxim 'honesty is the best policy', was shaking her head negatively. Fortunately, I hadn't inherited her compulsive truthfulness.

'Yes. Josie is my grandmother.'

I sensed Gran had turned to look at me, and I only hoped that none of her incredulity was visible for the receptionist to see.

'She's been taken up to C4, the elderly patient unit. If you take the lift, then turn right and keep walking, you'll find it.'

'They didn't say how she was,' Gran said quietly, addressing her words to the closed lift doors as it carried us up to Josie.

'That doesn't mean it's bad news.' I reached for Gran's hand, or she reached for mine, I wasn't sure which, and we held fast together for what felt like an interminable journey to the fourth floor.

I breathed in deeply as we followed signs for the ward, my lungs filling with the smell of the hospital. A nurse buzzed us into the unit; another directed us to the reception desk; and a third motioned us, with an apologetic hand, to wait as she finished up a telephone call. It seemed wrong that all these people, these strangers, knew the fate of the woman Gran loved, and yet we were still in the dark. Finally, the nurse behind the desk finished her phone conversation. There was a kindness in her eyes and an air of calmness that soothed like a salve on a wound.

'She's still a bit disorientated and confused, and quite sleepy from the drugs we've given her for the pain, but I'm sure she'll be delighted to see you.' I don't know how Gran felt, but I was just happy to hear Josie still being spoken about in the present tense.

The nurse led us a short distance down the corridor to a bay of eight beds and nodded to the one in the furthest corner. A shape, so slight it could easily be mistaken for a rucked blanket, was barely discernible beneath the covers. If it wasn't for the froth of grey curls on the pillow, I wouldn't have known who it was. But Gran did.

Something very strange happened as we crossed the bay to reach Josie's bed. Gran suddenly seemed to draw on an inner well of strength. Her hand fell away from mine and all at once she was walking taller, straighter and even faster as she hurried to the side of the woman she loved.

'Well, there you are,' Gran declared as she approached the bed, as though Josie had been guilty of playing a mischievous game of hide-and-seek rather than being occupied with evading death that day.

The nurse had been right, Josie was doped up to the eyeballs. Her focus was clearly off and I had no idea how many of us she actually saw approaching the bed, but that didn't matter because there was only one person she needed to see, and she was right there beside her. Gran reached for Josie's hand, which was lying slackly on the hospital mattress. Carefully avoiding the canula embedded into the papery skin, she squeezed her fingers and then bent down and very tenderly kissed Josie on the lips. It was the most beautiful thing I think I had ever witnessed, and suddenly I was crying.

Despite my best efforts to stifle it, a tiny sob escaped and Gran looked over her shoulder at me.

'Hush, Mandy. None of that now. Josie is going to be absolutely fine.'

Josie's lips were moving soundlessly, as though the events of the day had robbed her of speech, but her eyes never once left Gran's face. She was looking at her in a way I hoped someone would one day look at me. As though a world gone wrong was suddenly put to rights, simply because I was in it.

I excused myself, mumbling something about giving them some time alone, but in truth I had a feeling I was about to start bawling and I really didn't want to do that in front of them. I half stumbled back on to the main ward and headed blindly in the direction of the exit, only to be brought to an abrupt halt when I barged into the solid wall of someone coming the other way. Two strong arms tightened around me, which would have been decidedly overfamiliar if they hadn't belonged to the boy who was proving more important to me with every passing minute.

'Hey. Hey, Mandy. It's me.'

I nodded dumbly into the wall of Jamie's chest, my tears soaking into his T-shirt. Without releasing me, he managed to manoeuvre us both into a small day room for the patients. Thankfully, it was empty. He sat me down on a cracked vinyl-covered armchair, and dropped to a crouch at my feet. His eyes were troubled as he looked up at me.

'No. It's not that,' I quickly assured him, between hitching sobs that were finally slowing down. 'Josie's okay. Gran's with her now.'

Jamie let out a long, slightly uneven breath. 'Phew. You had me worried there for a minute.'

'Sorry,' I whispered, and then almost lost it all over again as he tenderly reached up and began wiping away my tears with the pad of his thumb. Mascara smudges mingled with the oil ingrained inside the whorls of his fingerprints. 'I must look a mess,' I said, with a shaky laugh.

Jamie shook his head, his blond hair swinging, mimicking that thing photographers do with wind machines. 'Never more beautiful,' he contradicted quietly. It was a lovely compliment from someone who turned every head they passed, and I would treasure it later, once we knew for sure that Josie was going to be okay.

The passage of time was marked not by the clock, but by the growing accumulation of empty vending machine cups on the table. Gran was still at Josie's bedside, and I was beginning to think we'd need a crowbar to prise her away from it. I drifted between the ward and the day room, splitting my time between the two people I cared about. Josie was surrounded by a disturbing number of tubes, monitors and machines that bleeped alarmingly whenever she moved.

'They're only there to help her,' Jamie said reasonably, putting aside an ancient copy of a gardening magazine he'd already flicked through half a dozen times as we waited. 'Although I remember being scared shitless the first time I saw my grandad hooked up to that many machines.'

I caught hold of his hand, and threaded my fingers in his. 'I forgot to thank you for saying that before to Gran. It really helped her.' I leant in and kissed him, which felt like a much better way of showing my gratitude. 'You never talk about your grandfather. I feel bad that I didn't even know he'd had two heart attacks.'

Jamie's eyes held mine, and something flickered in his.

'Three, actually. In the end, he had three. But your gran didn't need to hear about the last one.'

His meaning was clear, and I opened my mouth to say *I'm so sorry* or *That's really sad*, and no one could have been more surprised than me when instead the words that tumbled out of it were: 'I love you.'

We were frozen in the moment. Jamie's eyes were locked on mine, and my heart was beating so loudly I could no longer hear the muted sounds of the ward or the monitors. All I could see was Jamie, all I could feel was Jamie, and then suddenly the moment was shattered as the day room door flew open and another, altogether more familiar, voice broke the spell we were under.

'Mandy! Where the hell is your grandmother?'

'Dad!' I cried, breaking away from Jamie as though I'd been electrocuted. Beyond my father's suited shoulder, I saw the top of my mother's head. 'And Mum,' I added unnecessarily. My face was hot with embarrassment from what they'd just seen, and possibly even heard. 'What are you both doing here?' They entered the day room, which suddenly seemed uncomfortably overcrowded.

My father dug into his jacket pocket and withdrew a crumpled sheet of paper. I recognised the familiar slant of my handwriting. '"Have taken Gran to the hospital",' he read, waving my note around as though he was a barrister using it as evidence in a court case. It was easy to see the fear beneath the anger, which my carelessly composed note had caused.

'Oh,' I said guiltily. 'I see what you must have thought. I should probably have written "Have *gone with* Gran to the hospital".'

'You think?' Dad asked with unexpected sarcasm. 'Do you realise I spent most of the drive here believing it was my mother who'd been taken ill?' His voice was an irate growl, but I knew it was just a defence to cover up how worried he'd been.

'Your mum couldn't get through to anyone at Sunnymede, and it wasn't until we were almost here that we discovered your grandmother was just a visitor and not a patient.'

'Your phone is turned off,' Mum reproached quietly.

'I thought you had to do that in hospitals,' I replied, in what was probably a very flimsy defence.

Dad made a noise like an angry bear. 'So where is your grandmother right now?'

My eyes flashed briefly to Jamie's, but there was nothing he could do to make this scene any less uncomfortable.

'Gran is with Josie right now. She's not left her side since we got here.'

More ursine noises. Fortunately, Mum was much more sympathetic. 'How is Josie doing now?'

My dad shot her a look, but she flashed one back of her own and he backed down.

'It was a heart attack, which isn't great at her age, but I think she's more comfortable now. Shall I tell Gran you're here?' I asked, reluctant to leave Jamie alone with my parents, but even more worried about taking my father to Josie's bedside.

'Please,' said my dad expressively.

I flew from the room as though there were flames at my heels.

Gran didn't want to leave Josie, and only agreed to do so when I promised to sit with her until she returned. Two pairs of worried eyes followed Gran as she went in search of her son. I tore mine away from the corridor when I felt Josie reach for my hand.

'I'm so sorry, Mandy, for causing everyone so much trouble.'

I looked down at the frail old lady who held my grandmother's future happiness in her hands.

'Josie, nothing could be further from the truth. You don't have to apologise for anything. All *you* have to do is get better as soon as you can. That's all any of us want.'

I never did find out what Gran said to my dad, but it was a considerably chastened and mollified individual who was waiting for me back in the day room after Gran had once again resumed her position at Josie's bedside.

Dad cleared his throat several times, as though there

was a troublesome obstacle in there that was blocking the words he was trying to get out. I think it was called pride.

'I understand you were the one who drove them to the hospital this afternoon?'

I liked the way that Jamie stood up a little straighter as he prepared to be taken to task by my father. There was nothing of the boy about him as he stood there waiting for whatever was coming his way; he was all man.

'Yes I did, sir.'

My father's eyes flickered in what I liked to think was surprise at the deference in Jamie's reply. Dad didn't have a violent bone in his body, but even so when he began to raise his right arm, I instinctively flinched. But there was no need to have worried, for in a move I'd never have predicted in a million years, he held out his hand to Jamie.

It hovered in the space between them for several moments, purely because I don't think Jamie could quite believe what he was seeing either. Then, almost in a rush, he placed his slightly oil-stained hand in my father's waiting one. My eyes must have been virtually on stalks as the muscular arm decorated with tattoos solemnly shook the one covered in a Marks and Spencer Italian silk suit.

'Thank you for taking care of my family today. I really appreciate it.'

'I was happy to help out,' Jamie replied, giving me a 'see-this-wasn't-so-difficult' kind of look.

But I knew Dad far better than he did, and leaving it there would have been one miracle too many for the day.

'Well, I'm sure you must have somewhere else you need to be now, having spent so much time here already. So please don't feel you need to stay any longer.'

It was an artfully polite eviction, but an eviction nonetheless. Dad was a bit of a chess fanatic, and he was looking so pleased with himself that I was almost expecting him to utter a self-congratulatory 'Checkmate' under his breath.

But Mum was one step ahead of him, as I was beginning to realise was actually always the case.

'That's a great idea, Gerald. Why doesn't Jamie take Mandy home, and we'll wait here until visiting time is over and then drive your mother back to Sunnymede?'

I almost felt sorry for Dad, who realised too late how expertly he'd been outmanoeuvred in his very own game.

'I'm sure you must both be starving,' Mum continued, 'so why don't you pick up a pizza on the way home?' She nodded meaningfully at my father, who in a daze realised he was left with no other option but to extract his wallet. Poor Dad, he had the look of a man who was replaying the scene in his head, wondering how it had all gone so horribly wrong.

'That's okay, sir,' said Jamie, as Dad tried to pass him a twenty-pound note. 'I can pay for our meal.' I truly don't think I'd ever been more proud of him than I was at that moment, and also – surprisingly – a little sympathetic for my dad.

We did pick up a pizza on the way home, but Jamie drew the line at letting us eat it in the car. 'Pete's a reasonable bloke, but he won't be happy if the courtesy car smells of mozzarella and anchovies in the morning.'

As it was still not yet dark, we decided to have an impromptu picnic supper in the park. Jamie spread his denim jacket on the ground in lieu of a blanket, and we sat on a grassy slope overlooking the boating pond, which was glistening as though shot through with gold as the sun sank lower in the sky.

'Will your dad give your gran any grief on the way back to the home?' Jamie asked, tearing off an enormous triangle of pizza from the box between us.

'Not if my mum has anything to do with it,' I replied, sinking my teeth into a considerably smaller piece.

'Maybe all of this will turn out to be a good thing?' Jamie suggested optimistically, in the way of someone who still hasn't fully grasped the way my dad's mind worked. 'You know, maybe thinking his mum was sick, and then learning it wasn't her, will have made him realise how much he cares about her, and that he only wants her to be happy.'

'Do you spend all your free time reading Mills and Boon books or watching movies on the Lifetime channel, by any chance?'

Jamie laughed good-naturedly, but understood my reference.

'Dad *does* want Gran to be happy, but only in a way that's acceptable to him. So, quietly grieving for Grandad in a respectful widow kind of way is fine, but telling the world that she's fallen in love with another woman... *not* so much.'

'It's a generation thing,' Jamie said, nodding towards the final slice of pizza, asking permission to eat it if I was done. It was a continual mystery to me how someone who ate that much could possibly have practically no fat on their body – or at least the bits of it I'd seen.

'I think it's more of a Gerald Preston thing,' I replied with a resigned sigh as I began gathering up our empty drink cans and the pizza box. The sun was now all the way set, and I was suddenly very, very tired. It had been quite an exhausting day.

Jamie got to his feet and extended a hand, pulling me up and against him. His body was taut and firm against the soft planes of mine and as his arms tightened around me, my face was already tilting up, ready for his kiss.

'You taste of pizza,' I murmured quite a few minutes later.

'Should I apologise?' Jamie asked, throwing an arm around my shoulders as we began to walk back to the parked car.

I smiled up at him in the darkness. 'No. Never.'

26

'Frank is dead.'

I looked up from the keyboard, the final notes of
Für Elise still reverberating in the air. For once the residents'
lounge was empty except for my grandmother and me. I
looked at her blankly, and hated the way Dad's continual
insistence that she was suffering from early dementia kept
intruding into my thoughts. It was certainly there now after
this peculiar non sequitur.

'Frank... my tortoise?' I asked hesitantly, because I could
think of no one else with that name. Not that my suggestion
made much more sense than Gran had, because I'd been
reliably informed that Frank had 'gone to live on a farm' at
least ten years ago.

Gran gave a small snort of laughter, which thankfully
dispelled my fears in an instant. She was still here, one
hundred per cent. 'No, Mandy. Not your tortoise,' she
corrected patiently. 'I'm talking about Frank, as in Mary
and Frank.'

'Ohhh,' I said, as I successfully plucked the face of the

Sunnymede resident from my memory banks, and then immediately followed it with another 'Oh', this one more sorrowful. Mary and Frank were one of the few married couples in the home. They'd moved in several years ago, and were so devoted you'd be forgiven for thinking they were joined at the hip. They did everything together, and were often found sitting huddled close at the back of this very room while I played. I'd even seen Frank sitting beside his wife in the compact hairdressing salon Sunnymede provided for its residents.

Coincidentally, that was where Josie was right now, and to be honest I was surprised Gran hadn't wanted to accompany her, because since Josie had come out of hospital the two of them had become every bit as inseparable as Mary and Frank.

I felt guilty for having briefly forgotten who Frank was, and also genuinely saddened as I wondered how Mary would cope without him. A shiver ran through me. It was the same every time a Sunnymede resident passed away. It felt like death was a predator on the Serengeti, picking off the weakest of the elderly one by one. And every time it happened I felt as though I was one dreadful step closer to losing my grandmother.

'That really is sad,' I said.

'Frank was in a lot of pain,' Gran said pragmatically. 'And now he's not.' I realised it didn't matter how regularly I visited Sunnymede, I'd never be as sanguine about dying as its residents were. Not that Gran had felt that way when she'd almost lost Josie. Far from it.

'The reason I mentioned Frank is that it ties in with some news I have.'

I leant back on the piano stool and eyed my grandmother warily. 'More news, Gran? I'm not sure we've all fully recovered from the last surprise bulletin yet.' Dad certainly hadn't, but Gran knew that anyway.

My grandmother smiled, looking suddenly more than a little coy. 'What I have to say is connected to that in a way, and also to Mary.'

'I don't follow you.'

There was a look of suppressed excitement twinkling in her eyes. Whatever she was about to tell me was clearly important to her.

'With Frank gone, Mary's decided to move out and live with her daughter.'

She paused for a moment; there was nothing whatsoever wrong with her dramatic timing. 'Which means their double suite will shortly become vacant... and the management team have asked if Josie and I are interested in taking it.' She was looking at me now with a child-on-Christmas-morning kind of anticipation. 'What do you think?'

What I *thought* was that this time it might be my *dad* who'd have the heart attack, but there was no way on earth I was going to say that to her. I'd walk barefoot over hot coals rather than extinguish that look from her face.

'I think that sounds absolutely wonderful, Gran, if that's what you and Josie both want.'

To be honest, the more I thought about it, the more sense it made. Gran was hardly ever to be found in her own room these days. Despite the home having an excellent team of qualified nurses, Gran was happier keeping a close eye on Josie. And it wasn't hard to understand why.

It was only when Josie was well on the mend that I learnt

it had actually been Gran who'd found her, collapsed on the floor of her room. If Gran hadn't decided to knock on her friend's door when she did... well, it could all have ended very differently. So I understood why sharing the double accommodation made perfect sense. But it was more than that, which I quickly realised when Gran began to speak in an almost wistful voice.

'It would be very nice to share our "goodnights" and "good mornings" without having to walk down a corridor to do so. And after what happened, it makes you realise you never know how many of those you have left.'

'Don't say that, Gran,' I pleaded, sliding my arm through hers as we walked back to her room.

'Life's precious, sweetheart. We shouldn't waste a single minute of it.'

Gran waited until the door was safely shut on her suite before revealing a concern that she obviously hadn't felt comfortable voicing in the more public areas.

'The thing that's troubling me, Mandy,' she began, already looking a little flushed, 'is I'm not sure what people will think of us "moving in" together.'

I hadn't really thought of it in those terms, and when I did I could feel my cheeks heating up in a race to match the colour of Gran's. This really wasn't a conversation anyone should be having with their grandmother.

'Will people think that Josie and I are "living in sin"?' she asked.

'I don't think anyone calls it that any more, Gran,' I said, trying to shut the door on some very unnecessary visuals that were trying to push their way into my head. 'Nobody thinks anything at all about people living together these days.'

'Well, they did in my generation.'

I opened my mouth to tactfully remind her that we were actually in a different century now, but she shot me down with a very effective winning argument. 'And everyone at Sunnymede *is* from my generation, not yours.'

As much as I wanted to make light of Gran's concerns, because they seemed so groundless to me, it was impossible to ignore the worry lingering in her eyes. Gran and Josie were the least likely people on the planet to be cast in the role of Scarlet Woman, and yet I suspected that was what she was afraid of.

There *had* to be a solution, and there was, a glaringly obvious one, and surprisingly it wasn't me who found it, it was Josie, who joined us a moment later fresh from her visit to the hairdresser. She kissed Gran on the cheek and then kissed me too, which was a new thing, but really rather lovely, as it felt as though we were already becoming part of the same family. As she did so, the magazine she had tucked under her arm slipped free and tumbled to the floor. I bent to retrieve it.

'They said it was all right for me to take it back to my room and finish reading it,' she explained on a rush, believing my furrowed brow was because she was in possession of this week's edition of *Hello!* magazine. But that wasn't the reason. Wheels were turning in my head; ideas forming and slotting into place. Of course. How perfect. Why did I not think of this before?

I held the magazine where it had fallen open on a double-page spread of two well-known actors, both dressed in

Daz-white designer suits, exchanging their vows in the grounds of a stately mansion.

'That's it!' I cried, practically bouncing on my feet as the solution to everything was quite literally set out before us. 'There's the answer to your problem.'

Two sets of cataract-impaired eyes turned my way, their faces equally mystified.

'You should get married.'

'Have you lost your mind? Have they?'

Dad's reaction was disappointing, but hardly a surprise.

'As if my mother's head wasn't filled with enough crazy ideas, you had to go and add one more.'

'Getting married isn't crazy. Not if they love each other.' Dad was looking at me as though I might possibly be someone he'd never met before. My eyes dropped guiltily to my plate, but there was no help there among the lamb chops and peas.

'I thought after what happened with Josie you finally understood how important she is to Gran,' I said, addressing my words to my dinner. A single tear plopped silently into my gravy, swiftly followed by another.

'As a friend,' Dad muttered tersely, attacking his own chop ferociously, as if it had personally offended him.

'I think it's quite clear by now, Gerald, that your mother's feelings for Josie go much deeper than that.'

Dad's eyes flew to Mum. *Et tu, Brute?* they seemed to shriek.

'I know Gran was a bit taken aback when I first mentioned it...' I began, slow to realise I was slipping my own head into a noose. My voice trailed off as Dad slowly turned his face towards me.

'So you admit this was all your idea? You and those misguided idiots at the home. What were they even thinking of, suggesting that they should share a suite?'

'Oh, I don't know, Dad. Being supportive, maybe? You should give it a try sometime.'

'Mandy.' It was a single word, but I recognised Mum's tone from a thousand childhood reprimands.

'Sorry,' I mumbled. 'But Gran needs someone in her corner and I just want her to be happy – that's the only reason I suggested it. And I'm sure they'd have thought of this themselves... eventually,' I defended. My eyes were once again swimming with tears. There were two dads now instead of one, and both of them looked furious.

Would Gran and Josie have come up with this idea if I hadn't planted it in their heads? I couldn't say for sure. And admittedly there *had* been a long awkward moment of dumbfounded silence when I'd suggested the marriage idea.

Gran's eyes had dropped to the magazine in my hands. 'I rather thought that kind of wedding was only for famous people and celebrities?'

'No, Gran. Not at all. Same-sex marriage is for anyone who wants it. It's been legal here for years.'

She was shaking her head from side to side and Josie's face was locked in wide-eyed astonishment. They weren't ready for this, I realised, far too late to take it back. Maybe it *was* a generation thing. Or perhaps it was too soon after Grandad, or too much for the Sunnymede residents to accept. I was so busy feeling pleased with myself for having found a solution that I'd failed to notice I'd crossed a big fat line. I might have done it with the best of intentions, but I'd suggested something that had no place coming from me. It should have come from them.

They needed to discuss this in private, and I hastily made a flimsy excuse about having left my sheet music in the lounge and exited Gran's suite almost at a run. The last thing I saw as I shut the door were the two elderly ladies, wearing matching stunned expressions, staring at each other.

There really is only so long you can pretend to be looking for something that isn't lost in the first place. After twenty minutes in the residents' lounge, I realised I was going to have to go back and face the music. Pun totally unintended. I knocked lightly on Gran's door, my rehearsed apology for interfering all cued up and ready to go. But the words died on my lips when I saw them sitting side by side, holding hands. Josie's wrinkled cheeks were damp with tears and as she lifted up a hand to wipe them away I saw my grandmother's signet ring was now sitting on the third finger of her left hand.

Josie's smile was radiant through her tears as she looked at me. 'I've never had a proposal before. At my age, I never thought I'd hear anyone say those words to me.' And then she was crying again, and so was Gran, and so was I. It was one of the best moments of my life.

Unlike the one right now at the dinner table, which definitely felt like one of the worst.

'I've had enough of this,' declared my dad, getting to his feet so abruptly that his chair almost tumbled over. It wasn't entirely clear whether he'd had enough of the situation or his dinner, which, despite being his favourite meal, had scarcely been touched. 'I'm going out for a walk.'

My mother glanced at the rivulets of rain streaming down the kitchen window.

'In this?'

I don't think he'd even noticed the torrential summer storm, but once he'd made up his mind about something, it took a miracle for Dad to ever change it. Perhaps it would have been better for everyone if I'd remembered that a little earlier myself.

'But *apart* from watching countless episodes of *Don't Tell the Bride*, what do you actually know about organising a wedding?'

'That's not enough?' I asked, stifling my laugh so that it wouldn't travel beyond my closed bedroom door. On the other end of the phone, Jamie chuckled warmly.

'All I have to do is not have the ceremony on a football pitch, hold the reception in a rugby club, or get the bride dropped in by parachute.'

'Piece of cake then,' said Jamie.

'Ugh... cake, I forgot about that,' I said, reaching for a notepad where my scribbled 'to do' list was growing worryingly.

'Well, if you need a chauffeur, count me in,' Jamie assured. 'I'm sure Pete would let me borrow the car again if you want it.'

I sighed softly. Who knew that planning a wedding involved so much preparation? Not that I regretted telling Gran and Josie that I was happy to be their unofficial wedding planner, but perhaps I should have given a bit more thought to what I was actually taking on.

A light warning knock on the door gave me just enough time to whisper a hurried goodbye to Jamie, before Mum slipped into my room. She was carrying a mug of tea, the Preston family equivalent of a white flag. In a way I hoped looked entirely nonchalant, I flipped over the notepad so that it was face down on the duvet.

'How's Dad? Has he calmed down yet?'

Mum motioned for me to move up and perched on the edge of my mattress. I was suddenly thrown back a decade, to a time of bedtime stories and cuddles goodnight. How much simpler it had been to be a good daughter back then.

'Your dad is fine,' said Mum with a sigh. 'Just as long as no one mentions the words wedding, or double suite, or even the name Josie.'

'He was so good when Josie was sick though,' I sighed. 'Arranging and paying for a cab to take Gran to and from the hospital every day. I really thought that meant he was coming around to the idea.'

Mum raised her eyebrows. They were neat and light brown, and could hold entire conversations without her lips ever needing to move.

'Well... I'd *hoped* he had,' I completed sadly.

We were both silent for a while and then Mum glanced down at the notepad on the duvet beside me. I'd often suspected mothers had X-ray vision, and this just confirmed it.

'You're going to help her arrange it, aren't you?'

There was no point in lying, she'd know straight away if I was.

'I have to, Mum. She has no one else to do it for her.'

Mum nodded, as though this was entirely what she had suspected. 'I can't help you, Mandy, you know that, don't you? It would hurt your dad too much.'

This time it was my turn to nod. Asking for her assistance would put her in an impossible position, making her choose between two people she loved. And there was already far too much of that going on in our family at the moment.

'I know that, Mum. Don't worry.'

'Have you thought about how much this will all cost? Weddings are expensive and most of Gran's money is set aside to pay for Sunnymede.'

There were pound signs next to each bullet point in my notebook, and every one of them had a question mark beside it.

'Not really. I'll find the money from somewhere.'

Mum got to her feet, and her smile as she looked down at me meant more than anything she could ever say. She put her hand into her pocket, drew out an envelope and passed it to me. I lifted the flap, gasping softly when I saw the bundle of crisp, bank-fresh twenty-pound notes.

'It's not much,' she apologised, 'but it will get you started.'

My head was bobbing up and down, because at that moment words were beyond me. She didn't need them anyway; she knew. She bent and kissed the top of my head and suddenly I wished I really was seven years old again.

'Thank you, Mummy.' How many years had it been since I'd called her that? Too many.

'This is just between you and me,' she whispered, giving me one last hug before heading towards the door.

I flopped back on the pillows after she'd gone, my head

still spinning. All my life people had been telling me how very much I was like my grandmother, Amanda. And as much as I'd always loved hearing that, tonight, for the very first time, I really hoped that I was also a great deal like my mother. Because she was amazing.

27

The office was bright and filled with sunshine. Although I'd visited Sunnymede hundreds of times over the past five years, it was the first time I'd ever been inside the manager's office. I'd waited nervously outside her room, feeling very much as though I'd been summoned by the head teacher. Not that I was familiar with that particular sensation – although I'm sure Jamie could tell me what it felt like.

'Mandy,' said Mrs Blackwood, extending an arm to shake my hand.

I did a quick swipe of mine against the side of my jeans before completing the ritual. There was absolutely no reason to be nervous, and yet I was. On an anxiety scale, this scored way higher than the bunch of exams I'd recently taken, or even a root canal.

'Do come in,' the manager urged, nodding to a straight-backed chair on one side of the desk, while she slid on to her leather swivel one. She offered refreshments, but after a quick glance at the document-strewn desk, I politely declined. Being anxious always made me clumsy, and drowning her paperwork with coffee wasn't going to help win her over.

Mrs Blackwood's immaculately styled bob swung gently from side to side as she spoke.

'I understand from your grandmother that you're intending to help organise a wedding, and that you hope to hold it here?'

My fingers curled into tight fists, the nails making tiny half-moon indents in my palms. Were my plans about to be scuppered before they'd even begun? I realised too late that I should have spoken to this woman *first* to get her approval. It was a stupid rookie error.

'Yes. Gran and Josie don't really know where to begin. Not that I do either, I've not arranged a wedding before, but you know... I'm happy to google away until I find out what I need to do.' God, I was babbling like an idiot. If this was a job interview, I'd definitely not be getting the position.

Mrs Blackwood looked at me for a long moment, her face as inscrutable as a poker player's. 'What can we do to help you?'

The breath left my lungs in a rush, and relief made me sag in the chair like a deflating crash dummy.

'I thought you were going to say we couldn't go ahead.'

To her credit, Mrs Blackwood looked genuinely mystified. 'Why on earth would you think that?'

I could feel my cheeks growing hot, which had absolutely nothing to do with the warmth of the room.

'Well, you know, what with it being a same-sex relationship... I wasn't sure if the other residents would find that kind of...'

Mrs Blackwood laughed. 'I think you'll find that by the

time most people have reached their eighties they've pretty much seen or done everything. Old age is a bit like a Kevlar vest – not much shocks you by then.'

'That's really great to hear. Gran's news hasn't been quite so well received at home.' Was I being disloyal, sharing personal family issues with this woman? Probably not, for it seemed she already knew.

'Yes, I've had a couple of... interesting... phone conversations with your father.'

I gave an embarrassingly noisy gulp.

'I'm sorry about that.'

Mrs Blackwood waved my apology aside with a neatly manicured hand. 'Oh, please don't worry about that. Disgruntled relatives go with the territory.' Her face softened then, as she leant a little closer towards me. 'We're used to dealing with family grief and the different ways it can manifest.' I frowned, not following her meaning. 'I'm no expert, but perhaps your dad's issues are tied up with the loss of his own father?'

How was it possible that this woman, this virtual stranger, had seen through the bluster and anger and realised that, beneath it all, Dad might still be unbelievably sad?

'Anyway,' continued Mrs Blackwood, steering our conversation back on track. 'We've held several celebration ceremonies here at Sunnymede in the past, and we'd be delighted to host Amanda and Josie's. Although they *will* have to visit a registry office too.'

I nodded. I'd done my research and understood that a registry office ceremony would be needed to legalise the marriage.

'But this will be Sunnymede's first wedding with *two*

brides,' continued Mrs Blackwood enthusiastically, 'and I can't tell you how excited the staff are about it. Your grandmother and Josie are both very popular. If you'll allow it, quite a few of us would like to attend the wedding.'

'Oh, absolutely, the more the merrier,' I cried.

I left the manager's office almost in a daze and practically skipped along the corridor to Gran's room. For the first time, I was starting to feel incredibly excited.

'Let me have another look at that list,' asked Gran. Some new lines joined the ones time had left on her brow as she began flicking through my notebook. Admittedly, the number of itemised bullet points had continued to increase alarmingly and now covered almost two lined pages.

'Surely we don't need all these things,' Gran protested, trying to reach for my pen to begin an edit I was sure I wouldn't like. I refused to hand it over.

'You might not *need* them, but wouldn't it be nice for you and Josie to have them?'

Gran's expression softened like butter in the sun. 'You are such a sweet girl, Mandy. And I really do appreciate all this work you've done, but it's not the *getting* married, it's the *being* married that we're both looking forward to. And you don't need flowers or cakes or a big fancy frock to do that. And besides, I've done all that before,' she reminded me.

'Josie hasn't.' I could have argued with Gran until well past midnight, and I doubt I'd have found a more compelling point to make.

'We'll cut some things,' I compromised, rapidly scribbling through *Invitations, Sugared almonds* and *Printed serviettes*.

But when Gran tapped her finger beside an item I'd written in bold capital letters, I dug my heels in with the obstinacy of a mule.

'Gran, you *have* to have a new dress. You're the bride – well, one of them.'

'I've several perfectly nice outfits in my wardrobe that I've hardly worn. I could dress them up with a new hat. I *do* love a hat.'

'But Gran, if you don't wear a wedding dress then Josie won't either.'

She looked at me for a long, contemplative moment, but I'd won that round and we both knew it.

I leant over and hugged her warmly. 'Why don't you at least let me *try* to find you a dress, and then if I can't get one, you can wear something you already own.'

'With a hat,' she added determinedly. 'It's not a wedding without a hat.'

I'd walked the length of the high street twice before despondency began to set in. I didn't even bother venturing inside the exclusive bridalwear shops. My budget was way too limited for those. I had hoped to find something bridal-*ish* in one of the high street chains, but after four hours of shopping I had to admit I'd failed.

I thought when I met Jamie for lunch I'd be carrying an armload of carrier bags, like Julia Roberts in *Pretty Woman*. Instead, as I slipped on to the bench seat beside him in the burger bar, I didn't have a single purchase.

'No luck?' Jamie asked, giving me a sympathetic hug.

'I feel like I'm letting her down.'

'Of course you're not,' he defended loyally.

I picked dolefully at my fries when they arrived in their little metal basket. It was a sad day when even triple-fried potato couldn't cheer me up.

'How important *is* it to find a dress, anyway?'

I lifted my head and looked at him as though he was speaking in a language I'd never heard before. It was probably Martian.

'Oh,' he replied, backtracking rapidly with a look of apology.

'It's not like shopping for some second-hand car repair manuals you know, it's far more...'

My voice trailed off and the burger bar suddenly faded out of focus as I remembered standing in a charity shop, where something had snagged my attention and called out to me, even though I wasn't entirely sure what it was. All I knew was that it was white and flowing and somehow it felt as though I was *meant* to see it. I stood up so abruptly my fries flew everywhere.

'I have to go.'

Jamie looked around in confusion. Several customers on adjacent tables did exactly the same. 'Are you sick?' he asked worriedly, starting to get to his feet.

'No. No. I'm fine. Or I will be. Stay,' I urged, pushing my hand firmly against his shoulder. 'Finish your lunch.'

'But where are you going?'

'To buy a wedding dress,' I replied, already weaving through the tables and practically running in my haste to reach the exit.

★★★

In a film, the dress would have been on a mannequin in the shop window, but there was nothing on display except a teetering pile of board games and a collection of mismatched crockery. There was a snaking queue of customers at the counter so I headed straight for the clothing racks, certain that's where I would find the dress. A white dress should have been easy to spot, and yet I spun the carousel rack several times before admitting it wasn't here. Had they sold it already? Did it even exist in the first place?

I joined the queue for the counter, shifting anxiously from one foot to the other until it was finally my turn to be served.

'Hello,' I began. My voice sounded every bit as jittery as the rest of me. 'Do you have a wedding dress for sale?'

The woman shook her head.

'No, I'm afraid not. We hardly ever get them in here. People either keep them or sell them privately.'

Disappointment crashed over me like a breaking wave. I turned to go, but something stopped me. 'Could one have come in without you knowing about it?'

She gave me a look. *Way to go, Mandy. Tell her she's incompetent at her job, and then she's sure to want to help you.*

'It's only that I was in here a couple of weeks ago and there was a couple who I thought brought one in. The woman was in a wheelchair.'

The shop assistant was looking at me now as though I was a shoo-in for the Most-Troublesome-Customer-of-the-Day award.

I turned sadly towards the door. 'Oh well, never mind. It was always a bit of a long shot.'

I was one step away from the street when a different voice called out to me.

'Wait!'

I turned and immediately recognised the woman who'd just emerged from the back room. She was the volunteer who'd served the couple I was talking about.

'I remember those people, and you're right, they *did* bring in a wedding dress.'

I could feel the excitement fizzing through me, and my smile was growing so wide it was already making my cheeks ache.

'I'll see if we still have it.'

She was gone for quite some time, but I waited with a degree of patience I'm not usually known for. Finally she emerged, carrying a box that looked familiar.

'You won't believe it. It had somehow got buried beneath a pile of pet blankets,' she explained, setting the container down on the counter. 'If you hadn't asked me to look for it, I doubt we'd *ever* have found it.'

Her fingers were working on the fastenings of the box, and it took a superhuman effort to restrain myself from pushing her hands aside so I could open it quicker. Finally, the lid was freed, and as she unfolded the shroud of tissue paper, I looked down at the dress my grandmother was always meant to wear. Don't ask me how I knew that, I just did.

'I'm afraid there's a small tear and a few marks on the hem, made by the wheelchair, I believe,' the assistant volunteered.

'That's fine,' I said, scarcely giving the flaws a second glance.

'It's a very good make. It originally came from Fleurs, the expensive bridal shop,' the woman continued, pushing for a sale that was already a foregone conclusion.

'May I?' I asked, lifting the dress from its box and holding it up to catch the light. The delicate silver embroidery and scattered crystals twinkled under the overhead fluorescents.

'Would you like to try it on?' asked the assistant.

I shook my head as I began folding the cloud-like fabric back into the box. 'It's not for me, it's for my grandmother. But I can already see it will fit her perfectly.' And it would, because it would also fit me. As tempted as I was to try it on, I knew I never would. Somewhere out there was a dress I would one day wear to my very own wedding. But as beautiful as this one was, this wasn't it. This dress was Gran's.

'You found a dress!' To his credit, Jamie sounded genuinely delighted. His arms circled me in a hug that practically lifted my feet from the pavement.

'Not *a* dress, *the* dress,' I corrected on a laugh, almost giddy with a combination of elation and relief. 'Gran is going to love it.'

'So are we all done now?' There was a hopefulness in his voice that revealed I'd not made a shopaholic out of him yet. Perhaps that would have been one miracle too many, even for today.

'Well, I still need to arrange for flowers and buy a hat for Gran – she seems to think the marriage will be annulled if she isn't wearing one. But you don't have to spend the rest of your Saturday helping me. I realise it's not much fun for you.'

'Are you kidding me? Shopping for flowers and dresses and er... other wedding stuff... it's what I live for.'

I smiled. How could Dad not see that as far as boyfriends went, this one was practically perfect?

'Well, there's a bridal salon at the end of this road,' I said. 'It's way out of my price range, but...'

'You're feeling lucky?'

I lifted my head and dropped a kiss he hadn't been expecting on his lips.

'I am now.'

Through the window, Fleurs was an explosion of white. It was a bridal version of Aladdin's cave, with lace, chiffon, satin and a generous helping of bling. Little girls all over the world dreamt of places like this – some big girls did too. It was quite a surprise to discover I might be one of them.

I stepped back on to the pavement with a sigh. Jamie's hand fell from my waist as he took my place at the glass, hands cupped against the pane to cut out the glare of the afternoon sun.

'I'm going to say you *definitely* can't afford anything from here,' he declared, his breath forming an oval cloud on the pristine glass.

A sharp rapping sound made us both jump as a face appeared on the other side of the window. The woman, dressed entirely in black, was a dramatic silhouette against the white background. Her hair gleamed like the polished ebony of piano keys. And if looks could kill, Jamie was dead on the spot.

He flashed the woman one of his guaranteed-to-work

dazzling smiles. Nothing. Not even a glimmer of a response. It was the first time I'd ever seen him fail. With a mouthed *Sorry*, he wiped the glass clean with the sleeve of his denim jacket.

Feeling suddenly far less positive, I reached for the dress box that Jamie had been carrying under his arm.

'Why don't you wait out here for me? I have a feeling I'm not going to be long.'

She was scary. No, she was more than scary, she was like a character in a fairy tale, the kind that gives little kids nightmares. It was just as well I'd decided to venture into Fleurs alone, as I very much doubted that oil-stained car mechanics were permitted to cross the threshold. Come to that, I'm not sure I was entirely welcome either.

'Erm... I'm sorry about that... the window thing, I mean. I couldn't see if you were open.'

'We *are* open,' the woman confirmed with a glacial smile. 'Although I'm afraid we cannot accommodate walk-ins. Fleurs operates on a strictly-by-appointment system. Do you have one?'

It was quite obvious that we both knew I didn't.

'Erm no. I don't. I was just wondering if you sold hats – for brides, that is?'

The woman had the kind of nose that was perfect for looking down at people, and she was doing so right now. Her eyes flicked briefly towards the door, as though this might be a very un-funny prank that had now run its course.

I sighed. This had definitely been a mistake. I crossed the oasis of grey carpet to the door, my shoulders slumped. 'I only asked because I've just bought one of your dresses for my grandmother from a charity shop and was hoping you might have a hat that would go with it.'

Gwendoline Flowers clearly had several issues with that sentence.

'You've purchased a Fleurs gown?' Surprise number one.

'Yes, a few minutes ago.'

'From a…' She hesitated, her lips struggling to form the words. 'From a *charity shop*?'

'Yes.'

'For your grandmother?'

I nodded.

Her head inclined at an angle that looked quite precarious, she said, 'How intriguing.' She looked at the cardboard box beneath my arm. 'Is that the dress?'

My fingers tightened on the cardboard container, as though she might be about to rugby-tackle it from me. I placed the box in her outstretched hands and she carried it to an antique desk in the corner of the shop. Her nimble fingers made short work of the fastenings. By chance, I happened to be looking at her face at the precise moment she peeled back the protective layer of tissue paper. I saw her professional mask falter, slip, and then dissolve away as if it had never been.

'This dress…' Her voice was clearly shocked. 'I *know* this dress.'

It was a curious comment, and one I had no answer to. Saying nothing seemed the safest option at this point.

She nodded to a velvet-covered seat. 'Please sit down. Tell me about the woman who is going to wear this dress next. Tell me everything.'

'I thought you were never coming back. I was getting ready to launch a rescue mission,' said Jamie, when thirty minutes later I emerged from the shop in a daze. In one hand I held the box containing Gran's wedding dress, in the other a bag bearing the Fleurs insignia.

Gwendoline Flowers had listened to my story without interruption. Without intending to, I'd somehow told her everything: about Gran, about Josie, even about my dad. By the time I was done, I was highly embarrassed to realise my cheeks were damp with tears I hadn't even noticed had escaped.

'Do you know, I believe I *do* have a hat that will go with the dress,' she announced, swivelling from me on a delicate black stiletto heel.

She returned moments later carrying a gorgeous satin pillbox hat with a birdcage veil dusted with tiny crystals. She held it up and I caught a glimpse of a swinging price tag before she quickly ripped it off. But not so fast that I hadn't seen how much it cost. My heart had plummeted, because I already knew the hat would suit Gran perfectly.

'I… er, should probably have mentioned that I don't have very much to spend on a hat.'

'Well, you're in luck, as this hat is from last season's collection and was about to go into our sample sale.'

'Really?' I asked, my incredulity so obvious it was practically laughable. 'That's really kind of you, but I still doubt I can afford it.'

'The hat is now twenty pounds.'

'But it's worth way more than that – I saw the price tag.'

'You really haven't grasped the concept of haggling, have you?' Gwendoline asked, the trace of a smile playing on her lips. 'You're meant to talk me down, not up.'

In a daze, I withdrew the notes from the envelope in my bag and passed them to her. She wrote a receipt and wrapped the hat in tissue paper, as though this was a perfectly normal transaction, which we both knew was far from the truth.

As she walked me to the door, her eyes dropped to the box I was carrying. 'The dress you've bought is quite special. It has a history and your grandmother will actually be the *third* bride to wear it. Perhaps one day I'll write my memoirs and tell its story. Or maybe I should allow it to keep its secrets.'

She was talking about the gown as though it had a life and a will of its own, and while that should have really freaked me out, for some reason it didn't. Surprising myself almost as much as I did her, I turned at the door and impulsively hugged this woman who was a dressed-in-black fairy godmother.

'I can't thank you enough for this.'

I got the impression that Gwendoline Flowers didn't 'do' emotional and, as moving as the moment was, she wasn't about to start now.

'The dress found you and your grandmother. All I did was help with the accessories.'

'You did more than that,' I contradicted as she opened the shop door and gently ushered me from the premises.

28

There was an elephant in the room. A great big one. Its presence was so expected we should probably have set an extra place at the table and invited it to join us.

'More meat, anyone?' Dad asked, getting to his feet. My plate was still laden, but I nodded enthusiastically. Beneath the cover of the table I gave Jamie's ankle a subtle kick and he hastily added his voice to mine.

'Yes please, Mr Preston, it's delicious.'

That was probably the moment when Dad should have said, *Please, call me Gerald.* Instead, he just picked up the platter and headed for the kitchen.

The moment the door swung to a close behind him, the conversation switched back to the topic that had been held on 'pause' since my father had entered the dining room. It felt like a scene straight out of a Richard Curtis film, which is a lot less amusing in real life than it is on the big screen.

Today was the last Sunday of the month, a date when Gran always joined us for a home-cooked roast. It was also six days until the wedding, and was probably Dad's last chance to voice his disapproval. In an act of genius or total lunacy (I still couldn't decide which), Mum had suggested I invite Jamie to join us: *Your dad is far less likely to say anything negative about Gran's wedding with Jamie present, and he won't be hostile to Jamie in front of your grandmother.* She'd smiled at me with the delight of someone who'd just cured a disease, and I didn't have the heart to point out a third scenario, wherein Dad went for a double whammy and decided to have a go at *both* of our guests.

The last few weeks had been quite tense at home, with Dad doing an outstanding impression of an ostrich by pretending the wedding simply wasn't going to happen. He'd taken to leaving the room whenever the W-word was mentioned, or turning up the television to eardrum-damaging levels to drown out the conversation. It was a middle-aged man's equivalent of sticking his fingers in his ears and trilling *La, La, La, La.* But even he must surely realise that nothing short of an act of God could stop the wedding now.

'Mum's managed to get the stains out of your dress and done an amazing job on repairing that small tear,' I confided, my voice low.

Gran's eyes went fondly to her daughter-in-law, whose efforts to help with the last-minute preparations had of necessity been highly covert. 'That's really kind of you, Natalie. Thank you so much.'

Last night, Mum had pulled me into the spare bedroom, where Gran's wedding dress was hidden in a suitcase beneath the bed. She'd flipped open the clasps to reveal a gown now restored to its former glory. My enthusiastic reaction made me sound like I was auditioning for a detergent commercial, but she really *had* done an amazing job.

'And what's this?' I'd asked, picking up a small beaded bolero that she'd added to the suitcase.

'I thought Gran might like it as her "something borrowed". As incredible as your grandmother is, even *she* might struggle to pull off a strapless dress in her seventies.'

'Good point,' I'd said, giving her an enormous hug, which thanked her in ways I'd never be able to find the right words to do.

'I just wish I could see it on the day,' my mother said now, her voice a whisper and full of regret.

'You can,' I insisted.

A warm, wrinkled hand covered mine on the tabletop. 'No, she can't, sweetheart. Your mother's loyalty is to your dad. He's hurt and confused by my decision, and your mum needs to be with him. I understand that.'

'I just wish I could—'

The door swung open and Dad came in carrying a replenished platter.

'You wish you could what?' he asked his wife, setting down the dish and reaching for his glass of wine. Was I the only one who'd noticed he'd already refilled it several times more than he usually did?

'Make Yorkshires as good as the packet ones,' Mum replied, with the kind of quick thinking that made me realise she was far better at this undercover stuff than I would ever be. As much as I was looking forward to Gran and Josie's wedding, life would be far less stressful when it was over and done with.

'Is your father in the motor trade too?' Dad asked, which, apart from 'More potatoes?', was the first question he'd asked Jamie directly.

'No, sir. He actually runs his own management consultancy company.'

I could practically see the wheels and gears realigning in my dad's head as he assimilated that information. That's the thing about accountants, they like to file things: tax forms... VAT returns... people into pigeonholes. Jamie wasn't conforming to the background he'd obviously created in his head.

To be fair, today he didn't look like he'd ever set foot inside a greasy workshop. I'd actually done a double take when I'd slipped out to meet him at the end of our street an hour ago. His blond surfer-style hair had been effectively tamed with a product he didn't usually use, and he was formally dressed in smartly cut trousers, a long-sleeved shirt and even a tie.

I'd felt like I was kissing a candidate for a bank manager's job when he pulled me into his arms. Thankfully, this virtual stranger still kissed just like Jamie did.

I'd leant back in his hold, and he'd read the look on my face with surprising accuracy. 'Lose the tie?' I'd nodded and grinned. 'I told Mum it was too much. But you know what mothers are like.'

I thought I did, but mine was continually surprising me these days.

With two shirt buttons undone, the top of one tattoo was just visible, but when Jamie went to refasten his shirt, I'd stilled his hands by covering them with my own. The skin of his chest was warm beneath my fingers and was having a curious effect on my own internal thermostat. Jamie's heart was beating beneath my palm in a quickened thud, which was either from nerves about the forthcoming lunch or a result of holding my body so close to his. I knew which one I wanted it to be.

'We should go,' Jamie had said, pushing me away from him with obvious reluctance. He turned to pick up the bottle of wine and bunch of flowers he'd set down on a wall and held them before him, as though waving a white flag, as we crossed the threshold and entered my house.

Dad was too well mannered to be overtly impolite, but I think Jehovah's Witnesses and door-to-door salesmen may possibly have received more enthusiastic welcomes at our door than my boyfriend did. Fortunately, Gran had filled the breach and had warmly embraced Jamie and thanked him once again for helping us out when Josie had been ill.

'I hope she's feeling better now?' Jamie asked politely, as we moved into the dining room and took our places at the table.

'She is.'

'Just in time for the wedding,' Jamie said unthinkingly. My dad's brows joined together to form a single disapproving line and he disappeared off to the kitchen, muttering something about a corkscrew. Hopefully to use on the wine and not Jamie, although it was hard to say for sure.

'Sorry,' Jamie said quietly, as the Preston family women eyed each other with virtually identical expressions.

'You did nothing wrong,' Gran assured him, giving his forearm a kindly pat. 'I'm the one who's put him in this bad mood, not you.'

To his credit, Dad returned to the room with an attitude reset and I could see he was clearly trying to make an effort. 'You were practising something on the piano quite late last night, Mandy.'

My eyes flew to Gran's old upright, which occupied one corner of the dining room. On the music stand was the piece Gran had asked me to learn in order to play at her wedding ceremony. A fact I'd obviously not shared with Dad.

'Sorry. I'll try to keep it down in future.'

Surprisingly, his eyes softened and he turned from me to look at his mother. 'It's that Pachelbel piece, isn't it?' he asked her, rather than me.

'I'm surprised you knew that, Gerald.'

He shook his head, and a small, unexpected smile appeared on his lips. 'You used to play it all the time when I was younger. It feels like the soundtrack of my childhood. You always said how much you loved it.'

'Pachelbel's Canon in D,' Gran said, looking at her son with the kind of love that only a parent knows. 'It's always been my favourite. Which was why I asked Mandy to—'

The unseen elephant gave a warning trumpeting cry, and whatever Gran had been about to say was instantly changed.

'That's why I asked Mandy to learn it.'

Dad gave a small but meaningful nod. He knows. I know he knows, I thought, watching as Dad stood up and began gathering the dirty plates together. Why can't he reach out to her? Why can't he see how much it would mean to her if he just accepted her choice?

★ ★ ★

We had to wait until both my parents were busy loading the dishwasher, fortuitously refusing all offers of help, to tell Gran the good news about the wedding flowers.

'I know we said we'd probably have to make do with whatever we could pick from the garden,' I told Gran, my words tumbling out on a rush in case the kitchen duties didn't take as long as I hoped.

We'd moved from the dining room to the lounge and I was excited to share the news that the last missing element of the wedding plans had miraculously fallen into place. And I hadn't done a thing to make that happen. It had all been Jamie.

Wedding flowers sorted

was the text he'd sent me two days ago.

Will pick you up at 3.30 to explain

The hands of the clock had been particularly sluggish as I sat through the rest of the afternoon's lessons to find out what he meant by that intriguing message.

He was parked outside the school gates in a car I didn't recognise.

'Stole another one?' I teased as I slipped into the passenger seat.

'We're taking it for a test drive to check the repairs,' he'd replied, a smile playing around the lips I'd just kissed. It made me want to do it all over again.

'So what did you mean about having sorted the flowers?' I asked, swivelling in my seat as I realised we were now in a part of town I didn't know very well.

We were stopped at traffic lights, and in answer Jamie took one hand from the wheel and slid it behind me. His fingers grazed the inch of bare skin between the hem of my T-shirt and the waistband of my jeans, but that wasn't his target. His hand slipped into the back pocket of my Levis. As pleasant as the sensation was as his fingers explored the confines of the pocket, I was mystified.

'Are you looking for something specific?'

The lights changed and his hand went back to the wheel as we pulled away. 'The card that woman gave you.'

I looked at him blankly for a moment and then remembered the soggy rectangle of cardboard I'd retrieved after accidentally leaving it in the pocket when the jeans went through the wash cycle. My mouth fell open into a small O as I realised too late how significant that ruined business card could have been. 'Oh bugger, that woman we helped had a florist shop, didn't she? I'd forgotten all about that.'

'Luckily for you, she *didn't* forget,' Jamie said, sounding just a little bit smug. I was prepared to give him that, because I thought I could see now where our unexpected mystery tour was going to lead us.

'So this morning she turns up at the garage to get some work done, which is weird because she's not a regular customer, but even more bizarre is that she sees me and instantly recognises me. I have no idea how she remembered who I was.'

I smiled, loving the way he was truly unaware that he

had *that* kind of face, the kind that women of all ages would *always* remember.

'So I figured, what the hell, there's no harm in asking, is there? So I told her about the wedding you were planning for your gran and how you still hadn't sorted out the flowers, and she said she'd be happy to provide them. That's where we're going now,' he declared. 'Or rather where we are now,' he corrected, pulling into a parking space directly outside the shop with the very unusual name: Crazy Daisy.

As much as I didn't want to burst his bubble, one look at the area told me that even with a generous discount we weren't going to be able to afford to shop for wedding flowers here.

'She said not to worry about it,' Jamie said, with so much confidence that I found myself climbing out of the car and joining him on the pavement. Still feeling as though we were probably wasting everyone's time, I let him take hold of my hand and lead me into the shop.

The owner, whose name was Beth, was absolutely lovely. Apparently Jamie had already given her the date of the wedding, and even though it was only a few days away, she assured me it shouldn't be a problem. She led us to a rustic-looking bench beneath a beautiful abstract painting of poppies and passed me a leather photograph album with the label 'Wedding Arrangements' on the cover. I opened it up and instantly fell in love with the first bouquet I saw, and then felt my heart plummet as I saw the discreet price label beside the photograph.

I shut the album and passed it straight back to her, anxious not to take up any more of her day.

'Everything in here is going to be beautiful, I can see that, but there's no way I can afford any of them, even if you were able to discount them.' I gave a small helpless shrug. 'I've only got twenty pounds left to spend.' I got to my feet, but before Jamie could join me Beth placed the album in my hands once again.

'Don't look at the prices,' she said with a smile. 'Just pick which ones you like. When they equal the amount I'd have had to pay a garage to come out to fix the tyre on my car, I'll let you know, and we'll call it quits.'

I chose two matching bouquets, buttonholes and corsages for the guests and even a table arrangement, and the owner of Crazy Daisy never once said it was time to stop.

As I explained it all to Gran, I couldn't help but feel there was something almost magical about this wedding, and the way everything had fallen into place. The dress, the hat, and now the flowers had all just simply presented themselves, as though I was somehow meant to find them. There was now only one thing missing that would make the day complete for Gran, I thought, as my eyes turned towards the kitchen. The day lost a little of its colour as I acknowledged there were some wishes that even an army of genies couldn't make come true.

29

Icried the first time Gran tried on her wedding dress. In keeping with tradition, Josie wasn't allowed to see it before the big day, and had been banished from the room before I lifted the lid from the dress box. Gran had looked down at the Fleurs gown for a very long time without saying a single word. Finally, she'd turned to me, her faded green eyes sparkling in exactly the same way my own had begun to do.

'You found it, Mandy. You found the dress I was meant to wear. It's absolutely perfect.'

'You don't even know if it will fit yet,' I'd replied, my voice oddly thick.

'It will fit,' she'd said, with a serenity I don't think I'd ever heard from her before.

And of course it had.

I therefore assumed I'd be immune when seeing her in the dress for the second time. I was wrong. It's just as well my mascara was the waterproof type, I thought, as Gran swam in and out of focus, making the task of fastening the lacing at the back of the dress an unexpected challenge. For a pianist, I was strangely all fingers and thumbs as I struggled to cinch the dress against Gran's slender frame. Although, as it turned out, I didn't need to worry about my keyboard-playing skills today.

'What's this?' Gran had asked when I'd passed her the slim plastic CD case when I arrived at her suite that morning.

'Pachelbel's Canon in D,' I said, running my finger beneath the title on the case. 'Your wedding music.'

'I can see that, Mandy. But *why* do we need it? I thought you were going to play it as I walked down the aisle?' It wasn't exactly an 'aisle' in the true definition of the word, more of a walkway between two rows of decorated chairs in the residents' lounge, but I knew what she meant.

'I know, Gran,' I said, taking her hands in mine. I immediately noticed the absence of the wedding ring my grandfather had given her. It must have been an especially poignant moment when she'd slipped it from the finger where it had lived for over half a century. 'I've practised the piece so many times I can play it note-perfect without the score,' I assured her, 'but the thing is... I don't want to be sitting down at the piano watching you walk up to meet Josie on your own. I want to walk beside you. I want to have your arm linked in mine.' Oh God, I was starting to well up again. People were right: weddings *do* make you cry. 'I want to give you away, Gran. Please say you'll let me.'

I think it was a 'yes' she mumbled in reply, before gathering me into her arms with surprising strength for a woman in her seventies.

'Oh my darling girl, of course yes. I would love that.' Gran's usually steady voice was decidedly choked, something I tactfully pretended not to notice.

The CD was now in Jamie's care, and was hopefully cued up and ready for him to press the 'play' button the moment Gran and I appeared at the doorway of the lounge.

Beth from Crazy Daisy had been extremely busy, transforming the room where the ceremony was to take place. The first thing I noticed was that there appeared to be far more flowers than I remembered ordering, but when I hesitantly questioned this, Beth brushed it aside, telling me they were from a cancelled order that she hadn't wanted to go to waste. For a supposedly astute businesswoman, she really was a terrible liar.

At home, the wedding day had begun awkwardly. I'd been buttering a slice of toast, careful not to get crumbs on the pale-blue silk sheath dress I'd borrowed from Mum.

'Isn't that your mother's?' Dad had asked, coming into the kitchen in his usual Saturday morning attire: old faded shorts and a T-shirt souvenir from a concert he'd attended before I was even born. It was his lawn-mowing outfit, and as he surveyed the clear skies with an approving nod, there was no need to ask if he'd had a last-minute change of heart.

'Yes. Mum said I could borrow it.' My chin was lifted as if in a challenge, but he simply gave an insouciant shrug and returned to the task of choosing which box of breakfast cereal to pull from the cupboard.

'It's the one I wore at that wedding last summer – you remember the one, where the girl from your office called it off at the last minute?'

Dad had his back to us, but I saw his shoulders tense up beneath the heavy metal tour dates etched across his T-shirt as Mum added: 'Let's hope the wedding today has a much happier outcome.'

While Jamie was loading the dress box on to the back seat of the car he'd borrowed, Mum walked with me to the door, pausing to give me an extra-long hug. 'Tell your Gran I wish her all the happiness in the world and that I'll be thinking of her this morning,' she whispered in my ear.

There was really no need to speak softly, for Dad was already firing up the Flymo, the drone of its motor obliterating the sound of our words. For a single moment he looked up and our eyes locked. He wanted to say something, I *know* he did, but pride was like a paralysis, seizing up his tongue, his throat, and working its way down to his heart.

'Well?' asked Gran, performing a careful twirl before me in the suite she would no longer occupy from this day forward.

'You look beautiful, Gran.'

Gran turned to study her reflection in the mirror. The jewels of the designer gown caught random rays of sunlight streaming through the window and enveloped her in a nimbus of twinkling gems. She reached for a pair of pearl-drop earrings, and was hooking them into place when a soft knock at her door heralded the arrival of Mrs Blackwood, Sunnymede's manager.

Gone was her usual pencil skirt and smart blouse. Today she was wearing a brightly patterned floral dress, with pink satin peep-toed shoes. She was dressed for a wedding, and she wasn't the only one. Every member of staff I'd seen that morning had forgone their usual workday clothing. As I journeyed back and forth between Gran's room and the lounge, I realised there seemed to be an unusually high number of staff on duty that day. It was only later that I learnt that even employees who weren't rostered to be working had given up their free time to attend. It was the kind of support that made my heart sing and my lower lip want to tremble.

Of course, Gran and Josie knew nothing of this yet, as neither of the Sunnymede brides had set foot outside of their respective suites all morning, and wouldn't be doing so for another half an hour yet.

'I just wanted to let you know that the registrar has arrived,' Mrs Blackwood informed us, stepping into the room and smiling broadly at the elderly woman in her care. 'You look radiant, Amanda,' she declared, crossing the room to give Gran's wrinkled cheek a gentle kiss.

Mrs Blackwood struck me as a woman who seldom cried, but even her eyes were suspiciously bright as she shook her head, as though reminding herself of the purpose of her visit. 'The registrar asked if she could see a copy of your wedding certificate.'

'I have it on the table over there,' Gran replied, turning to retrieve it, but I was closer.

'I'll get it,' I said, reaching for the document. But as I went to place it in Mrs Blackwood's outstretched hand, I froze as a very familiar name in the witness column caught my eye. I drew the certificate back towards me.

'Mum?' I questioned, my voice soft with wonder. '*Mum*

was at the registry office to witness your wedding on Thursday?' For the first time that day, Gran looked a little less than comfortable.

'She was,' she admitted quietly, her eyes dropping to her pretty white silk shoes.

'But I thought you said you didn't want any of us to be there? That it was just a quick legal formality?'

Gran's eyes were soft, and I knew she was remembering a treasured moment that belonged solely to her and the woman her son had married. 'That *is* what I said, but I think your mum wanted to show her support for Josie and me,' Gran explained. 'I had no idea she was going to turn up.' Her eyes flew to Mrs Blackwood, and you didn't need to be Sherlock Holmes to work out who Mum's accomplice had been in all this. 'But I'm very glad that she did.'

As I walked down the corridor to Josie's room, I kept thinking about how much it had meant to Gran having Mum as a witness to her wedding, and how brave it was of Mum to have done that. It must be hard supporting someone you love as much as I knew she did my father, when you also knew they were in the wrong. And yet however grateful Gran was for her daughter-in-law's support, I knew that just one kind word from Dad would have meant so much more.

One of my favourite carers in the home was helping put the finishing touches to Josie's wedding outfit. With help from the staff, Josie had purchased a beautiful oyster-coloured floor-length dress online, and looked lovelier than I'd ever seen her look before. She'd waited a very long time to be a bride, and her joy that this day had finally arrived was so great it transformed her.

Both brides had been visited by the hairdresser that morning, and Josie's wispy curls had been tamed with copious amounts of hairspray, which meant the small feathery fascinator set at a jaunty angle on her head was practically glued in place.

'Josie, you look absolutely lovely,' I declared, rushing across the room to hug her before she attempted to meet me halfway. For her to take a tumble today, of *all* days, was absolutely unthinkable.

Josie's response was to blush a charming shade of bubblegum pink, and my heart ached a little as I realised how infrequently she'd been told those words throughout her life.

'How is Amanda?' she asked, with a degree of breathlessness caused by neither angina, emphysema nor any other respiratory complaint. It was pure unadulterated excitement.

'She can't wait,' I told her truthfully.

I reached for the small gift bag I'd been hiding behind my back. 'I've brought you a little something,' I told her, feeling suddenly shy as I placed the shiny bag in her hands.

'Oh Mandy, you didn't need to do that,' she said, her quivering fingers rummaging in the bag to find the item hidden amid the nest of shredded tissue paper. After a few moments' searching, she found and withdrew the shiny gold tube. I watched as decades slowly peeled away, leaving her looking like a child on Christmas morning with a surprise stocking gift. Very carefully she pulled the tube apart and twisted the base, her smile broadening as the pillar-box red lipstick came into view.

'You are bold enough to wear any colour of the rainbow,'

I told her warmly. 'Don't ever let anyone make you think that you can't.'

In answer, Josie took a small wobble-free step towards me and hugged me just as tightly as Gran had done earlier that morning.

'What would make me happiest of all is if someday you were able to think of me as your *second* grandmother,' Josie admitted, sounding close enough to tears that she was likely to take me down again.

I squeezed her back, just hard enough for her to know I meant every word. 'I already do, Josie.' Even the carer was reaching for a tissue, as I repeated the words that were completely true. 'I already do.'

Perhaps by the time you've almost reached your ninth decade nothing really fazes you, for it was *my* hands rather than Gran's that were trembling as I passed her the delicate lily-of-the-valley wedding bouquet.

'Are you ready?' I asked.

Gran paused for a moment, bathed in a wide shaft of sunlight that was streaming in through the window. She looked ageless, timeless. Whoever had worn this dress before her could not have looked more beautiful in it. It simply wouldn't have been possible. When the dreadful day came when eventually we would lose her, *this* was how I would always remember my grandmother, I promised myself.

Her eyes scanned the room, lingering for a moment on the photograph of my grandfather on the shelf beside her favourite chair. She breathed in and then slowly exhaled. 'I am.'

We walked side by side down the carpeted corridor towards the lounge, Gran's hand tucked firmly in the crook of my arm. We'd already had word that Josie was safely in position in one of the two flower-decorated chairs positioned at the end of the aisle.

The lounge had large double doors that were currently thrown open, and through the gap I could see that the room was filled to capacity. There was a riot of colour within, from both the flowers and the brightly attired wedding guests. As we approached the threshold I saw Mrs Blackwood give a small nod to someone within the room. Suddenly, with perfect synchronicity, everyone bent down to gather something from beneath their chair. Gran and I wore matching mystified expressions until the guests began to straighten in their seats. Every single person in the room had put on a hat. Admittedly, some were not the usual wedding style – I spotted at least two flat caps and even a fez – but every head wore some sort of headpiece.

Mrs Blackwood was setting a small neat pillbox upon her own smartly coiffed hair. 'Someone once told me it's not a proper wedding without a hat.' Her eyes were warm as she looked at the woman I was beginning to suspect might be her favourite resident. 'And this is a *proper* wedding, Amanda. Your Sunnymede family are all delighted to be sharing this special day with both of you.'

Gran's smile never wavered, not even for an instant, but for a second I glimpsed a fleeting sadness I wasn't supposed to see. Her real family should be here. I shouldn't be the only one to witness this. The weight of my family's absence felt like a boulder on my shoulders.

Within the lounge, I searched for and found Jamie's face. There he was, poised beside the CD player, looking unbelievably handsome in a shirt and tie. His eyes met mine and his smile grounded me, and then suddenly the grin was gone, wiped from his lips, which were now slightly parted in surprise.

The weight on my shoulders now felt almost physical, which was hardly surprising, because that's exactly what it was. It was the weight of a hand halting me from stepping forward. I looked down. Those were fingers I recognised: they'd mended my bike when it was broken; they'd taught me how to catch a ball; they'd held my hand when we crossed the road.

Dad? What was he doing here?

I spun around, my expression unknowingly identical to Jamie's as I took in the smart suit, shirt and tie. He didn't look like a person who'd come with the intention of speaking up when they asked if anyone here knew of any just cause or lawful impediment...

He cleared his throat, and it was only in those moments before he spoke that I could see he was nervous. 'Mandy, if you don't mind, I believe this is *my* job.'

With a suaveness I really don't think I'd seen in him before, he gently removed Gran's hand from the crook of my arm and tucked it within his own.

'Hello, Gerald,' Gran said softly, pride and love battling it out to see which emotion would sit on her face as she looked at her son. It was a draw.

'Sorry I'm late, Mum.'

I think all three of us knew he didn't just mean to the ceremony.

'You're here now, my love, and that's all that matters.' There were questions to ask and apologies to be made, but this wasn't the time for either. Gran turned to me. 'You don't mind, do you, Mandy?'

I kissed her cheek, and then Dad's, loving them both so much that I wanted to freeze this moment for ever. 'Just give me a minute to get to the piano,' I said, weaving among the rows of guests to reach the place where Jamie had already moved in readiness. He held out the piano stool and remained behind it as I lifted the upright's lid. Without the sheet music, and with my eyes blurry from tears, it could all have gone horribly wrong. But it didn't. I played better than I'd ever played before or since. I played for the woman who'd taught me so much more than just scales and arpeggios; I played for the woman who'd shown me that when every voice speaks up against you, there's only one you should listen to… the voice in your heart.

30

'Has it sold yet?'

Jamie's arm disappeared from around my shoulders as fast as a python slithering into the undergrowth as my mother entered the lounge. I pressed the refresh button again on my phone's screen and shook my head sadly.

Mum set down the coffees she'd been carrying on the low table in front of us, and Jamie reached for his. He was now a frequent enough visitor for my parents to know how many sugars he took in his drinks, and yet he still jolted away from me as though I was radioactive whenever they came into a room. Still, I suppose it was early days. 'You just need to give them time,' Gran had advised me recently. 'That's what I'm doing.' It was good advice, and it seemed to be slowly working for both myself and my namesake.

'I still think you've priced it too low,' said Jamie, sitting back carefully on the settee cushions. He held his drink warily, as though carrying nitroglycerine. Admittedly, it would take very little to ruin the light beige fabric, so I couldn't really blame him for being cautious. Some days it struck me as funny that Jamie still believed his entry into the Preston household was so precarious that even a coffee spill could see him permanently excluded. Other times, it felt too close to the truth to be amusing. *One day at a time*, as Gran would say.

'It's the same with cars,' Jamie continued, tensing up just a fraction as my father entered the room and settled himself down in his favourite armchair. 'If they're too expensive they won't sell, but if you don't ask for enough, people automatically think there's something wrong with them and that they're being conned.'

'There's nothing wrong with Gran's dress. It's absolutely perfect,' I defended hotly, frowning as I stared at the tiny box on my eBay screen that told me that with less than two minutes until the auction ended, there was still no one who wanted to buy the gorgeous Fleurs wedding gown. 'And it's not about making money. That's not why we're selling it. We're going to give it all to charity anyway.'

I could practically see my father shudder at those words. They must have been like a dagger thrust deep into his accountant's heart.

'It's about the dress going to the right bride.'

'Like the wand finding the right wizard?' Jamie teased gently, quoting another of my favourite childhood authors. My youthful reading really *had* been all about dragons and magic. His hand briefly covered mine where it lay on the no-man's-land space between us on the settee cushions.

'Exactly.'

Dad set down his newspaper and reached for something on the table beside him. 'I think the F1 qualifier is about to start,' he announced, pointing the device in his hand at the large-screened television in the corner of the room. Dad, whose only interest in cars was whether they successfully conveyed him from A to B, was once again holding out an olive branch to Jamie. Today it took the shape of a TV remote control. It *was* early days, but anyone could see he was definitely trying, with both Jamie and Josie.

With the sound of roaring car engines filling the room, I turned my attention back to the screen on my phone.

'What if no one wants to buy it?' asked Mum, settling herself down on the other settee. 'What will you and Gran do with it then?'

'You could always keep it and wear it at your own wedding.'

Was I the only one who'd heard Jamie's momentary hesitation as he hastily changed what had started like 'our' and ended up as 'your'? I looked across at the armchair where my father was wearing a look not dissimilar to the one rabbits have just as the car headlights are bearing down on them. We'd come a long way in the weeks since Gran's wedding, but clearly we still had a way to go.

'I'll just keep relisting it. The right person will find the dress, or the dress will find the right person.' I waited to see which of the people I loved most in the world would laugh at such romantic nonsense. None of them did.

'How long left, babe?' asked Jamie, his attention torn between the big screen with the speeding Ferraris and the small one, which still hadn't shown a single bid.

'Fifteen seconds,' I said, a small tinge of disappointment lacing my words. 'Ten, nine, eight...' I could feel a tension thrumming through me, which was crazy. If the Fleurs gown didn't sell, all I had to do was list it again.

'Seven, six...' The countdown was beginning to feel as tense as a NASA launch.

'Five, four... three...'

The Formula 1 cars faded away; I could hear nothing except the thudding of my heart as I watched my phone. And then, with only two seconds to go, the screen finally changed. I gave a totally out-of-proportion jubilant cry and looked up with an enormous grin.

'Sold,' I declared happily.

And so it began, all over again...

Acknowledgements

I'd like to start by thanking the TV planners and programmers for bringing so many weddings shows to the small screen. Without my fascination for *Don't Tell the Bride*, *I Found the Gown* and *Say Yes to the Dress* I might never have had the idea for this book. But once it was in my head, it definitely stuck. One dress, three brides. I was already planning the weddings, and couldn't wait to invite you all to join me.

A huge thank you to my publishers for allowing me to stray a little off-piste with this one. I am very fortunate to have Laura Palmer as my editor, who fell in love with this story. Her support and that of the creative and enthusiastic team at Head of Zeus was, as ever, amazing.

Heartfelt thanks goes to my incredible agent Kate Burke and to the talented and tirelessly hardworking team at Blake Friedmann Literary Agency.

The last year or so has been a strange and lonely time to write and publish a book. And as great as our Zoom chats have been, there are some people who I've missed dreadfully. I am incredibly lucky to call these talented, funny, and loyal women my friends. Fair warning, Kate Thompson, Fiona Ford, Sasha Wagstaff and Faith Bleasdale, once the hugging begins it may never stop.

There are so many author pals I can't wait to reconnect with, and far too many prosecco-fuelled lunches that we've missed. I hope we get to rectify that very soon. Paige Toon, Kate Riordan, Holly Hepburn, Catherine Isaac, Heidi Swain, Milly Johnson, Alice Peterson, Kate Furnivall, Juliet Ashton, Penny Parkes, Anstey Harris, Iona Grey, Isabelle Broom, Gill Paul. I am really looking forward to seeing you all again.

Debbie Keyworth and Hazel Davies, thank you both for always replying with an enthusiastic 'yes' each time I ask you to read one of my books before the rest of the world gets to see it. I always breathe a little easier when I know that you have enjoyed it.

I raise a virtual glass to my very good friends for their love and support, and I'm looking forward to the day when we can sub it out for a real one. Thank you for always being in my corner, Sheila, Kim, Christine, Barb and Annette.

Finally, thank you to my family. To Kimberley for her advice and inspiration and for having the best ideas, and to Luke for almost managing not to roll his eyes whenever the conversation comes back to the world of books (it does that a lot, I must admit). And lastly to Ralph, who provides me with endless cups of tea, cooked meals, and more patience and love than I deserve. He was the reason I bought my own wedding dress thirty-six years ago... and it remains the best decision I ever made.